Duff knew what w... been no reason to cheat. Jack's lies in the rough had been good enough that he might assume Duff had been improving them all along. Now, however, he'd know better. It was too bad. Jack was a nice guy; he didn't deserve to lose this way. And if he did, so too did Duff lose the financial help Jack had promised him. Duff's toe was resting directly behind the ball, all he had to do was push. He remembered the old pro's words: *You never know till you face the test. . . .*

THE BIG TOUR

ROBERT UPTON

BERKLEY BOOKS, NEW YORK

THE BIG TOUR

A Berkley Book / published by arrangement with the author

PRINTING HISTORY
Berkley mass-market edition / December 2002

Copyright © 2002 by Robert Upton.
Cover design by Judy Murello.
Interior text design by Julie Rogers.

ISBN: 0-425-18758-6

BERKLEY®
Berkley Books are published by The Berkley Publishing Group, a division of Penguin Putnam Inc., 375 Hudson Street, New York, New York 10014.
BERKLEY and the "B" design are trademarks belonging to Penguin Putnam Inc.

PRINTED IN THE UNITED STATES OF AMERICA

10 9 8 7 6 5 4 3 2 1

Out here the wind was a force that seized the mind.

—Don DeLillo, *Underworld*

And the wind shall say: "Here were decent godless people:
Their only monument the asphalt road
And a thousand lost golf balls"

—T. S. Eliot, "Choruses from 'The Rock'"

I

After winning his first professional golf tournament, Duff Colhane spent the night in a federal jail in Miami.

It wasn't at all what he had expected. He had assumed he'd spend the evening back at the Doral, surrounded by sportswriters and pretty girls, drinking champagne from his silver loving cup while fending off agents with lucrative endorsement offers. Instead he was seated in a hard chair in a bare office fending off questions by a couple of federal agents in New York suits who wanted to know about drugs and an old girlfriend, and no matter how many times he told them he didn't know anything, they just kept asking over and over in different ways. Of course he wasn't under arrest; they just wanted to ask him a few more questions, they kept saying. But it was plain that he might be arrested if he didn't cooperate, so he spent a long night balancing on a thin line between civic duty and personal loyalty to an old girlfriend. When he was finally exhausted and unable to go on answering their questions, they offered to give him a cot so he might get some sleep and maybe remember things a little better when he woke up.

He knew just from watching television that he was free to leave at any time or call an attorney, but doing so might only make him look guilty, so he took the cot. After all, he wasn't guilty of anything just because Gena was fooling around with drugs; the feds knew that. It simply wasn't the sort of thing a PGA player did. He might throw a champagne bottle out of his car after winning a tournament, or cheat on his income tax, or engage in a little insider trading, but not drugs. Never that. It just didn't match the profile of the golden boys of golf, the privileged young men who pal'd around with presidents and CEOs and movie stars. And they knew it. He could see it in their eyes: the envy, the admiration . . . He had duped them; they had no idea he wasn't a country-club kid, but rather the son of a Montauk fisherman who in no way matched the public image.

Or had he been found out? he wondered, as he lay on the hard cot, thinking over the questions they had asked him. Is that why I'm here? Am I under arrest for posing as a gentleman? he asked himself, as he closed his eyes tightly against the overhead light.

The sun was lying just above the hill bordering the 18th fairway when the skinny kid in cutoff jeans hauled his bag up onto the tee. He shaded his eyes with one hand and squinted at the sun. Still time to get in the last hole and hit a couple of bags of balls on the range before going home to make dinner for his dad. He pulled his driver from the bag, a beat-up club some twenty years older than himself, and let the torn bag of mismatched irons fall to the ground with a solid clank. When he looked up the last fairway, with the poplar-tree shadows stretching across the grass like broken comb tines, he saw a great crowd assembled around the green, waiting anxiously to see who would be the next United States Open champion: the highly favored Tiger Woods, who had beaten back all his challengers save one over the first three days; or the unknown young amateur from the Montauk Municipal Golf Course who had quietly worked his way—after a disastrous opening-round 76—to within one stroke of the leader going into the final round.

And what magnificent golf these two players have shown the fans so far today. Coming to the 18th hole, Woods is 5 under par on today's round over this extremely difficult Montauk Golf Course, the first municipal course ever to host a U.S. Open; while the local amateur, who caddies here when not competing in amateur events is—and this, folks, has got to be one of the most amazing feats in golf history—also 5 under par, just one stroke back of the great Tiger Woods! Young Duff Colhane, the son of a local fisherman—that's his proud father right there in the captain's cap, standing beside that beautiful young girl, Gena Hall, whom I'm told is Duff's high school sweetheart. . . .

Wish I'da gone to a school like that.

Don't we all, Ken Venturi. Tell us, Ken—you've watched this young man for three days—what are his chances of overcoming his one-stroke deficit to Woods on the last hole and forcing a playoff?

To tell ya the truth I don't know, but I talked to him this mornin' and I'll tell ya one thing, he's got confidence—ya might even say eeze cocky. And young—this kid did'n even know who I was—heek I don't think he even knows who Tiger Woods is! And ya know what—I don't think he cares! I'll tell ya one thing, if I had to say one thing about him I'd say eeze cocky, and a little cockiness can be a good thing, but too much can be a bad thing.

He's getting ready to hit. Kind of reminds you of Nicklaus, doesn't he, Ken, the way he stands behind the ball, one shoulder hanging down, staring down the fairway?

T' tell ya the truth I don't think he patterns hisself after nobody. Cocky . . .

The boy stood behind the ball, right shoulder hanging low, staring intently at an imaginary blade of grass more than 250 yards away, then approached the ball at an oblique angle, like a banderillero moving toward a charging bull, intent on placing the sticks while gliding fearlessly and gracefully over the sharp-tipped horns. He took one practice swing and addressed the ball, his plan firmly in mind: bring the club back slowly, then smoothly down and through the ball, finishing with the hands high and the bellybutton pointed squarely at that blade of grass more than 250 yards down the fairway, then watch it hit and dance another 35 yards before coming to rest on a tuft of grass. But alas, something went awry, the club struck the earth a split second and a fraction of an inch before the intended time and place, and the ball squirted up weakly and landed softly in the right rough, at a place far short of its intended destination.

He's popped it up, Ken, he's popped it up!

That's what I was sayin'; that's the thing about confidence, sometimes ya don't have enough, sometimes ya got too much, and havin' too much can be worse 'n not havin' enough! I'll tell ya one thing though, right about now Tiger's smellin' the blood of a tender young amateur.

Tiger's about to hit—there it goes—the crowd loves it! Is 'at any good!

No, it's going left, Ken, it's hooking into the trees! Uh-uh, look out . . .

Unlike life, in golf you get a second chance, the boy said to himself, as he approached his ball. A cynical attitude for one so young, the priest had chided when Duff let slip this despairing sentiment during his enforced counseling—something his father thought he needed after his mother's death. Actually it was his father who had needed counseling, which Duff guessed he got at Sal's with his fishing buddies. But Duff was too young to drink, so he had to go to counseling. According to the ground rules laid down by the priest, he was supposed to just say whatever was on his mind at these sessions, although he soon learned that wasn't at all what the priest had in mind. If Father Dolan thought he was being cynical or somehow blaming God for his mother's death, he twisted his words until they meant something else, and Duff had to agree that that's what he'd meant in the first place or he'd never get out of his office. He grasped right away that the priest wasn't there to help him but to help God, to see that He didn't get blamed for Duff's mother's cancer—even though the young priest didn't seem to know any better than Duff why God shouldn't take the fall.

In fact it seemed to the boy that Father Dolan was having a problem of his own at the time, and it was important that Duff say nothing to rattle him any more than he already was, so he was careful to never let him know how really pissed at God he was. Not just pissed because of what God had done to his mom, but also because of what He had done to him. It was a selfish thought and he was ashamed—he should only be thinking about his mother—but he couldn't help sometimes thinking about himself, about how he was no longer part of a family. Everybody else had two parents, like a perfect loop, but now it was just him and his father, like a broken wheel bouncing down some rutted road with all the other wheels rolling smoothly by, going to some wonderful place he didn't know about and couldn't get to anyway because his wheel was broken.

Duff had listened quietly to everything the youthful priest had had to say, until the last session—when he was winding up with his message of hope, telling the boy that in spite of his misfortune he could be whatever he wanted to be—when finally Duff had had enough. His mother was dead, his father was a charter captain who'd lost his fishing boat, and this priest was telling him he could be the president of the United States.

"I don't get that," he'd said, shaking his head. "I can be a fisherman or a house builder or work in a real estate office or something like that, but I can't just be whatever else I wanna be. I mean I think that's pretty much decided when we're born, don't you, Father?"

"What—what kind of—of Presbyterianism is that!" the young priest spluttered, staring aghast at the portrait of infinite possibility he had just painted on the air, now hopelessly torn by this—this heretic! "We are all born with the precious gift of free will; we are all responsible for our own choices! We can't blame God or anyone else for our mistakes! Do you understand that?"

Duff understood but he didn't believe. Nor could he understand why the priest had gotten so angry over the opinion of a kid, until the following year—when Father Dolan abruptly left the priesthood to marry the pretty nun who taught the first grade at the church school.

He had been given a second chance, he realized when he saw his ball in the rough, but he wasn't entirely sure what to do with it. If he managed to get a 3-wood cleanly on the ball he would have a short shot to the par-5 hole; but get a little grass between the club and the ball and he'd be faced with another very long shot. Two good long irons, on the other hand, would put him safely on the green in three. He looked across the fairway at Tiger's ball, deep in the woods—he'd have to chip out. . . .

What would you do if you were in that young man's position, Ken?

I'll tell ya, if I was in his position I'd hit two long irons to the green, have a chance at birdie, come away with no more'n a par and hope Tiger makes bogey, and I'll tell ya why: 'cuz if Colhane dubs a shot, Tiger knows all he's gotta do is make bogey to win. But as long as Colhane's in position to make par or better, Tiger's gotta go for it, it puts the pressure on him, ya see.

It looks like Colhane has decided to go with the 3-wood!

Well, I'm not about to second-guess a player—it's his decision, that's why he's down there and I'm up here in the booth—but I gotta tell ya, I don't like that play.

As Duff stared at his ball, nesting down in the rough

like a quail egg, he suddenly realized that on the last day of the United States Open this rough would have been tramped down by the great crowds roving over the course, and so, to make the conditions as nearly similar as possible, he nudged his ball up on the grass just a bit.

Confidence is good, ya gotta think you're better'n the other guy, but too much confidence can be bad.

He's taking a 3-wood! He's going for it!

Cocky . . .

What a shot! Right at the pin! He'll have just a short pitch!

A great shot, but I got a feelin' that ball musta been settin' up better'n it looked from here.

Unfazed by Tiger Woods's venomous gaze, Duff waited while the golfer pondered his second shot. Needing at least a par to hold his 1-stroke edge, he had no choice but to attempt the nearly impossible, a low power fade through the narrow opening in the trees, bouncing off the hump on the right side of the fairway with enough force to bounce through the U.S. Open rough and back out onto the fairway. In all the years Duff had played the Montauk Muni, it was a shot he had managed just once.

What would you say Tiger's chances are, Ken?

I hafta say not very good. But I'll tell ya one thing, if I had to choose one player on Tour to make this shot, it'd be Tiger Woods.

Here it comes—through the trees—off the hump. . . . What a shot!

Like I said, if I had to choose one player. . . .

When Duff doffed his cap to the older man, the crowd showed their appreciation. And a few minutes later, when the young amateur chipped in for an eagle to win the U.S. Open, the crowd went nuts. Duff was in the middle of his acceptance speech when the pro called to him from the shop.

"What is it?" he called back.

"The cops called. Your old man's in jail again!"

• • •

"Mr. Colhane. . . . Duff, Duff, wake up!"

Duff opened his eyes to discover a dark man in a floral shirt shaking him by his shoulder. "What . . . who are you?"

"Raymond Martinez. I'm your lawyer."

"Lawyer . . ." Duff pulled himself up and swung his stocking feet to the floor. It took him a moment to realize where he was. "Did the PGA send you?"

The lawyer shook his head, as if it were a dumb question. "Your agent called me. I've been trying to get to you, but they've been stalling me. Did they tell you you had the right to an attorney?"

"Yeah—I'm not sure . . . I mean I know I had the right, but they told me I wasn't under arrest, they just wanted some information."

Raymond Martinez shook his thick, black pompadour and sighed wearily. "That's why you need a lawyer."

"I don't even know a lawyer."

"Well, now you do," he said, sitting next to him on the cot. "What're they after?"

"They asked me about Gena. . . ." he began, then halted. "You got some identification?"

"*Now* you get careful . . . Yeah I got identification," he said, digging into his back pocket for a shiny black wallet with silver tips at the corners. He withdrew several cards, flipping them onto the cot like a blackjack dealer. Duff read them. He was allowed to drive a car in Florida, practice law there, and he was a member of the ACLU. "And I graduated from Stetson Law School in 1992, but that's on my wall in Little Havana. You want me to represent you or not?"

"I guess so. . . ."

"I appreciate your confidence," he said, sliding the cards back into his wallet. "Now tell me what they asked you. And more important, what you told them."

Duff began with a preface of ignorance and innocence,

just as he had with the feds, before moving on to the specific questions. Gena Hall was a girl he'd gone to high school with. Girlfriend? She had been once, not now. Who was her boyfriend now? He wasn't sure. Was it Monte? Maybe. Who was Monte? He ran a restaurant in New York and East Hampton. Drugs? He didn't know. What did Gena Hall do for money? She was a model in New York. Had he ever seen her picture in a magazine, watched her on the runway? He hadn't. Had he ever taken money from her? Maybe a little now and then, he couldn't remember exactly. Cash? He thought so. He was having a hard time remembering, he was exhausted.

"That's when they told me I could take a nap and when I woke up they'd have a few more questions for me. I wanted to go, but I knew if I tried they'd arrest me."

"Bastards. . . . But it sounds like you did okay. I know you aren't telling me everything, but that's okay too, you got New York street smarts. I'm goin' upstairs and I'm tellin' 'em to shit or get off the pot. That's a legal motion that'll either get you busted or get you busted outta here. Okay with you?"

"You're my lawyer," Duff replied.

"And don't forget it," Raymond said, getting to his feet. "Anybody come down here and ask if this is your decision, any shit like that, you tell 'em to talk to Martinez."

Duff said he would.

When his lawyer left, either to spring him or get him busted, Duff lay back down on the cot and tried to relax. He put his arm over his eyes and thought of what Martinez had said—New York street smarts. So he hadn't duped them after all. All that hard work over all those years, learning how to talk, what fork to pick up, what to wear, and all he had to show was New York street smarts? And he wasn't even from New York.

As a young boy, upon opening a borrowed book to an unknown world only a short distance away, Duff Colhane

discovered that a terrible injustice had been done him—
he'd been given to the wrong father and it was up to him
to do everything in his power to correct it. It was a very
old book, scattered through with illustrations of gentlemen
from another era in plus-fours, argyle socks, two-tone
shoes, plaid sweaters and neckties and jaunty caps, swinging hickory-shaft spoons and mashie niblicks at gutta-
percha balls; while lovely girls in diaphanous dresses
stood on tiptoe to watch excitedly, and ladies in sun hats
and cocktail dresses sat on the porch with gentlemen in
white suits, highballs in hand.

He had come across the book while browsing through
the Montauk Library on a winter afternoon while a fero-
cious sou'easter rattled the windowpanes in the sash and
hurled sleet and hail across the roof with the fearful sound
of a flogging. The book was filled with golf stories by
writers he'd never heard of, stories about rich kids who
went to country-club dances in fast roadsters and drank
drugstore gin while going from party to party. There were
stories about men who made fortunes on Wall Street and
played matches with their friends for hundreds of dollars,
and their wives were prettier than movie stars. All the
houses were castles and the country club was a heavenly
kingdom where music played constantly, and all the beautiful people laughed delightedly at their witty chatter, and
glasses tinkled and Japanese lanterns cradled the beautiful
dancers in a warm light of golden promise for all the cold
nights to come.

The boy was almost breathless after finishing the first
story by someone named John O'Hara. He knew vaguely
of such grand places as O'Hara described, had driven by
the stately Maidstone clubhouse with his father and
watched the rich sonsabitches walking the fairways. His
father had taken a lot of them out fishing on his boat, the
Night Star, and they were all sonsabitches who couldn't
get up to get their own beer let alone boat a fish, and they
had a way of talking past him and looking right through
him as if he wasn't even there—until they needed help

with their fish. There were hundreds of reasons to hate the rich, and Duff had heard them all. After finishing the second story, however, by someone named F. Scott Fitzgerald, about a caddie who wins the love of the beautiful daughter of a member of the exclusive Sherry Island Golf Club, Duff decided that despite his father's opinion of these people, he had to somehow get into one of those wondrous places and see for himself just how bad they really were.

The Montauk Municipal Golf Course, just a couple of miles from home, was no Sherry Island Golf Club, but if he could just learn the game, the rest might somehow follow. And that's how it happened that a motherless kid in sneakers and jeans presented himself to the golf pro one early spring day—a day when piles of wind-driven snow still lay in the hollows and bunkers scattered across the fairways like flocks of sheltering sheep—and asked for a job, any kind of job.

The Irish professional sized the boy up. The lad was Irish, Duff Colhane, that was a plus. Pleasant enough looking, although with a bit of an underbite that gave him a determined look, perhaps defiant, which would be a minus. Too, he didn't have much need for a boy until the season got into full swing over the Memorial Day weekend. . . . But, being a skillful golf hustler as well as a professional, Teddy McGill recognized a mark when he saw one and therefore decided to extend a penurious offer to the boy. When the skinny kid hesitated, Teddy was afraid for a moment that he'd misread the apparent hunger in the boy's eyes.

"What's the matter, lad, the pay's not to your likin'?" he'd asked in his Dublin brogue.

"No, sir, the money's fine," the boy answered. "But I wanna learn how to play."

A fair trade, the little Irishman decided, shaking his hand. Then, before he could change his mind, he took the boy into the bag room and fixed him up with a bag and a mismatched collection of clubs. He showed him how to grip the club and how to swing it, and told him he'd be free to play in the evenings after he'd finished with his duties for the day.

"Can I start now?" the boy asked.

The pro glanced through the window at the pockets of snow dotting the course and replied, "If you're that daft."

Duff was indeed that daft. He showed up each morning before dawn to get in some practice before the first golfers started arriving, then continued to play from closing time until after dark.

"Won't your mother be gettin' angry with me with your comin' home so late?" the pro finally had to ask.

"My mother's dead," the boy answered, with a defiant thrust of his jaw.

"Sorry. Your father then, won't he mind?"

"No."

If he wanted to be a boy without a past, that was fine with the pro. He showed up on time, did his work without complaint and didn't ask for more money. Time on the golf course was all he wanted. By the end of the summer he was shooting in the high 80s, and the following summer, when he was 14, he managed to break 80 for the first time. Teddy, an only child himself with no children of his own, didn't know enough about kids to know if his employee was a prodigy or just a grinder. Certainly he had never seen anyone, amateur or professional, who practiced so long and hard as that boy. His taped hands were blistered and bloody from spring till fall—Teddy once suggested he take a break to replenish his red blood cells—but his obsession never diminished.

Duff couldn't understand how the pro could think hitting balls was work, when to him it was the greatest pleasure life had yet shown him. Hitting a golf ball was one of the few things in life that could be done perfectly, over and over again, or never once. And if he hit a bad one there was always the next one, the eternal promise of for-

giveness and salvation. On the range he was a Zen archer,
shooting the first arrow directly into the center of the
bull's-eye, then splitting it with the second. He was a
Samurai warrior, alone, dedicated only to his discipline,
repeating the same swing over and over and over, splitting
the arrow in two again and again and again.

The following summer he became distracted by a girl.
Gena couldn't understand why he wanted to be by himself
so much of the time, and although he told her he didn't
like it either but it was necessary if he was going to be a
good player, the truth was he enjoyed being alone. Often
when he was hitting balls he found himself thinking about
things he might otherwise never think of—about how
he'd like to have friends and yet be alone, about whether
his mother was in heaven watching him or just rotting in
the grave—problems like that that had no solution but had
to be thought about anyway.

He also thought a lot about Gena Hall. Sex, of course,
would be an even greater pleasure than hitting golf balls,
but so far he had only glimpsed its power and possibility
while pressed tightly against her on a cold evening on the
beach. It was mysterious; like the golf swing, there were
things going on that he couldn't understand, things he
couldn't step back from and observe. Gena had eyes so
dark he couldn't see the pupils until he got very close,
and then it was too late, they were like tidal caves he
wanted to dive into. She didn't know it yet, but she had
the power to get him to do almost anything she wanted
him to do, which sort of thrilled and frightened him at the
same time.

He thought it would be nice to be married to her and
sleep in the same bed and be able to make love to her
whenever he wanted—which would be just about all the
time—but there was a big price to be paid for that, he
already knew. Even the married guys who weren't much
older than he was and had never wanted to do anything
but get married and live in Montauk and go fishing—even
they had a kind of sad look when Duff saw them pulling

the kids along like trailing anchors, as if they were trying
to get someplace else but didn't know where, and even if
they did, it didn't matter because now it was too late anyway. Despite Father Dolan's counseling, Duff didn't yet
know what he wanted to do with his life, but he knew he
wouldn't stay in Montauk and be a fisherman like his
father. He would like to be a professional golfer, but he
knew the odds against that, and wanting it would only
bring bad luck so he tried never to think about it. Sometimes he thought he might like to form a band—that way
he could take Gena along as a backup singer—but not
being able to play an instrument, he knew that wasn't very
realistic either. Maybe he'd be a lawyer, only he'd heard
that would take four extra years of college, and he didn't
know where the money would come from. He didn't even
know where the money for college would come from, but
he'd get it somehow. The one thing he knew for sure was
that he was going away to college. That was going to be
his ticket out.

Although Gena had lived in Montauk for several years,
she was not a local and never would be, as the waiting
list was at least two generations long. Not that Gena ever
aspired to such status. For it was apparent from the day
when she first dropped unexpectedly into their midst, like
an exotic bird that had somehow become detached from
the flock, that she was only passing through. There were
several pretty girls in Duff's high school class, but Gena
Hall was a beautiful young woman—the most beautiful
young woman he had ever seen. Before enrolling in
school during the middle of the year, Gena had been a
summer person, staying with her parents in their shingled
cottage on a bluff above the Old Highway overlooking
the ocean. Her mother was a plain-looking, conventional
nurse who found herself somehow married to a musical-
comedy actor blessed with matinee-idol looks but a bus-
and-truck talent. Between Broadway understudies and
dinner theater tours opposite one or another aging Hol-
lywood star, Keith Hall managed to earn a tenuous live-

lihood from the theater which, combined with his wife's earnings as a surgical nurse, allowed them to buy a small summer place in—if not the Hamptons—Montauk. The actor was on the road more than half the twenty years of their marriage, often playing the part he'd understudied on Broadway the year before, almost never in town when the good parts in the new shows were being cast, never rising beyond his reputation of always dependable. Maritally, however, he proved less than that when he returned from a tour of *Same Time Next Year* to announce that he'd fallen in love with his costar, a '70's TV child actress who'd amassed a small fortune in residuals. When her parents divorced and her mother got the summer house (and little else), they moved their meager things from Manhattan to Montauk and became permanent East Enders. Or at least her mother did. For Gena was by then already a committed New Yorker and intended to get back to Manhattan just as soon as she could. Almost as much as anything else, it was their shared ambition to get out of town that had brought he and Gena together, Duff supposed. One by one all the high school swains had presented themselves to her, only to be driven away in turn by her indifference. She wasn't deliberately unkind, but there was an unintended glow of amusement in her appraising brown eyes that urged all to abandon hope and escape quickly with what dignity remained. Despite her aloofness, she and Duff shared a strong attraction, but they each understood that it was only to last until graduation, when they were destined to go off to bigger and better things.

Through their high school years they watched from a distance as their classmates paired off with feverish impatience, making summer glandular connections intended for a lifetime but doomed to cool with the first frost. It was a chaste but dangerous time for a couple of sexually charged kids intent on avoiding domestic bliss at all cost, but they unconsciously managed to somehow construct a kind of sexual obstacle course that served their unstated purpose. They attended art films (Gena's description) at the Sag Harbor Cinema, and exchanged books and listened to music at her house while her mother was at work, but rarely attended dances or parties with their classmates. Except for a bit of tongue kissing and awkward groping that Gena always curtailed gently but firmly, they came nowhere near the line so many of their classmates had already crossed.

"I don't see why we shouldn't," Duff finally said on a late spring afternoon in her bedroom when they'd come very close. They'd stripped down to their underpants and lay grinding against one another until, as he was about to come, she pushed away, snatched up her bra and clothes and bounded into the bathroom.

"We went too far," she said, snapping her bra closed.

"Or not far enough," he groaned. "I thought actors were supposed to be terribly sophisticated, able to take a lover on a whim and drop him just as quickly."

"You're thinking of my father."

"Actually I'm thinking of myself . . ."

"My father's a terrible actor," she went on. "When he started to lose his looks he knew it was all over, so that's when he decided to marry Pie Face." That was her mother's name for the sitcom actress, and it was apt. As a teenager, a flat freckled face could be cute, but on a surgically altered, middle-aged face it was a youthful grotesquerie. "He says he didn't marry her for her money, that she's really a great actress who never got her chance and he wants to see that she gets it. What a joke. . . . That's why I can't make love to you, darling," she said, striding out of the bathroom in bra and panties. She was tall, with muscled legs and buttocks and a broad back from summers on the beach, swimming in the surf and playing volleyball with the summer people. Despite her hard body, her breasts, to which he'd only recently been granted complete access, were heavy and soft as pillows, and they would drive him mad. He wanted them with him always, to stroke and squeeze and kiss; he wanted to go to sleep with his head between them and wake up with a hard nipple in his mouth. But now there was nothing soft about her. She stood over him, feet planted wide, fists resting on the gracefully curved ledge of her hips, her abdomen hard as a wall. "Just because my father's a bullshitter doesn't mean I am. I know that once we make it we're hooked. College, golf, acting—none of that'll mean a thing anymore. All we'll be able to think about is each other."

"That's all I can think about now. . . ."

"Poor baby," she purred, dropping down beside him on the bed. She fixed her dark eyes on him and asked, "Would you rather we stopped seeing each other?"

"No," he said, twisting his head slowly from side to side like a hooked fish.

On a late fall day during his last year of high school, Duff stood on the practice tee of the Southeastern University golf course with about 50 other high school hopefuls from around the country, knocking balls as far down the range as possible, while the college coach walked slowly down the line, stopping briefly to appraise each player before moving on to the next. He was accompanied by a student with a clipboard, from which he recited the vital statistics of each player as they got to him. For some the list of accomplishments was fairly long—high school team records (everyone Duff had met was, like himself, captain and number one man) outside tournaments, lowest competitive score, etc.—while for most it was cruelly short. For these were the aspirants, the high school athletes who wanted to play for a golf powerhouse like Southeastern University, but had somehow been overlooked by Coach Waylin's scouts and had failed to receive an offer of scholarship for their services. Several of them had flown in from California and Texas, so eager were they to play for Southeastern, some accompanied by their fathers or high school coaches to act as caddies in today's 18-hole tournament for the last available scholarship on the South-eastern golf team.

Duff had known the odds were long against when he had piled his clubs into Teddy McGill's Cadillac the day before and made the long drive down, yet there was always the chance that this could be one of those days when, for no known reason, he'd get in the zone and shoot a 66. He'd never shot 66 before, but he'd shot 70 with a stupid double-bogey on the last hole. Okay, maybe 66 isn't realistic, he thought as he reared back and crushed a drive more than 300 yards down the center, but I know I can play with anybody here.

"Hey, Slingshot!" a voice called, and Duff looked up, along with several other golfers in the vicinity. It was Forbes Witherspoon, the student with the clipboard, the number one man on the team. He'd heard all about him (far more than he wanted to hear in fact) from the other hopefuls in the dormitory the night before, high school players who knew everything about every good college player in the country, and little else, it seemed. He was runner-up in the United States Amateur that year and, one of the high schoolers reported, the longest hitter in college golf. Duff's reply, that Witherspoon used to be the longest hitter in college golf, was greeted by stony silence. Although only amateurs, they were already practiced in the touring professional's code of feigned humility. Forbes Witherspoon was tall, unusually so for a golfer, and thin, with sun-bleached blond hair that almost fell over one eye, from behind which he now seemed to be staring amusedly at Duff.

"Yes, you in the khaki sho-ahts. Ah don't seem have you on mah papuh." He sounded more like a Southern historian narrating a Civil War special on PBS than a golfer.

"I only decided to come at the last minute," Duff said.

"Had yoah haht set on Stanfuhd, did you."

"Hahvahd, actually," Duff replied. Prissy fuck. "The name's Colhane, Duff Colhane."

"Duff—?"

"Not Slingshot."

"Wheah you from—Slingshot?"

Duff sighed wearily and teed up another ball before replying, "Montauk."

"You a fishahman?"

Duff shook his head. "A golfer."

"A golfah. . . . Titles?"

"I was Suffolk County Junior champion for the last three years and—"

"The joonyuh champion!" Witherspoon exploded gleefully.

"And runner-up in the Long Island Amateur."

"A joonyuh champion and a runnah-up. Lowest competitive scoah?"

"Sixty-six," Duff said.

"Was that on a joonyuh co-ahse?"

"Shinnecock Hills," Duff responded. The bigger the lie the better.

It got the coach's attention. He watched Duff hit two long ones, one left and one right.

"You're long, but are you straight?" Chip Waylin, who'd been a short but straight hitter while playing on the PGA Tour, asked.

Duff shook his head. "It has a little draw at the end," he said, carving the perfect pattern in the air with his hand, the pattern which even the best of players aspire to all their lives.

"Oh, I want to play with him," Forbes Witherspoon said, flashing an eager grin.

They moved off and Duff hit another ball, this one longer than the last though not so straight. When he looked back he saw the coach watching, probably thinking of what Harvey Penick said to Tom Kite when he caught him enviously eyeing a big knocker: The woods are full of long hitters. It was good advice, Duff knew—he swung much too hard at the ball and often strayed from the fairway (or raced headlong)—but he wasn't yet ready to start holding back. Hitting the ball farther than everybody else might not be the object of the game, but other than knocking the cover off a baseball there was no feeling in sport that could equal it.

A short while later he hit one like that off the first tee while the coach watched, a long low riser with a right-to-left hook that didn't hit the turf so much as ricochet off it, then bounced and ran to a stop more than 300 yards down the fairway.

"Ah'm impressed, Slingshot," Forbes Witherspoon said, as he stepped up onto the tee after him.

Their other two players—a kid named Talifaro from Jacksonville, whom Witherspoon had promptly named Tally, and a black caddie from Augusta, whom he'd dubbed Looper (as PGA Tour caddies were called)—had already hit their balls about 260 yards down the middle. He teed his ball up and looked back at Coach Waylin, slumped comfortably on his golf cart, big cigar in his mouth, watching each of the nervous players as they teed off. Whether intended or not, his presence resulted in an unusual number of bad drives.

"If Slingshot's going keep that up, I think we'd better have a chiropractor waiting for him on the ninth green, Coach."

"You just make sure you don't hurt yourself," his coach warned.

Despite his coach's advice, it was apparent from the first hole that Forbes Witherspoon did not intend to be out-hit by a high school kid, least of all a Yankee fisherman from Montauk, New York. Time after time he knocked the ball well down the fairway, occasionally longer than Duff, but usually not. Through it all, Tally and the Looper watched with awe, both of them running off eight straight pars without once earning the honor to hit first off the tee. Duff and Forbes both birdied the short par-4 first hole, followed by seven straight pars for each of them (although both had to scramble a bit when their tee shots found the rough a couple of times) and they were both 1 under par coming to the par-5 ninth hole. When Duff led off there with a Brobdingnagian clout that brought him to within eagle distance, Forbes Witherspoon had to shake his head, too, at the incredible length of the Montauk Slingshot. Forbes teed it up and hit a fine drive that ended up 30 yards behind Duff's ball.

"There must be something in the air from Plum Island that gives you Montauk boys that monster strength," Forbes remarked as they walked side by side to their balls.

Duff had been surprised when the Southerner knew where Montauk was, but to know Plum Island, a highly secretive government research station off the Montauk shore, was even more improbable. "How do you know Plum Island?" he asked, glancing sideways.

"I've sailed those waters," Forbes replied. "My family has a summer place on Martha's Vineyard."

"Umm," Duff grunted.

"You know the Vineyard?"

"Sure. I sail up there all the time."

"You have a boat?" Forbes asked, seemingly more excited to meet a sailor than a golfer.

"A few, actually." His front yard was littered with boats his father had salvaged with the intention of repairing, but seldom did he get around to it. At times he went so far as to bring his tools out into the yard, but this was invariably followed by a six-pack, followed closely by a bottle of bourbon, which ended ultimately with unmended boats in the yard and rusty tools in the boats. "I prefer the schooner."

"Schooner . . . ?" Forbes asked, staring at his playing partner as they walked. "How big is she?"

"The captain says she's eighty feet, but I never measured her. What kind of boat do you have, Forbes?"

"A day sailor," Forbes answered gloomily. Duff felt his curious eyes on him as they walked. "What's your father do, Duff, if I might ask?"

"Sure, Forbes. He's in marine salvage, but mostly he

just invests in things. What about your father, what's he do?"

"Insurance," Forbes replied, with apparently little more enthusiasm for it than he had for day sailors.

Forbes hit a 3-wood for his second shot, which he came up out of, slicing the ball into the narrow creek that meandered down the right side of the fairway before turning sharply in front of the green. Could be the turning point, Duff said to himself, as he idly trailed his hands over the clubheads while studying his shot. He realized he wasn't playing against Witherspoon, but rather the whole field. Yet if he beat Southeastern's number one man, there was an excellent chance he'd beat the field. He calculated that he could easily reach the green in two with a 3-wood, but if it landed hot it would run through the green, down the hill in back and into the trees; whereas a well-struck 1-iron would clear the creek and run up onto the green, leaving him with a putt for eagle, or an almost sure birdie. Anything less than well-struck, however, would almost certainly find the creek, leaving him with a par at best, or more likely a bogey. The 1-iron felt right.

He knew the instant he struck it that his intuition had been correct. The ball fairly screamed as it rocketed off in the direction of the green, across the creek and onto the bank, where it scrambled up the slope like a frightened duck and flopped weakly onto the green, inching along to within 25 feet of the hole.

Chip Waylin was seated on a cart beside the ninth green when Duff crossed the bridge and walked up onto the green, putter in hand. He didn't know if the golf coach knew he was 1 under par to here and putting for an eagle, but after Forbes started talking to him and he felt the coach's eyes on him while he was crouching down to line up his putt, he was sure he knew. And when he made the putt for eagle for a 3-under-par 33 on the front nine, he thought he might be in the zone, might shoot 66 for the first time in his life. He thought he might be a Southeastern golfer.

•   •   •

When they got to the 16th hole and Duff was still 3 under par, he and Forbes began making plans to get together on Martha's Vineyard over the summer. Forbes knew all the girls who summered there and he would see that Duff met the prettiest of them, and together they would attend all the best parties. He didn't know what he would do if Forbes insisted on visiting him at the fishing shack he and his father lived in, but he wouldn't worry about that now. He had done the nearly impossible. He had made the Southeastern golf team and it didn't matter that he had bullshitted the number one man. The only thing that mattered was that he had beaten him. Forbes had gotten it to even par after bogeying the ninth hole, which they'd heard was the second lowest score so far; while the Looper, who had bogeyed only one hole and parred all the others, was apparently in second place behind Duff. The black caddie, who hadn't given himself much of a chance, was quietly pissed that on the day he was playing over his head, his playing partner was having the round of his life.

However a short while later, after Duff had double-bogeyed the last two holes for a round of 73, and the Looper had birdied 18 for an even par round of 72, both young men were stunned by the sudden shift in their fortunes. After fairly staggering off the 18th green, Duff stood staring numbly at the Titleist score sheets for a long empty moment, while the other players congratulated the black caddie. The Looper would be attending Southeastern University on a full scholarship in the fall, while Duff, known briefly as the Slingshot, would be off to peddle his skills in a lesser market. He had stupidly blown it, trying for eagle-birdie on the last two holes and a 66, when all he needed was two safe pars for a strong 69—or just two bogies for a 71!—and the scholarship would have been his.

"Bad luck, Slingshot," Forbes Witherspoon said.

Duff turned to the golfer standing beside him and said, "I guess the Vineyard is out."

Then he walked to the bag stand, picked up his clubs and headed for the players' parking lot. There was no need to go back to the dorm; he had taken his overnight bag with him, knowing unconsciously perhaps that he wouldn't win today. Yet he so easily could have, and he knew this loss was something that would stay with him for the rest of his life, like Doug Sanders's missed tap-in-putt on the last hole to lose the British Open by one stroke. Twenty years later Sanders said it no longer bothered him as much as it used to, that sometimes an hour went by when he never once thought about it.

He threw the clubs onto the back seat and slammed the door, then got behind the wheel and started the engine with a pained howl of pistons and valves. He got in line behind a funereal procession of disappointed players, parents and caddies, and made his way slowly to the gate where a guard collected their temporary parking passes. Their brief stay at Southeastern, the splendid athletic dorm and dining hall and the magnificent golf course, was finished. It wasn't the end of the world, he told himself; he would play someplace else, a smaller school. He wouldn't get the kind of financial aid he would've gotten at Southeastern, and the competition wouldn't be as keen or the coaching as good, and he wouldn't be the kind of player he would've been if he'd played at Southeastern, but he would survive it. He would make up for the lost time and opportunity, and one day in a PGA event he would face Forbes Witherspoon again, and he would beat him, just as he would've beaten him today if he hadn't been so determined to prove he could shoot 66.

He handed the campus policeman his temporary pass and pulled the red and white Coup DeVille out onto the entry road in a hail of spitting gravel, punctuated by an angry squeal as he raced around the horseshoe-shaped, magnolia-flanked drive. As he circled recklessly by the stately Georgian clubhouse, he saw some fool on a golf cart headed straight for him, and slammed on the brakes, drawing to a squealing stop within just a few yards of the stopped cart.

"You drive a car like a golf ball, don't you, Slingshot!" Forbes Witherspoon called.

"You trying to get yourself killed? What do you want?" Duff demanded.

"Somebody wants to talk to you," Forbes said, indicating a place beside him on the cart. "So why don't you just leave your daddy's big-ass car right there and come with me."

"Yeah, sure . . ." Duff replied.

He pulled the car to the side, got out and climbed up onto the cart with Forbes.

Forbes parked the golf cart at the rear of the building and led Duff through a maze of basement corridors to a door marked PRIVATE. He knocked once and opened the door to a high-windowed room where Coach Waylin and another man were seated at the end of a long table. Duff stepped inside, and without any instruction, Forbes closed the door, leaving him alone with the two men. The coach studied him for a moment, with a faint smile or smirk— Duff couldn't tell which—and said, "Well, Slingshot, looks like your rubber broke on those last two holes."

"I got snagged on those tight fairways," Duff said.

"I'll mention it to the golf course architect next time I see him," Chip Waylin said, indicating the chair opposite his companion, a sunburned, thickset, middle-aged man wearing a red golf shirt with the Southeastern University logo emblazoned over the left breast. The shirt made him look like a shiny boiled sausage.

"This is Mr. Cawthon. Mr. Cawthon played golf for Southeastern—a few years ago."

"About thirty years ago," the old alum put in.

"But you'd be a fool to give him one a side," the pro warned.

The ex-varsity man smiled and asked, "What happened to you out there today, son?"

Duff shrugged. "I just ran out of fairway."

"Big hitter are you?"

"Length is my strength."

"Yeah, you're a big strong boy," the stocky man said, appraising his broad but thin upper body. "You lift weights?"

Duff shook his head. "I hauled a lot of clam rakes when I was growing up."

"Yeah, I ate a lot of those clams when I was up there. And lobsters. Man, I love those Montauk lobsters. What's the name of that big restaurant you got up there, the one out on the fishin' docks?"

"Gosman's?"

"Yeah, Gosman's. You'd like that restaurant, Chip."

"I'm not much of a fish eater," the golf pro said.

"Chip's a meat-'n-potatoes guy," the alum remarked with a conspiratorial grin. "But we didn't ask you here to talk about food, did we, Chip."

The golf coach shook his head. "You do that often, Slingshot, shoot yourself out of a golf tournament like that when you got it all but won?"

"Almost never," Duff answered, which wasn't entirely true. When he had a long lead he had a tendency to back off, then start playing again in earnest when the competition caught up. Teddy McGill said it was a failure of concentration, but Duff wasn't sure. It seemed that no matter how hard he concentrated, he just wasn't a very good front-runner.

"Bad timing," the coach said, shaking his head. "You know, don't you, all you needed was two bogeys to beat that black boy."

"I'm sorely aware of that," Duff replied.

"Two bogeys and you could've had yourself a full scholarship. And that's a shame, because I think you're a damn sight better player than him. Unfortunately there's nothing I can do about it, the National Collegiate Athletic Association limits the number of scholarships I can give out. That's why I keep one spot open and have this tournament every year—just in case there's somebody out there I overlooked. I expect the best player to come out of the pack, but I know it doesn't always work out that way. I know that, so that's why I always keep the coach's prerogative. If I choose to, I can ignore the results of the competition and pick you for the last scholarship." He stopped, letting Duff hang on his words for a hopeful moment, then resumed. "But because the winner is black, I got a real problem with that. If I give that black kid's scholarship to you, the NAACP will have my scalp, and the NCAA will take what's left. I think you get the picture," he said, gesturing helplessly.

Duff nodded slowly. He supposed the coach was just trying to be a nice guy, calling him in to explain his predicament, but he wished he hadn't; he was only making it worse. Now the big guy was talking, telling him how sorry he was, when all Duff wanted to do was get in his car and get the hell out of there.

". . . But there's more than one way to skin a cat," the alum was saying. "The school might not be able to give you an athletic scholarship, but there's nothing to say you can't just enroll in school and try out for the team this fall."

"Nothing except that I don't have the money to enroll here," Duff informed him.

"No, but I do."

"You . . . you'd pay my way . . . ?" Duff asked.

The alum leaned back in his chair and crossed his thick arms. "Room board and tuition, for as long as you're on the team."

Duff knew from the expectant look on the face of both men that the offer was a serious one. Perhaps illegal, but serious.

"Whattayasay, Slingshot?" Chip Waylin asked.

"I say yes!" Duff replied.

•   •   •

At dusk, yellow gashes of exploding light appeared silently and ominously against the blue-black sky above the road ahead. When the Cadillac hit the wall of rain a short while later, it was like thrusting a surfboard through a big Montauk breaker, and he quickly slowed the car to a crawl, moving slowly through a forest of falling water, past randomly stacked cars, their red lights blinking oozily in the silvery headlamp light. The storm would set him back an hour or two, but he wouldn't let it bother him. What was a little rain to a guy with a four-year scholarship to Southeastern University?

But this was no little rain, he was beginning to realize. The raindrops fell on the car like stones and jumped up off the flooded pavement like maddened dancers in silver capes, illuminated by a pair of spotlights that barely penetrated the watery darkness. When a lighted rest stop appeared suddenly and felicitously at the side of the road, he pulled gratefully onto the off-ramp and into the vast parking lot—all but filled with cars and vans—that surrounded the fast-food restaurant beneath the glowing golden lights. He found a parking space at the back of the pack, then reached over the seat into his golf bag for his rain suit. He removed his shoes and socks, got into the rain suit and dashed for the restaurant.

The lobby was crowded with gloomy travelers, like irritable wet birds interrupted on their annual northern migration. He walked past the sign requiring shirt and shoes, took a tray and started down the food line. Except for the baked beans and hot dogs and a pan of macaroni and cheese, most of the hot dishes had been devoured by the ravenous pilgrims who had preceded him, so he settled for a cellophane-wrapped tuna sandwich on white bread and a large cup of coffee. The only empty table in the place was piled high with used paper plates and plastic cutlery and wadded napkins, which he pushed aside to make a small space for his paltry dinner. No matter, it was just something to do until the storm cleared; in the fall he would be eating sumptuously at the training table in the athletic dorm with his teammates. For now, not even the fat couple and their five squabbling kids at the table next to him, all of them wet as swamp rodents, could bother him.

After almost an hour, when the rain began to lighten—somewhat at least—Duff decided it was time to go. He pushed his way through the crowd gathered at the front doors and plunged again into the rain.

When he put the key in the door and found it already unlocked, he was briefly confused. It wasn't like him to leave the car unlocked, unless in the confusion caused by the storm . . . ? When he looked into the back of the car and saw no golf clubs, he knew in a depressing instant that he must have done just that—or else they'd broken in. It didn't matter how they'd gotten in, he had stupidly left the clubs on the back seat where they could be plainly seen, even in a nearly blinding rainstorm. There were few things that could have ruined the greatest day of his life, but losing those golf clubs—which he had carefully weighted and balanced, re-shafted and re-gripped until they were as perfectly pitched as a Stradivarius violin—was certainly one of them. He raised his clenched fists to the wet heavens and let loose a litany of angry curses that was answered by a bolt of lightning and a peal of thunder that shook the asphalt beneath his feet, but failed to turn up the missing clubs.

His father was standing in the yard with a cup of coffee when Duff arrived the next morning, appraising a boat, as if this might be the day to sand and paint her and sell her to an unsuspecting summer person for an unconscionable sum. In fact he'd been pacing in and out of the house all morning, looking down the street for the golf pro's red Cadillac, anxious to be there for his son when he got home with the bad news. Sam was sure the news would be bad—all those players from all over the country competing for one spot—and he was angry with Teddy for filling the boy's head with crazy ideas. God knows, Sam said to himself as he watched his son climb stiffly out of the car, he had let his son down often enough; he didn't need strangers doing it to him, too.

"Hi, Dad," Duff croaked, as he walked toward him.

"How was the trip?" Sam asked.

"Great, Dad, just great!" his son beamed.

"You won?"

"No, but I . . ." he began, then stopped, noticing his father's right hand wrapped around the coffee mug, big and red as a chela, with scraped knuckles still oozing. "What happened?" he asked, already knowing the answer.

"Ah, some fuckin' candy ass . . . Threw my tip on the ground because we didn't catch no fish, so I popped him."

"You hit a client!" Duff exploded. His father had been fired from most of the fishing boats in Montauk at one time or another for insulting clients, but until now he'd confined his fights to the locals.

"It's all right, he ain't gonna sue. He told Cap'n Delaney he would, but there's no way. He'd just embarrass himself all over again with his Brooklyn buddies. Wanted me to think they were in the mob just 'cuz they had names with a lotta vowels . . . Shit. If he was a mobster he wouldda had a gun—he wouldda shot me when he started losing the fight."

"There was more than one, and you thought they might have guns?" Duff asked, incredulous. "They could've killed you!"

"When an asshole throws your money on the ground, you don't think about that. A guy insults you like that, you gotta fight him," his father said, thrusting his barge-prowed jaw out for emphasis. He had the same underbite as his son, but Duff had his mother's finer jaw. "Anyway, I'm gonna cut back on the drinkin'."

"Good."

"Whattaya mean good?" he said, turning that wild eye like a panicked horse to its rider. "I ever hit you when I was drinkin'?"

"No," Duff admitted. According to Grandpa Duff, he and his mother were the only two people safe in Montauk when his father was drinking.

"Then don't be a smart-ass. And don't feel bad about the golf scholarship. Those assholes in the pink pants only started playin' golf *after* they got rich, not before. You got it all cocked up," he said, starting into the house.

"Not me, Dad. I intend to get rich by playing golf. I got a sponsor!"

"Sponsor . . . ?" he asked, stopping and turning.

"Some rich alum. He's paying my way, room, board and tuition!"

"Now why the hell would anybody wanna do that?"

"Because he wants me on the team," Duff answered wearily as he walked into the kitchen.

His father was no more impressed by his accomplishments than Forbes Witherspoon had been by his junior championships. Golf was foreign to the fisherman, a la-di-da game for sissies and social climbers, and Sam Colhane didn't want either one of them in his family. If it weren't for the money he made working at the golf course, Sam would have put an end to it long ago. Now it was too late, that crazy Irish pro had filled the kid's head with all sorts of crazy ideas and nobody was going to change him. Duff filled his cup and extended the pot to his father.

"Yeah," Sam replied. He crossed the room and waited while Duff filled his cup. "So you didn't win the scholarship but this rich alum is takin' up the slack, is that it?"

"That's it."

Sam stared at his filled cup and nodded. "And what happens if you don't make the team?"

"No play, no pay," Duff answered with an easy shrug. "But don't worry, I know I can make the team. I would've won the tournament and beat their number one man if I hadn't gotten crazy on the last two holes. But it doesn't matter, the coach saw me, he knows I can play."

"So why didn't he give you the scholarship instead of gettin' some alum to pay your way?"

"The winner gets the scholarship, those are the rules. The only thing that matters is that I'm getting a free ride to Southeastern."

"No, that's not all that matters; not to me," Sam said. "If somebody's offerin' to pay for my son's education, I got some serious questions about that. Like just who the hell is this guy and where's he gettin' all this money from?"

Duff took a deep breath and exhaled audibly. "His name is Earl Cawthon, he used to play on the golf team. Chip says his family has a lot of gas leases."

"Chip . . . ?" Sam asked, as if smelling rotten fish.

"The golf coach."

"And this guy's got gas stations . . . ?"

"Natural gas, in the ground," Duff said, pointing to the kitchen floor.

Sam nodded, considering natural-gas leases. "And he wants to give you what—twenty or twenty-five thousand a year?"

"Not that much . . ."

Sam thought about it some more, then shook his head. "I don't get it, what's in it for him?"

"He's an alum, wants to see the team do well, likes to hang out with the players . . ."

"Is he a fag?"

"No, Dad, he's not a fag. He's just a gung ho alum with school spirit."

"Bullshit. Nobody gives a kid that kinda money and don't expect something for it; that ain't human nature." He walked to the sink, piled high with the dishes that had accumulated while Duff had been away, and looked through the window at the small sandy patch that was their backyard. There was a kicker in the deal, there had to be, but he didn't know enough about big-time college sports to figure it out, not golf anyway. He knew some of the Yastrzemskis from Bridgehampton, had listened to them brag about Carl's big deals, bonuses, options and spokesman contracts and such, but that was professional baseball, not amateur golf. Still, Nicklaus and Palmer and Woods and some of those guys made even more money than Yaz. . . . That's it, the guy wants to manage my kid's career!

"You didn't sign anything with that guy, did you?" he asked, spinning suddenly around.

"Just a school application," Duff replied. "Chip said he'd walk it through the admissions office."

"Chip . . . I'm talkin' about a management contract, anything like that. . . ."

"Dad, I'm not turning pro, I'm just playing on the golf team. Believe me, that's all Mr. Cawthon is interested in."

"For now."

"Don't worry, if anybody asks me to sign anything I'll run it by you first," Duff assured him.

"Good," Sam said with a satisfied nod. "You remember that. 'Cuz no matter what you think, nobody invests a hundred thousand in somebody and don't expect a return somewhere down the line." He splashed his coffee in the sink and went to the refrigerator for a beer. He popped the top and took a long drink, then had a sudden idea. "What happens if this guy goes broke or just decides he don't wanna pay you no more? Did you think about that?"

Duff shrugged. "I guess that'd be the end of it."

"Bullshit! What kind of a deal is that! Before we go any further with this thing we gotta have a lawyer."

"No, Dad, I don't want a lawyer," Duff replied firmly. "Mr. Cawthon's a Southern gentleman. He'd be insulted; it'd kill the deal."

"Then I say let him! If he's afraid to talk to a lawyer it's because he's got something to hide."

"Dad, we made a deal. I'm not gonna change it now!"

"You made a deal! What happened to not signin' anything without runnin' it by me first?"

"I don't understand you!" Duff wailed. "I got a chance to go to college for nothing and you're trying to kill it!"

"I'm not tryin' to kill it! You got offers from other colleges—colleges around here—I didn't try to kill them, did I?"

"Is that it? You don't want me to go to Southeastern just because it's not near here?"

"That's not what I'm sayin'!" Sam shouted, crushing the empty can in his hand. "It's not just the distance, it's the difference. The South is like a fuckin' foreign country. What happens if you meet a girl down there?"

"What happens . . . ?" Duff repeated.

"You fall in love and you get married, right?"

"I suppose . . ."

"Then you think she'd wanna come up here and live with your friends?"

"My friends . . ." Duff repeated uncertainly. "What have my friends got to do with this?"

Sam turned away and went for another beer, and suddenly Duff thought he knew. Incredible! All these years I thought he wanted nothing more than to have me out of the house so he could have his girlfriends over all night—and he probably did—and now he's afraid he's going to get his wish! He's afraid I'll go away and disappear into the South and never come back.

"Dad, I'm not getting married, I'm just going away to school," he said gently. "I'll be home at Christmas and spring break and I'll be here all summer. Nothing's going to change," he went on, as his father stood in front of the refrigerator, watching suspiciously out of the corner of one eye.

"Nothing's gonna change . . . ?"

"No, Dad, nothing's going to change," Duff assured him.

He was lying and they both knew it, but it was the thing a son had to do.

They lay in two picket-fence rows, like swords in a dueling academy, thin shafts of glinting steel and dull graphite connected to heads of space-age metals—except for a few stubborn blocks of burnished wood, still glowing, defiant as coals on the hearth amidst the ice-cold, high-tech promises of ever longer and straighter shots. The old pro smiled almost invisibly when his young student reached reverently for one of these pear-shaped, wooden veterans. Duff gripped the handle lightly—just as Teddy had taught him on the first day he'd picked up a club several years before—gave the shaft a testing wag, then slowly turned the age-hardened wood this way and that, letting the light play off the glossy dark finish like sunlight on a chestnut thoroughbred, then placed it reluctantly back on the shelf. She was as beautiful as a Bugatti, but she would win no races.

Teddy McGill nodded as Duff's hand went to the most lethal-looking saber in the arsenal, its glittery shaft as hard and stiff as diamond, its face a massive chunk of sculpted titanium that looked as if it might serve to forge horseshoes as well as drive golf balls.

"That'd be the one," the pro confirmed. "Extra long, extra stiff and extra heavy. Excalibur itself."

And I'm King Arthur, Duff said to himself as he took the driver down from the shelf. When he gripped and shook it, he heard thunder rolling across the sky. "Sounds like rain," he commented.

"I heard nothin'," Teddy replied.

"I like the feel of it."

"It was made for you."

"How much?"

Teddy shrugged as he turned and walked to the counter. He never remembered the price of his own stock, nor did he sell much expensive equipment at the public course. His players, locals and city people who only played on vacation, mostly bought cheap beginners' sets or were content to rent clubs for the few times they would play, but he always liked to display a few premium sets in the shop, if only to give the place a professional look. And the driver that Duff had in his hand indeed had that look.

"The suggested retail price is six hundred dollars," he said, running his finger down the price list. "The spoon and the cleek"—the Irishman favored the Royal and Ancient terminology over the modern 3-wood and 4-wood—"should be about five hundred dollars apiece—but I can't find them listed here. . . ." he mumbled. It was perhaps just as well that the little Irishman didn't sell many clubs, as he was scarcely a businessman by nature. "Figure another coopla thousand for the irons and a bag—did they steal your shoes, too?"

"Both pairs."

"Then the whole kit and caboodle should cost you about three grand."

"Three thousand . . ." Duff repeated miserably. He knew Teddy wouldn't charge him the retail price, but with only a couple of hundred dollars to his name and the caddying season not yet in full swing, he wasn't even in a position to begin negotiations. Sadly, he replaced the driver in the rack.

"Just a minute," the pro said. He took the driver from the rack and extended it horizontally in two hands, tantazingly, to his putative customer.

Duff stared longingly at it, shining beautifully in the morning light through the shop window, and slowly shook his head. "I'm broke."

"Since when have you not been? But not to worry, lad, I have a plan."

Before he could ask about the plan, Duff allowed the pro to place the driver in his hands. One way or another, it had to be his.

The clubhouse lay at the top of a winding drive bordered by a low stone wall, an imposing old pile anchored stolidly atop a promontory overlooking a wide bend of the Hudson River. Built in the early nineteenth century from great blocks of the same sand-colored stone that lined the drive, it had served originally as the family home of a

Dutch merchant who had grown fabulously wealthy in the fur and timber trade.

"The fookin' Dutchman had a dock right down there," Teddy continued, pointing through the windshield as they crested the hill, "where he kept a steamship for goin' in and out of New York if you can believe it."

Duff stared down the hillside, dotted by great oak and beech trees that had been there even before the Dutchman had cleared the site for his mansion. Since then, however, enough of them had been cleared to carve 18 rich green fairways across the rolling hillside. When they stopped in front of the clubhouse, a uniformed bagboy took their clubs from the car while a second attendant took the car to the visitors' parking lot. Duff had never played or even seen Hudson Oaks, although he had played a few of the jewels in the Westchester County Crown—Winged Foot, Sleepy Hollow and the Westchester Country Club. He found them all to be a challenging but fair test of golf— even if lacking the mystery and complexity of the great seaside courses of the East End: Shinnecock Hills and the National Golf Links, where the wind seemed to blow in four directions at once and still the fog concealed the fairways; while the bunkers, like ghostly outfielders, repositioned themselves under struck drives. The narrow, tree-lined fairways of Hudson Oaks would be less tolerant of the long driver's mishits than those of the short hitter, Duff thought, as he stared down the gun-barrel 18th hole from green to tee, but the lush fairway looked as if it would receive a shot like a goose-down pillow.

"If you can play Westchester, you can play Hudson Oaks," Teddy had said, when proposing his plan the previous week.

It was to be a money match against a gambler called Blackjack Stricker—who had beaten Teddy out of a couple of thousand dollars in Florida the previous winter— and the Hudson Oaks pro. Like most golf pros, Teddy believed that perpetual summer was as much a perquisite of his profession as complimentary green fees and, being

a bachelor with few needs, managed to find a teaching
job and cheap digs somewhere in Florida every winter.
The tanned Irishman always seemed amazed when he got
back to Montauk in the spring to find that those poor souls
who had stayed through the harsh winter hadn't frozen to
death or been eaten by starving wolves. But Teddy didn't
go to Florida just for the weather. What skill he lacked
as a businessman—and his salary at the Montauk Muni
was a meager one—he usually made up for in the off
season, hustling golf games with the wealthy amateurs in
Naples and Palm Beach, players who, given enough
strokes, were sure they could beat even the best professionals. Some of them were quite good players with
single-digit handicaps, but even the wealthiest of them,
bankers, lawyers and brokers for the most part, had a tendency to let the backswing get shorter and quicker as the
stakes got bigger; while the seasoned professional, who
often lacked the money to pay off should he lose, maintained the rhythm and tempo that separated him from the
amateurs. Hustling golf on two continents, Teddy had
come across a lot of amateurs with greater physical skills
than himself—there were few touring pros who could hit
a ball as far as Duff—but none with the nerves and con-
sistency of the professional.

Blackjack Stricker was a player of limited ability who
unfortunately understood that quite well; but he was—and
this was even more unfortunate—one of the most skilled
gamblers Teddy had ever come across. Jack had little interest in the mechanics of the swing but a keen interest
in the mathematics, and wouldn't play a match until he
was given a more than a comfortable number of strokes.
Teddy knew Jack would demand too many strokes of him,
but he was hoping to make up for it with his gangly,
teenaged ringer.

"I put up the money, I take the winnings or the loss,"
Teddy had proposed.

"And what do I get?" Duff asked.

"You get your clubs at the wholesale price, right now,

and you can pay for them by the week, over the course of the summer."

It was a good offer, but knowing how badly Teddy wanted this game, Duff knew he could do better. Teddy's weakness as a gambler was his pride. When Duff beat him out of a mere $6 for the first time just the summer before—winning all three points of a $2 Nassau match, the first nine holes, the second nine and the 18-hole total—Teddy demanded a rematch the very next day. It took the master a long time to accept the harsh fact that his student was finally capable of beating him, at least some of the time. Having lost once to Stricker, the practical gambler should know enough to avoid him in the future, but Teddy, Duff knew, would keep coming back until he beat him.

"How much did you lose to him last winter?" Duff asked.

"What makes you think I lost?"

"Come on, Teddy. . . ."

"About two grand," the pro admitted.

"Okay, I'll play with you," Duff countered, "providing all winnings over three thousand dollars goes to the purchase of my clubs."

"In other words if I win I get to pay for your clubs. . . ."

"It should make us both play harder," his potential partner pointed out.

"It's a fine wager for you, but I can't say the same for myself," Teddy complained halfheartedly. "But I'll do it."

Duff had known he would.

"Duff!" Teddy called from the doorway, motioning him to follow.

They walked down the carpeted hallway, past an enormous dining room where a corps of white-coated attendants were unfurling the linen tablecloths and setting out the engraved silver and crystal. Beyond the French doors lay the patio and pool—silent and empty on this spring weekday—yet Duff was easily able to envision the privileged youth who would soon fill that gilded frame, for

F. Scott Fitzgerald had already described it vividly for him on a wintry day years before. Past the pro shop, crammed with more stock than a Nevada Bob's, they descended a long flight of stairs to a basement room where rows of tall mahogany boxes, each with a brass nameplate, stood like coffins awaiting interment. A very old black man escorted them to an anteroom filled with lockers without nameplates, and pointed out the shower room reserved for guests. He asked if they wanted a cup of coffee, which Teddy declined for both of them as he pressed a $5 bill into the clawlike hand.

Teddy said little as they changed shoes and started out to the practice range, so Duff, too, held his tongue. He had a lot to win but nothing to lose, while Teddy stood to lose more than he could afford. The pro claimed to play best when under the most pressure, yet he'd suffered some disastrous Sunday crack-ups during the several years he'd managed to scratch out a living on the Pro Tour. Teddy was in his mid-forties now and, like thousands of other golf pros all over the country, hopeful that by the time he reached 50 and was eligible for the Senior Tour, his game would somehow move to the winning level that had eluded him the first time around. His inspiration was Jim Albus, a one-time Staten Island municipal golf course professional who quit his job to go out on the Senior Tour, where he promptly beat the likes of Nicklaus and Trevino and quickly made more than a million dollars in prize money. When Duff suggested that Albus might have also been a great player when younger but unable to afford the insecurity of the Pro Tour, Teddy went into a silent depression for several days. The cruelly seductive Senior Tour, it was beginning to seem to Duff, was the National Basketball Association for old white guys. Teddy was not the kind of player to blame others for his bad play, but nevertheless, Duff didn't want to say or do anything that Teddy might later blame for their loss—should they lose.

Their bags, strapped to a cart, were waiting on the practice tee with their caddie when they arrived, but there was no sign of Jack Stricker or his partner, the club pro. They had already warmed up and were waiting on the practice green, ready to go whenever their challengers were ready, their caddie informed them. They each hit a bag of balls, beginning with the wedge and working up to the driver, then boarded the cart and drove wordlessly up to the practice green where their opponents waited.

Blackjack Stricker, with bulging neck and florid jowls, looking like a college lineman gone to seed, rumbled across the green with a big grin and outstretched hand. "How ya doin', Teddy?" he called.

"Very well, thank you, Jack," Teddy said, taking his hand with the respect and cordiality peculiar to gamblers, even while each knows the other is intent on taking a great sum of money from him.

"And this must be your ringer," Jack said, turning his grin on Duff. "Jack Stricker."

"Duff Colhane. How do you do, sir?"

"Hey, none of that sir crap!" He laughed. "How am I gonna beat somebody who calls me sir? What happened, Teddy, all your old partners give up on you?"

"It's true," Teddy said, with an expression of great sadness. "I've lately been playin' so poorly that I'm forced to rob the cradle for new partners."

"He may be young, but I hear he hits it a ton," Jack Stricker said, looking his opponent up and down.

When Teddy had called to propose a match with an unknown kid, Jack had phoned some of his gambler friends from Shinnecock and the Atlantic and the National for an assessment of the boy's game, but none of them knew anything about him, which wasn't surprising as very few teenagers had the money to play with middle-aged millionaires. Teddy claimed the kid was a 6 handicap—which meant he was probably no more than a 3—but Blackjack Stricker had to know more before consenting to a rematch with the wily Irish pro. He had, after all, very nearly beaten him and his pro in Florida, even after

Jack had allowed himself a most generous and thoroughly unjustified handicap. Learning nothing about one Duff Colhane from the members of the exclusive East End golf clubs, Jack next phoned some of the club employees he knew, the keepers of the gate who allowed each other onto their exclusive domain for an occasional evening scramble. It was a kind of informal employee's exchange program that went on among the assistant pros, caddies and greenkeepers at many private clubs, of which only a few members were aware, usually the better players who enjoyed the keener competition provided by these kids. Jack Stricker was aware of the practice because he had been one of these kids himself while growing up in the shadow of Sing Sing Penitentiary, playing quarter skins with his fellow caddies at Sleepy Hollow in near darkness. Now he was a member of the venerable Hudson Oaks Golf Club, a wealthy real estate developer who played $100 skins in the daylight. This young man, Duff—strange name—reminded him a little of himself at that age—or how he imagined himself at that age: trim and lithe with a determined set of the jaw. He even looked a lot like his son, who, unfortunately, had not inherited his father's predilection for the game.

Jack called his pro over, a young man named David Lambert, with a Florida tan and very white teeth. Lambert was the new assistant. Teddy had never played with him, but he had also called a few pros in the area to get the book on him. He was long: if his driver was working, he could be formidable; if it wasn't, he could shoot a big number. He was, Teddy remarked to himself at the time, a player much like his own partner. The four men exchanged handshakes on the center of the practice green, like fighters meeting in the ring, then walked to their carts and drove to the first tee.

Duff and Lambert stood at the back of the tee, swinging their big drivers slowly, like heavy scythes, while their partners stood between the tee markers, reaffirming the previously fixed terms of the match. Once all the intelligence had been gathered, Teddy had reluctantly agreed that Duff would play to a 3 handicap, Jack to a 7, and the two pros would go off at scratch.

"Thousand dollars three ways—automatic presses . . ." Golf talk for big money floated to the back of the tee.

It was a Nassau match, an 18-hole contest worth three points at a thousand dollars each; one point going to the team winning the first nine-hole match, one point for the second nine-hole, and one point for the overall winner of the entire 18-hole match. If the match were tied after the front nine, the back nine was then pressed, meaning it was played for two points. If any team went two holes down in the match, a separate challenge automatically issued, whereby a separate match was begun from scratch, to be decided at the end of the first or last nine holes. If Stricker and Lambert lost all 18 holes, Duff calculated while whistling Excalibur through the air, he and Teddy would win eight press bets worth eight thousand dollars, besides the three-thousand-dollar Nassau! Duff knew the chances of winning all 18 holes were extremely remote, but if they could just win the Nassau and a couple of presses, they would have five thousand dollars, enough to satisfy Teddy and leave him two thousand toward his new clubs, bag and shoes. One way or the other, at least that much money would change hands today, Duff guessed.

"Being our guests, we'd like you to have the honor of teeing off first," Jack said, sweeping his hand over the perfectly manicured teeing ground.

Duff thanked him and started across the tee to the markers.

"No," Teddy said, pointing to the driver in Duff's hand and shaking his head. He could not afford to have his partner gun his first shot into the trees, then waste one or two holes trying to collect himself. Statisticians might claim that each stroke is equally important, but golfers know the first stroke is the most important one of the round. "Hit three-wood, lay up short of the bunker," the pro instructed.

"That bunker's not in play," Duff said, confident that he could carry the sand with Excalibur.

"The advantage is not sufficient," Teddy decreed.

"It's at least a two-club difference," Duff argued. And the way he was hitting his new driver, there was no reason he shouldn't risk the longer shot.

"All this strategy on the first hole—I'm afraid we're in for a long day, Dave," Jack Stricker remarked to his partner as he pulled a long cigar out of his golf bag.

"Okay. . . ." Teddy sighed, stepping back to give his partner room. He didn't like the play, but neither did he want to upset his teammate on the first hole of the match.

Duff took two practice swings, aligned his shot and stepped confidently up to the ball. He took the driver back, heard the sharp tinkle of cellophane at the top of his backswing, and skyed a drive that settled softly under the front lip of the bunker.

Cooly silent, Teddy selected a 3-wood and knocked it short of the bunker in the center of the fairway. Stricker did the same, while Lambert, relaxed at having his partner safely in the fairway, hit driver over the bunker and left it in the first cut of rough.

"Good shot," Duff said, as they walked to their carts.

"Thank you," the pro replied perfunctorily, as if he expected to be saying it for the rest of the round.

"Listen to me," Teddy began patiently, as he drove down the first fairway. "It's my money, I call the shots."

"He crackled his cellophane," Duff protested.

"And before this match is over he's liable to grab you by the balls. You're playin' a hustler now, not a schoolboy."

"You mean 'cheater,' don't you?"

"If the money's enough, anybody will cheat," the golf pro assured him. "Now are you goin' to listen to me or are we goin' to lose this match?"

"We're goin' to win," Duff imitated, as Teddy stopped the cart near his ball.

Teddy hit a 4-iron safely to the center of the green,

while Duff was forced to blast a wedge over the front lip of the bunker, followed by a 7-iron to the back of the green. From there he 2-putted for a bogey while all the others made par. The master didn't have to say anything to his student as they drove to the second tee; the virtue of patience was plainly to be seen.

Playing conservatively off the second tee with a 1-iron, Duff parred the hole, as did the others; and they arrived at the long par-5 third hole, where Duff and Stricker each got one stroke, with the match unchanged.

Teddy watched his drive land well to the right of the last oak tree guarding the dogleg-left fairway, then turned to his partner and said, "Now hit the driver as hard as you can."

Duff reared back and deliberately halted at the top of his swing, half expecting to hear the crackle of cellophane or glimpse some movement behind him, but this time he wasn't distracted. Nevertheless, he glanced Stricker's way as if he had been, just to put him on notice, then stepped back to his ball and flushed it, drawing it well past and around the lone oak.

"You sure got all of that one," Dave Lambert said, as he watched Duff's ball taking the short but dangerous route home.

Stricker whistled. "They told me he could hit the shit out of it. . . ."

After Jack and Teddy hit their second shots safely to within easy reach of the green, Stricker and his partner walked up to have a look at Duff's lie before deciding on their shot. If the lie was good and their opponent stood a chance of reaching the green in two, Lambert would have little choice but to go for it himself. And even if Duff might not be able to reach the green in two he could probably clear the menacing pair of eyebrow bunkers that lay sentinel some 40 yards in front of the green, leaving him a short chip to the hole; whereas Lambert, lying 20 crucial yards behind the amateur, had to either explode a perfect 3-wood over the eyebrows or, with great luck, thread a low driver shot through the narrow opening.

"Take out your driver," Teddy said softly.

"I can't hit the driver off that lie," Duff said knowingly. He had practiced the shot on the driving range the day he got the club and found that it lacked the loft to get the ball airborne off any but a perfect lie.

"I know that, and you know that," Teddy said. "But Jack Stricker doesn't."

Duff smiled faintly as he pulled the headcover from his driver and slid it out of the bag. He had forgotten that his partner was also something of a gamesman.

Stricker looked Duff's way, saw him swinging his driver back and forth, like an angry cat switching its tail, and made his decision.

"Go for it," he ordered his partner.

Lambert cracked a perfect fairway driver!—except for the few blades of grass that got between the clubface and the ball and took a few yards off the shot, not a lot, just enough to deliver the ball to within a few inches of the top of the eyebrow and from there send it trickling down the face of the bunker, ending finally in a fateful heel print, hard up against the lip of the bunker.

"Bad luck," the gambler said. "Live by the sword . . ." Were he aware just how bad his partner's lie was, he might not have been so philosophical.

After watching his opponent's ball settle in the bunker, Duff put his driver back in the bag and replaced it with the 3-wood. He took it back in a long arc until, near the top of his backswing, something moved behind him and the clubhead moved a fraction of an inch off its intended path and the ball hooked left like an errant rocket, dropping out of sight in the thick rough short of the green.

"You moved!" Duff charged, turning on the golfer behind him.

"I don't think so," Jack Stricker said.

"I saw you."

"Or if I did I'm terribly sorry—I had no idea. . . ."

"I'm sure you didn't mean it, Jack, but could you be a

bit more careful?" Teddy asked, politely but pointedly.

Protesting his innocence all the way to his ball, Stricker took out a 7-iron and lashed it to the back of the green, very near the hole. Teddy took a hurried shot with his wedge, caught it a little fat and left his approach on the front of the green. Lambert tried the impossible and ended up taking two shots to get out of the bunker, while all Duff could do out of the deep grass was blast it to within 40 feet. It was all academic, as Stricker easily 2-putted for a natural-par net birdie and their team had a one-hole lead.

Over the next few holes, while their opponents enjoyed the honor, Stricker began walking off the tee a split second before Duff made contact, resulting in tee shots that trickled into the damp rough. When Duff complained, the hustler apologized and thanked him for pointing it out, then did the same thing on the next tee. Duff managed to convert for par on the short par-4s and the par-3, but bogeyed the long par-4 seventh hole, as did Teddy.

When they came to the par-5 ninth, the team was two down and on a press. Both the host players knocked 3-wood to the flat part of the fairway, just short of the church pew bunkers, as did Teddy. When Duff reached for his 3-wood, Teddy stopped him.

"I'll get the par, you go for the birdie," he said, then turned to Stricker. "And would you try to hold your position just a bit longer, Jack?"

"I'll wait here till you call me," the golfer promised, taking a second cigar from his bag.

"And please don't crinkle your cellophane," Duff added.

"I think it's beginning to get a little touchy out here," Stricker remarked to his partner.

Duff hit a big drive that looked like it might be enough, until a spray of sand in the last church pew announced otherwise.

"It was a good try," Teddy said gamely but with little enthusiasm as they started up the hill. He had very much

wanted this rematch with Jack Stricker, so much so that
he had given up too many strokes, he was beginning to
worry. Lose your head, lose your money. . . . "We've got
to bear down, partner," he said, laying a hand on Duff's
shoulder as they walked to his ball. "We have to birdie
this hole and win the fookin' press anyway, then get 'em
on the back."

When they rounded the dogleg, they saw a small group
of spectators gathered around the ninth green, waiting to
get an update on the big-money game before setting out
to play their own $5 Nassau. After Stricker's second shot
failed to bounce out of the damp rough on the high side
of the fairway, as it ordinarily would, and Lambert left
himself with more than 150 yards to a severely sloped
green, Teddy thought he glimpsed some light at the end
of the fairway. Before hitting his shot, he walked up to
the last bunker to have a look at his partner's lie. To safely
hit it over the lip of the bunker, Duff could hit no more
than a 6-iron, both players agreed. Duff would make five,
maybe four if he got lucky, and Teddy would hope for a
birdie.

However, when Teddy returned to his ball he had another thought. If he could hit a perfect fairway driver, he
might be able to bounce the ball up onto the front of the
green, leaving him with an almost sure birdie, or possibly
even an eagle. They'd still lose the front nine by one hole,
but at least they'd win the thousand-dollar press bet. He'd
hoped for better on this front nine but it was scarcely an
impossible position.

Duff stood to the side of the church-pew bunker and
watched Teddy, as he adjusted his stance to a ball that lay
several inches below his feet. Duff didn't like this play at
all, but it was Teddy's money. . . . And when he watched
his professional partner come up and out of the shot, just
a fraction of an inch but enough to send the ball on a
sickening arc from left to right, he was suddenly afraid
the money was lost. He hoped for a second that the ball
might catch the right bunker, but it soared over it, caught

the downhill side and leapt into tall grass that had never before seen a mower.

"Fook! Fook, fook, fook!" Teddy shouted, beating the ground with the offending driver.

Teddy double-bogeyed the hole while everyone else parred it, Stricker's for a net birdie. The team lost the press and was three down on the Nassau going to the 10th hole.

"Jack's strokes are killing us," Teddy muttered.

Not to mention his cellophane, Duff thought. "We'll get 'em on the back," he said.

But it was not to be. The team lost the back by one hole despite Duff's 2-under-par 34. Teddy's grudge match with Blackjack Stricker had cost him four thousand dollars on top of the two thousand he'd already lost.

"When am I gonna learn you never give seven strokes to a guy who carries a one-iron," Teddy grumbled on the dolorous drive home. Other than an occasional ejaculated obscenity, that was about all he said.

Duff, who'd set off in the morning expecting to win a free set of golf clubs but instead now owed the pro two thousand dollars, said little more. The 1-iron had nothing to do with it. You just don't play for money against a guy who crinkles his cellophane.

Gena said she'd rather die than attend her senior prom.

Duff was all right with that, but Gena's mother was devastated. She had missed her own graduation dance 25 years before and was convinced that that was why her romantic life had taken a downward slide, resulting finally in her husband throwing her over for Pie Face, and she was not going to stand by and watch the same thing happen to her daughter. She couldn't explain it, but there were certain things required of a woman—rituals of behavior that had to be observed, attitudes that must be concealed—and so far her daughter had shown little respect for these conventions. In fact she was openly contemptuous of them. She insisted that she and Duff were just friends, yet she refused to see anyone else. She was so beautiful she could have any boy she wanted, but she wanted nobody! She just wanted to be an actress, probably marry an actor like her father and end up with what . . . ? Not that a boy who wanted to be a professional golfer was a bargain. . . .

She had just about given up all hope of getting her daughter to the prom when she happened upon the beaded black gown in the hospital thrift shop, a beautiful and incredibly expensive dress from Saks that some too-rich Hampton socialite had donated to charity after only a few wearings. It was the perfect dress—cut too low but she could do something about that—that any girl, especially an exhibitionist like Gena, would be unable to resist.

And she was right. Once Gena saw herself in the dress, saw how it set off her long lean lines and sun-kissed cleavage, she was smitten. She had to have it and someplace to wear it just as soon as possible, even if only to her senior prom. In fact, she finally realized, that was the perfect place. This slinky, daringly cut, shimmeringly beaded black dress, standing alone among the white and peach taffeta like a daring and graceful exclamation point, would serve wonderfully as her final farewell.

"Of course I'll have to pull it together in front," her mother said, inching the bodice closed.

"You'll do no such thing," Gena said, pulling away.

"Gena, your bra will show!"

"Mother!" she exclaimed, and flounced out of the room.

Duff was puzzled by her change of heart—he'd had a hard time finding a tux at the last minute—but happy that she'd changed her mind after seeing her in her distinctive prom dress. From the moment they entered the gym, well after the dancing had begun, all eyes were on her.

"Let's show them something," Gena said, as she slipped into his arms and began to dance.

"Like Scott and Zelda," Duff said, as they glided among their classmates, the boys staring admiringly at Gena, the girls glaring.

"Didn't she end badly?" Gena asked.

"Died in a fire in a mental institution."

"I must be thinking of somebody else."

Debby Harris, who'd been the queen of the class until Gena matriculated and would never get over it, danced by in a cloud of pink chiffon and called over the football captain's shoulder, "We thought you wouldn't be caught dead here!"

"You mean I haven't died and gone to hell? Don't you think her mother's wedding dress looks nice on her?" Gena said as they danced away.

"Snob," Duff said.

"Just making the most of what I've got, that's all. The only thing I'll ever inherit from my father is his good looks, and that's my ticket to New York. That's not snobbism, that's the American way. Did I ever tell you you're a wonderful dancer?" she asked, as they moved gracefully across the gymnasium floor.

"I've been working on my tempo," he replied.

Later, after Debby's somewhat drunken date worked up the courage to cut in, the log-jam was broken and all of Gena's spurned suitors lined up for a last consolation dance with her, imagining what might have been, while their girlfriends chatted gamely among themselves. As the evening was drawing to a close, marked by slower, romantic numbers, Gena's sad admirers drifted back to their dates—they knew the rules—and Duff got her back. He wasn't annoyed, in her reflected light he only looked that much better. The band was playing "I'll Be Seeing You," closing in on "Good-night Sweetheart," the evening about to draw to its sentimental conclusion. Their classmates in rented tux's and virginal white gowns (some destined soon to be wedding dresses) stood locked in close embrace, some with tears in their eyes, swaying like grass in a faint breeze. Most of the guys had removed their clip-on bow ties and opened their shirts, and a lot of them were drunk after too many trips to the parking lot.

"After you win the U.S. Open, will you ever come back here?" Gena asked, her lips close to his ear.

"I suppose I'll have to if they rename the Montauk Muni after me," he answered. "What about you, will you make a guest appearance after you're a big movie star?"

"I'll order my pilot to fly low and tip a wing on my way to Cannes," she answered.

"The people will be thrilled."

"It's more than they deserve."

"I'll Be Seeing You" drifted to a close, and the orchestra drifted softly into "Good-night Sweetheart" as the white-coated band leader addressed the graduates in a mellow baritone voice reeking with sincerity. He told them they'd been a great audience, congratulated them on their graduation, wished them joy and prosperity in the future, and reminded them that his band was available to play wedding dates. Then the music swelled and the dancers clutched tighter, and Gena lifted her head from Duff's shoulder and raked her eyes across the dimly lighted gym.

"Just look at them," she said. "The poor bastards are so happy—they have no idea their best years are already behind them."

"They're happy because they're going to go off somewhere soon and make mad passionate love," Duff pointed out.

"Relax, you'll get your strokes."

"I don't want strokes. I want a real game."

In a voice mockingly sweet, she replied, "You know I'm saving it for the man that I marry."

"The shame of it is, you're saving it for some struggling young actor who doesn't deserve you half as much as I do."

"Probably true," she allowed. "But at least I'll have the satisfaction of knowing that I didn't rob a promising young golfer of a brilliant professional career."

"As I told you before, you've got a greatly inflated idea of your power over me."

Her laugh was a silent puff against one ear. "Did you ever see 'The Blue Angel'?"

"You mean those Navy pilots?"

"No, darling, it's a movie—about this uptight German who falls in love with a cabaret singer, Marlene Dietrich, and she ruins his life."

"But I'm not an uptight German."

"But I'm a Marlene Dietrich," she said, grasping and spinning him in a flashing pirouette as the brass section squeezed out the last bittersweet notes.

The dancers applauded, then the girls excitedly hugged and congratulated one another on the successful completion of their first significant rite of passage, while the boys dug out their car keys. Some were going to a party at a friend's, while others, the big spenders, were going to Gurney's for a late supper and an early morning walk on the beach. Duff and Gena had made no plans.

"Let's go to Leo's party," she suggested, as they walked across the parking lot to her Fiat roadster. It had been her father's summer car until he had given it to her to sort of soften the blow of his divorce from her mother. It had seemed an unusual though not unwelcome token of appeasement at the time—until she later learned that Pie Face had given him a Mercedes to celebrate the same divorce, and he had no room for two cars in the city. He was an exasperating father as well as husband, equally capable of unconscious cruelty or unusual generosity. Although still in the honeymoon stage, he had persuaded Pie Face to allow her to stay with them in their New York apartment until she could find a place of her own, which had doubtless required a lot of nagging, as Pie Face did not like beautiful, long-legged blondes anywhere within camera range; not even a daughter.

"Leo Hover?" Duff questioned, as he released the roof catch on the passenger side. Leo lived in a tiny house beside the railroad tracks with his mother and two younger sisters. Leo was the class screw-up, a bright but lazy student and a great athlete who would rather work at the gas station after school than waste time on the practice field, despite the pressure from coaches and teachers. Duff admired his spirit but was careful not to get too close, as Leo was a daredevil and a schemer whose exploits usually caused greater harm to his friends than to himself. "Where's Leo throwing a party?"

"You'll see," she said, folding the roof down.

She started the engine and roared backward, nearly hitting Cindy Koslow who had left her glasses at home on prom night.

"Hey watch it!" Cindy's date called, as Gena shifted and squealed away.

Duff pestered, but she wouldn't tell him where they were going as she headed into town and turned on the Montauk Highway. At the edge of town she pulled off the highway and around the back of the darkened Shell station where several pick-ups and customized cars were parked. The rear windows were covered, but a dull red light seeping through the seams and the throb of heavy metal from within left no doubt—this was Leo's party.

Gena turned off the engine and asked, "Cool?"

"Do you really think this is a fitting end to the golden years of high school?" Duff asked, as he nevertheless climbed out of the car and followed her through the side door and into the marijuana-smoke-filled lube room.

There were few couples in formal dress, mostly guys in leather and denim, some with matching girls, more without, clutching long-neck Buds and passing roaches back and forth. Marijuana was the theme; this wasn't the party for the college-bound. Most of the guys had graduated or dropped out of school a few years earlier and were making good money building big houses in the Hamptons, and would continue to do well until the stock market went south, when they'd go back to cutting lawns and clamming and clipping food stamps.

"Gena, do we really want to be here?" Duff asked.

"I promised Leo—" she began.

"Gena—Duffy!" Leo, in his trademark black leather jacket, burst through the crowd like a chorus boy in West Side Story, big white teeth and dull blond pompadour, long arms open wide. "Glad you could make it!" he cried, gathering them both in his arms and kissing Gena on the cheek.

"Where else would we be?" Duff replied, while Gena struggled good-naturedly against Leo's powerful embrace. He was like a friendly gorilla welcoming them to his zoo.

"Where else indeed!" he shouted over the heavy rock emanating from the boom box on the tool shelf. "We got the admissions director from Princeton right over there, the one hoggin' the joint; and Harvard right here. . . . And now we got Gena Hall, the hottest chick in Montauk and all the Hamptons, and her date, Tom fuckin' Cruise! You must know some fancy undertaker," he said, fingering Duff's satin lapel. "How was the dance?"

"Okay."

"Everybody missed you," Gena said.

"And I'll always miss them," he said. "So what now? Life on the wicked stage and golf college, right?"

"Right," Duff said, as Gena nodded.

"Good luck. But if it doesn't work out you can always come to work for me. Meanwhile mingle, get yourselves a beer. . . . Or something else if you like. This chick is so hot," he added, as he moved off.

"He's mad."

"Can we go now?" Duff pleaded.

"Now who's being a snob? Mingle, make some new friends, get us a beer," she said, moving off.

"Where are you going?"

"To cop a toke."

Duff said nothing. Marijuana made her amorous. Lately they'd begun smoking it in her room during their afternoon trysts and each time she'd allow him to go a bit further, until it seemed she was almost ready to give in. He even suspected that this was the night she'd been waiting for—graduation was more momentous than either of them let on—and he was therefore carrying a pack of condoms in his tux jacket, just in case. So if she wanted to smoke a little grass to get in the mood that was okay with him. As for him he didn't need anything. He was already getting hard just anticipating his graduation gift.

He stepped carefully around the lift and oozed through the crowd to the stationary tubs where the beer was stored. He pulled a bottle from the ice water, unscrewed the cap and took a long drink. He had shared some bourbon with Jerry Cruz in the men's room earlier, but the glow was long gone, and he felt the need for an added boost. Not too much. He'd read that alcohol inhibits sexual performance, and while he could scarcely imagine such a thing—he and Judy Thomas always got blotto before they did it—he didn't want to do anything to mess up tonight.

"Hey, preppie, how was the dance?"

Duff turned to a thinly bearded kid in a frayed denim jacket cut off at the shoulders to reveal a dripping dagger from shoulder to bicep.

"Not bad, townie," he replied.

He knew it was dumb to get in a fight and wreck a rented tux, but he was his father's son, he couldn't help himself. But this guy was just a bluffer who'd had too many beers, he quickly calculated. And familiar. Right! He was the scrawny kid who'd been a couple of years ahead of him in high school—the one who wouldn't shower after gym class until some guys threw him in the shower and scrubbed him with floor brushes.

"Spotless . . . ?"

"You remember me?" Nick Spoto asked, wide-eyed. His nickname was all that had distinguished him during his four years at Montauk High.

"How could I forget you. . . ."

"You're the golfer, right?"

"Duff."

"Duff, right—how ya doin'?" he asked, reaching for his hand.

"Fine," Duff answered, shaking hands.

"You still playin'?"

"Still playing. What are you doing?"

"I'm workin'—workin' with Leo," Spotless answered, with a backward thrust of his head.

"With Leo . . . Doing what?"

"This and that."

"This and that . . . Anything legal?"

"You a cop?" Spotless grinned.

"No, Spotless, I'm not a cop," Duff said, as it suddenly came clear. Gena's pot, the promise of cocaine . . . Leo Hover was her connection. He was dealing drugs, right here. This was no party, it was a fucking drug bazaar! And the way it was with Leo, he and Gena would get busted and nothing would happen to him.

"You lookin' for the chick you come in with?" Spotless asked.

"Yeah, you see her?"

"She's hot, man."

"So I've been told. Where is she?"

"She'll be back."

"I know she'll be back. Where is she?" Duff demanded, clamping his hand around Spotless's dripping dagger.

"Hey, be cool!" Spotless whined, trying to extricate his arm from the golfer's strong grip. "She's with Leo!"

"Where?"

"Try the john."

Duff released him and pushed heedlessly through the crowd, making for the men's room on a wake of angry complaints. He burst into the office, past Leo's startled lieutenants, and pulled hard against the locked bathroom door.

"Gena! Open the door!"

"Just a sec!"

A moment later the door opened and Gena emerged with Leo.

"Hey, Duff . . ." Leo greeted.

"We're going," Duff said, grabbing Gena's wrist.

"Hey, man, you just got here," Leo protested.

"We gotta go," Duff said, pulling Gena after him.

"If you gotta go . . ." Gena called back, as Duff pulled her through the door and out into the night.

"You knew what was going on in there!" he charged.

"It's just a party."

"A drug party."

"So they were doing a little coke; who isn't?"

"I'm not." He stopped at the car, turned her face to him and peered into her dark eyes. "You did a line of coke in the john."

"Lighten up," she said, pulling away.

"Did you make a buy?"

"I bought a little something for us, yeah."

"Get rid of it."

"What . . . !"

"I'm not getting in the car with you while you're holding."

"Duff, you're overreacting," she warned, anger rising in her voice.

And blowing my chance to make it with you, he reminded himself. He wasn't squeamish about drugs, most of the kids in their class had experimented with them, some quite seriously. But he didn't want to get caught holding, not now, not when everything was finally perfect, not when he was about to go to Southeastern. And in a fishing village where drug smuggling wasn't that unusual, the cops were especially vigilant. They would soon discover Leo's drug operation and close it down, maybe even send him to jail. Yet it was unlikely they knew anything yet. Hell, he'd only discovered it himself a few minutes ago. There was, he had to admit, little risk in getting in the car with her, and the possibility of great reward.

"Okay, let's go," he said, opening the door for her.

She puckered up and kissed him lightly on the lips before sliding under the wheel. She started the car and drove out the way they'd come in. Before they'd gone a hundred yards, the revolving roof light of a Montauk police car pierced the darkness like a prison beacon.

"Get rid of it!" Duff ordered, as she pulled the car to the curb.

"Be cool," she said.

The cop got out of the patrol car and swaggered up to them. Duff recognized him in the pulsing light—the same cop who had once arrested his father over a drunken brawl in a bar—and he just hoped to God the cop wouldn't make the connection.

"License and registration," he droned.

Gena handed them to him and waited quietly while he studied them. When he compared her to her license photograph, she smiled her thousand-watt smile. Don't overdo it, Duff said to himself.

"How was the prom?" the cop asked, handing the papers back.

"Great."

"Fantastic," Duff added. He was going to let them go.

"Had anything to drink?" he asked, peering into Gena's eyes.

"No, sir," she smiled.

"Then why are your eyes dilated?"

"Must be all the excitement, graduation and all . . ."

"Because we don't drink at all," Duff assured him.

"Your name Colhane?" the cop asked.

"Yes, sir," Duff answered weakly. He knew. The old man was a lush so the kid has to be.

"You run outta gas?"

"No. . . ."

"Then why'd I see you comin' outta that gas station?"

"We were just cutting through the lot," Duff said.

He cocked his head at Gena and asked, "That right?"

"That's right," she answered with a big smile.

"Step outta the car, please," he said, opening Gena's door.

"You too, Colhane. Just stand up on the curb. You got any objection to a search?"

"Yes," Duff replied.

"No," Gena replied, almost simultaneously.

"She don't seem to mind," the cop said.

Duff said nothing as the cop stepped in front of Gena. She held her arms out and smiled invitingly, her beaded purse swinging from her right hand. What the hell was she thinking of? The cop looked her over like a horse buyer, then ran his fingers lightly down both sides of her skin-tight dress before stepping back and looking down at her cleavage.

"I'm not wearing a bra, so I can't be hiding anything there," she said in a teasing voice.

The cop reddened and looked away. When he took her purse, Duff knew it was all over. Gena was going to be busted for drug possession, but worse, he would not be going to Southeastern. The cop dumped the contents of the bag on the hood of the Fiat, sorted through everything, tasted her face powder, then put it all back and returned the bag to her. Amazing! Where the hell was it?

"Now what about you?" the cop said to Duff.

Duff shrugged. "Fair is fair."

He frisked Duff more closely, up and down both legs, checked his socks, then started through his jacket pockets. He found the condoms and held them up for Gena's inspection.

"Wishful thinking," she said.

The cop frowned and returned them to the suspect. He was obviously not pleased at the thought of the drunken fisherman's kid getting it on with a beautiful girl like that.

"Okay, you can go," he said. They thanked him and got into the car. "But a word to the wise . . ."

"Yes, Officer?" Gena smiled.

"I know what's goin' down around here."

"Yes, sir," she said, then started the car and drove slowly away.

When they were safely down the road she repeated in a deep voice: "I know what's goin' down around here."

"I give up, where is it?"

"Someplace I knew he'd never look."

"In your panties?"

"I'm not wearing any panties."

Duff swallowed hard. Tonight was the night.

To celebrate Duff's eighteenth birthday, his father and Rita Soames insisted on taking him to Sal's for a drink. Sam hadn't proposed anything to celebrate his acceptance to Southeastern or even so much as congratulated him, but on his eighteenth birthday a Montauk fisherman's son had to have a drink with his father at Sal's, a ramshackle saloon on the fishing docks that looked as if it had been assembled of flotsam and jetsam washed up on the beach over the years, which was at least partly true. The original shack, built by the present owner's grandfather before the war, had seemed to grow on its own over the years, like a mushroom in the damp air, adding cell after cell as more sportsfishermen came each year in pursuit of the big one. The dingy walls were hung with their faded photographs, proud sportsmen and their captains posed beside their near-record catches, champagne and beer bottles clutched in their hands. There were several pictures of Sam Colhane on the walls, standing straight and slim as a U-boat commander in black turtleneck and billed hat on the deck of the Night Star, the boat he'd lost after his wife died and the drinking got worse. Looking at him now, his thickened body and flattened nose, you'd never know he was the handsome young man in the photographs, Duff thought, as he studied the one behind the bar. Back then he'd looked like Mountbatten; now he looked like a battered old salt who drank too much, just like so many others. It was an occupational hazard among the fishermen who gathered in Sal's over the long winter when the ice clamped down and the boats couldn't go out and there was no other work to be had. Most were able to cope, turn it on in winter when sobriety was least required, then off in summer—or at least keep it to a workable flow.

Sam, however, was one of those without the luck, only able to turn it off when the money stopped.

Looking at his own reflection in the mirror beside the youthful image of his father, Duff wondered if he had the luck. He didn't drink often, but at parties where the beer was plentiful, he enjoyed getting a buzz on, even getting a little drunk, but he was always able to turn it off until the next party. He didn't know for sure what he might do if there were a party every night, but he figured he could handle it. Anybody who'd gotten a free ride to Southeastern certainly had the luck.

"So, birthday boy, what'll you have to drink?" Rita asked, hauling her full body up onto the bar stool next to him.

Rita was a waitress at Gurney's. She wasn't especially pretty, but she was always smiling as if somebody had just told her she was—or else it was because she knew that with a body like hers a plain face was no great drawback. Rita was technically married—to a handsome Portuguese man who had drifted down from Provincetown one year when the fishing was bad up there, then drifted up to Georges Bank one year when the fishing was good up there, and was never heard from again. "Probably shacked up in an igloo with some Eskimo girl," Rita joked, which wasn't far from the truth. In fact he was living in St. John's with a half-Aleut prostitute, now reformed except in the winter when things got slow in Nova Scotia and she took on a few select clients. If Sam would marry her, Rita would get a divorce, but he never mentioned it so she hadn't bothered. There were more than a few Montauk fishermen who'd marry Rita Soames in a minute, but as long as Sam was around, she had no wish to marry anybody else. She'd been madly in love with Sam since high school, and when he'd married Amy Duff, which was understandable as she had been the prettiest girl in school, Rita had wanted to die. But when instead it was Amy who died, just a few years after Rita had married her Portuguese fisherman, she wasn't terribly upset about it. For a while she felt a little guilty, but she couldn't help being elated at having a second chance at Sam Colhane even though she was second choice, and even though she was now an inconveniently married woman. She waited until Amy had been in the grave for a week, then came calling on Sam with a pot of mine-strone and stayed for the afternoon. She didn't think her husband ever knew she was carrying on an affair with Sam, yet he had become unusually quiet shortly before leaving for Georges Bank, which made her sometimes wonder. It didn't bother her though, as she was no more unhappy about her husband leaving than she had been about Amy Duff's death.

"I guess I'll have a beer," Duff replied.

"Oh come on, honey, it's your birthday!" Rita bawled, clamping a hand over his thigh. "My God, you're like a rock—have a daiquiri or something sexy like that."

"No daiquiris," Sam said. "He'll have a beer and a shot back. Make it an Irish whiskey, in honor of your mother."

Duff knew his mother never drank, but he wouldn't argue. He didn't like the taste of whiskey, but he drank it dutifully while Sam's friends cheered the birthday boy. Then someone bought another, then still another, until it looked like it wouldn't end until the birthday boy passed out. But after the third the ruddy-faced man in the cap-tain's cap, who was sitting conspicuously at the bar with only a Coke in front of him, spoke up.

"He don't need no more," Captain Dobbs said, and the bar grew apprehensively silent.

They all watched as Sam stroked his big jaw, as he had a familiar habit of doing when he was getting angry, then sighted down the bar at the unsolicited advisor. "Andy, it's the boy's birthday," Sam said, in a surprisingly mild manner.

"And many more to him," Andy said, lifting his red can. "And to his father."

Sam picked up the shot glass intended for his son and raised it. "And to you Cap'n Dobbs."

The tension broken, the babble resumed.

"Bring out the cake!" Rita hollered.

"Cake . . . ?" Sam said.

The cooks at Sal's could make a hamburger or fry fish and that was about all. But a moment later, when the cook came out with a huge crabcake with 18 lighted candles, Sam gave Rita a hug and a kiss as the assembly broke into "Happy Birthday." When they finished, Duff blew out the candles and Rita cut the cake into wedges and passed them around, first to Duff and Sam, then to the others. As soon as Duff finished his beer, there was another one sitting on the coaster in front of him, the foam sliding down the glass, and it looked very inviting. He was getting drunk but he didn't mind, it was the easiest way to get through the evening.

Some time later, Rita threw an arm over his shoulder and pressed her big breasts against his back. "So what'd you wish for?" she asked.

He twisted and looked blankly at her. He had wished for nothing. He wished this party would end; wished his father hadn't thrown it in the first place; and he wished he would never end up a fisherman—although these were hardly the kind of wishes he could admit to anyone here. Besides, there was no danger of his staying here now, not now that he was headed for Southeastern in a few weeks.

"I wish I'd make enough caddying so I could buy a car," he improvised. He'd so far made almost enough to pay for his clubs, and if the rain held off he'd have a few hundred dollars saved when he left for school.

"I'll mention it to your father," she said.

Duff grinned drunkenly and lifted his glass. The only thing his father could give him was a leaky boat, but to Rita he was the man from whom all God's blessings derived. It was reassuring that love could be so blind even into middle age. Crazed with love for Gena Hall as he had been at 15, at 18 he had become sadly disillusioned.

"Actually there's one other thing I wish," he added after a moment.

"What's that?"

"I can't tell you."

"Whattaya mean you can't tell me—we're family. Come on. . . ."

"Anyway it's not gonna happen, not now."

"What's not gonna happen—tell me."

"Just between you and me . . . ?"

"Waitress's honor," she said, extending her open hand.

"I wish I could've made it with Gena Hall."

Rita's chin dropped. "You didn't?"

"Nope," he said, shaking his head sadly.

"The girl must be mad!" she exclaimed, clapping his face in her hands. "Either that or you didn't really try."

"Believe me, I tried."

"How far'd you get?"

"Rita, I can't tell you that," he said, shocked.

"Course you can, we're family."

"That's why."

"Don't be silly, tell me. You do any petting?"

Duff laughed. "Petting . . . ?"

"Did you feel her up?" she asked impatiently.

"Sure."

"Where?"

"In the car—her house . . ."

"Where on her body! Here?" she asked, hoisting her big breasts in the air. Duff stared and nodded. "Did you get your hand in?" He reddened and shook his head. "Jeez—why not? Once you get your hand on it no girl can stop. Stupido, don't you know that?" she said, rapping her knuckles on his head. "Youth—why's it wasted on the young. . . . You know what a clitoris feels like or I gotta show you?"

"I know."

"Then you go back there and you get your hand on it and you don't stop until she squeals. Then, Duffy my boy, then she'll follow you anywhere. Take your aunt Rita's word for it."

"Thanks, Aunt Rita," Duff said, sliding off the stool. He'd had enough, he was going home.

"And you better pray your old man never hears about this!" she called after him.

"What—hear about what . . . ?" Sam demanded.

Duff awakened the next morning with a head full of pain and remorse. What could he have been thinking of, telling Rita about his love life—or lack thereof? he asked himself as he fumbled through the medicine cabinet looking for some aspirin. Sam, who claimed he never got hangovers (and to prove it, was snoring contentedly in the next room at the moment) rarely had them in the house. After a few fruitless minutes, Duff abandoned the search, soaked his head under a cool shower for a long time, and set out for the golf course.

"Got inta the beer last night, didja?" Teddy needled when he showed up for work.

"It was my birthday."

"That would explain it."

"Don't worry, you'll get your money's worth."

"You can start by bringin' up some carts. If you're not too drunk to drive," he added, as Duff started out of the pro shop. "Wait, I got a message for you!"

"From who?" he asked, daring to hope it might be Gena. He hadn't heard from her all summer, not since she'd left for the city after their angry breakup on prom night.

"From Jack Stricker."

"Another match?"

"Not with me," the pro said, resolutely shaking his head. "He's playin' Larry Prescott at Shinnecock next Sunday and he wants you to caddy for him."

"Sure," Duff said. Larry Prescott was one of the biggest gamblers on the East End. If Jack beat him, Duff knew he'd be well paid.

"Here's his office number and his home phone," Teddy said, sliding a slip of paper across the glass display case.

"Thanks a lot," Duff said, walking back to the counter, reaching eagerly for the numbers.

"But there's somethin' you should know." Teddy said, covering the paper.

"Yeah?"

"Caddying for Jack Stricker is like workin' for an escort service. Nobody says you have to go to bed with the client, but if you do you'll be better paid."

"He'll expect me to cheat?"

Teddy shook his head. "Jack fancies himself an honorable man. He'll not come right out and say it, but he'll make it plain that you'll make more if he wins than if he loses. Mind ye, I'm only tellin' you so you'll be prepared."

"Then you needn't have bothered because I won't cheat for him—not for any amount of money," Duff said, with a defiant thrust of his prognathous jaw.

The old pro smiled. "But you never know till you face the test, do you?"

Duff picked up the scrap of paper and stuffed it into his pocket. He knew.

It was if nothing had happened. She phoned him at home quite late one night and told him she was coming out and would like to take him out to dinner on Saturday night. There was a lot of noise in the background—she was in a bar and couldn't hear him very well and she was in a hurry—so he didn't get much information.

"I'll pick you up at about nine!" she'd shouted, then quickly signed off.

At nine thirty on Saturday night, wearing new khakis and a white golf shirt, Duff wandered among the beached boats in his front yard and waited for Gena. At ten he decided she wasn't coming. She'd probably been drunk or stoned and forgotten she'd made the call, or maybe it was her way of getting even. Not that she had anything to be angry about. She'd led him on, teased him until he decided finally not to take it any longer, and calmly suggested that perhaps they should stop seeing each other. He'd only meant it as a ploy and was somewhat dismayed when she took him up on his offer, but still he thought they had parted friends. Apparently their relationship was more complicated than that.

He stepped up onto the porch and was about to open the door when she pulled the Fiat to the curb and jumped out, calling his name loudly. She wore a silk scarf over her hair and dark glasses, and the standard models' uniform for that summer in the Hamptons—a little black T-shirt and white jeans that fit like skin.

"Sorry I'm late, darling!" she called, striking a goofy pose for him as he started down the path. She greeted him with a quick kiss, then stepped back and whipped off her scarf and shades.

"Jesus!" he gasped. Her formerly long, caramel-colored hair was now short and streaked with blond; her once major-highway eyebrows had been tweezed down to a dirt road; her hollowed cheeks were painted peach, and her lips looked like melting cinnamon balls.

"Like it?"

He nodded. "Very nice."

"Golfer . . ." she muttered. "Get in the car."

He sat in the passenger seat and closed the door a second before she roared off. "What brings you back?"

"I wanted to see my beau."

"I thought you were mad at your beau."

"Now why would you think that?" she asked.

"You didn't phone."

"Neither did you."

"I didn't have your dad's number."

"I'm not staying with him anymore. I've got a great apartment on the Upper East Side."

"That was quick."

"I did my first commercial."

"Congratulations. What is it?"

"A shampoo for short hair. That's the reason for this

do," she said, brushing her hand through her hair. "Only they cancelled the damned product so it won't run."

"So you cut your hair for nothing?"

"Not for nothing!" she protested. "I got a shooting fee. Plus it was good experience."

"I thought you were never going to do commercials."

"I changed my mind. It might not be acting acting, but it is acting."

"So how's the acting acting going?"

"It isn't. Not yet anyway. I've been too busy."

"I thought that was the reason you went to New York, to become an actress," he reminded her.

"Some people have to make a living. I don't have a golf scholarship, you know."

He wanted to tell her that if she hadn't rented an expensive apartment she might not be so busy, but he didn't. He had the feeling that New York wasn't quite what she'd expected—maybe Pie Face had thrown her out and she'd been forced to find another place.

"Where are we eating?" he asked when she turned right on the Montauk Highway. It was so late he was afraid they'd end up at the all-night diner.

"Monte's," she answered.

"Monte's!" he exclaimed, pulling against the seat belt. It was the hottest and most expensive restaurant in the Hamptons, the exclusive reserve of the rich and the famous. "What makes you think we'll get in there?"

"I hang out at Monte's other restaurant in the city. He told me to come by any time I was in the Hamptons."

"Yeah, like let's do lunch. This is Saturday night in the height of the season, celebrities only."

"Don't be such a clam digger," she said, patting his hand.

"Okay . . ." he said, sliding down in the seat.

The parking lot was filled with exotic cars, and the bar was packed with the beautiful but not so famous, waiting hopefully for what . . . ? Romance, love, attention, a table? Fat chance. Gena strode confidently through the crowd, pulling Duff after, suddenly calling, "Monte!" as the maitre d' stepped from behind his podium to block her way.

A dark, balding man, gym-toned muscles bulging beneath a well-opened black silk shirt, looked up from a table of the beautiful and famous he'd been attending and, to Duff's amazement, signaled her over. She gave Duff's hand a tug and they stepped behind the rope and into the sanctum sanctorum. The owner greeted her expansively with a buss to both cheeks, then turned to Duff with a heavy-lidded, bemused expression.

"And this must be the high school boyfriend," he said, clamping Duff's hand in a show-off grip.

"I guess so." Duff winced.

Monte released his hand and led them to the owner's table at the back of the restaurant. "Always keep this table for high school boyfriends," he said, indicating the boyfriend's chair. Then he hooked an arm around and Gena and said, "Let's go backstage."

"Be right back," she called over her shoulder, as Monte hauled her into the kitchen.

Duff leaned back in his chair and tried to look as if he ate here all the time, while looking across the room at the crowd who did. There were a few familiar movie faces and professional athletes scattered among a sea of anonymous models and silver-haired men in blue blazers, laughing and talking, eating and drinking—as blissfully unaware of the mounting costs as the architects who built their houses. Why would Gena want to blow a couple of hundred dollars in a place like this? he wondered. To show him that she'd arrived? It wasn't like her, she was never impressed by this sort of thing. Or had she changed that much over the summer? When a waiter brought a bottle of champagne to the table, Duff quickly told him he hadn't ordered it.

"Monte did," the waiter said, popping the cork.

What the hell, he said to himself, as he lifted the glass.

It felt like Alka Seltzer but tasted like something out of this world.

A few minutes later Gena emerged from the kitchen with Monte, his arm around her, both laughing loudly over something. He sat at the table and poured two more glasses of champagne while they continued their giggling conversation, Monte speaking in short, scarcely intelligible bursts that broke Gena up, but which Duff could scarcely understand. It was if he were telling jokes in a foreign language to which Gena knew the punch lines.

When Monte left, Duff asked, "What was that about the high school boyfriend?"

"Well, weren't you my high school boyfriend?" she asked, perusing the menu.

"So it was just something you mentioned—at the models' bar?" he asked, envisioning the girls having a laugh at the expense of the homeboy.

Gena placed the menu in front of her and slowly looked up at him. "Is something wrong?"

"I'm just asking."

"Because ever since we got in the car, you've been grilling me."

"I'm sorry, I though I was just inquiring politely after you."

"Bullshit! You disapprove of everything! The high school boyfriend, the models' bar, 'I thought you went to New York to be an actress . . .'! You manage to find fault with everything I've done!"

"No, Gena, you're wrong," he answered, shaking his head slowly but surely. "I'm just a sounding board. If you disapprove of what's bouncing back, your problem's with yourself, not me."

"I don't have a problem, you have a problem!" she said, thumping her breastbone.

"You think life's a golf match and everybody plays by the rules. But I'm not a golfer, for me there are no rules. I have to make them up as I go along."

"Gena, everybody has to improvise, even golfers. If I

gave you the impression I don't approve of what you're doing, I'm sorry, I didn't mean to. And if I did, you'd have every right to tell me to go to hell because it's none of my business."

"You think I'm sleeping with him, don't you," she charged.

"Who?" he asked, knowing full well.

"Monte."

"No, I don't think you're sleeping with him."

"What makes you so sure?"

"Because I know that if you were you wouldn't bring me here to flaunt it."

Her combative expression dissolved as she reached slowly across the table for his hand. "Such a sweet, sweet boy," she said.

"Shall we order?" he asked, pulling his hand away. Nothing could be plainer—she was fucking Monte's brains out.

They ate lobster and drank another bottle of Dom Perignon and some kind of brandy that Monte sent over after they'd eaten. He had to know the high school boyfriend wasn't of legal age, but it didn't seem to worry him. This was Monte's after all, where not even the chief of police could get in without a reservation. Duff awaited the bill with fascination and dread—even though Gena had made it clear that the dinner was on her—but no bill ever came. Before leaving, Monte took Gena back to the kitchen again, and when she emerged, leaning heavily on him, Duff could see that she was too drunk to drive. What the hell was she doing—she who had left town a virgin, despite the high school boyfriend's best efforts—trading sex for dinner?

In the parking lot she handed over the keys without any fuss, even though Duff was none too sober himself. She flopped into the front seat of the roadster, laid her head back and looked up at the full moon.

"Let's go to the beach," she said.

• • •

She walked barefoot across the wet sand, white jeans rolled to her knees, then stood and waited to be chased up onto the dry beach by the next crashing wave. Duff sat on the blanket on the dune, waiting for the wave that would surely catch and soak her. He was amazed that in spite of all she'd had to drink she was still bursting with energy. Nor could he believe that Gena would pass him over for an oily guy like Monte, no matter how rich he was.

Meanwhile she was playing tag with the ocean just like an innocent little girl, waiting till the last second then rushing away from the grasping waves. When a particularly large wave loomed up in the moonlight like a giant crocodile, she squealed and staggered up the steep wall of sand, and this time he was sure the ocean would catch her. But once again she managed to lurch to the high ground as the surf grasped at her bare heels before slipping back down the wet, glistening sand. Amazing. Sober, she would have fallen long ago; drunk, she managed to escape every time.

Suddenly she shrieked and he looked up to see her against the frothy wall of a big breaker a moment before it fell on her with a dull slap and swallowed her up. Duff leaped up and ran toward the water, but she emerged safely in a moment (she was a strong surf swimmer) and staggered up onto the beach, shaking her arms like a wet duck.

"All that time in New York, you've lost your sense of timing," Duff said.

"The dreaded sea puss got me!" she laughed and spluttered as they walked back to the blanket.

Duff picked it up and snapped it in the air, then held it open to her, like a bath attendant. She wrapped it around her, blotting her clothes and rubbing her hair dry, then spread the blanket and sat.

"I just hope this didn't get wet," she said, as she dug

into her pocket and pulled out a plastic sandwich bag.

In a flash everything came clear to him—the trips to the kitchen, the laughing jags, the energy. "Did Monte give you that?"

"Monte give me—!" she exclaimed. "Why do you think we got a free dinner?"

"You gave him drugs for dinner . . . ? Gena, that's dealing!"

"Just trading."

"What the hell's the difference?"

"About twenty-five years," she laughed.

"That's not funny. You could've gotten us both in a lot of trouble."

"Relax, golf boy, your college will never find out."

She dipped the one long nail of her little finger into the bag and came out with a speck of white powder which she brought to her nose. Pressing one nostril closed, she drew it in with a quick sniff. "Wow," she said softly. She dipped her finger in again and held it up to Duff.

"No thanks."

"Come on, it won't make you an addict—or ruin your putting swing. Hurry up before it blows away."

Duff looked at the pile of coke on her proffered finger, bowed his head, pressed a finger against one nostril and inhaled with a quick, sibilant sniff. "Wow," he said.

Gena watched him intently, her wide eyes glistening in the moonlight. "Is it happening?"

"Yeah."

"Wild . . ."

"Yeah."

Suddenly she jumped to her feet. "I'm going in!"

"What!"

"Swimming," she said, pulling her T-shirt over her head and dropping it in his lap.

She slid her wet jeans and panties down over her hips and stood over him, naked, taunting, feet planted wide. He wasn't prepared—he had never seen her completely naked before, only in her underpants through which he had glimpsed her pubic hair, thick and dark as the hair on her head had once been—but now she had no pubic hair!

"You shaved . . ." he said, staring fixedly.

She smiled and stroked herself lightly. "Occupational necessity. You like it?"

"Yeah."

When he reached out to touch her she danced back, turned and ran down to the water. He quickly kicked off his shoes and scrambled to his feet. He felt a dizzying rush as he struggled out of his clothes, whether from alcohol or coke or sex—or maybe everything all at once. He didn't know this feeling—a kind of reckless daring in search of release. He heard a long howl that rose unbidden from his lungs and trailed after him like a blazing comet as he streaked across the sand, splashed through the shallows and dived into the incoming wave, coming out on the other side and stroking madly down the moonlit lane that stretched to the horizon.

When he finally stopped, nearly breathless, and treaded water while waiting for his wind, he saw he was farther from shore than he'd imagined, out in the deep water where the big sharks roamed. He pictured himself silhouetted against the moon, circling sharks below, then lay back on the water and howled defiantly at the moon. He was bulletproof, afraid of nothing. He was out of breath and his arms were heavy as waterlogged timbers, but nothing could harm him. Not sharks, not fatigue, not drowning . . .

"Nothing!" he shouted.

"Duff!" Gena called faintly from somewhere in the dark.

"Coming!"

He rested a bit more, rising and falling on rolling swells—one moment in a black tomb of water, the next atop the ocean hill—then stretched out flat and stroked for shore. Fearless though he was, his arms were nevertheless heavy as he struggled against the riptide that was

carrying him downshore, away from the place where Gena
waited for him with her smoothly shaved body. His graceful stroke had become awkward, he gulped water when
he lifted his head for air and for a time lost sight of any
shore lights.

Stop fighting, ride the rip, he reminded himself.
Shouldn't have sniffed dope. Shit! He stretched out on the
water and took off like a cork on the tide, with no idea
where he was being taken. Finally he saw a great light
flickering red and yellow in the distance—a beach fire,
not very far away. He was gliding toward it.

He heard his name and looked shoreward and saw Gena
splashing through the surf, running naked beside him, her
hairless body glowing white in the moonlight. He began
to stroke, first one hand then the other, reaching for shore,
for Gena's smooth shaved flesh.

Suddenly she was in front of him, wading out to gather
him in her arms and pull him up onto the beach where
they collapsed in a gasping heap. When they looked up
they found themselves surrounded by clothed people with
beer cans and hot dogs, staring silently at these two naked
people who had washed up from who knew where.

"Hi," Gena said.

First one spoke then they all spoke, asking if they were
all right (they were) where they'd come from (up the
beach) if they needed anything (wasn't it obvious?). They
offered them beer and hot dogs (they declined) then
watched as they got to their feet. There was an audible
gasp at the sight of Gena's hairless part, as if they feared
she'd been shorn by the surf. They invited them to warm
up by the fire, rest a bit, but Duff said they had to get
back, then they turned and started off. Sadly the party-
goers waved, their backs to the fire, as the naked cast-
aways faded into the darkness.

Their embarrassment gave way to laughter as they
lurched down the beach, stifled at first, then increasingly
raucous, finally uncontrolled as they collapsed helplessly
on the blanket. They squirmed and wriggled and rolled

around on the blanket, clutching themselves—until they found each other. They embraced, their mouths met, straining fiercely, hoarsely together, then parted and went off on a mission of discovery. They grappled like wrestlers, or dancers, gentle but violent, graceful but tortured, harsh groans of love issuing from their twisting bodies. She was endless, a twisting labyrinth of possibility and pleasure from which there was no exit. He would bury himself in the salty soft smoothness of her and remain there forever.

At dawn they awoke, their bodies sealed tightly together by the glues of love, like a pair of barnacled mollusks washed up by the sea. He opened his eyes to see her watching him, one eye open, one closed, a smile working at her swollen lips. He winced as they unlaced their limbs. His head throbbed with champagne, he was chafed and burning, his mouth was bruised and his tongue felt as if it had been torn up from the floor of his mouth, and he'd never felt so wonderful in his life.

"Wow," he whispered hoarsely.

"Wow," she replied.

"You sure you feel okay?" Jack Stricker asked his caddie as they started down the first fairway at Shinnecock.

"I'll be okay," Duff assured him. Scattered clouds shaded the morning sun and a cool breeze was blowing in off the ocean, yet he was already wet with perspiration and white as winter.

"You look terrible."

"Don't worry about me, worry about the game," the caddie advised.

"Yeah, right. This is the big one, Duff. We win this one, we'll both be in clover. I'm gonna need your help."

"In what way?" Duff asked. *Ask me to cheat so I can go home and go back to bed.*

"Any way you can."

"I'll do my best," the caddie replied. I'll carry the bag, find the ball, tell you what club to hit and which way the green breaks.

"Good man," Jack said, with a light chuck to the shoulder.

When they arrived at Jack's ball, which lay some thirty yards behind Larry Prescott's drive, he pulled an iron from the bag without consulting his caddie and left it short of the green.

"Shit, I hit that good!" he complained, slamming the club back into the bag.

Duff shook his head. "You never had enough club."

"Why the hell didn't you tell me that before I hit?"

"You didn't ask."

"Look, I'm not one of those players who resents unsolicited advice, okay? I want you to help me any way you can. I thought I made that clear, for Christ's sake."

Larry Prescott knocked his ball onto the green, and when they went to the second hole Duff's bag was 1-down. Jack was pissed, until his caddie coached him to a solid par and he went to the third all square.

"Teddy tells me you got a golf scholarship to Southeastern," Jack said, as he watched Prescott's ball roll onto the third green. "Nice shot, Larry."

"Not exactly a scholarship, some alum's paying my way," Duff grunted as he hoisted the heavy bag to his shoulder.

"Very nice. Who's the sport?"

"Mr. Cawthon."

"I'll be damned!"

"You know him?"

"If they play for money, I know 'em. And Earl Cawthon's a big-money player. Matter of fact I was supposed to play with him in the Vegas Calcutta, but we decided to pass this year."

"How come?"

"Too much cheating."

Too much cheating for Blackjack Stricker? Duff mused, suppressing a grin. Must be a Hell's Angels tournament. Jack asked how he'd met Earl, and Duff told him about his nearly great round at the Southeastern tryout.

"Too bad about the last two holes, but that was a hell of a round. If you need anything, I want you to give me a call," Jack added.

"Thanks."

"I mean it. I just wish my kid would go out and do something like that. The way he's going he might not even get into college," he muttered, as he eyed his next shot. The ball lay about 10 feet off the green, either a chip or a putt. A skilled player would chip it, intending to make it; while an unskilled player would putt it, just trying to get it close.

"What would you do?" Jack asked his caddie.

"I'd chip it," Duff answered. Jack nodded. "Give me the six-iron."

"Uh uh," Duff said, handing him the putter.

"You said chip it!"

"I said *I'd* chip it."

Chastened, the golfer putted the ball across the short grass onto the green and to within three feet of the hole, then tapped it in to tie his opponent. "Good call," he said.

By the time they reached the sixth hole, Duff was feeling worse than ever and had to go into the trees to stick his finger down his throat.

"You and your buddies must've put away a lot of beer last night," Jack remarked when Duff appeared, chalk white, from the woods.

"Not my buddies," Duff, no beer-drinking high school kid anymore, replied.

"You were out with your girlfriend?" Duff nodded. Jack stopped at his ball and looked at his caddie. "What'll I hit?"

"All you've got. Just get it over the pond."

Jack said that a well-hit 3-wood would go over the green (and it would) but Duff insisted he hit it. He hit it poorly (as his caddie guessed he might), but it cleared the water and made the front of the green. When Duff complimented his player on a good shot, his player didn't correct him.

"Your girlfriend likes to drink?"

"My girlfriend likes to do everything," Duff responded.

"Good for you. But if you want to be a professional golfer—and I'm sure you do—you're gonna have to stay away from the booze."

"I don't drink very often."

"But when you do you drink a lot?"

"Sometimes."

Jack nodded surely. "Take it from a guy who knows—that shit can waste you."

"I know that," Duff responded with a telling sigh.

"Your father?"

"Yeah."

Jack had gathered as much from Teddy. "That's another reason to stay away from it. How old are you, Duff?"

"I was just eighteen."

Jack nodded approvingly. "My son was just sixteen. You remind me a lot of him."

"I'm sure that's a compliment," Duff said. But from Jack's pained look it was apparent that his son was not yet a great source of pride.

At the ninth hole Jack went one up on the Nassau, winning the front side, which was worth a thousand dollars. It was a five-way Nassau, so the back nine was worth two thousand and the overall match was worth another two thousand. Automatic press bets—after a player went two holes down—were worth another thousand each. Although Jack maintained his poker face, he was in a buoyant mood after winning the front nine.

"You want a Coke or something?" he asked his caddie as they walked to the clubhouse.

"No Coke," Duff answered. "But could I have a beer?"

"Beer?" Jack asked, halting at the steps and turning.

"It'll make me feel better. This'll be my last," Duff assured him.

"Just remember that," Jack said before starting up the stairs.

"Could you make it two?" Duff called after him. "For Mr. Prescott's caddie. He's afraid to ask."

Grudgingly, Jack entered the small bar at the end of the clubhouse, emerging a few minutes later with two cans of beer. Duff stashed one of the cans in Jack's bag and drank the other as he hurried to the top of the hill at the 10th fairway to await their tee shots. By the time both players arrived at their tee shots, well short of the hill, Duff was already into the second beer and feeling a little light-headed. The way Jack stared at him as he walked to his ball, Duff was afraid it showed, and he pulled himself erect, the alert and dutiful caddie.

But Jack Stricker was thinking of something else entirely while staring appraisingly at his caddie. He was thinking of his own son, just a couple of years younger than Duff but not half the golfer. And he was thinking of the Vegas Calcutta. He hated to miss it, he had played in it every year for ten years and hadn't won a thing. There were some phony handicaps and a bit of cheating in any big-money tournament—and this was as big as it got—but lately the Vegas had gotten completely out of hand. Until a short while ago he was convinced that there was no way he was ever going to get back any of the money he'd lost to those sharpers—almost a hundred thousand dollars, he estimated—but suddenly a faint possibility had begun to glimmer in his mind. It was an unusual and risky idea, yet simple. So simple in fact that the more he thought about it, the more he realized it was fucking ingenious!

Due to a couple of mental errors on Jack's part, the back nine was all even when the players arrived at the last hole. He had become so preoccupied with his plan to win the Vegas Calcutta that he was having a hard time concentrating on the match at hand. He had to put this

drive in the fairway, his caddie had reminded him before
starting down the fairway to await the fateful shot. Even
Corey Pavin, in the shot seen round the world, required
a 4-wood from the fairway to reach the green and win the
'95 Open. Anything in the rough by either of these amateurs was a bogey at best, possibly even a double.

Prescott was first to hit. It started left and his caddie
moved into the rough, then backed out as the ball faded
and settled nicely on the edge of the fairway. "Shit!" Duff
exclaimed, as Prescott's caddie, suddenly sure of a big
tip, grinned at him from across the fairway. They both
knew the pressure would be too much for Stricker. And
it was. Duff watched helplessly as the ball sliced over his
head, caught the edge of the fairway and dived into the
right rough. It could be a very bad lie, down in a nest, or
half way decent, sitting up on the grass, Duff knew as he
ran after the ball. He saw when he got there that it was
worse than he could have imagined. The ball was not just
down in the grass, it was down in a fresh divot. It would
be all his player could do to advance it a short distance
with a wedge. If the ball had rolled just an inch farther,
it would've ended up atop a natural grass tee with a clean
furrow behind, affording him a clean shot to the green,
Duff realized as he surveyed the dismal scene. Or even if
the thoughtless player ahead of them had repaired his
divot, Jack might've stood half a chance of getting his
ball close to the green. But as it was he had almost surely
lost the match. It was indeed a cruel game.

Duff knew what was expected of him—Prescott's caddie was far enough away that he could move the ball
without being seen—and if he didn't Jack would know
he had failed him. Until now there'd been no reason to
cheat, Jack's lies in the rough had been good enough that
he might assume Duff had been improving them all along.
Now, however, he'd know better. It was too bad, Jack
was a nice guy, he didn't deserve to lose this way. And
if he did, so too did Duff lose the financial help Jack had
promised him. His toe was resting directly behind the ball,

all he had to do was push. But he wouldn't, not for any amount of money, he reminded himself, as he remembered the old pro's words: You never know till you face the test.

"How's it look?" Jack asked as he approached the ball. Duff didn't answer. Jack looked at the ball, then at his caddie. "Another inch and I'd've been fucked."

Larry Prescott watched with disbelief as his opponent's ball soared up and out of the rough and onto the green. He was still thinking about that shot, wondering how Jack could've brought it off, when he pulled his approach into the left rough. From there he took a double-bogey and lost five thousand dollars to Blackjack Stricker.

Duff put the clubs in the trunk of the black BMW and waited while his happy employer pulled a wad of bills out of his pocket. They were all hundreds, thousands of dollars in gambling money that Jack had been prepared to lose in a game of golf, more than enough money to pay for a year of college.

"We make a good team," Jack said, as he pulled one bill from the stack.

"You played well," Duff said.

"I was a little distracted on the back nine."

"But you managed to keep it together," Duff said, closely watching the magician's hands as he lightly fingered a second bill. Magic! Duff exclaimed silently as he peeled the second bill from the pile.

"I was thinking about the Vegas Calcutta," he said, not yet handing over the money.

"Yeah?" Duff said, watching him slowly slip still another bill from the deck.

"How would you like to play as my partner?"

"Go to Las Vegas?" It wasn't possible.

"Everything on me," Jack said, sliding a fourth bill loose. "If we win, you get twenty-five percent."

"Twenty-five percent of what?" he asked, his eyes on

the money, four hundred dollars in the magician's right hand, thousands more in his left.

"First place is worth fifty thousand. Plus the Calcutta pool of course. You know how that works?"

"Not exactly."

"Everybody bids on the teams and the owner of the winning team takes the pot. That's always worth at least a hundred thousand. So figure you'll make about forty thousand for a weekend's work. If we win."

"Forty thousand dollars!" What was the catch? There had to be a catch. "What if we lose?"

"You've gained some valuable experience and had a nice weekend in Las Vegas," he said, pulling another hundred-dollar bill from his left hand. He was now waving five hundred dollars under Duff's nose.

Duff could smell the money, all forty thousand dollars, but he knew there had to be a reason he couldn't take it. It was just too easy.

"Why me?" he asked. "Why don't you take somebody who can pay his own way—like Larry Prescott?"

"Larry's no pressure player; you are. And more important, with you I play well."

Duff didn't think he'd played all that well. But his opponent had played worse, so he was right not to take Prescott. Duff was ready to grab the money and take Jack up on his offer, until he remembered the reason he couldn't. "If I won I'd lose my amateur status," he said, shaking his head sadly. All that money . . .

"You don't win. I win. If I choose to make a gift to you, that's strictly between us," Jack explained.

"I don't think it works that way."

"Of course it does. Earl Cawthon's paying your way through school, isn't he?"

"Yeah."

"And that doesn't violate your amateur status, does it?"

"No, but that's not . . ."

"It's exactly the same. When you and Teddy McGill beat some sucker out of a few hundred bucks, you don't ask the USGA if it's okay to take the money, do you?"

"Of course not, but . . ."

"Well this is no different, except the stakes are a little higher."

"A lot higher."

"The amount doesn't mean a thing because the USGA and the NCAA are never even gonna hear about some cockamamie Calcutta in the desert. Believe me," he said, pushing the five one-hundred-dollar bills into Duff's hand, "there is no risk."

Duff looked at the money, then at his benefactor. "I'll have to ask my dad."

"Of course," Jack said. No lush was going to turn down forty grand.

The gambler was right. Sam saw no reason his son should pass up a chance to make forty thousand dollars, and what the USGA and the NCAA didn't know wouldn't hurt 'em, and they could all go fuck themselves anyway. Accordingly, two weeks later Duff found himself seated in the first-class section of a jet plane bound for Las Vegas to play a big-money game with Blackjack Stricker. Being his first time in a plane, he was careful not to attempt to adjust the lights or air until he'd watched Jack do it. He affected the air of a jaded, first-class frequent flier as the plane taxied onto the runway, while at the same time paying close attention to the pretty stewardess who, to a recorded message, mimed the emergency procedures in case of an accident. When the captain finally announced that they were ready for takeoff, he clenched the armrests and pressed back against the seat as the plane raced down the LaGuardia runway and rose up into the blue sky. Relieved to feel the plane safely in the air, he leaned forward and watched the boats on Flushing Bay become smaller and smaller as the jet banked and swung around into the setting sun. He had the feeling his life was just beginning and it was going to turn out just like one of those stories by F. Scott Fitzgerald.

"You ever been to Lost Wages?" Jack asked, as the plane reached cruising altitude.

"No—that's one place I've never been," Duff answered.

"Chump city. Bunch of mugs from the Midwest lined up to give away their money, then get back on the plane and go home and beat up the old lady. You don't gamble while we're there," he said, raising a warning finger.

"Right," Duff said. Apparently playing golf for a hundred and fifty thousand dollars wasn't gambling. Anyway, he had no intention of throwing his money away on the craps tables if they won the Calcutta. Forty thousand dollars! He still couldn't believe it. Even if they only won second prize he'd still make enough to buy a good used car.

"And no drinking," his partner added. Duff nodded. He should've told Jack it was something he'd eaten, like his father always did. "You want a Coke or something?" Duff said he'd have one, and Jack called to the stewardess for a Coke and a Black Label. "It relaxes me," he said, when he caught his partner eyeing him.

"You don't want to be too relaxed tomorrow," Duff said. For forty thousand dollars he didn't want a shaky partner.

Jack smiled and replied, "Don't worry, I got a good partner."

"It's the guy with the high handicap who wins these tournaments, not the scratch player," Duff reminded the gambler unnecessarily. Duff's job was to make a few birdies if he could, while Jack made par for net birdie, but above all to hold par when Jack bogied or double-bogeyed.

"I know," Jack said, still smiling.

When Duff had his drink and was settled back in the big comfortable seat, he discovered why Jack was smiling.

"By the way, there's something I forgot to mention."

"Yeah?"

"You won't be playing under your own name tomorrow."

"What are you talking about?"

"I entered you as my son, Jimmy Stricker."

Duff turned in his seat and stared incredulously at his partner. "You're telling me this now—after we're in the air!"

Jack waved his drink dismissively. "I didn't think it was that important."

"Not important! You're asking me to cheat!"

"Keep it down," Jack cautioned. "And listen to me. This is Vegas, not some USGA event. These guys may be amateur golfers, but they're professional gamblers. Cheating is an accepted way of life. Getting caught is the only thing that's unacceptable."

"It's not acceptable to me."

"Oh no? When you caddied for me, did you move the ball?"

Duff hesitated. "Once."

"Once, twice . . . It's still cheating."

"This is different."

"It's no different," Jack said. "Duff, I'm telling you, we're not going up against a field of sportsmen, we're going against a bunch of hustlers and ringers. Hell, the guy who won last year was teamed up with one of his Japanese customers with a 16 handicap, only it turned out later he was a pro on the Asian Tour."

"I don't care if they're a bunch of thieves and murderers, I'm not playing under a phony name," Duff replied.

"Not for forty thousand dollars? Think about it, Duff."

"Not for anything. I'll play under my name and my handicap, but not as your ringer."

"My ringer. At least my ringer's an amateur."

"Yeah, and if I get caught that's all I'll ever be."

"Is that what you're worried about—getting caught? Because I promise you, there's nothing to worry about. They've already checked my son out, they know he's a legit twelve at Hudson Oaks and there's not a soul in Vegas whose ever seen him before. Here, look at this," he said, thrusting a few cards at Duff. "It's his school ID, library card, club membership, handicap card. This fuzzy picture could even be you, not that I'm gonna show it. Who's gonna question it? Nobody!"

"No," Duff said, pushing the cards away. "I'm not going to do it."

"So what am I gonna do now, turn the plane around?"

"That's your problem. I'll do as I agreed, I'll play under my own name and to my own handicap, but no other way."

"That's just great! You're gonna play to scratch against a bunch of fucking hustlers."

"They can't all be hustlers."

"No, they're not all hustlers. Some are worse. You know how a lot of these guys make their money?"

"No, and I don't care."

"Drugs."

"Come on."

"I'm not talking about dealers, I'm talking about the money launderers, the guys in the nice suits and shiny shoes, the bankers and accountants and lawyers. You have no idea how deep this shit goes. As an example, there's a guy in this tournament, a respectable dealer in art and antiques, went to Yale or some place like that, and you know where he makes his money?" Duff shook his head. "He sells Picassos and Hepplewhite credenzas to Colombians for cash, duffel bags full of twenty-dollar bills. Then he and his wife—one of those Park Avenue ladies who lunch at Mortimer's and go to fashion shows all the time—they go to Vegas for a week and they go to all the casinos, buying five-hundred-dollar chips with twenty-dollar bills. They win a little, lose a little, mix it all up and go back home with all their money nicely washed and ironed. You feel guilty about taking money from people like that?"

"They can't all be crooks," Duff replied sullenly.

"Show me a guy willing to lose all that money and you can be pretty damn sure he didn't come by it honestly. It's guilt money, that's why they have to gamble it away. It's a moral test. If the money comes back, they're forgiven; if it doesn't, they've been properly punished."

"Is that why you do it?" Duff asked.

The gambler shook his head. "I'm not a religious man. I believe only in the law of probability. I don't take unnecessary risks and I wouldn't ask you to do this if I thought there was any chance we'd be caught."

It might be safe, but it was still wrong. While the plane soared ever closer to Las Vegas, Duff recited the reasons he could not be part of a dishonest gambling scheme, while Jack in turn hammered away at each of his points. By the time they reached Chicago, the argument had been considerably distilled. Jack insisted that Duff's absolutist view of morality, while commendable in the world at large, had no place among the comparative ethicists of Las Vegas who would do unto others whatever they could and therefore deserved no less from them.

Somewhere over Colorado Duff had to admit to a certain logic in Jack's argument, especially when weighed in tandem with the psychological truth that all gamblers unconsciously wish to be punished, and beating them in the Calcutta might be considered by some a kind of medical service. And besides, he needed the money a lot more than they did. Suddenly the lights of Vegas came into view, like a golden glowworm on the dark desert, a long stem of pulsing incandescence.

Fifteen minutes later they were inside the terminal, among the package-tour hopefuls hauling their vinyl-piled luggage carts, like latter-day prospectors in search of the bonanza. On the drive to Caesar's Palace in a complimentary limousine, Jack's carefully reasoned argument gave way to begging. Winning this tournament meant everything to him; it wasn't just the money, it was a matter of honor; it was a chance to avenge himself against those cheating sonsabitches who'd been taking his money all these years.

"Okay, I'll play," Duff suddenly assented.

"You will?"

"I'll play as your son, and like your son."

"What do you mean?"

"I mean I'll shoot just what a twelve-handicap would be expected to shoot, somewhere in the mid eighties."

"What the hell good will that do us?" Jack wailed.

"That's the only way I'll play. Take it or leave it."

Jack looked at him, taking his measure, then replied, "Okay, I'll take it."

"You will?"

"I've got no choice," the gambler answered glumly.

Duff was puzzled. He'd been sure Jack would spurn the offer. But the gambler, a keen student of human nature who felt he knew the boy better than the boy knew himself, was betting that he was the kind of player who couldn't bear to lose, not even under an assumed name.

After checking into their rooms—Jack had the high-roller's suite, Duff the connecting room—Jack inspected Duff's clubs, counting to make sure he had no more than 14, a violation of the rules that could cost them the tournament.

"What's this?" he asked, removing an iron from the bag.

"My one-iron."

"A twelve-handicap with a one-iron? You might just as well get caught with a PGA card as this," he said, handing it to him. "Put it in the closet. I don't even want the maid to know you got it."

"What difference does it make what I'm carrying if I shoot eighty-six?" Duff grumbled, as he stashed the club in the closet.

"Just playing it safe, that's all," he said, pulling the adjoining door closed.

Downstairs in the conference room where the Calcutta auction was about to begin, the air was heavy with cigar smoke and greed as Duff followed his *father* around the room, politely shaking hands with tomorrow's competitors. On a large white board at the head of the room, the names of the 18 teams were posted. Duff found his assumed name with an adjusted 9 handicap beside it, and Jack's with a 7 handicap. His eyes traveled disinterestedly down the board, until he came to a familiar name that brought a gasp.

"I gotta get outta here!" he exclaimed.

"What's the matter?"

"Earl—Mr. Cawthon!" he stammered, pointing at the board.

"Oh shit."

"You said he wasn't gonna play!"

"He must've changed his mind. Who's he playing with?" Jack asked, peering at the board. "Never heard of the guy. The sonofabitch must've found a ringer!"

"Jesus!" Was there one honest player in the whole field? Duff wondered, as at that moment Earl Cawthon appeared in his Southeastern golf shirt.

"Jack Stricker!" he called, advancing with an amiable grin and an outstretched hand. Then he recognized the young man at his side and the grin gave way to a puzzled expression. "Duff?"

"Hello, Mr. Cawthon."

"What are you doin' heah? He caddyin' for you, Jack?"

"Earl, I'd like to talk to you," Jack said, looping an arm over his shoulder. "Jimmy, you wait here."

"Jimmy?" Earl Cawthon asked as Jack led him away.

Duff stood stock-still in the middle of the room and waited for the hotel to come crashing down on him. It might just as well, because his life was over. No risk! Shit.

After 15 or 20 minutes had passed like a day, Jack, smiling assuredly, returned with Earl Cawthon. He still looked a bit confused, but when he wished them luck and walked off, Duff was incredulous.

"What did you tell him?" he demanded.

"The truth," Jack replied airily.

"And he's not going to report me?"

"Earl's in no position to report anybody. I told him I knew his partner was a ringer, and if he reported me I was gonna report him."

"You said you never heard of the guy," Duff reminded him.

"So I bluffed him."

"I don't like it . . ." Duff began, as Jack brought a finger to his lips.

"There's somebody you have to meet. Martin!" he called.

A tall, olive-complexioned man in a dark suit and dark glasses, accompanied by a shorter bull-necked man in a Hawaiian shirt, walked slowly across the floor to Jack. "Good to see you, Jack."

"Good to see you, Martin," Jack said, shaking his hand.

"You remember Paulie."

"Sure," Jack said, shaking the hand of the torpedo-shaped man in the bright shirt.

"We were glad to hear you changed your mind," Martin said.

"Yeah, I decided to give it one more shot," Jack said. "As long as Walton's got no Japanese pro this year."

"We don't hafta worry about Walton no more," Paulie said.

"You threw him out?"

Martin shook his head. "He had an accident."

"Sorry to hear that," Jack said.

"Yeah, we was all broken up," Paulie said.

"This your boy?" Martin asked.

"Jimmy, say hello to our host," Jack instructed.

"How do you do, sir?"

"Our first father-son team," Martin said, inspecting

Duff through his dark glasses. "Twelve handicap at Hudson Oaks?"

"Yes, sir."

"Good luck," he said, then walked off with Paulie.

"Who are those guys?" Duff asked.

"One's a lawyer, the other's a union guy."

"Mafia?"

"Hey!" Jack cautioned. "They're just a couple of legit guys playing the Calcutta."

"Like us. What'd he mean about that guy having an accident?"

"I have no idea."

"You know what I think?"

"Don't even say what you think," Jack said, squeezing his arm tightly and steering him to a table. "Let's just sit quietly and wait for the auction to begin, okay?"

"I don't like this, Jack," he said, looking around the room. Suddenly all the golfers looked like mobsters.

"We made a deal," Jack reminded him.

"What if Mr. Cawthon changes his mind? What if he tells Martin?"

"Don't worry, Earl's not going to tell anybody anything."

"How do you know? What'd you tell him—that he'd have an accident if he did?"

"You're getting excited, take it easy. Earl is cool. He understands that if you get caught up in a cheating scandal, Southeastern will lose a very good golfer. And the last thing Earl wants to do is to hurt his alma mater. So just sit back and relax, everything is under control."

No, things were getting out of control, Duff knew. Okay, he'd stay and he'd play, but he'd be damned if he'd play well. Better to have Jack Stricker pissed off at him than Martin and Paulie. A moment later, in a voice made even raspier by the public address system, Paulie instructed the players to be seated for the auction.

"Can you hear me in the back?" Martin Howard called out over the microphone. He waited while the golfers got to their seats, then briefly welcomed them to the annual Las Vegas Calcutta Golf Tournament. Then the bidding began. The teams were auctioned in the same order as play: Martin and Paulie first; Jack and his son last.

"They get a lot of strokes," Jack commented when the Martin-Paulie team went to themselves for a staggering eleven thousand dollars.

But even those teams getting precious few strokes were going for enough that it was soon clear the Calcutta pool might exceed one hundred thousand dollars. When Earl Cawthon refused to bid for his own team and they were picked up by a stranger for just thirty-five hundred dollars, it was apparent that he expected Jack and Duff would win. Knowing this, Duff expected Mr. Cawthon to bid on their team, but he didn't. Nor was anybody else much interested. Jack was awarded the team for just two thousand, the lowest bid of the evening. Even so, the total Calcutta pool came to $114,000. It was almost enough to allay Duff's fears.

Jack Stricker was strangely quiet the next morning as they drove to the golf course. Even though Duff had made it clear the night before that he was going to play like a true 12-handicap, he was nevertheless surprised when Jack didn't resume his entreaties the next morning. Sooner or later, he knew, it had to be coming.

After checking in and warming up, they proceeded out to the first tee with their Mexican caddies, where Jack introduced him to their playing partner, J. T. Purdy.

"Jeeter to my friends and customers, Jimmy," J. T. said, shaking Duffs hand. "Your boy's no Jap pro now is he, Jack?"

"My son's a legit twelve."

"Just like my partner. Say hello to Charley Taylor, boys."

Charley Taylor, an extremely fat man, waddled across the tee and shook hands. Like Duff, he too was a first-time competitor, and like Duff he'd also been thoroughly checked out by the handicap committee. He'd reportedly been a very good player while growing up in Georgia, but after moving to Texas his handicap had shot up like his weight. A player who'd methodically worked his way down from a 36 to a 12 handicap was fairly predictable; but a player who'd worked his way up from a 3 to a 12 was dangerously unpredictable, always capable of going on a youthful birdie binge. But Charley Taylor's scores for the current year, none lower than 81, had finally satisfied Martin and Paulie that he was just another aging athlete who had forsaken the pursuit of laurels for the pleasures of Kentucky bourbon and Texas barbecue. However, after watching the fat man take a few practice swings, Duff was sure he was a ringer.

"What you say to a little side bet, Jack?" Jeeter asked. "Say a thousand dollars a man?"

"Make it five and you got a bet."

"No!" Duff said.

"You're on."

"Remember, Dad, I'm a twelve," Duff whispered as their opponents took the tee.

"So's Charley," Jack replied.

Does he really believe that, or is he just trying to get me to bear down? Duff wondered, as he watched Jeeter slice a drive into the desert.

"Don't just stand there, go get it!" he shouted to his caddie, who was waiting well down the fairway. "Those Mex's are good caddies, but they're scared shitless of snakes."

"You're gripping the club too tight, Jeeter," Charlie advised as he took his place on the tee. "Just remember how your first whore held your cock, cuz that's all the tighter you got to hold it."

"How am I gonna hit the sonofabitch holding the club in my mouth?" Jeeter said.

Charley made a surprisingly big turn for a man of his girth and smoothly stroked the ball far down the fairway.

No doubt about it, Duff decided, the fat man was a ringer.

Jack teed his ball up and calmly stroked it safely down the middle. Duff followed with a shot about 10 yards short of his partner. Jack said nothing as they drove to their balls. The first hole was a long par-4, the kind a 12-handicap couldn't be expected to reach in two strokes. Accordingly, Duff took his 3-wood out and hit a high shot that settled softly well short of the green. Jack followed with a 3-wood that bounced and ran almost to the green.

"Good shot," Duff said.

"Somebody's got to hit one," Jack said.

Jeeter's caddie found his ball, or one like it, and Jeeter managed to chip it off the desert scrub and back onto the fairway, from where he hit his third shot into the greenside bunker. His partner, however, hit a 4-iron that settled softly about 15 feet from the pin.

"He's no twelve," Jack said.

"So call off the bet," Duff urged.

"I'm no welsher. Hit your shot."

Duff had a full sand wedge to the green—the kind of shot that usually landed like a ballerina and danced to the hole on pointed toes—but this one skittered across the stage like a baggy-pants comedian and tumbled into the pit. From there he chipped on and 1-putted for a bogey, while Jack did the same for par. The fat man, however, knocked in his 15-footer for a birdie, net eagle!

"Even a blind pig finds a chestnut now and then," the fat man said.

But the blind pig continued to find chestnuts until, after six holes, his team was 4 under par, while Jack and Duff were just 1 under, all of it owing to Jack.

"When you said you were going to shoot in the mid-eighties, I thought you meant for eighteen holes," Jack said, after his partner hit another erratic drive off the seventh tee.

"I'm playing like a twelve," Duff reminded him.

"Yeah, but Taylor's playing like a three."

"That's not my fault."

Jack gestured impatiently and ordered, "Take the cart, I'll walk."

Duff drove the cart to where his caddie waited in the rough beside his ball. It was sitting up nicely, he could probably hit it to the green if he wished. The fat man, lying in the center of the fairway again, almost surely would. Jeeter and his ringer were going to cheat Jack out of ten thousand dollars and possibly even win the Calcutta, but there was nothing he could do about it. He no longer had any moral compunction about playing his best—he doubted there was an honest handicap in the bunch—but he still wasn't willing to risk his ass just to save Jack ten grand. He watched the fat man knock his second shot onto the green to within birdie range, then, despite a great urge to answer the shot, laid his own ball up short to within bogey range.

At the end of nine holes they were 3 under par—quite a good score considering Duff's bad play—while Jeeter and the fat man were an incredible 6 under. Martin and Paulie, who had already finished, were leading the tournament at 10 under par.

"Shit, last year Walton and his Jap pro only shot eight under," Jeeter said, peering at the scoreboard. "But don't you worry, Charley, we can beat that."

Knowing he got four shots on the back nine and his partner got five, Jeeter was reasonably sure they'd better Martin and Paulie by at least one stroke.

"Jeeter!" a voice boomed from the direction of the clubhouse.

It was Martin, with Paulie at his side, motioning to Jeeter to join them. Jeeter pointed to the 10th tee and made a swinging motion, but Martin continued to beckon.

"Fuck! I'll meet y'all on the tee," Jeeter said, then turned and walked sullenly to his cart.

Fifteen minutes later Jeeter returned gloomily to the game. "You ain't gettin' no more strokes, Charley."

"Bullshit!" Charley wailed.

Jeeter shrugged helplessly. "Martin just got off the

phone with some asshole at your club. He told him you might be a twelve in the computer, but everybody in the club knows you're no more than a three. So Martin says you been sandbaggin' and you got to voluntarily relinquish the five strokes you had comin' on the back nine."

"That ain't right!" the fat man wailed.

"Charley, you're talkin' to me now, remember?" Jeeter said, patting him on the shoulder. "Under the circumstances, Jack, feel free to call off our bet."

"You're Goddamned right—"

"No!" Duff said.

"Jimmy, we're three down."

"I know, Dad, but I think I'm going to play a lot better on the back nine."

"You're sure?"

"Positive."

Jack stared appraisingly at him for a moment, then turned to their opponents. "We're doubling the bet, gentlemen."

Jeeter looked to his partner, got a faint nod and replied, "We're down."

Duff was gambling that the fat man's anger would undo him, at least for the first few holes, while he would run off a few pars and get the match back to even. Getting five strokes to Charley's none, Duff was confident he could win four of the next nine holes and capture the match without putting himself at risk. Maybe he was no more honest than Charley, but what the hell, this wasn't golf. It was just a high-stakes craps game played on grass, and all the players had shaved dice. If a player gets caught cheating, he's not even thrown out of the game, he's just stripped of a few strokes and sent back out to play. This wasn't golf, it was something else, a game with which Duff was unfamiliar.

Charley led off, hitting a vicious duck-hook deep into the left rough. He and Jeeter both bogeyed the 10th hole while Duff parred it, followed by a birdie at 11 and another par at 12, and suddenly the match was even.

"You're pressin'! Stop pressin'!" Jeeter chided through clenched teeth, as they walked to the 13th tee.

"If you'd get in the fuckin' game, I wouldn't have to press so hard," Charley replied.

"I'm tryin', Charley, I'm really tryin'," Jeeter assured him.

"If that fuckin' kid's a twelve, I'm Tiger fuckin' Woods."

"Just stop pressin' Charley, stop pressin'."

"You say that one more fuckin' time, Jeeter . . . !"

When Charley hit his second shot stiff to the 13th hole for an easy birdie, it looked to Duff as if they would lose a hole—until he hit his second shot to within 15 feet and made the putt for a birdie to tie.

"Jack, I think we gotta adjust here," Jeeter said, after a conference with his partner.

"What the fuck are you talking about!" Jack shot back.

"Jack, let's not bullshit each other—your boy is no twelve."

"And your boy is?"

"Okay, let's say we were both a little off on our math. And that being the case, we think Jimmy should voluntarily relinquish his remaining strokes in our little match— just so there won't be no trouble in the big match."

"Are you threatening me?" Jack demanded.

"I reckon you could say that."

"Dad, it's okay!" Duff said, stepping quickly between the two of them. "I'll give up my strokes."

"I think that's the honorable thing to do," Jeeter said.

"It's fuckin' blackmail, that's all it is," Jack grumbled, reluctantly stepping back to allow Duff the tee. It was a short but narrow par-4, no more than a 1-iron and a firm wedge. Duff made a vicious pass with the driver that left the ball just short of the green.

"Holy shit," Charley breathed.

Duff pitched to within a few feet of the 14th hole for a tap-in birdie, then followed up with pars on 15 and 16. Freed of the weight of dissimulation, he was swinging heedlessly, thinking only with muscle and adrenalin.

Neither was Charley Taylor, however, an uninvolved spectator. Apparently pleased to be finally playing in a fair game, he ran off two pars and a birdie, bringing the match back to even and getting the team to 7 under par as they headed for the 17th tee.

The fat man led off with a beautiful drive that settled softly near the right rough, which Duff answered with an even prettier shot to the opposite side of the fairway. Both Jack and Jeeter hit poor drives, but it didn't matter, it was down to a 2-hole match for twenty-thousand dollars between Duff and the fat man.

"Just pick it up and get out of my way," Charley advised, after Jeeter shanked his third shot into deep rough.

Jack hit a solid 3-wood but still came up well short of the green, while Charley hit a 5-iron that leaked into the thick rough to the right of the green. When Jack saw the ball disappear into the grass, he was sure Charley stood little chance of getting up and down. All his partner had to do was hit it safely to the center of the green and 2-putt for a par and the win.

However, when he discovered his partner's ball lying close beside a sprinkler head, he was not so sanguine.

"I'm taking relief," Duff announced.

"Wait a minute!" Jeeter hollered, rushing over to have a look. "It don't look to me like that sprinkler head's in your way."

"What the fuck are you talkin' about!" Jack protested. "There's no way he can hit that ball without hittin' the sprinkler head!"

"Shit, he's got a good two-inch clearance there," Jeeter said. " 'Course you're free to ask Martin for a ruling— see how he feels about giving relief to a twelve handicap who's two under for the last seven holes."

"You prick!" Jack shouted.

"You're right about that, Jack. For twenty thousand dollars I can be a mighty big prick. Now you want to hit that shot or call for a ruling?"

Again Duff stepped between the two men. "I'll hit it, Dad," he said, pulling his wedge from the bag. Forget the sprinkler head, just put a good swing on it, he told himself, as he took his stance. He brought the club back smoothly, then brought it down with a sweet rhythm that ended abruptly with the clank of steel on steel that sent the ball skittering across the fairway, through the rough and out into the desert.

"Goddamn!" Jack gasped. He was staring down at the divot where the earth had been torn away to reveal a previously concealed flange extending two inches around the top of the sprinkler head.

"Guess you should've called for a ruling," Jeeter said, turning his back to Jack and walking off.

Jack lunged, pulled Jeeter around to face him, and swung. The blow missed Jeeter's jaw but landed solidly in the center of his chest and both men went down, thrashing wildly about on the grass. Jack was astride him, fist high in the air, when Duff pulled him off. While Duff held him back, Charley went to the aid of Jeeter, who was lying flat on his back, eyes bulging, gasping hoarsely for air.

"He can't breathe, he's havin' a heart attack!" Charley cried.

"I hope he fucking dies," Jack said.

"Somebody get a doctor!"

The Chicano caddies stood in a tight cluster some distance off, wanting nothing to do with a bunch of crazy gringos who'd bet twenty thousand dollars on a golf match and then try to kill each other.

"Let me see," Jack said, pushing Charley aside. He leaned over Jeeter and asked, "Can you hear me?" Jeeter grunted unintelligibly. "He's okay, he just got the wind knocked out of him. Get up!" he ordered, struggling to pull Jeeter to his feet.

"I don't think we should move him," Charley warned.

"He's gonna finish this fucking match," Jack grunted,

as he pulled his opponent to his feet, "even if I have to carry him."

"I'm up—get away from me!" Jeeter gasped, pushing Jack away. "Crazy bastard!"

"Prick!"

While they hurled curses back and forth, Duff walked across the fairway and out into the desert to survey the damage.

"Saguaro," his caddie said, pointing out into the desert.

Duff didn't know what he meant until he saw his ball resting against a tall cactus and realized it meant "hopeless." He tried to chip it back to the fairway, but managed to get it only as far as the rough, where it was truly saguaro. Now it was all up to his partner, who was still squabbling with Jeeter.

From fifty yards out, Jack hit a soft sand wedge, hoping to loft the ball onto the green and roll it slowly to the hole. But the ball never got up in the air. It whizzed through the grass like a snake on a mission, then slowed suddenly and rolled up onto the green where it collapsed.

"Lucky sonofabitch!" Jeeter wailed.

"The old bump-and-run," Jack replied.

Charley had a long putt which he safely lagged to within two feet and tapped in for par. Jack's putt wasn't much shorter, all downhill with a big left-to-right break.

"What do you see, partner?" Jack asked as he surveyed the putt.

Saguaro, Duff said to himself, as he nevertheless squatted down to observe the line. He got to his feet, pointed to an old ball mark about four feet outside the line and said, "Hit that and it'll go in."

"That far?" Jack questioned.

"Trust me."

Jack addressed the ball uncertainly, brought the putter-head back and rapped the ball sharply, well out past the old ball mark.

It was going off the green, Duff thought, as he watched the ball climb up the side of the hill like a kid on a skateboard, until it all but lost its velocity, then fell back on an oblique line and raced straight for the hole. It was going much too fast, he thought, as he watched it hit the back of the cup, jump high in the air, then spelunk to the bottom of the hole.

Jack hooted loudly enough to be heard at the clubhouse, while Jeeter and the fat man stared silently.

Head shaking in disbelief, Duff said, "Nice putt."

"Yeah, even if your read was a little off," Jack replied.

They were one down with one hole to play. Duff walked to the front of the elevated tee to have a look at the final hole. It was a par-5 that doglegged right around an artificial pond with a fountain in the middle—one of those cookie-cutter finishing holes that seemed to come with every new course—a tantalizing risk-reward hole. Go the long way and it required three shots to the green, but take the shortcut over the corner of the pond and the green was reachable in two. Playing off the members' tee, Duff knew he could easily clear the water and put himself within birdie range; provided he didn't knock the ball through the fairway and out into the desert among the dreaded saguaro trees.

"You go first," Duff said.

Getting a stroke on the hole, Jack was reasonably sure he could make net par if he could avoid the water on the right. And if he did, Duff could go for the birdie. He chose his trusty cleek, the club least likely to go right on him. This turned out to be one of those rare times, however, when his faithful 4-wood let him down.

"Play it safe," Jack advised his partner, after watching his ball splash into the pond.

Duff looked over at Charley, who was swinging his big driver back and forth, slowly and surely, and knew instinctively that nothing less than birdie would win here. He picked a spot on the fairway on the far side of the pond and hit the ball right at it. He was afraid when he hit it that that he had struck it too well and, a moment later, as he watched the ball bound across the fairway and

out onto the desert, his worst fear was confirmed. He was
not only out of birdie range, he was probably out of par
range.

Knowing this, Charley put his driver back in the bag
and knocked a 3-wood safely down the center of the fairway, as did Jeeter.

Jack was furious but silent, until Duff attempted to
board the cart. "You walk," he said, then motioned Duff's
caddie to take his place beside him.

Duff worried, as he scraped through the rocky desert
with his spiked shoes, that his caddie might not even find
the ball, but there it was, sitting up nicely on a gravel pile.
He would at least be able to chip the ball back out into
the fairway. But his caddie already had the 3-wood out.

"*Mira,*" the caddie said, pointing the way to the green.

Duff got behind the ball and looked. There was indeed
a narrow opening between the cactus and palm trees between him and the green, which looked to be about 250
yards away. While he was considering his play, Jeeter hit
his second shot into the water, while the fat man hit his
to within 160 yards of the green, from where he would
likely par or maybe even birdie the hole. Duff looked
across the barranca to where Jack sat watching from the
cart.

"You want to have a look at this?" Duff called.

"Go for it, partner."

Duff took two practice swings, anchored his spikes into
the rocky soil and let it fly. He hit the ball solidly off the
gravel pile and looked up to see it heading in the general
direction of the green. At the last it started to hook, then
disappeared over the hillock guarding the front-left side
of the green and never bounced.

Duff heard a howl from the clubhouse veranda, and saw
why when he emerged from the desert. His ball was lying
on the edge of the hole, just a fraction of an inch away
from a double-eagle. All the contestants were coming
down from the clubhouse to see for themselves if it could
be true that Jack Stricker's kid had almost holed out his

second shot from somewhere out on the desert. And the two most interested spectators were Martin and Paulie, Duff realized with a sudden, sinking sensation. That tap-in-eagle would put him and Jack at 11-under-par. They had edged Martin and Paulie by one stroke to win the Calcutta. He looked helplessly at Jack—who was bounding around the green like Tom Watson after he'd chipped in on Nicklaus to win the Open—and wondered what he could do. Yip a putt that's already leaning over the hole?

Duff walked out onto the green as if it were thin ice and nudged the ball into the hole for an eagle-3, less his handicap stroke, for a net-2. There was a weak cheer from the crowd—they were gamblers, not sportsmen—and suddenly Jack was beside him, smiling like a proud father.

"Go back to the hotel and wait for me," he ordered.

Martin and Paulie were sitting alone at the clubhouse bar after the money had been given out, trying to figure out how a 12-handicap could hit a ball out of a gravel pit to a green 250 yards away, when Earl Cawthon walked slowly into the room. Earl, too, had been trying to figure something out. He'd been trying to decide if a boy who'd enter a golf tournament as a ringer was the kind of boy he wanted playing for Southeastern, even if he was one of the best prospects he'd ever seen. At first—after Jack had explained that Duff was only standing in because his son had gotten sick and he was going to play just like a 12-handicap—he'd agreed not to say anything. But after the way the boy had played, he'd regretfully decided that Duff Colhane wasn't the kind of boy he wanted at Southeastern.

"I think there's something y'all ought to know . . ." Earl Cawthon began.

Jack Stricker walked into the hotel lobby with more than a hundred thousand dollars in a plastic briefcase tucked tightly under his arm. He was thinking about that shot from the desert, knowing it was one of those events he'd remember for the rest of his life. Duff had hit one hell of a shot, no doubt about it. But the man who'd moved the ball so his partner would have a clear shot at the green and then teed it up nicely on a pile of gravel deserved more than a little of the credit himself. This pleasant reverie was alarmingly interrupted by the sudden appearance of Martin and Paulie rushing purposefully up to the front desk, which caused Jack to duck quickly behind a wall of slots. He watched from his hiding place as Paulie spoke briefly but intimidatingly to the clerk, who reluctantly fished a key from under the desk and handed it over to him. Then, their flushed faces seething with fury, Martin and Paulie dashed for the elevators.

Jack waited until the elevator doors closed and then, hiding his face with the plastic case, walked hurriedly out the front door and jumped into a waiting cab.

Duff was stretched out on the bed, trying to distract himself with an old movie, when finally he heard Jack enter his room. However, it wasn't Jack he saw when he opened the door to the adjoining room, but Martin and Paulie.

"Where the fuck is he?" Paulie shouted, advancing across the room, his face glistening with rage.

"I don't . . ." Duff began, as Paulie snapped him forward and head-butted him across the room.

He found himself lying on the carpet, staring at his 1-iron in the closet, while a bass drum pounded painfully in his head and he tried to make sense of what was going on. Somebody was throwing stuff around—Martin and Paulie—looking for Jack, for the money. Plane tickets— Martin was shouting about plane tickets. . . .

Now the 1-iron rose up from the carpet and he heard Paulie's shouted curse, followed by a mysterious though dreadful pain, as if a shrapnel grenade had gone off in his hand. Then he was alone in the room and the pain was becoming unbearable, and when he looked at his bloody hand he saw splintered bones sticking through torn flesh. Then he saw black.

Duff sat slumped in a wheelchair outside the emergency room, his body numbed by morphine, his mind ablaze with visions from hell, while he awaited the surgeon who would piece together his splintered fingers. The wounded and the sick came and went, or sat nearby groaning with pain, while the healthkeepers whizzed about like soccer players in a game that had no ball. A man in Gucci loafers passed by on a gurney in an unnaturally slow and endless procession, flanked by attendants in blood-splattered whites shouting soundlessly, as if words might heal. But then he saw in one, terrible, clarifying moment that they were not lifesavers but pallbearers, accompanying the man in Guccis to his grave. A nearly naked Chicano, clutching his torn guts, performed a slow dance in front of him, while a young blond man with slashed wrists, accompanied by his pregnant wife, tried vainly to applaud, and a shrieking woman with a bloody child in a white dress called for more. At times he was able to will himself a spectator watching detached images floating through the halls of memory, like nightmares from which he would soon awaken, but all the time he knew that the starving wolf waiting beyond the door at the end of the dark corridor was as real as death.

Finally he heard his name, soft and quiet as smoke in the forest. It took some time to realize that the sound was gurgling out of the man on the gurney beside him, and longer still to recognize that the swollen, split-lipped, missing-tooth mouth from which the sound had issued, was Jack Stricker's.

2

After a long winter layoff,
each club feels like a broomhandle,
and each ball when struck transmits
a shock up the shaft, causing the player
to think he has hit a lump of iron.
Golf is not much fun during this period;
but it is a period we must endure to
enjoy the pleasures beyond.

BOBBY JONES, *ON GOLF*

The New York specialist, a 9-handicap at Winged Foot,
smiled sadly when the boy voiced his plans to play professional golf. Reasonable use was the best the hand surgeon could offer. His broken fingers had been carelessly
baled together by the Las Vegas surgeon, most of the
joints in his right hand would never articulate normally.
With proper therapy he might still be a good recreational
golfer, but the nerve damage—more the result of careless
surgery than the original trauma—had messed up the cir-

cuit board, as he put it to his lay patient. From now on his right hand would have something of a mind of its own. It would do crazy things its owner didn't intend—like duck-hook a drive out of bounds, or yip a putt clear off a green—the kind of thing a recreational golfer could live with but not a touring pro. Perhaps he should think of becoming a club pro, the doctor advised.

Duff was willing to accept that his doctor knew a lot about bones and muscles and nerves, but what did a 9-handicap know about the golf swing? Or about him? By next summer he'd be playing again, better than ever. Besides, if his hand really had a mind of its own it would've picked up a knife and plunged it into Jack Stricker's heart by now.

After more than a year of reflecting, however, Duff had come to realize that he could not blame Jack entirely for his injuries. Jack had deceived him, but he had been all too willing to be deceived. Jack had also paid for his surgeries and his weekly therapy sessions in New York, as well as given him money to get by, and all this made it hard to keep on hating him. In fact Duff had come to both pity and admire Jack, because while Duff had learned his lesson, he knew that Jack never would. For Jack Stricker was a romantic, a man who believed in luck no matter how much he claimed to be a realist, a man who would go off to Vegas to joust with windmills at the drop of a glove. And, Duff had to remember, it was he who had carried his lance.

Much as the broken hand hurt, the thought that he would never attend Southeastern University was an injury that would never heal. Four years of intense competition under Chip Waylin's tutelage was to have been the last step in his training program before stepping out onto the PGA Tour. From the country club to the university to the U.S. Open, that was the gentleman golfer's path to fame. But it would not be his. His way would be the blue-collar way: satellite tournaments, the Dot Com Tour, PGA Qualifying School. . . . There would be no staying with the families of friends from college while playing the Tour, no dinners across the table from the beautiful sister who would drive him to the golf course the next morning in her graduation-gift roadster. Instead he'd stay in cheap motels with bikers and roving militiamen and hope to God his wreck of a car would get him to the tee on time. For a young man who had been drawn to the game by its trappings of wealth and glamour, it was indeed a cruel irony.

But being familiar now with both the rich and the poor, and having been disappointed by both, it no longer mattered as much as it had. He would never fully trust anyone again, not even his caddie. Maybe it was even a blessing to forego the forced camaraderie of college golf and the hypocrisy of the notion of the team player. Whether on the golf course or on a sinking ship, it was every man for himself, the young man now knew. That was the Las Vegas truth.

On his trips to New York for therapy over the winter he stayed with Gena in her Upper East Side apartment. He thought she'd disappeared forever from his life when she'd returned to New York without a word after their night on the beach, but she'd called him from the city after hearing from her mother what had happened to him. She told him she was very sorry that he wouldn't be going away to college, and when she saw his stitched hand after the first surgery she was horrified at what they'd done to him. Duff assured her that it wasn't as bad as it looked, and that by summer he'd be playing golf again. She said she believed him, and that was when Duff realized she wasn't a very good actress after all.

Gena had never enrolled in acting classes, had become a model instead and was obviously doing very well at it. She was living by herself in a large apartment in a door-man building with a gym and a swimming pool, surrounded by beautiful and successful young singles. He and Gina spent their days and nights lounging around the pool or the apartment, until one of her many friends would call to invite her out for a drink or something. At first Duff was annoyed when she insisted on going alone, but they weren't people he'd enjoy meeting, she assured him, just people in the business who might have a line on a job. And she was never gone for long.

For a beautiful young woman with a lot of money and a lot of friends, Gena often seemed oddly sad. They did some coke when he stayed with her—it was a condition of his tenancy—but not enough to account for her gloomy moods, he felt. When he dared to mention it one night after they'd done a line and made love, she laughed and suggested that the cocaine was perhaps affecting him.

Duff knew better but decided to let it lay. Cocaine obviously wasn't the high for him that it was for her, although it was a good auxiliary therapy, he was beginning to feel. He tried not to worry about his bionic hand when it balked at putting the pegs in the holes, but there were sometimes desperate moments in that defenseless time between waking and sleeping when doubt clamped suddenly down on his windpipe like a pair of murderous hands in the dark. With Gena's magic vanishing powder, however, all doubt disappeared. He was unbeatable on the course, insatiable in bed, and able to slay any dragon fate put in his way. It filled him again with the same heedless daring he'd experienced that night on the beach when he'd raced naked into the big breakers and swum far out into a rough sea with the giant sharks. But in Gena Hall's apartment on the Upper East Side of Manhattan there was no ocean, so he floated down softly on Chardonnay and Heineken and awaited the healing that was sure to come soon. Druggy delusions could be dangerous, he knew—they induced Gena to believe she would go back to acting—but they were such pleasant relief from the old people at the rehab center and the gloomy assessment of his 9-handicap doctor. And it was nothing he wouldn't gladly give up when it was again time to play golf.

Yet while walking the Montauk golf course on one of those unusually warm late-winter days that pop up like crocuses in the park, he found himself thinking more about coke than golf, and decided it was time to get back to business. He would miss Gena—he doubted that she would return to Montauk in the summer—but he sensed it wouldn't last much longer anyway. Lately she went through the motions of love with him with a detached passion that only signaled the end.

They were lying in bed after just such an experience when he told her he wouldn't be coming to New York anymore, that he had to remain in Montauk and get to work on his golf swing. She said nothing for a while, just picked up his hand and, with her long, coke-serving nail, traced the still-pink scar along his middle finger.

"Feel anything?" she asked.

"A little."

"Enough to play professional golf?"

"Eventually," he said, pulling his hand back. He'd gotten used to the doubts of his doctor and his father, but until now he'd thought Gena was behind him. "It'll take time."

"Maybe a lot of time." She threw her leg over his hips and sat up heavily on him. "Until then, why don't you stay here with me?"

"What would I do in New York?"

"You could work with me."

"I'm not the model type."

"Neither am I," she said, stretching for the jar on the nightstand, pressing her breasts against his face. She sat back on him, dipped her nail into the jar and sniffed a quick bolt of lightning. "Aahh ... !" she exhaled deliciously. She extended the jar and he shook his head.

"What do you mean—neither am I?" he asked.

"I think you know."

He supposed he did, but like the doubts about his hand,

he'd tried to deny it. He hadn't asked why there were no magazines around with her picture in them, or why her agent never called, or why so many friends from Monte's did. "You're dealing."

She leaned over him to replace the jar, then settled back down on his thighs. "I perform a vital service to the modeling industry," she said archly. "I could get you in on it."

"Forget it."

"You'd make a lot of money." He shook his head. "It's not as if you'd be hooking innocent kids, you know. I mean fucking models—they're all users. They can't eat or drink or they'll blow up, so they do drugs. Somebody's got to supply the demand, why not us?"

"Because it's illegal. Because they put you in jail for it."

"They don't put pretty young girls in jail just for carrying a little dope. And I don't sell it, somebody else collects the money."

"Monte?"

"I can't tell you that unless you're in. But I promise you, there's no risk."

"That's what Jack Stricker told me. You see what I got for listening to him."

"That was a mistake, this is an opportunity. And it's not a lifelong occupation, you know. It's just a chance to make a lot of money in a very short time. When I have enough I'm going to quit and start acting classes," she announced, tossing her hair back over her shoulders.

"And how long will that be—two years, five years?"

"Whatever it is, I can cut it in half if you'll come to work for me."

"For you! I thought we were going to be partners."

"Yeah, we would be. You'd be the distributor and I'd be the supplier."

"You mean I buy the stuff from you for a thousand dollars and sell it to somebody else for two thousand?"

"More like ten thousand," she corrected.

"And you buy it from Monte for how much—a hundred dollars?"

"More than that."

"How much more?"

"That's none of your business. I supply the product and the leads. I think I deserve something for putting you in business."

"Yeah, you're a regular Amway lady."

"You bastard!" she cried, slapping him hard across the face.

When she swung again, this time with a closed fist, he stopped it with his right hand, setting off a stab of pain that jolted him up and sent her flying off the bed and onto the floor.

"Are you okay?" he asked, scrambling after her.

"Get your fucking hands off me!" she screamed. "You think you're going to play golf with that hand? Forget it, you'll never be a fucking golfer."

"Maybe not. But I'll never be a fucking pusher either," he said, getting to his feet and starting into the bathroom.

"You'll be a fucking loser, that's what you'll be! Loser, loser, loser! You hear me?" she screamed as he slammed the door. "You're a fucking loser!"

Duff stared at the scarred hand while she hurled insults at the closed door, then looked at his reflection in the mirror.

"You're a winner," he said in a softly assured voice.

He carefully wrapped his injured fingers around the handle of the wedge, then slowly executed his first practice swing. No serious pain, just an unfamiliar sensation, as if the hand had found itself in a strange place and was in need of directions. Not since his first lesson, when Teddy had tugged his small hands into the correct position on the club, with the Vs of both hands pointing to the right shoulder, had he experienced any uncertainty about the golf grip; it was as natural as gripping a toothbrush. Now he had lost his muscle memory; he had to look at the right hand to know its position.

It'll take time, he reminded himself as he continued to swing the club in a slow metronomic motion, slowly lengthening and extending the arc, warming and softening the muscles on this cold March day. When he felt ready, he propped a ball up on the winter-ravaged grass and prepared to take the first shot of the season, a soft lob, nothing ambitious. But he shanked it, skittering the ball obliquely across the grass and setting off a ringing pain in his injured hand. After giving it a rest, he repeated this ignominious shot several more times before finally hitting one on the clubface. Some shots skittered along the ground and some rose in the air, some went left, some right. In the past he could tell the height and direction of a shot without looking at it, just by the feel of the ball on the club for a fraction of a second. Now he knew nothing until he looked up and found the ball in the air. The circuit board was truly messed up.

He had expected to hit a couple of bags of balls on the first day, but before he'd gone through one bag the throbbing pain in his hand forced him to stop.

It'll take time, he reminded himself as he set out to pick up the shag balls.

A week later, on a day when a fierce sou'easter was blowing grainy fog over the dunes and craters of the Montauk Muni, Teddy McGill drove into the parking lot in his road-streaked Cadillac and parked in front of the sign that read simply: PRO. The town was not going to invest in anything more specific when it was never certain— given the lowly salary—that it would be the same pro from year to year. There was a time when Teddy would have agreed with the town—it was indeed to have been but a short-term job, just until the sour swing sweetened and he could get back out on the Tour. But that had been more than ten years before, and in that time the swing had only gone from sour to bitter. Now he could only live with the hope that one day the fluid swing would magically return in time for the Senior Tour, and he would never again have to return to the Montauk Muni on a wintry spring day when the wind was howling in from the sea, blanking out everything with a wall of gray fog. But for now—not having been nearly so successful with the Florida gamblers as in winters past—he was glad to be back.

The fog hit him in the face like wet sand as he climbed out of the car. He hauled his clubs and duffel bag out of the trunk and started up the stone steps to the deserted clubhouse. When he stepped onto the spike-scarred deck, he stopped suddenly and listened. For a moment he thought he'd heard the sound of a golf ball being struck, but it was only his imagination playing tricks on him.

Or else the wee people was havin' a game, he said to himself, as he found the key in the niche above the door where he'd left it in the fall. He opened the door and stepped into the cold room and was about to close it when he heard the sound again. There could be no doubt about it, some loony was hitting balls on the practice range.

"Now just what sort of idiot do you suppose . . ." he muttered, as he walked to the back door and threw it open. Here on the seaward side the fog came rolling across the range like stampeding ghosts, engulfing everything in its path.

"Hullooo!" Teddy called into the gray stuff. "Who's there?"

"Duff Colhane!" came the reply.

"I might've guessed," he said, as he treaded carefully down the wet slope. "Where the hell are you? Make some fookin' noise will ye!"

"Over here!"

He found him, wet as a duck, hair plastered down, waving his hands like a beacon.

"What in the name of God are you doin' out on a day

like this when you can't see the fookin' ball in front of
your face?"

"That's the idea," Duff said, advancing with outstretched hand. "I'm working on feel."

"As well as a case of pneumonia," Teddy said, taking
the hand gently.

"Don't worry, you won't break it," Duff said, showing
him the hand.

It was white as a fish's belly except for the angry blue
lines where the surgeon had cut, and the place where the
red blood was seeping around the nail of one finger. Band-
Aids covering broken blisters were wrapped around two
other fingers.

"How many times must I ask you not to bleed on the
grass?" the pro said, nudging a ball into position with his
toe. "Let me see you hit one."

His student hit a few soft lobs, some fat, some thin.
The pro couldn't be sure of the direction, as the ball was
quickly swallowed up by the fog, but the former zip and
crispness was sadly lacking, he could plainly see.

"Not bad for the first time," he charitably allowed.

"I've been out here for a couple of weeks," Duff replied.

"Well—it takes time," the pro said gently.

"I challenge you to a match on Easter Sunday."

"How many strokes do I get?" the pro asked.

"What—you'd take strokes from a cripple!"

"You know better than to ask for sympathy from a
gambler," the pro laughed, when in fact he was saddened
very nearly to tears.

Duff wasn't ready to compete on Easter Sunday, nor even
by Labor Day. He practiced every day until the course
was covered with snow, then retreated inside to diligently
perform his exercises, while Teddy retreated to Florida to
prepare for the Senior Tour. Neither of them thought the
other stood a chance, but on the day of Teddy's departure,

they embraced warmly and wished each other luck. Jack Stricker, too, was convinced that Duff was wasting his time, yet he continued, somewhat grudgingly, to pay his medical expenses. He was understandably relieved, yet dubious, when Duff reported in the spring that he had finally regained most of the strength in his right hand.

Unfortunately, however, the strengthened hand continued to stubbornly demonstrate a mind of its own, occasionally sending the ball on a path uncharted by the mind. But this was happening less and less, he was convinced. And even if a few shots did miss the fairway once in a while, he could usually scramble a par. However if a putt moved only a small fraction of an inch, it would result in the loss of a stroke nearly every time, and this was intolerable.

He tried everything to cure his jumpy nerves. He tried putters of every length, from knee-high to chin-high; he tried blade putters, mallet putters, and several Rube Goldberg contraptions that defied description. He tried putting reverse-handed, one-handed, left-handed and side-saddle; he tried the overlapping grip (double and triple) the interlocking grip and the reverse overlapping grip, and finally even tried putting with both hands laced together as if in prayer. Sometimes, usually at the end of the day, he was sure he'd found the cure, only to discover the next day that it was just another quack remedy. Yet he remained hopeful. It just takes time, he told himself over and over.

His father, however, was not so patient. He cornered Duff one morning in the kitchen before he could get off to his caddying job.

"I saw Teddy McGill yesterday," Sam said, leaning in the kitchen doorway in his boxer shorts, arms crossed over his hairy chest.

"Yeah?" Duff said, looking up from his cereal.

Sam walked across the linoleum floor and poured a cup of coffee, then came and sat in the chair opposite him.

"And I get the idea from him you haven't been levelin' with me."

"I don't know what you mean."

"I mean whenever I ask, you always tell me you're hittin' the ball good as ever, but that's not what Teddy says. He says your nerves ain't gettin' any better and you're never gonna be able to play like you used to."

"When did Teddy become a doctor?" Duff asked, skidding the chair back and getting to his feet.

"He's a golf pro. He knows golf."

"But he doesn't know me. My hand's getting better, I'm just not quite ready," he said, placing his dishes in the sink and opening the hot valve all the way.

Sam walked to the sink and turned off the water. "I know I forfeited a lot of rights with you, and believe me, I ain't tryin' to put pressure on you now. Okay?" Duff nodded and glanced at his watch. "But I'm worried you might be puttin' too much pressure on yourself. I'm worried about when you get three or four years down the line and it ain't happenin' for you, what're you gonna be doin' then? Caddyin'?"

He took a breath and replied, "I'm going to be a touring pro."

"And I hope you make it. But if you don't . . . All I'm sayin' is, you should have another string in your bow. You should be goin' to college."

"With what?"

"If you wanna go I'll find the money. I been workin' a lot lately."

"I know, and I appreciate the offer. But I'm not going to college."

"Then a business."

"What business? The fish business?"

"What's wrong with the fish business?"

"Nothing, if you want to be a fisherman. But I don't want to be a fisherman, I want to be a professional golfer. And I'm going to be late for my caddying job," he said, looking at his watch.

Sam clamped a hand on his son's wrist. "I just want you to promise me one thing."

"What?"

"That you won't do yourself in because of your pride. I want you to promise me that if at any time you feel like you might wanna learn the fishin' business you'll come to me. Will you promise me that?"

"Yes, I promise." He felt his grip loosen and broke for the door, then stopped and turned. "Thanks for the offer."

"Forget it," Sam said, waving him off.

After carrying doubles for 36 holes at Maidstone, Duff, propelled by a fear of fishing, returned to the Muni to look for a new putting stroke. He tried the Langer method until it became almost too dark to see the hole—left arm extended down the shaft, right hand clutching his bicep to the handle—but he continued to jerk the ball left and right. It should be very simple, just take the right hand out of the stroke, he told himself, as this time he tried placing the right hand very lightly atop the left so it couldn't work independently. He tried it and missed again.

"Shit!"

It was getting too dark to see the hole, time to go home, try again in the morning. He grabbed the club in a tight baseball grip, all ten fingers clutching the handle, and slammed a putt at the farthest hole he could still see. Amazingly it went in. Blind luck. He lined up a 10-footer and tapped the ball gently, then watched it run like a squirrel on a telephone wire and disappear down the hole, followed by three more! This was the one grip he'd never tried, a notoriously unreliable one that allowed the right hand to roam freely, the very opposite of what he required. It was the instinctual grip of all first-time golfers, one they'd continue to use until afforded the benefit of instruction. It was a powerful grip, capable of producing long drives or disastrous snap-hooks. He didn't know why—it was a contradiction of the basic physical principles of the golf stroke—but his right hand was a neutral force, a thoughtless follower of the left. It had to be a fluke, yet he was making putts from every length! He moved around the green like a basketball player with a hot hand, sinking everything he put up, nothing but net!

"Hallelujah," he whispered fearfully.

Then it occurred to him—if the grip works with the putter, why not the rest of the clubs? He grabbed his driver and sprinted down to the practice range, teed it up and let it fly. The ball exploded off the clubface and drove straight as a bullet through the darkness. He couldn't see the ball but he knew, he could feel it.

"I'm back!" he shouted at the dark sky.

When Duff announced his intention to qualify for the U.S. Open, Teddy was at first gently discouraging. There would be thousands of players from all over the world playing two 36-hole elimination events for fewer than a hundred open places, and they wouldn't all be young amateurs like himself, either. And even if he did somehow manage to survive the first cut, he would then have to face all those hundreds of well-known professionals who weren't among the paltry 50 or so exemptions granted by the USGA.

"And besides that," he added, when it was plain his argument was having no effect, "when they get a look at that goofy baseball grip of yours they'll laugh you right off the course."

"Let them laugh! You saw me hit the ball!" Duff shot back.

"I saw you hit it on the range; I haven't seen you hit it in competition."

"Then come to Boston," Duff said, turning and walking out of the pro shop.

●　　●　　●

The sun was glowing dully through the morning mist when Duff pulled his father's old truck onto the dewy grass and followed a long line of cars across the field to the area labeled CONTESTANTS PARKING. He parked at the end of a long row of cars and stared through the windshield at the grim-faced players and their caddies filing past in the gray light, silent as troops going into battle, keeping cadence by the rhythmic clank of steel clubs. The young players had Sunday bags naming their college, hauled by a friend or a father; while the older players, middle-aged stockbrokers who spent more time at the golf course than at their desks had professional caddies lugging their big leather bags, hung with club tags and baggage-claim tickets—campaign ribbons for battles fought at exotic golf clubs in foreign climes.

Duff climbed out of the truck, threw his bag on his shoulder and joined the ranks of marchers, all intent on the clubhouse at the top of the hill where the USGA flag twitched sullenly in the light breeze. He checked in at the reception tent and then went down to the locker room to change shoes—where he ran into an old friend.

Forbes Witherspoon was standing in front of an open locker, almost a head taller than any other golfer in the line. He looked much older than when Duff had last seen him, and not half so ebullient. He'd come onto the Tour right after graduating from Southeastern and had played rather well his first season, but over the past few years Duff hardly ever saw his name in the *Times* again. He thought he might've quit and gone into the family insurance business, until last winter when Duff had seen his name in the paper again—among a list of touring pros who'd had to go back to Q-School to regain their playing cards. Now here he is trying to qualify for the Open just like me, Duff thought, as he stepped forward, hand outstretched.

"Hello, Forbes."

Forbes turned with a ready smile that slid away as his eyes moved from the familiar face to the scarred hand.

"Hiya, Slingshot." He turned to the players nearby and asked, "You guys know Slingshot?" They didn't. "Slingshot was all set to go to Southeastern, but instead he went to Las Vegas and got himself a busted flipper. Who you caddying for, Flipper?"

Duff's offered hand closed suddenly into a fist, then slowly opened again. "I'm here to qualify."

"Under your own name or somebody else's?"

"It'll be the one at the top of the score sheet," Duff said, as he turned and walked to his locker.

Forget about Forbes, just play golf. Your grip is solid, your swing is sound, Duff assured himself, as he looked down the fairway one last time before taking it back and letting it fly. He knew without looking, just from the feel, that it was dead solid perfect. He picked up his bag and walked buoyantly off the tee with his playing partner, a stocky insurance broker from Boston named Josh Levy. Josh was a veteran, this was his fifteenth attempt to qualify for the U.S. Amateur, all of them unsuccessful thus far. Because the golf course was soft after the heavy spring rains and therefore favorable to the long hitters, Josh estimated it would take at least 3 under to advance to the second-stage qualifier.

"Then I'll shoot four under just to be on the safe side," Duff had replied.

He both meant it as a joke and didn't; talk the talk you gotta walk the walk—but Josh didn't smile. He too had once been a brash young kid, setting unrealistic goals for himself both on and off the golf course, then watching forlornly as the scores grew higher and the disappointments multiplied. He was pushing 40, he had lost a wife and two jobs to golf and hadn't yet qualified for an Open, and this he knew would probably be his last chance. He wondered how long this cocky young kid would keep trying, and how much he'd lose in the process. Not long and not much, he decided, after noticing the kid's goofy base-ball grip.

However, after watching the boy mortar a wedge to within 10 feet of the hole and calmly stroke it in for birdie, he wondered if perhaps this kid might have some-thing more than a big mouth. And when he made the turn at 2 under par, jamming in putts like a nerveless teenager, Josh was certain of two things: This kid was going on to the finals, and Josh was going back to his desk. Unless he could get unusually lucky over the last 27 holes, make seven or eight birdies and an eagle—it wasn't impossi-ble. . . .

Several hours later Duff stood in the scorer's tent staring incredulously at the scoreboard. His name, with a 69 be-side it, was at the top, just where he had told Forbes it would be. His fellow competitors—there was hardly one in the field who didn't know now who he was—watched with a jealousy bordering upon respect as he moved about the clubhouse and grounds, shaking hands and accepting congratulations from the same USGA officials who had greeted him with stone-faced anonymity just a short while before. He hadn't changed, it was only their perception of him that had changed, he understood. And yet, however illogical it was, he couldn't help feeling that he was not entirely the same person who had shown up that morning with no more than a little hope and a lot of fear. This was the day everything had finally come together, the day he had finally emerged a finished golfer. He was going to the U.S. Open!—if he could continue to play well this afternoon.

"You need a caddie?" someone called, as Duff searched through the bags outside the clubhouse. He looked up and saw poor Josh Levy, who had shot 81 in the morning round.

"Where is he?"

"Right here," Josh said. "I withdrew."

"I can't afford a caddie," Duff replied uncertainly. He assumed it was a free offer, but from the look on the poor man's face, he might need the money.

"No charge," he said, picking up Duff's bag. "I just want to be able to tell the guys at the club that I got Duff Colhane to the U.S. Open."

"You can carry the bag, but if I want advice I'll ask for it."

"I understand," Josh said, hoisting the bag to his shoulder. "But if one of my pals ever comes up to you on Tour and tells you how they know the guy that got you to the U.S. Open, you play along with it, okay?"

"Deal," Duff said, extending his hand.

When Duff learned that he would be paired with Forbes Witherspoon for the last round, he was both pleased and concerned.

There could be no more fitting a finish to the day than to trounce Forbes as well as qualify for the Open, yet he was concerned lest his personal feelings overwhelm his judgment.

"Forget about everything else, we're going to the Open," Josh said, as they walked to the first tee where Forbes waited.

He had changed to a bright yellow shirt and was pulling on a matching new glove. He stared wordlessly at Duff while he pumped his hand, stretching the leather, waiting perhaps for the contender to speak first. But Duff said nothing as he dug into his bag for a wrinkled glove. When the group ahead hit their second shots, the official stepped up onto the tee and asked, "Ready, gentlemen?"

Both players nodded.

He introduced both players to the small gallery, then said, "Mr. Colhane will play first."

Forget about Forbes, this is for the Open, Duff cautioned himself as he went through his pre-shot routine, then stepped up to his ball. There was a gasp from the small crowd as the ball exploded off the clubface and started down the right side of the fairway, then veered sharply left and settled in the left rough.

No matter, Duff thought, as he snatched up his tee. He would hack it out of the rough and onto the green and make the putt for bird. He was invincible.

Several weeks later, when the U.S. Open was being contested on the west coast, Duff was standing at the stern of a fishing boat in the middle of the night, gliding past Gosman's dock, through the narrow, stone-piled breakers marking the inlet, and out onto the dark sea. The boat, a 50-foot convertible with a two-story tuna tower rising up like a ladder to nowhere, was riding low under the weight of extra fuel and stores, and when they rounded Montauk Point a fine spray began breaking over the bow, hitting Duff in the face like rock salt. Yet he remained at his post. His father and Captain Dobbs were in the pilothouse, warm and dry, drinking coffee and eating donuts, but Duff preferred to remain alone on the open deck. He could see them in the fuzzy glow of instrument light, heads bobbing, talking of fish. If he went in they would stop talking, out of sympathy for his own fish that got away. They'd say kind things, as they'd been doing for weeks—that he shouldn't worry, that anybody could have a bad round now and then—and he didn't want to hear that. He'd rather stand alone on the deck in the breaking spray.

If it had been just one bad day, he wouldn't be here. But every day since his ignominious breakdown had been a bad one. He could play several holes perfectly, then suddenly the putter would go off in his hands and the ball would skitter blindly away. Just when he thought his troubles were over—and for long stretches they were—the damned hand would reach up and grab him by the throat. It'll take time, he again reminded himself, looking up at the sliver of moon that had appeared briefly between scudding dark clouds. And until then he'd be a fisherman.

After they passed the last marker and pointed out to

sea, his father emerged from the pilothouse and climbed down to the deck.

"You're gettin' soaked out here," he said, sliding his hand over Duffs wet cheek.

"It's refreshing."

"You feelin' seasick?"

"I'll be fine, don't worry."

"Yeah, you'll be fine," Sam said, patting his cheek. "I'm gonna go below and rack out for a while, so you go up and keep Andy company, okay?"

"Sure," Duff said, and started up the ladder.

His father had been pleased when he asked to go fishing, but he sensed that Andy Dobbs wasn't entirely convinced by his sudden vocational change. Captain Dobbs was as devoted to fishing as Duff was to golf.

"Want some company?" Duff asked, stepping through the hatch.

"If you like," the captain said, staring straight ahead at the waves in the bow light.

Duff climbed up on the stool beside him and watched the breaking waves smashing against the bow. "Looks like we're going to get some weather."

Andy nodded, seemingly pleased at the prospect. "Let's hope it holds till we get to the Canyons."

It was to the Canyons—the deep ocean holes off the Continental Shelf where a school of giant tuna had been spotted the day before—that they were headed. Andy Dobbs was as excited as he ever gets, but not surprised by the fishing report. After the first nor'wester of the fall pushed the warm coastal waters offshore, the big tuna invariably followed, out beyond the Shelf and down into the deep waters of the Canyons lying at the edge of the Gulf Stream where, with any luck, they would soon boat a giant. The conditions were good for tuna, even if a bit uncomfortable for fishermen, with a 20-knot wind blowing out of the west (an easterly wind was bad for fishing, Andy knew from experience, although he didn't know why). Most people, even a lot of experienced fish-

ermen, assumed that fair weather was best for giant tuna,
but not Andy Dobbs. He couldn't prove it, but Andy knew
after nearly forty years of deep-sea fishing that overcast
skies and a little chop made the tuna a vicious hunter.

Sam Colhane, a principal critic of Andy's arcane fishing theories, didn't believe this. Sam believed that tuna
were like people: they liked the sunlight and smooth warm
water; they ate when they were hungry, and they made
love when the opportunity presented itself. To Sam it
made no sense to fish in bad weather, knocked about by
cresting and running waves, when any sensible tuna was
hunkered down out of the ebb and flow, ready to eat when
the sun came out and the sea calmed.

But Andy insisted that tuna were as complicated in their
own way as fishermen in theirs, and to catch them required great discipline and intelligence. Discipline to—
when they were on the bite—drop everything else and
run for the boat, and the intelligence to outthink them. It
was a solid combination, discipline and intelligence, one
as essential as the other. It required no genius to know
that a wily tuna wouldn't strike a stale butterfish exposing
a hook, or a lure trailing sea grass; but it required discipline to haul in the line and clean the lure and replace the
bait. Show up every day and do things the way they ought
to be done and you'll be a success, Andy believed. Anything less was just trusting to luck, something his rich
clients could afford but not him. Neither could his friend,
Sam Colhane, yet he did. He didn't know about the boy,
he'd never fished with him. He liked him well enough, but
nice boys don't necessarily make good fishermen. And
there was that gimpy hand . . . Sam insisted it was strong
as ever, but Sam was the boy's father; he'd say that.

Duff peered through the wet glass at the gray shaft of
spotlight poking through the endless darkness that surrounded them and felt a sudden cold shudder. Being alone
with Andy made him feel somehow vaguely uneasy. Either that or the ocean did. The thought that they could be
swallowed up in that dark sea in a matter of minutes and

never heard from again always filled him with a strange mix of fear and anger. Random death was a part of life, but drowning at sea was as lonely and ignominious a way to go as he could imagine.

"You ever fish the Canyons?" Andy asked.

"A few times," Duff said. He went out once on an overnighter, ran into some heavy weather and became violently sick and vowed he would never go again.

"How'd you like it?"

"I loved it."

Andy looked at him and nodded dubiously. "But you never go out with your old man. . . ."

"I've been busy with golf—until now."

"Umm," Andy grunted. He couldn't understand how anybody would want to do anything else when he could be out fishing. "How's your hand?"

"Good," Duff said, opening and closing it for him. "Almost a hundred per cent."

"That your reel hand?"

"Yeah."

"Umm."

Andy went back to watching the waves, and Duff assumed the conversation was finished. He was deep in thought, thinking of that missed birdie putt on the 19th hole that had started it all, when Andy resumed the conversation.

"There's still some good money to be made fishin'," he said. "Despite what you always hear. As long as a man knows what he's doin'. And does it," he added.

"Yeah, I'm sure," Duff agreed.

"Your father knows what he's doin'. Only trouble is he sometimes lets the booze get in the way."

"He's cut back lately."

Andy nodded. "On account of you. He has your best interest at heart, you know."

"I know."

"I guess it wasn't always that way, but . . . If he had somebody to keep him on course, he could still be one of

the best fishermen around here." He looked sideways at
Duff and asked, "Know what I mean?"

"You saying you think I could keep him from drinking?" Duff asked. He was the last person in Montauk his
father would listen to.

"I think you could, if you had a professional responsibility to each other."

"Professional responsibility . . . You mean you think I
ought to go into the fishing business with him?"

"There's worse ways to make a livin'."

"Yes, there are."

"And it'd give him back his self-respect—be in business with his son, have his own boat again . . ."

"A boat costs a lot of money."

"I got some money."

"You?"

"I could loan you the down payment, go guarantor on
the rest. I was talkin' to Cliff Smalley—he says he's interested in gettin' out and movin' to Florida, if he could
find a buyer."

"That's very kind of you," Duff mumbled.

"He might even carry some short-term paper."

"I appreciate your offer, Andy, I really do. But you
have to understand, I think I've got a future in golf."

"After the way you broke down the last time?"

"That was an aberration."

"Aberration . . ."

"A one-time thing."

"I know what it means. I don't wanna be unkind, but
it seems to me a player that can't qualify in an amateur
tournament don't have much future in the pro ranks. Or
am I missin' something?"

"It takes time," he said, clenching and unclenching his
hand.

"I thought it was almost a hundred per cent."

"It's good enough for fishing," Duff replied. It was obvious that his father had sent him up here so Andy could
grill him, and he was getting hot. "Not that fishing re-

quires anything less," he added in an apologetic tone.

Andy nodded, apology accepted, as a big wave broke over the bow and splattered against the port glass. "Aren't there a lot of young fellows out there just like you—only they got two good hands—thinkin' they can play professional golf?"

"Yeah, quite a few."

"That Irish golf pro told your dad the odds are a thousand to one."

"I don't think the odds are that—"

"And that's if you got two good flippers. So it seems to me it wouldn't hurt to have somethin' solid to fall back on."

"Maybe," Duff allowed. "But if I had a fishing business to fall back on, maybe I wouldn't work so hard at golf."

"Yeah, I can see where that might hurt you," Andy allowed, nodding slowly. "But it might hurt Sam a lot more."

"If I was as sure as you that this would help Sam, I might be interested, Andy. But I don't think it would. Dad had his own boat once, remember? And that didn't stop him from drinking."

"That's not the same," Andy replied surely. "Sam went on a drunk after your mother died and I could understand why. But that was a long time ago, now he's got somethin' to take her place."

"Rita?"

"I'm not talkin' about Rita."

"Me?"

"That's right."

"I don't think so," Duff said, shaking his head.

His father had scarcely noticed him while he was growing up, it was his grandmother who came over to clean up his father's messes and feed him and wash his clothes and get him off to school. It isn't his fault, he misses your mother so much, if only you could have known her. . . . Duff grew up hearing excuses from aunts and uncles until he became convinced that no one, not even a son, could ever make up for what Sam had lost. Duff didn't blame his father, he even loved him in a pitying kind of way, but he could never invest so much of himself in Sam Colhane as Andy required.

"Nobody could ever take my mother's place with Sam," Duff said surely.

"I'm not sayin' anybody could take Amy's place," Andy replied. "I'm just proposin' a business relationship. I'm askin' you to give him a second chance. Promise me you'll at least think about it?"

"I'll think about it," Duff said.

Andy looked at him out of the corner of his eye but said nothing while Duff stared straight ahead at the dark sea. They plowed on in silence, except for the monotonous hum of the powerful engines and the sound of water slapping the hull and whooshing past. Duff was thinking of his mother, of the stories he'd heard so often that they'd become memories. He saw himself toddling about the yard, handing her clothespins while the wind blew the sheets and her dress and her long brown hair. He saw her at the beach, wearing the same black bathing suit she wore in the picture of the two of them that rested on the bookshelf in the living room, holding his hand while he stumbled in the shallow surf. He saw her on her bed in the hospital, pale as an angel, and he felt her arms wound lightly around him and her cool lips on his cheek. And finally he saw her face before him, her very beautiful face, the one his father carried in his worn wallet, calm and reposed as a statue in church.

"Andy?"

"Yeah?"

"What did you mean before, when you said you could understand why my father behaved like he did after my mother died?"

"You'd only have to've seen her to know the answer to that one," Andy answered, as the boat yawed suddenly and pitched them both to the side.

"Beautiful?" Duff asked, knowing she was. He had

grown up hearing it from everyone who had known her, and she shined like a movie star even through the cheap faded snapshots that were all that remained of her.

"Prettiest girl I ever saw," Andy said, with the finality of a connoisseur. "There wasn't a boy in Montauk wasn't in love with Amy Duff. And she was such a nice girl, she could make us all think we stood a chance. Until Sam Colhane come along anyway. I can tell you, it was a sad day for a lotta young men on the East End when Amy Duff got married."

"What about you, Andy—were you one of the sad ones?"

"I wasn't so much sad as angry," he replied, with a surprising trace of bitterness still. "I don't mean I was angry with Sam for marryin' her—that was her choice— but I got mad at the way he started treatin' her after that."

"What do you mean?" This was the first he had heard that his parents' marriage had been anything other than idyllic.

"I don't mean that he abused her or anything like that. He just started takin' her for granted, leavin' her home alone with you while he went bar hoppin' with the boys. For all of us guys who were in love with Amy Duff, that seemed a terrible waste. I think your father kinda enjoyed makin' us suffer, if you wanna know the truth."

"He started drinking *before* she died?" Duff had always subscribed to the romantic notion that his father had been abruptly plunged into alcoholic despair at the tragic and untimely death of a wife whom he had loved more than anything else in life, even their son.

"Not like later. But lookin' back you could see it was buildin' even then. All it took was somethin' like that to push Sam right into the arms of old John Barleycorn. I can tell you, it had a soberin' effect on me when I saw Sam lose his boat. I haven't had a drink since. Now I got my own boat and Sam's got nothin'."

"You and Sam used to drink a lot together." Duff said, both question and statement.

"A hell of a lot."

"And you were able to quit, just like that?"

"Cold turkey."

He looked at Andy—big, red and bulbous—and tried to picture him as he might have looked 25 years before, sitting at the bar with Sam, both drinking a hell of a lot. He could envision his father drunk and raucous, out of control, but not Andy. Andy sat like a sphinx, tight as a tick, pushing drinks across the bar to his drinking buddy. Why? To prove to Amy Duff that she had married a drunk who'd never amount to anything, when she could have had Andy Dobbs, master of his own boat? And now that she was dead and gone, was he trying to make up for what he'd done by helping Sam and his son to get a fishing boat?

"I'll think about what you said," Duff promised.

They reached Block Canyon at the edge of the Continental Shelf just as the sun was rising out of the sea like hot blown glass. Andy punched up the GPS for an exact location, then nodded, pleased with his dead reckoning skills. They were almost directly over the edge of the Continental Shelf. Shortly after he reached the edge and pulled back on the throttle to begin the slow search for tuna, Sam climbed sleepily up the ladder and asked, "Breakfast ready?"

"Cook's day off," Andy said.

"Been hearin' for years about this great cook he's got, but every time I sail with him she's off," Sam winked at his son.

The slowed boat was rocking steeply in the twenty-knot swells and the morning sky was overcast, just what Andy had wanted and Sam had not. Sam rubbed his eyes and peered at the fishfinder. The screen was blank, but still he asked, "See anything?"

"Water's too cold yet," Andy answered.

It was less than 50 degrees, Duff noted. Even though

he wasn't a fisherman, he knew just from growing up around them that even the biggest bluefins wouldn't venture into water that was less than 60 degrees. Moving left and right as they were along the Shelf, Andy was looking for a warm core eddy from off the Gulf Stream where the bluefins should be lurking. When they spotted some floating eelgrass and sargasso weed and the water changed from green to blue, Andy said they were getting close. And when the temperature gauge jumped suddenly to almost seventy degrees, he announced, "I think we've found the happy fishing grounds." A few minutes later he pointed to some shadowy activity on the screen and said, "There they are."

"Big?" Sam asked.

"Fifteen- or twenty-thousand-dollar size, I'd say."

"So let's get one."

Duff couldn't see much of anything. They left him at the wheel of the slow-trolling boat while they went down to the cockpit to dribble some chum and chunkbait over the stern. Twenty minutes later they saw their first fish.

"Big fuckin' blue!" Sam called up to the wheel.

Quickly they baited two lines with live bait fish, pushing a thin wire through the eyes and wrapping it around a hook pressed tightly against the forehead, then dropped them over the stern amidst the chopped fish and began pulling line off the reel. When the rods were set, Andy returned to the wheel and sent Duff back to man the smaller rod. His father strapped him into the standup tackle and Duff fitted the butt end of the pole into the gimbal on the heavy belt. The professionals had decided earlier that the younger Colhane would man the short line, while Sam would handle the longer line from the fighting chair, supposedly because the nimbler man could flit more easily about the deck and keep the lines clear in the event of a double strike. Duff worried, however, that they had assigned him the minor role because they were afraid he might not be able to reel in the long line with his weak right hand.

"Just make sure you hold it tight," his father warned, tugging at the shoulder straps. The most embarrassing and expensive thing that could happen to an unsuspecting neophyte was to have his tackle snatched from his hands by a large tuna or shark.

Duff gripped the handle tightly and waited while his father climbed into the big game chair and strapped himself down. Then while Andy pushed the boat slowly ahead, they trailed out their line, Duff to a hundred feet, Sam to the two-hundred-foot mark. They were going deep for the monster bluefin, the three- to five-hundred pounder, or even larger, that would fetch several thousand dollars from the Japanese buyer waiting on the dock. This late in the season the big tuna was both scarce and at its best, it's deep red flesh larded with the summer fat that sushi eaters prized. The Japanese broker might pay as much as $30 a pound for a good fish, a seemingly astronomical sum were it not for the thousands of Tokyo businessmen waiting to pay more than that for just a few slivers at lunch the next day.

Duff trailed his bait off the starboard side, keeping his hook as far from the center line as possible, while Sam continued to throw chunks of bait fish over the transom and Andy looked over his shoulder for tuna while trolling at a few knots. They'd been expecting a quick strike after watching the big bluefin come to the top and take the bait fish, but for the next half hour they saw no sign of fish. For a while Andy tried surging—quickly throttling down and letting up, hoping the fish might mistake the sound for frenzied feeding and come to the top to investigate—but nothing happened. Duff said as little as possible while they searched for fish, answering his father's comments and observations with no more than a murmur. He was thinking about Andy's offer, growing increasingly angry at his father's imagined part in it.

Thinking he was reading Duff's silence, Sam said, "The big bluefins are spooky. That's how they get big. When you hook a tuna you'll see the others followin' along when you're pullin' him to the boat, just watchin' and rememberin'. Then the next time they wanna swallow a fish they're gonna make sure it's not attached to a line that's attached to a boat."

"You really think they're that smart, do you?" Duff said.

"It's a fact," Sam said, quietly confident. "A hundred years ago they could catch a tuna with a hook at the end of a rope. Nowadays you better have an invisible leader and monofilament line and your hook better be up on top, outta their sight line, or you're just wastin' your time. Fish learn from experience, you see, just like people."

"Not all people."

"True, some people are dumber than fish."

"Did you know Andy wants to put us in business together?"

After a moment's silence, Sam answered, "He mentioned it, just in passing."

"Just in passing . . . Is that why you brought me along? Were you hoping I'd get the fishing bug?"

"Why not? What else are you gonna do?"

"You know what I'm going to do, I told you. I'm going to play golf."

"No, Duff, you're not gonna play golf," Sam said, shaking his head slowly from side to side. "The doctors say you're not gonna play; Teddy McGill says you're not gonna play; everybody but you knows you're not gonna play. You gotta start makin' some plans."

"I've made my plans and they don't include fishing. If Andy wants to put you in the fishing business, that's fine with me. But don't expect me to go along just to take care of you."

"Take care of . . . ! You think I went to Andy because I wanted your help?"

"Why else?"

"I went to him because I wanted to help you. I was never able to do anything for you before, but now I thought I finally could. So I went to Andy and asked him for a loan so I could stake you. You think that was easy for me?"

"Why didn't you ask me first? If I want to be a fisherman I'll get my own loan."

"You think Andy or anybody else would loan money to buy a fishin' boat to somebody with no experience? That's the only reason I was goin' along—to teach you the business. I didn't do it for me, I did it for you!"

"Thank you very much, but you should've talked to me first and saved yourself the embarrassment. Because for the last time, I'm not going be a fisherman, I'm going be a golfer."

"Duff, for God's sake, wake up before it's too late," he pleaded.

At that moment Duff felt the strike and managed to tighten his grip on the pole as the reel shrieked and the line ran out. "Fish!" he cried.

"Let him run, don't hit him yet!" Sam hollered, as Andy throttled back until the boat was scarcely moving.

With the drag only lightly on, the line unfurled with an urgent whine that made Duff want to stop it, to haul back on the pole and hook his fish, but he knew better. Don't yank the bait out of his mouth while he's just carrying it, wait till he takes it. But at the rate the line was disappearing—his fish had to be a big fast one—he couldn't wait much longer. Just when he thought Sam had forgotten him—he was busy reeling in his own line—he shouted, "Now, hit him!"

Duff lowered his pole and braced his knees against the transom, and when he hauled back it felt for a moment as if he'd hooked an anchor. Then he was nearly snatched off the deck as the fish hauled back and the reel, with the drag heavy, began spinning off line and Duff braced his knees against the transom and fought to keep his balance, to keep his body leaning back, away from the transom, while the fish hauled in the opposite direction, intent on either pulling him into the sea or taking the boat to the bottom of the ocean.

"He's sounding!" Andy called from the flybridge.

"Slack off the drag, give him line!" Sam said.

Duff eased off on the drag and watched the line vertical down as the fish dove even deeper. His father was behind him now, his own line reeled in, a hand under Duff's shoulder strap, ready to pull back should the fish threaten again to yank him out of the boat. This was a big fish. Sam was sorry it hadn't taken the long line so he could work it from the fighting chair—although some giant fish had been known to tear a fighting chair out of the deck along with its hapless occupant. Anyway, the chair was no longer an option as the stand-up pole was too short for it, the line would saw against the chines or the props and break the moment the fish neared the boat. They would have to fight him with the short pole, keeping the fish away from the boat; hard work but not impossible—several hundred-pound fish had been taken on standup gear by strong, agile sportsmen. And although this fish was big, maybe even two or three hundred pounds judging from the depth he was seeking, the two of them, taking turns if necessary, could manage him. If only he stays hooked, Sam silently prayed.

"He's taking all my line!" Duff cried, when he sensed the chrome axle was about to appear at any moment. And yet the line continued to sing out.

Sam glanced at the reel and reluctantly ordered, "Put on the drag!"

Duff applied the drag and watched, as if he were skidding helplessly toward the edge of a cliff, as the spinning line drew to a stop—with just a glint of chrome axle beginning to shine through. He lowered the rod and managed to turn a bit of slack onto the reel before the fish pulled back furiously, bending the pole until he thought it would break. Then Andy began backing the boat slowly and Duff was able to dip the pole and wind on a bit more line—until the line was almost vertical and Andy had to pull forward to keep it out of the props.

"Work him, Duff, work him," Sam urged, still gripping

the shoulder strap tightly. "Get some line on."

Duff tried to wind, but it was as if the line were hooked on the Continental Shelf several hundred feet below them—until the big fish chose to go deeper, and then he knew he was hooked into something live and huge and strong.

"More drag!" Sam ordered, when the reel began to turn slowly.

"I can't, the pole will snap," Duff gasped. A sudden pain in his right hand was now running up his arm like an intermittent electric shock.

"If you give up any more line we'll lose him anyway. Haul!"

Duff braced his knees and lowered the rod until the tip was almost in the water, then hauled back with a great guttural heave, reeling a few precious inches of line onto the reel before the fish pulled angrily, flailing the rod crazily in the air. He did it again, then again and again and again, for almost an hour, painfully acquiring only a few yards of line after all that time. It had been cool when he started, but now he was soaking with sweat under his light jacket which he wished he could somehow discard. The pain in his hand and arm was now accompanied by a dull ache in his back and shoulders, and suddenly he was incredibly thirsty.

"Some water," he said.

"You want me to take it for a while?" Sam asked.

"No, just water!" Duff barked.

"Can I let go of you?"

"Yeah."

Duff held the bending pole still while Sam went for the water bottle. He held it to Duff's mouth while he drank greedily, then poured some on his head when he'd had enough to drink.

"You're sure you don't want a break?"

"I'll tell you if I want a break," Duff grunted, pulling again against the big fish. It was his fish, he'd boat it.

Yet an hour later the fish was hardly any nearer the

boat than it had been. The hand and arm had gone mercifully numb, but the ache in his shoulders and back had now moved down into his hips and legs. Andy had now joined Sam in occasionally suggesting that he give the pole to someone else, but Duff wouldn't give it up and they wouldn't force him. They might be fishing commercially at the moment, but they were sportsmen—it was Duff's fish as long as he wanted it.

Although no one had seen the fish, the older fishermen were sure it was a very large bluefin, perhaps as big as three or four hundred pounds. Duff would take their word regarding species, but he was convinced, after struggling for more than two hours to dislodge this monster from the bottom of the sea, that it was at least twice that size. An eight-hundred-pound bluefin was unlikely but not impossible. The record rod and reel tuna was fifteen hundred pounds, and a few weighing nearly a ton were sometimes netted by commercial fishermen.

Suddenly the line went slack and, after a confused moment, Duff began to reel in line, yards and yards of it, while Andy and his father shouted encouragement. His right hand was numb but working, even if it seemed to belong to someone else, while his back and legs felt like the the morning after the first day of football practice.

"He's running out of oxygen!" Andy shouted. "He's coming up!" Duff assumed the battle was nearly over—when he broke the surface he'd begin working him to the boat.

But that wasn't the way of the giant tuna, he learned from his father. "Get all the line on him you can,'cuz after he gets some air, he'll head for the bottom again," Sam said. "Let him go but make him work for it."

"Shit," Duff muttered. He didn't know how he could go through this whole thing again, yet he would not give the pole to his father. Even while he reeled frantically and Andy backed up, the line was slanting way out, his big fish was coming up.

The sea rose first, like an underwater explosion, then

the shiny blue-black of the giant tuna, rising in a froth of silver, slowly and forever, then disappearing into the blue water, leaving nothing of himself but the tension on the thin line in Duff's hands. He had known it would be a big fish, and still he was so unprepared for the monster that had appeared and disappeared so quickly that already he could not be sure of what he had seen.

"Jesus Christ!" Sam said reverently as the dusky yellow tail fin disappeared in the dark water.

"Pay day! Pay day!" Andy shouted from the flybridge.

"How big is he?" Duff shouted.

"Five hundred pounds at least!" Andy called back.

"More like eight!" Sam corrected.

"Feels like more than a thousand!" Duff added.

"Easy—keep it taut," Sam cautioned. "We don't wanna lose him now." The line zizzed out as the monster went deep, then suddenly stopped, leaving plenty of line on the reel this time. "Tighten down. That's it. He'll start to circle now," Sam predicted. And he did. "He's gettin' tired. And disoriented, can't tell which way's up. Keep the pressure on the line, make him lay over. That's it. Now pump the rod, keep his head up. That's it, bring him up. Nice and easy. He may be confused but he ain't whipped, not by a long shot."

With each lazy circle Duff brought his fish closer to the stern, until finally he glimpsed him as he crossed the wake. He was enormous, almost as long as the transom, easily a thousand pounds. More than thirty thousand dollars! Half to Andy, the rest to him and his father—almost eight thousand dollars apiece! With the boat backing up slowly on the circling fish, Andy came down the ladder and went to the cockpit controls where he'd be closer to the action when the fish was brought to the boat.

Suddenly Sam was shouting, "Reel in! Reel in!"

Duff looked and saw the line laying slack and realized he'd lost his concentration; he'd been counting his money before his fish was in the boat. Instinctively he raised the rod tip, getting the line as far away from the stern as he could, then tried turning the handle. But the handle wouldn't move; it was frozen. Then, with his father shouting in his ear, "Reel in!" he realized it wasn't the handle that was frozen, but his hand. The boat was backing up on the slack line and he couldn't make his hand work. They were about to back over the line and he couldn't reel in. Andy was shouting at him to reel in while Sam was shouting at Andy to pull forward and nobody was doing anything. Except the fish.

Suddenly revived, the monster dove again, pulling the line away from the spinning props. It should be the monster's fatal mistake, Duff knew. He was getting a second chance and now it was up to him to capitalize on it. He managed to get the drag on and slow the fish's dive, but still his hand lay helpless on the crank, rigid as death. Then he felt his father and Andy at either side of him, incoherently admonishing while trying to wrestle the pole from his grasp, and now he was fighting two men and a monster fish, but he would beat them all. He braced his legs against the transom and leaned out over the water, keeping the rod out of their reach while risking a headlong plunge over the side. Wisely, both men gave up the struggle and grabbed for Duff's shoulder straps and pulled him back, tugging against the fish. Almost six hundred pounds of men pulling against several hundred pounds of fish at the end of a long line that would snap at the slightest mistake by the man in the middle. Duff knew he should give the pole to one of them but something within him wouldn't allow it. His hand was doing the thinking, telling his brain that it was as good as any hand in the world and it would prove it. It would shake off the cramp and reel in the big fish. And it would hit a golf ball as long and as straight as any other hand in the world. He was sure of it, he just needed time.

But there was no more time. They were shouting for the hand to do what it had to do. Haul him in! Now! No more excuses! Work you sonofabitch! Work!

Still the hand refused. "You're pissing me off!" Duff

grumbled through clenched teeth, not at the fish, as the men assumed, but at his goddamned hand. "Work, god-damn you!" he cried as the line went suddenly slack and he was sure he'd lost his fish.

Until a moment later when the great fish broke the sur-face once more, fixed his tormentor with a baleful eye and disappeared again under the sea. This was his last chance, Duff knew. He detached the clawed hand from the crank and pounded it against the rail, hard, again and again, until suddenly it opened like a flower. He quickly re-gripped the handle and began hauling in, expecting the hand to seize up again with each revolution. But when the line went taut and the hand continued to crank, Duff recog-nized that something had changed. Slowly but inexorably, he was moving the great fish to the boat in ever narrowing circles. They spoke softly and said very little, like men disarming a bomb, until Sam got the gaff in and they hauled their big fish aboard, when suddenly the tension exploded in a spontaneous cry of exultation.

On the way back in Duff sat in the stern with his fish while Andy and his father rode in the pilothouse, giddily speculating on how much their fish would bring. Twenty thousand, thirty—more? When Andy looked back at Duff on the spray-washed deck, Duff gave him a thumbs up and Andy nodded okay.

"That's one stubborn kid you got there," he told Sam.

Sam nodded.

"Must get it from his mother."

"Right," Sam said.

Gena lay naked on a table while a Jamaican woman with strong fingers and a face of melting tar vigorously kneaded her back muscles, talking all the time about this and that in a mesmerizing Reggae lilt. While growing up in Montauk she never would have dreamed of going to Gurney's Spa. It was something rich matrons from Oyster Bay or models from Manhattan did in the winter, not the locals who hunkered around the kitchen stove and hoped the oil would last till spring. But things change. Today she would casually peel several hundred dollars from a thick roll of twenties for a swim in the indoor pool, a workout, sauna, facial, manicure, pedicure and massage, and never give it a second thought.

Somewhere between sleep and wakefulness, while the Jamaican masseuse caressed her muscles like violin strings, her thoughts drifted to Duff. She'd intended to call him but learned after arriving that he was somewhere down south. Her mother had saved the article from the local paper telling how he'd almost qualified for the U.S. Open last summer, shooting the lowest score in the morning then blowing up in the afternoon. But he wasn't disappointed, he was sure he'd do well on the Minitour over the winter.

She was sorry, she'd wanted to see him, to apologize for the way she'd behaved at their final meeting. He was, after all, her first love (Monte didn't count), he would always be special. Even though they were both kids at the time, the decision to leave him and go to New York had been a difficult one for her, far more than she had let on. My loss, golf's gain, she quipped to herself. Now things were different, they were both sophisticated people, able to turn it on and turn it off at will. Too bad he wasn't in town.

A light smack on the bottom signaled that the massage was done, time for the next treatment. It was all so decadent, she felt an urge to apologize to the black masseuse, to let her know that she was not really one of them. But she was.

An hour later, still tingling with the pleasure of ministering hands and buzzing on a line of coke, Gena swept into the dining room wearing several thousand dollars worth of leather, cashmere and jewels, and called confidently for a table overlooking the ocean. Not unaware of the appraising stares of the spa ladies, she followed the maitre d' to her table, chin up, eyes straight ahead, just the way the supermodels sashayed into Monte's.

"Your waiter will be with you in a moment," the maitre d' said, sliding her chair under her.

Gena tipped him with her million dollar smile and turned her attention to the menu. Earlier she'd been famished, but now she felt more like another line of coke rather than lunch. Still, a girl has to eat. Oysters and champagne, she decided, closing the menu.

He saw her face as the menu came away and halted, looking left and right for an escape. But it was too late, she had him in her sights.

"Duff!" she exclaimed, jumping to her feet.

"Gena," he said, approaching warily. When she made a move to embrace him, he put the table between them.

"What are you doing here?"

"Isn't it obvious?"

"I had no idea you were working here. My Mom told me you were down south playing golf."

"I was—for a while."

"What happened?"

"It didn't work out."

"I'm sorry."

"Don't be. I'm a loser, remember?"

"Duff—you know I didn't mean that!"

"You said it plainly enough."

"That was the coke talking."

"Care to hear the specials?"

"Duff, please . . ." she said, reaching for his hand.

He pulled it away. "The broiled swordfish is especially popular with our models."

"I've really wanted to talk to you. Give me a chance."

"And have my throat cut again?"

"I've changed."

He looked closely at her dilated pupils. "Have you?"

"That's chlorine."

"I don't think so."

"Damn it, stop being such a tight-ass! Can't you see I'm trying to make it up to you?"

"Fine, your apology is accepted." He struck a professional pose, order pad at the ready. "Now would you like to sit and order?"

"God, you can be such a prick," she said, plopping onto her chair.

"Loser, remember? Your order?"

"Fuck you."

"I'm afraid that's not on the menu."

"What time do you finish?"

"Are you trying to pick me up?"

"It's winter in Montauk, you got a better offer?"

"You're such a sweet talker."

"What time?"

"Nine o'clock."

"I'll be here," she said, rising from the table.

"What about lunch?"

"I'm not hungry," she called over her shoulder.

The maitre d' watched curiously as his customer walked past him and out the door, then summoned his waiter with a curl of the finger.

"Why did that woman leave?"

"She couldn't find what she wanted on the menu."

"Which was?"

"Nose candy."

"Ah ha . . ." Catering to the many models who frequented the spa, he was not unfamiliar with the erratic effects of amphetamine abuse. "I knew she was trouble the moment she walked in," he said, waving his waiter back to work.

So when am I going to learn? Duff wondered, as he returned to his station.

At a few minutes after nine, Duff stepped out onto the cold dark parking lot and looked around for Gena. From the back of the lot came the high whining sound of a powerful engine turning over, followed by the blinding flash of headlamps as a car hurtled toward him and squealed to a stop.

He opened the passenger door and asked, "Would you like me to drive?"

"I'm not high, get in," she ordered.

He slid into the Porsche and attached the seat belt. "Nice car."

"It belongs to a friend."

"Monte?"

"If it's any of your business."

"Generous employee benefits package," he remarked, running his hands over the leather seat, soft as a glove.

"Would you like one?" she asked, making a tight U-turn and racing for the highway.

"No thanks."

"Tight-ass."

She turned sharply out of the parking lot and raced west along the roller-coaster hills of the Old Montauk Highway. The up-and-down motion caused his stomach to roll.

"I wouldn't want to hit a deer in this tin can," he warned.

To his surprise, she quickly slowed the car. They passed the string of motels at the edge of the seaside cliff and glided down to the main highway that ran flat and straight beside the open beach. A half moon hung out over the ocean, cutting a silver swath on the black water and frosting the breakers with vanilla icing. The car felt solid and powerful, and he liked it a lot, but he wouldn't say anything because it was Monte's. He also liked being back with her, but he wouldn't say anything about that either. Not just yet anyway.

"I'm really glad I ran into you, Duff."

"I'm sure."

"Honest."

"How's your mother?"

"Fine."

"What does she think about all this—the Porsche, the expensive apartment, all the money—where does she think it's coming from?"

"She doesn't ask. Unlike you."

She drove slowly through East Hampton and turned right on 114.

"Where are we going?" he asked.

"You'll see."

A short while later she parked the car on Main Street in Sag Harbor and led him to the National Hotel, a very old and expensive inn where she had earlier in the day reserved a suite. Duff moved hesitantly through the richly appointed lobby, as if afraid he might break one of the fragile antiques, then followed her up the stairs to their room.

"How much?" he asked, stepping into an exquisite room of brightly papered walls and lace curtains and antique furnishings.

"When are you going to stop worrying about money?"

"When I have some," he answered, sitting testily on the canopied bed. "And don't say anything."

"I wasn't going to," she said, pulling a vial from her bag.

They did a line of coke—for him a courtesy toke—then bathed together in a claw-foot tub and made love in the four-poster in front of a fire. Duff tried to remain dispassionate despite her fervor, until at last he could no longer hold anything back from her. Finally spent, they lay side by side staring at the tin-paneled ceiling, the bedclothes in a pile on the floor, the crackling fire and their deep breathing the only sounds in the room.

"Am I forgiven?" she asked.

"It's a first step."

She laughed softly. "I think you're finally ready for this. I think we both are. It was too much before, you know. It threatened to crowd everything else out. Do you know what I mean?"

"Yeah, I know what you mean." He remembered the hold she once had on him—probably still did—but he would never admit it to her. He had been scarred, nothing could ever hurt him again.

"We're older now, more sophisticated. We're able to keep this separate from other things."

"Like Monte?"

She exhaled audibly, irritably. "I was thinking about you, your career."

"Waiting tables?"

"Golf."

"I'd rather talk about Monte. Are you living with him?"

"I was wrong, you're not ready for this at all," she said, turning her back to him.

"Tell me."

"What difference does it make?"

"I have the feeling it could make a big difference. I mean first I get beaten up by the Vegas mob, then I have an affair with the drug dealer's girlfriend . . . ? A shrink might say I'm suicidal."

"Relax, he'll never find out," she promised. "And even if he did, I'd be the one to suffer, not you."

"Is he violent?"

"I can't talk about that."

"I'm not talking about his business, I'm talking about you. Does he hit you?"

"Not exactly."

"What do you mean, not exactly? Either he does or he doesn't."

"Anybody who does a lot of drugs gets a little excitable once in a while, but it's nothing I can't handle."

"It doesn't sound like that to me. It sounds to me like the situation is getting out of control."

"Bullshit," she said, turning back to him.

"No, Gena, you're bullshitting yourself," he said, sitting up. "He doesn't hit you, he's just excitable? You're living with him, but you're here with me?"

"God, you're such a tight-ass!" she wailed, springing out of bed. "I'm here with you now, tomorrow it might be somebody else. Try not to make a big thing out of it, okay? We need another hit."

He didn't, but he sniffed a small bit just to keep her calm. He put another log on the fire while she prowled about the room naked, her skin flushed and glowing in the firelight from the hot bath and sex and drugs.

"You're doing too much of that shit," he said, as he watched her pace.

"God! You shouldn't be a golfer, you know that? You should be a fucking social worker. Always telling other people how to live, then you go out and get yourself all fucked up."

"I don't want you to do the same, that's all," he said, squatting naked before the fire, waiting for the new log to catch.

"I know, I know . . ." she said. She came and crouched beside him and draped one arm over his shoulders. "I know I gotta get out, and I will."

"When?"

"Just as soon as I make a little more money."

"Don't push it, Gena."

"You're getting rather cautious in your old age, aren't you, darling? I mean what are the odds against making it on the golf tour—ten thousand to one?"

"That's why I'm free to advise—I got out."

"I don't believe that. Not you."

"No, not me. My sponsor made the decision for me."

"What sponsor, what do you mean?"

"Jack Stricker, the guy I went to Vegas with. He was covering my expenses on the Minitour until last month when he pulled out."

"Why?"

"Because I didn't make any money for him. We were supposed to split the purses sixty-forty but there weren't any. So, that's why I'm waiting tables."

"That's shitty!" she exclaimed. "That's really shitty. I mean how long did you play—a couple of months?"

"One season, and I didn't win once."

"Well, it takes time. I mean how long did Tiger Woods play before he won?"

"He won the Masters his first year."

"That's a big tournament?"

"Pretty big."

"Nevertheless . . ."

She was suddenly on her feet, pacing and raging at the unreasonable expectations of an ungrateful sonofabitch who would get him beaten up and then yank the financial rug out from under him. Duff made a weak attempt to defend his sponsor—for in truth the agreement to quit had been his as much as Jack's, maybe more—but Gena's coke-fueled diatribe would admit no interruption.

"How much does it cost to play?" she demanded.

"About a thousand dollars a week on the Minitour."

"Chump change. How much can you win?"

"I don't know—a couple of wins, a few top tens—more than a hundred thousand."

"So if he stuck with you he'd've made some money."

"Possibly."

"I'll sponsor you."

"What?"

"What was the deal, sixty-forty?"

"Yeah, but . . ."

"He got forty, you got sixty?"

"Yeah."

"With me, you get seventy, I get thirty."

"I can't."

"Okay, eighty-twenty."

"That's not it, I just can't take your money."

"Can't take my money!" she exclaimed. "Why? Because of how I get it?"

Duff shook his head. "That's not it. I just don't want to see you lose your money, that's all."

She laughed explosively. "I've got money coming in so fast, I buy expensive shoes just so I have boxes to store it in. Believe me, you don't have to worry about the money. All you'd have to worry about is winning."

"That's the problem," he said, climbing to his feet. He sat at the end of the bed, gripping the bedpost tightly in his good hand. "I can't win. I have some good early rounds, then this hand starts jerking me all over the golf course and I blow sky high. It was a joke—all the guys waiting for me to explode. They started calling me 'Flinch.'" There were times when he was alone and started thinking about it that he felt like crying, but so far he never had. Now of all times, sitting naked in the National Hotel with his high school girlfriend, he felt like he was about to lose it.

He felt the springs give and her warm thigh pressing against his as she took his damaged hand in hers. She whispered meaningless but comforting words as she lightly traced the surgical scars with her newly manicured red nails.

"Maybe it's not just the hand," she said. "Maybe it's the financial pressure, knowing you have to win to stay out there. You wouldn't have that with me backing you."

"It's not the pressure, it's the hand. It's just this fucking hand!" he cried, pulling it from her and thrusting it towards the fire. "I just have to accept the fact that it's never going to get any better."

She rested her chin on his shoulder and studied his hand against the firelight. "I can almost see right through it." She pulled his hand to her lips and kissed each fingertip, then placed it between her legs and squeezed. Then she took it out and examined it again, as if her ministrations might have brought forth a shining new hand. But it was the same battered hand that she now pressed against her breast. "I know a doctor," she said.

"So do I," he replied. "Lots of them."

"This doctor's different. All the models go to him. He prescribes things for energy and weight loss and things like that."

"I don't have a weight problem."

"He also treats a lot of jocks."

"Nor do I need steroids."

"He says there's a drug for everything, you just have to find it."

"Not for what I got."

"Why not try him?"

"I don't have the money."

"I have the money. If I'm going to sponsor you I want you in good shape. Come on—what've you got to lose?"

"Gena, right now the only professional skill I have is the ability to remember which plate goes with which customer, and I'm not about to ingest something that might jeopardize my last remaining gift."

"No, darling, you're meant for bigger things than that."

She wrapped her arms around him and pressed him down on the bed and kissed him the length of his smooth body. Then she was above him, rising slowly and falling back down, like a horsewoman taking the fences in the dark while lightning flashed behind her, streaking the tin ceiling with rippled gold, until finally she stiffened and cried out as Duff rose to her and they fell apart and their hoarse breathing mingled with the popping sounds of the fire and red sparks danced in their eyes.

"You'll always be my first fella," she said softly. "Will you stick with me?"

What did that mean? Taking her to the emergency room after an overdose? Getting her into detox? Finding a lawyer for her? He knew he should get away from her before she messed his life up even more than it already was, but he had no place to go.

"Yes, I'll stick with you," he said.

The doctor's waiting room looked like a storeroom for discarded mannequins, filled as it was with some of the same sunken-cheeked, limp-haired models who graced the pages of the old fashion magazines scattered about the room. There they sat, dim reflections of a glamorous illusion, riffling desperately through those old magazines for proof of their existence, twig-limbed and hollow-eyed, breasts unnaturally high, waiting with faith and hope for the chemical that would lower the appetite, raise the mood, sustain the illusion and stop time in its hoary tracks.

Duff watched as one by one they dragged themselves into the treatment room, then emerged a short while later, buoyant as Macy's Thanksgiving Day Parade balloons. He debated leaving. He wasn't one of them, a junkie, a vainglorious egoist who would deny fate. He was an injured athlete in need of medical aid, and he would almost certainly not get it here from a Dr. Feelgood. Yet he stayed, and when his name was called, he filed numbly into the treatment room.

Dr. Francis Promer perched on the corner of his desk and listened, chin in hand, nodding and murmuring occasionally as the young athlete recounted the long and painful ordeal that accounted for his presence in his office on this freezing winter day. Duff stared through the French doors at the bare maple trees in the garden while he bored himself once again with the overly familiar story. The trees seemed beyond awakening, too frozen and brittle for the sap of life to ever flow again. Like his patients, the well-conditioned and winter-tanned doctor appeared much younger than his nearly 50 years—judging from the date of his NYU Medical School diploma hanging on the wall (along with pictures of him at sport, posing beside a tarpon, a racehorse, at a tennis event and a pro-am golf outing). The wall facing the portrait gallery was covered with cabinets and chests upon which rested a variety of ominous syringes. There was a framed picture of a young girl on the desk, but no sign of a wife.

"My daughter is on contract, my girlfriends tend to be day players," the handsome doctor said when Duff remarked on the omission.

When Duff was finished with his medical history, the doctor patted the examining table and his patient jumped up like a show dog. He took Duff's hand in both of his, turning it from one side to the other, asking familiar questions of the veteran patient who replied easily in medical shorthand.

"Unfortunately, there's no medicine that can regrow nerves," the doctor said, letting Duff's hand fall. He walked to the swivel chair behind his desk and sat. Doctors liked to put something between themselves and their patient when delivering bad news, Duff had come to recognize. "Gena tells me you almost qualified for the U.S. Open, but you choked in the last round."

"I didn't choke," Duff answered irritably. "My hand began to spaz."

"And when you're playing in a tournament, at what point does your hand begin to—spaz?"

Duff thought for a moment before replying. "Usually at the end."

"When you're in contention?"

"A couple of times, yeah." There were always a few erratic shots during the course of 72 holes, but the big blow-ups always seemed to come on the last day.

"So what's the hand got to do with it?"

"What do you mean?"

"It sounds to me like you can't take the pressure."

"Bullshit!" Duff said, pushing off the table. "Until this," he said, waving the hand at the doctor, "I never choked. I needed the pressure, that's when I played best. It's not me, it's the hand. I've got a messed-up circuit board!"

"A messed up circuit board . . ." the doctor repeated. He leaned back in his swivel chair, laced his hands behind his head and stared at his patient. "You and Gena went to high school together?"

"That's right. What's that got to do with it?"

"She was your girlfriend?"

"Is that a medical question?"

"You asked about my wife. . . ."

"We dated."

"But not anymore."

"No. How do *you* know her? If I might ask."

"Through Monte. You know Monte?" the doctor asked.

"I've met him."

"I often eat at his restaurant. Gena's something of a fixture there. Along with a lot of models, actors, ballplayers . . . The place is hot."

"So I've heard. I take it you can't do anything about this," Duff said, raising his hand.

"I didn't say that. I might be able to do something for you; then again I might not. The question is, how bad do you want it?"

"Bad enough to try almost anything."

"Almost anything . . . What would you say to ripping out the whole circuit board?"

"No more surgery," Duff said, shaking his head.

"Not surgery, chemistry. I treat a lot of professional athletes—tennis players, baseball players, football players—especially football players. Admittedly, their needs aren't the same as yours, or my tennis or baseball players. They want no pain, no remorse, just attitude. And I'm able to give them that. I think I can give any athlete just what he needs, and that includes golfers. The trick is to find the drug that most successfully enhances the particular neuromuscular function required of your sport. And golf, as I know from my own sad experience, requires the nerves of a safecracker. Would you agree?"

"That's what I've heard."

"Which means we must retard the spark, so to speak. What we're looking for is a nerve block that won't rob you of all your strength. Or perhaps a second drug to offset the first . . ." He placed his elbows on the desk and his chin on his knotted hands while consulting silently with himself about the problem. "Yes, a combination . . ."

"You're not thinking of steroids, are you?" Duff asked.

"Steroids," he said, "are a banned substance. If I prescribed them, would you take them?"

What is this, some kind of a moral test? Duff asked

himself. Or is he afraid I might turn him in? He sensed
he had come to one of those important forks on the road
of life. Only a short while ago they were out of the question. Now he replied, "I'd have to know more about it."

Dr. Promer smiled. "I'm happy to say that steroids
aren't appropriate in your case. But neither am I entirely
sure what is," he added, scanning the cabinets that lined
the wall, as if the answer might lie there. "The point is,
I'm proposing to make you a guinea pig. And as with any
experimental treatment, there are risks. Most are fairly
predictable, but some might turn out to be a surprise."

"Like I might end up a vegetable?"

Dr. Promer smiled again and shook his head. "Experimental, not radical. The problem is this—when we relax
the peripheral muscles with a neuromuscular blocking
agent, we also unfortunately depress respiration, which
can leave you too weak to swing the club. And if the
dosage is too high it can depress the autonomic ganglia,
leading to a fall in blood pressure—even heart failure."

"Pass vegetable stage, go directly to death."

The doctor laughed shortly. "I assure you, none of my
patients has ever died of a drug overdose. We will experiment very carefully and very safely. There will be
some side effects and some of them will be uncomfortable, but they'll only be temporary—until we find the right
drug or combination of drugs, and the correct dosage."

"Uncomfortable side effects . . ." Duff mused. "Can
you be a little more specific?"

"They can be anything from," he said, gesturing inclu-
sively with his hands, "insomnia, sweating, skin rash,
cramps, impotence, dizziness, irritability . . . Unpleasant
perhaps, but nothing that can't be controlled. That's the
easy part. The hard part is finding a concomitant drug that
will artificially maintain respiration while the blocker con-
tinues to retard the nerves in your hand. It'll be a trial-
and-error method, but if you stay with it long enough, I
think we'll be successful."

"How long?"

The doctor shrugged. "Three or four months."

"I don't know, it sounds dangerous. . . ."

"I'll monitor you every step of the way."

"And expensive . . ."

"Gena told me to remind you that you're not to worry about anything."

Just my life, Duff said to himself. He had no illusions about Frank Promer: he just wanted a golfer to complete his roster of athletes and secure his place in the Performance-Enhancing Drug Sports Hall of Fame, and if he had to kill a few golfers to get there—so what? It was the risk-reward hole of all time. He could submit to the experiment, with all of its unknown risks and seductive promises, or go back to his job waiting tables. It was no contest.

"What have I got to lose?" he said.

Frank Promer's three- or four-month experiment turned out to be a year of madness. Some of Frank's concoctions made his patient sick and unable to eat, while others gave him an appetite that could only be satisfied by more drugs. Some pills caused hallucinations and nightmares that made him desperate to escape, while others filled him with glorious dreams from which he wanted never to return. With each new drug he became a different person. One would set him buzzing with aggression, sending his friends diving for cover, while the next would make him calm and still as casual water exasperating in his lethargy. There were a few brief days that filled him with hope, followed inevitably by long nights of despair.

Through it all, only Gena and his doctor remained encouraging. Both his father and Teddy McGill, who had taken him on as his assistant over the summer, begged him to give up the treatment before it killed him.

"You could be a club pro; it's a good life," Teddy pleaded, when he was sure his protégé would never play on the Tour with his damaged hand.

"Then why are you giving it up for the Senior Tour?" Duff countered, as he teed a ball up for another practice shot.

He was testing a new upper which Frank promised would eliminate the wild palpitations caused by the last one, and so far seemed to be working okay. After each setback Frank always came up with a new designer drug which he was sure would remedy the problem caused by the last—if only Duff would give it this one last try. And he always did—through the spring, summer and fall.

Meanwhile his golf game was no less volatile than his physical and mental well-being. When the downers held sway, he putted like Brad Faxon but lacked the strength to hit the ball any distance. And when the uppers dominated, he was a long but very loose cannon with no more feel for the game than a gorilla. Being a professional now (even though he'd only won a few thousand dollars on the Minitour) he was eligible to play in only a few regional opens over the summer, and he'd not played very consistently in any of them. But there were sometimes four- and five-hole stretches when the ball flew long and straight and the putts fell like hailstones and he knew, at least for a time, that he was the best player out there. After a particularly good day with still another wonder drug, he could hardly wait to get to the phone to tell Frank he'd finally found it, the magic elixir to soothe the demon that possessed him. But by the next day the wonder drug would prove to be a demon of its own, sending the doctor back to the lab to scramble up still another.

By late fall Frank had narrowed it down to a few brightly colored pills of various shapes and sizes that showed great promise, although the exact dosage was still a matter of art as much as science—and Duff was the artist. His body was a test tube into which he periodically poured chemicals, then waited for the results. Sometimes they were excellent, while at other times—depending upon how much he'd slept or how much or what he'd eaten, or any number of other mysterious variables—not

so good. When everything came together, he could feel
the tube glowing warmly within himself and he knew then
that he could either thread a needle on a bucking bull or
wrestle the beast to the ground. But when it didn't, when
the body for some reason balked at the mix or the timing
or some such, then he could smell the sulfurous stench of
still another failed experiment wafting from the tube. On
the good days, each swing repeated itself identically, his
drives found the fairway, his irons the green, and all his
putts were true. Gradually he began acquiring an instinct
for the medicine that cured—a hunger for the red pill, a
thirst for the blue—until, after a satisfying streak of
under-par rounds, he dared to think that his artwork, himself, was very nearly finished. And when he came from
out of the ranks to finish in the top ten in the Northeastern
Open, he knew he was ready to play.

It took him a few days to catch Gena at her apartment in
the city. She was in and out, spending a lot of time in the
Hamptons with Monte at the big beach house he'd recently purchased with his share of their drug profits. And
when she was there she spent a lot of time running around
with the celebrity coke crowd—a business requirement,
she explained. Duff was worried—she was using a lot of
her own product as well as running the risk of apprehen-
sion—but she told him not to worry, she would soon be
getting out of the business. Because it was hard for her
to get away from Monte, he only saw her at odd times.
Sometimes she would just show up at his house in the
middle of the night and climb into his bed while his father
slept in the next room. At other times he would find a
cryptic message at the pro shop naming a motel room and
a time, nothing else.

   "That girl's gonna get you in a lot of trouble," Teddy
had predicted after passing on a few notes.

   "Too bad you didn't know as much about Jack
Stricker," Duff answered.

Gena assured him there was little risk, that Monte wasn't the jealous type. Yet the precautions she took indicated to Duff that the drug dealer was a dangerous man. He knew Teddy was quite possibly right, that he should end it, but he couldn't.

They met at an out-of-the-way saloon near the Sag Harbor waterfront where Monte and his friends would never be seen. It was an unusually warm but dreary late fall afternoon, with the last of tropical clouds bouncing off the Long Island coast, soon to be replaced by the relentless winter westerlies. The ungainly scallopers were struggling in against the foamheads with yet another pitiable harvest, the result of Red Tide? development? Who knew? Watching as they rounded the breakwater and headed for the bridge, Duff remembered his own days at sea dragging a clam rake and felt a cold shudder that inflamed every sore muscle in his body. But he had no plans to haul a clam rake, or wait tables, or even be a club professional.

"Are you still interested in that business we talked about?" Duff asked, as he filled Gena's glass with champagne for the second time. It was all she drank anymore.

"You wanna work with me?" she asked.

"I'm talking about golf, remember?"

"Right, I remember, sure," she said, nodding effusively. "Whenever you're ready."

"I'm ready," he said, reaching into his pocket for the paper he had typed up in Teddy's office. "I drew up a contract like the one I had with Jack Stricker. . . ."

She shook her head and pushed it away. "No papers. Just tell me what you need."

What he needed was the three-thousand-dollar entry fee for the PGA Tour Qualifying School and more than a thousand dollars a week for the next several weeks, assuming he got past the first two qualifiers and went to the finals. The money was no problem as long as he'd take it in twenty-dollar bills, which he didn't mind. He would phone and tell her where he was going to be and she would FedEx the money to him. In return he offered her half his winnings for three years, but she would only take a fourth and he was free to pay her off and terminate the agreement whenever he wished.

"Then I guess we've got a deal," he said.

"You'll need something to get started," she said, reaching for her bag. She pulled out a thick, rubber-banded roll of twenties and passed it across the table to him. Duff thanked her and put it in his pocket. He had no idea how much it was. "By the way, how are you getting down?" she asked.

"I'm hoping Dad will loan me his truck."

"No!" she wailed. "You're representing me now, you can take the Fiat."

"I can't take your money and your car," Duff protested weakly.

"I don't need it, I've got Monte's Porsche. Which reminds me," she said, glancing at her watch, "I have to get back." She dropped five twenties on the table and got to her feet.

On the way to Monte's car she said, "I'm sorry we couldn't get together."

"So am I," he said, kissing her as she slid into the car.

He stood at the curb and waved as she disappeared down 114. When he got to his father's truck he removed the rubber band from the twenty-dollar bills and counted them. There were five hundred bills in the roll.

Duff's father was of two minds about his son's decision. True, he'd begun to shoot some very low scores in the fall, but that didn't mean it would continue. Sam had watched the experiments with the pills for more than a year, seen him half dead one minute, then so charged up the next that he couldn't sit still for a second. He'd seen him one day after a good round when God Himself couldn't convince him he hadn't licked it, then the next when he looked to have come back from hell. Sam wanted it to work for his son, but he was afraid this was just another phase of false hope, a bit more promising than the others perhaps, but bound to end just as badly sooner or later.

Yet he gave Duff his blessing when he drove off to the Country Club of South Carolina to play the first of three Q-School qualifiers. With more than twelve hundred able-bodied young men playing for thirty-five spots on the PGA Tour, what chance did one busted-handed kid have, no matter how many drugs he swallowed? He just hoped that when his son came back this time, he'd have grown a little more realistic.

Sam didn't hear from his son until more than a week later, when he phoned from a place called Gulf Shores, Alabama.

"What the hell you doin' in Alabama?"

"Getting ready to play the second tournament."

"You qualified in South Carolina?"

"Easily."

In truth he'd played 8 under par over four rounds, well down the leader board but good enough to advance, along with 22 other golfers, to the second stage. The traveling, or something he'd eaten the night before, had caused the uppers to wear off too soon the first day, and he'd been lucky to limp in with only one bogey over the last several holes, but he got the dosage straight the next day and played well over the next three rounds. It was a valuable lesson—from now on he'd always carry extra pills in his golf bag just in case he needed a quick fix to get him in.

"Congratulations," Sam said, striving for enthusiasm. He was glad he'd made it over the first hurdle, but he was still afraid he was riding for a fall.

Duff thanked him and asked him to tell Teddy he'd made it through the first round. Sam said he thought he'd left for Florida, but he'd call and see.

"I've got to go. I'll call you later, Dad," Duff ended

abruptly. Gena had loaned him her telephone credit card, but he didn't want to abuse the privilege.

When Duff phoned his father a week later, it was to tell him he was 9 under par after just three rounds and stood a good chance to be a medalist after the next day's final round.

"Just don't get too cocky," Sam warned.

"I've got the game, Dad."

"I always knew it, son."

This time it was Sam, feeling a sudden lump in his throat, who hung up quickly, even though Duff was in the mood to talk some more. He'd obviously taken too many of those red pills and he was blowing like a sou'easter. Just trim your sails son, Sam said silently to the dead phone.

It was the silence, that's what it was. That's what made the Q-School different from every other golf tournament in the world, Duff realized, as he hauled his clubs across the smooth lawn of the Grenelefe Golf & Tennis Resort in Haines City, Florida. There were scores of players chipping and putting on the practice green and hitting balls on the range, as well as officials and television people driving about on golf carts, and yet the place was as silent as the orange groves that surrounded the vast resort. Even at the Shinnecock Open the players had talked and joked before setting out to beat each other's brains out, but not here. These guys weren't playing to win a golf tournament, they were playing for their lives. They all knew that one bad shot over the next six days could mean the difference between the PGA Tour, where fame and fortune waited each week at the final hole; or the PGA Minitour, where most players were just hoping to make enough to get to the next tournament.

Duff dropped his bag in front of the scoreboard and

searched the score sheets for his name. When he found it, listed alphabetically on the top of the second sheet along with his hometown, he felt a sudden shock of relief. It hadn't been a dream, he had made it, he was one of the 168 finalists. No matter what happened, he was guaranteed at least a conditional Minitour card, and probably a fully exempt one. But if he could just finish in the top 35! When he'd signed up for Q-School he was just hoping to survive the first two cuts and earn an exempt Minitour card. Now, however, after finishing just three strokes behind the medalist at Gulf Shores, only a PGA card would do. In dreams begin bigger dreams.

Not that the Minitour wasn't a good one—the PGA Tour was rife with Minitour grads who had won a Tour event on their first year out—but it was still the minor leagues, something to be endured before going on to the majors. And I'm a major leaguer, Duff said to himself, as he scoured the board for a familiar name. He found more than a few, Tour players who had won big tournaments and millions of dollars but had to return to the Q-School because they'd slipped below the top 125 on the money list the previous year. Even though golf was more about losing than winning, being told you're no longer even good enough to compete with the winners was something else entirely. Near the end of the board he found a name with which he was very familiar, and at almost the same moment heard a familiar voice.

"Hi yah, Slingshot!"

"Forbes!"

"Yeah, it's me. Back at Q-School with the wretched and the damned," he said glumly. "All the same, congratulations to you. The hand must be okay . . ."

"You mean the flipper, don't you?"

"Listen, I'm sorry about that—I never even gave you a chance to explain. I looked for you after the tournament but you'd already left."

"When you play like I did you don't feel like staying around for the celebration."

"Yeah, after the morning round I thought for sure you'd be going to the Open."

"I decided to go fishing instead."

"I should've gone with you. I'll tell you, Slingshot, pro golf is a lot tougher than I thought it was gonna be. If you want some advice from a scarred old veteran, get out while you've got the chance."

"I'm here because I finally *got* the chance," he said, opening and closing the scarred hand. It felt good, he was anxious to get over to the range and hit some balls.

"You got a good physical therapist?"

"Even better . . ."

"Because I'm looking for one," Forbes said, stretching his back. "You still hitting it long?"

"And straight."

"You'll need it here. Believe me, these are the toughest one hundred and eight holes of golf you'll ever play in your life."

"I can't wait," Duff said.

"That's the spirit, Rookie."

Forbes wished him luck and walked over to the practice range where his caddie was waiting on the tee. Duff slung his bag over his shoulder, clubheads behind, the way the pros carried, and walked off in the direction of the caddie corral. Forbes Witherspoon was plainly not the same cocky guy he'd met at Southeastern, he realized. But what would I be like if I had to come back here after thinking I'd finally made it on the Tour? he wondered, as he planted his bag in front of the small group of hopeful caddies milling around behind the food concession.

There were several young white kids in the group, high school golfers who intended to be playing here themselves one day, and an older black man who had the look of a professional caddie. The youngsters were eager as puppies in a pet store when Duff questioned them, while the older man didn't seem that interested in the job. The white kids claimed to be familiar with both the South and West courses over which the tournament was to be played, while the older man admitted he'd never been here before.

"I was s'posed to be carryin' in the JC Penney at Innisbrook, but my bag pulled out so I come down here. Here, there—don't make no difference. I can size a golf course up in a practice round, do it all the time on the Big Tour," the old caddie assured him.

"How long you been caddying on the Tour?" Duff asked.

"More'n twenty years."

"You got the job," Duff said, setting off a groan from the white kids.

"Maybe I do and maybe I don't," the caddie said. "First I wanna know where you been playin'?"

The audacity! "I played the Minitour a couple of years ago. . . ."

"Couple a years ago? What about lately?"

"I had to sit out last year because of an injury."

"You win on the Minitour?"

"I had a couple of high finishes."

"High finishes on the Minitour . . . First time at the Q-School?"

"Yeah."

He removed his baseball cap and shook his head sadly. "How much you fixin' to pay?"

"A hundred dollars a day?"

He made a dismissive hissing sound and slapped his cap back on his head. "I'll carry for you for two hundred a day," he said, causing the puppies to yap competitively. They would work for 50, yet Duff chose to stay with the experienced man for two hundred. "Plus twenty percent of the purse," he added, setting off a howl from the white boys.

"You don't get that much on the Tour," Duff complained.

"On the Tour we don't even bother teein' it up for no fifty thousand dollars," the professional caddie informed him. "And you bein' retired for the last coupla years, you ain't exactly the favorite, if you don't mind my sayin'.

'Sides, you make it to the Big Tour, you ain't gonna feel
too bad about payin' me twenty percent."

He had a point, Duff knew. For this tournament wasn't
about money, it was about the chance to make money.
Hell, if he made the Tour, the caddie could have it all.

"Cash okay?" Duff asked.

"You been readin' my mind."

The old caddie figured he'd made twelve hundred dollars tax free and 20 percent of nothing, unless the kid
lucked out and earned one of the four-thousand-dollar
prizes for making the Minitour exemption—not a lot but
enough to get him to California in January for the start
of the PGA Tour. He hadn't so much as seen his player
hit a shot, but it was unlikely that a green kid without his
own personal caddie stood much chance against a bunch
of seasoned pros, many whom he knew from the Tour.

"Name's Sidney Tate," he said, extending his hand.

"Duff—Duff Colhane," he said, seeing for the first time
that the man had a gnarled hand. It felt like a dried root.

"Mashed it in a thrasher," Sidney said, a tiresome for-
mality. When Duff showed him his own scars, the old
man shook his head sadly. "I shouldda asked for three
hundred a day."

After a couple of practice rounds, Sidney not only knew
the fairway bounces and roll of the greens on each course,
he also knew the strengths and weaknesses of his player.
The kid was very long but he knew when to play conservatively, which was unusual in a young player with his
strength. Yet he seemed to have a strange way of sometimes letting his mood rather than strategy dictate the shot.
He'd play several holes slowly and cautiously, almost like
he was still asleep, then suddenly start swinging for the
fences, even though it was obviously the wrong shot in
that situation. Sidney had the feeling that sometimes his
brain clicked off for a while and his emotions took over,
or his muscles or something. . . . He didn't know, he'd

never seen anything quite like it. It must have something to do with the way he practices—everybody has their little superstitions and things—because nobody in his right mind is going to play that way in a tournament, Sidney knew.

"There's something I'd like to ask you," Sidney said, after they'd played two practice rounds together. They were seated at a table in a Shoney's outside Haines City, scorecards and yardage books sharing the table with chicken and pork chops. "But if it's somethin' you don't wanna talk about, you just tell me." Some players didn't want you in their head, some welcomed it. He wasn't yet sure about this kid, who sometimes listened but didn't seem to be hearing, and other times seemed to know what he was going to say before he'd even said anything.

"Yeah, ask me anything," Duff replied.

Until now he'd worked with pickup caddies whose only job was to carry the bag and keep up. But Sidney had been to the Big Show, he knew some secrets which he might divulge at any time, so attention had to be paid.

"During them practice rounds, when you be attackin' the hole one day, then layin' up the next . . . ? I mean that was just practicin', right? I mean when we go out there tomorrow, you got your mind made up on how you gonna play the hole, right?" Duff had the feeling that the usually reticent caddie was perhaps finally ready to divulge something important. He was obviously looking for something more than a simple answer to an obvious question about course management. The question was the caddie's way of opening a Socratic dialogue—obviously something more than a yes or no was required.

"Sometimes I have a plan," Duff began carefully. "Sometimes I think about every shot I'm going to hit the night before. But then when I get out on the course and one of the shots doesn't come off as I planned, I forget about the plan and start playing by feel. Is that what you mean?"

"Yeah, sort of. But what about right now—you got a plan right now?"

"Not a firm one."

"Not a firm one. . . ."

"You think I should?"

"That all depends . . ." the caddie replied. It was like psychology—you didn't want to tell the patient what to do, you just wanted to help him make up his own mind. That way if it didn't work, your ass was covered. "Some pros make a plan and stick to it, some play by feel," he went on carefully. "So I'd say you're right down the middle."

"Right down the middle . . ." he said, rolling the words around in his head, sorting through them for the full meaning.

"Yeah."

He stared silently into space for a long time before finally replying, "And that's where I want to be."

"Yeah. That's where you wanna be."

Duff nodded and smiled, picked up his fork and went back to his dinner. A professional caddie made all the difference in the world.

Although he had drawn a late tee time, Duff arrived at the West Course soon after sunrise the next morning, only to find the practice tee already crowded with players methodically and wordlessly lofting and drilling little white balls through the early morning mist. The nearby practice green too was packed with players, silently chipping and putting, their only sound the roiling of their bowels. Many of them hadn't been able to eat any breakfast while others had deliberately skipped it, afraid it might come up on them at the first tee, an embarrassing and not unusual occurrence at the Q-School. Duff's partner during a practice round, who was back for the eighth time, made nine on the opening hole one year, but got a reprieve when the round was washed out, only to come back the next day and make an eight.

"It's that kind of progress that keeps me coming back," he told Duff.

They would play 108 holes over the next six days, knowing that just one bad one would probably take them out of it. If they were to be among the low 35 to earn their Tour card (the consensus was that any score higher than 6 under par stood no chance) they would have to shoot birdies and pars and hardly a bogey. With 168 players in the field there were bound to be 35 hot hands out there, and Duff could only hope to be one of those lucky enough to find himself in the zone.

He found an open spot on the practice range and began slowly with the wedge, working his way back, thinking only of tempo. This wasn't the time to be thinking about the elements of the swing. It was exam time, too late to cram, you either knew it or you didn't. He swung with a clear head, letting his muscles do the thinking, listening to what they had to say. Whoosh. Whoosh. We're working smoothly, it's going to be a good day, his muscles told him. And he hadn't even taken his medicine yet.

Sidney showed up halfway through the drill and stood silently appraising his investment. He was beginning to think that his 20 percent arrangement, which he'd earlier thought meaningless, might even amount to something after all. This boy had the physical gifts, no doubt about it. But those goofy mood swings could be a problem. It was like caddying for Jekyl and Hyde, and even after their little talk last night, Sidney still didn't know quite how to handle the kid—or if he should even try. When he was charging he wouldn't listen, when he was floating he didn't hear. At times he wanted to grab him and haul him down to the ground, while at other times he wanted to light a fire under him, but he didn't dare try anything lest he blow the boy sky high. If he didn't know better he'd say the kid was doing coke or something, but that was just plain impossible. He knew of a few drinkers on the

Tour who managed somehow to keep it together, but there was just no way a cokehead could play this game. Sidney prided himself on being more than a bagger. He was a manager and a psychologist, but so far he hadn't been able to figure out what made this kid tick, and it frustrated him. His player wasn't getting full value. But if I ever do figure him out I might just have me a meal ticket, he thought, as he watched the kid lash a drive down to the farthest corner of the range. At this rate he was going to tire himself out before he even got to the first tee.

"How about we go hit some putts?" Sidney suggested.

Sidney was surprised when his player immediately handed over the driver. Now why can't he be that way on the course? he asked himself, as he followed him to the practice green.

From the first tee an official announced the first player in the tenth group of the day. There was no applause, no gallery, just a name hanging alone in the air for a fraction of a second. Some of the players on the practice green stopped putting long enough to watch the threesome hit off, like condemned men watching the execution of their comrades, then went back to their practice as players and caddies started down the fairway, accompanied by the martial cadence of clanking irons. Two of the players peeled off left and right into the moss-draped live oaks oozing through the dew-gray air, thinking perhaps that they were already finished. The first drive was the most important shot of the tournament: miss the fairway, catch the bus.

Now three new players, cigarettes dangling from their lips, stepped up onto the tee and waited nervously under a cloud of smoke while the two errant players ahead of them chipped back out onto the fairway. Knowing it wouldn't be allowed on the Pro Tour, many of the Q-School players smoked with a vengeance, flouted facial hair, sported wrinkled pants and golf shirts that bore no corporate logo, and cussed like caddies. But should they be among the chosen 35 come Monday, they would will-

ingly submit to the PGA charm school and emerge
scrubbed, shaved, coifed, smokeless and well-spoken as
all the other gentlemen of the Tour.

Meanwhile three more players and their caddies, also
smokers, crossed wordlessly in front of Duff on their way
to the first tee, like infantry to the front, a never-ending
supply of valiant but expendable warriors. Even now,
across the United States and abroad, fresh young recruits
were training to take their place at the front next year,
and the year after that and the year after that. Why? Didn't
they know the odds? The game was a flame to moths, but
Duff was fireproof.

He stood at the edge of the green, lagging very long
putts to Sidney who gathered them up and rolled them
back. First the long ones, then the short ones, Teddy had
taught him. Start out missing a five-footer and the nerves
are shattered for the rest of the day. He looked at his
watch—a little over an hour until tee time—then patted
his pants pocket reassuringly. But felt nothing! He had
left his pillbox at the motel. Then after a panicked moment, he remembered the reserve stash in his golf bag and
plunged in. He pulled out the glass vial and took stock of
the red and blue pills. There were, thank God, more than
enough to get him through the round.

"What you got there, Slingshot, some kind of voodoo
charm?" Forbes Witherspoon called out, as he and his
caddie approached.

"Hogan's ashes," Duff replied, sticking the vial in his
pocket.

"You'll need it," he said, continuing on to the driving
range.

You have no idea, Duff thought. He patted his pocket
reassuringly, then stroked another ball at the hole, jerking
it badly.

"You're jabbin', not strokin'," Sidney instructed.

"It's nothing to worry about," Duff assured him. "I'm
going to the clubhouse, I'll be back in twenty minutes."

Nothing to worry about? Sidney questioned, as he

watched his player walk off. If you're jerking the ball on the practice green, what do you think's gonna happen when you get out on the course?

However when Duff returned in 20 minutes, replaced the vial in his bag and began stroking short putts, Sidney saw that he was right, the hitch had disappeared. One after another the six-footers banged the back of the hole squarely and dropped. Gonna have to get me some of them Hogan's ashes myself, Sidney decided.

There was a small crowd gathered near the giant score-board when Duff and his two playing companions walked off the 18th green more than four hours later. Forbes Witherspoon was being interviewed by a stocky television announcer, Duff saw, as he walked past them on the way to the scorer's tent. Forbes had shot 69, the lowest score so far, he learned from the scorer.

"Unless you did better," she said, reaching across the table for his card.

"I did for a while," Duff grumbled.

She looked at his card, saw the double-bogey and shook her head sadly. "That's all it takes, just one bad hole . . ."

"I certainly hope not," he replied icily.

He had made the turn at even par (lipping out three birdie putts) and had felt he was on the way to a strong back nine—until he knocked his drive out of bounds on the par-5. He'd been forced to take an extra red pill on the back, as play had been slow and he'd felt the blue slowing him down, and that's what caused the rush that caused him to yank his drive and lose his temper.

Sidney had tried to calm him down but he'd lost his tempo and couldn't get it back until the bubbling in his blood slowed down, and by that time he'd made a bogey and he knew he was gone.

"We just need us a few birdies and we'll be right back in it," Sidney said after the bogey.

Yeah, right—I got a monster par-4 coming up, a six-hundred-yard par-5—out of bounds, a lake! So much for a professional caddie. He'd missed the Tour cut, all he could hope to do now was score well enough to get a fully exempt rather than a conditional Minitour card, and not even that excited him anymore. He had awakened this morning confident that he was the best player in the field, certain that he would be among the low 35 come Monday, and now he was no longer even sure he'd finish in the top 100. And if he didn't, if he finished among the conditional players who could only play a Minitour event when an exempt player was unable, then what business did he have even being here in the first place?

He didn't want to think about it. All he wanted to do now was get the hell off the golf course without seeing anybody, least of all Forbes Witherspoon.

"Hey, Slingshot!" Forbes called, as Duff emerged from the scorer's tent. "How'd you do?"

"Not as well as you. Congratulations."

"Sixty-nine, how about that!"

"Great score. I gotta go."

"What'd you shoot?" Forbes called after him.

"Seventy-six."

"Seventy-six!"

"Yeah, seventy-six," he said, continuing to walk.

He picked up a ham-and-cheese sandwich and a six-pack of Jax beer at the gas station minimart on the way back to the motel. There were several other players staying there, guys who couldn't afford to stay at the resort, but none of their cars were yet in their places. They had probably all played better than he and stayed on to practice for tomorrow, still hoping to go to the Big Show next year. He didn't need to practice his swing, he needed to practice taking his pills.

He went inside, closed the door and the curtains, plopped down on the bed and reached for the television remote. Television was the one luxury required by any golfer who had chosen this monkish profession. No, not a luxury, a necessity, providing no less solace and spiritual comfort to an errant golfer than a prayer book to a sinful monk. The purpose of the glowing image and inane chatter was distraction, not entertainment—which ascetics were not allowed anyway—and if it kept just one player from suicide it was worth it. Too, a player could watch CNN and call it education.

That was another thing about the golfer's life that annoyed Duff at this moment—he was surrounded by ignorance. Nobody could talk about anything but golf. He knew he was no intellectual (which was another thing that annoyed him—if not for golf he'd have gone to college and might well be an intellectual) but at least he read things besides golf magazines. In fact right now in the bottom of his duffel bag were several Penguin Classics he intended to start reading just as soon as he was able to clear his mind of golf.

He popped a can of Jax and took a long draft, then tore the cellophane from his sandwich and spread it out on the nightstand. He had a lot of other gripes about his chosen career, but he wouldn't list any more of them now. He wouldn't because he knew that had he shot 69 today instead of 76, he wouldn't be sitting here drinking cheap beer and watching Oprah while thinking about how unhappy he was with his life. He'd be on the range preparing for tomorrow, joking with his pals, maybe having a beer with them in the pizza bar afterward. . . . He took a bite of his sandwich and placed it on the night stand. That was another thing, the lousy food.

He was awakened later that night by a phone call.

"I hope I'm not calling too late," Gena said.

"No—it's okay," he mumbled, feeling for the light switch. It was 12:15.

She knew how much he needed his sleep and she would have called earlier but she'd misplaced his number and had to phone his father, and she just had to know how he did on his first day, she went on rapidly, apparently fueled by coke. "And I thought you were going to phone me and tell me how you did," she added.

"I'm sorry. I would have but it wasn't anything to phone home about."

"What did you shoot?"

"Seventy-six."

"What was the lowest?"

"Sixty-nine."

"So—you're only seven strokes behind."

"That's right." Her math was good, even stoned.

"You can still beat him!" she cheered.

"I don't have to beat the first man, just the thirty-fifth," he explained.

"What did he shoot, the thirty-fifth man?"

"I don't know. It doesn't matter, there are five more rounds. If I can shoot two under every day I've got a chance." Several hours ago he thought he was finished with professional golf, while now, laying it on for his sponsor, he was beginning to convince himself he had a chance. Must be something in that Jax beer.

"Can you do that?"

"I hope so."

"You hope so?" she questioned, faintly disapproving.

"I think so." If she wanted her money back, why didn't she just say so?

"I know you can," she said brightly. "Even the best horses can stumble coming out of the gate, but they can still win."

"Right," he said, feeling like Monte's jockey. "Thanks for the pep talk. I'll call you tomorrow and let you know how I did."

"Good luck!" she called, as he said good night and replaced the receiver.

He turned off the light, pounded the pillow and lay back down. Don't I have enough pressure already without having to cope with a disgruntled sponsor? he asked himself. That's just the way it was with Jack Stricker—he was only in it for the sport, the money meant nothing. They say they're only in it for the sport, but sooner or later they have to remind you that it's a professional not an amateur sport. That's another thing that annoys me— having to take money from a drug dealer.

Now his mind was racing; he'd never get back to sleep. Why had he told her he could do it? These were two of the toughest courses he'd ever played and the best players he'd ever faced. Worst of all, the pills weren't working like they should. He debated calling Frank Promer but decided it would do no good. The physician had come up with the prescription, it was up to the patient to administer it. Instead he took a blue pill and washed it down with a can of Jax.

Still he couldn't sleep. He lay in the dark thinking of the next round that would begin in just several hours. It was going to be a hard day and each one after that would be even harder. To last, a player had to shoot low in the early rounds, get the wind behind and then just sail in. He had missed that chance and was in danger of pressing and blowing it entirely.

Yet it wouldn't be impossible to shoot 2 under every day. Or even 3 or 4 under one day. Forbes did it, why couldn't he?

He knew why. Forbes was patient, he just let it happen. And lucky. Nobody shoots a great round without a lot of luck. But I can't afford to be patient or trust to luck. I'm too far back, I've got to make it happen. I have to attack the course, overpower it—go for the par-5s, grip it and rip it and go look for it. Shoot 66 or 86! That's my game plan. It's the PGA Tour or nothing!

When his player shot 2-under on the par-71 South Course the next day, Sidney was disappointed. It was a good score but it could've been even better if he'd listened to him, laid up when he told him to, gone for the middle of

the green instead of attacking every pin. Fortunately his
wild gambles paid off more often than not this time, but
there was little chance he'd be that lucky again. If only
the kid could be a little patient. He was just 2 over, if he
could stay there he'd probably make four thousand dollars
and be assured an exempt Mini card. But if he continued
to play like a gorilla on speed, trying to cut the corners
and hit it over the water, aiming for the sucker pins, going
for eagles but getting double bogeys—then he'd end up
with a conditional card and Sidney would end up with
chump change.

"Patience," the caddie had cautioned when Duff made
a stupid double-bogey after hitting his drive onto the
wrong golf course. They were then facing a delicate dogleg left that called for no more than a 2-iron off the tee,
and his player was still hyperventilating after that double-
bogey.

"Patience doesn't get eagles," Duff had replied, pulling
the driver from his bag.

He exploded a drive over the corner that took more than
a hundred yards off the hole—if it cleared the trees. His
fellow players were sure he hadn't made it—and his des-
peration was beginning to unnerve them—but when they
rounded the dogleg and saw his ball on the green, they
were incredulous. And when he made the putt for eagle-
2, Sidney held his tongue—until the next bogey.

That was the way it went for the next three rounds. All
Duff did was grip it and hit it, and all Sidney did was go
look for it—which wasn't always easy. Some drives settled beautifully more than 300 yards down the fairway,
while others ricochetted among the trees like pool balls
in the dark. And when he did find his ball, he was all but
certain to try and thread it through the trees and curve it
up onto the green somehow, rather than chip it safely out
onto the fairway, maybe still make par. Miraculously,
some of these shots came off, but many were disastrous.
He was an exciting player to watch—even his fellow

competitors became amazed spectators—but to a caddie on commission it was nerve-racking.

"If they was just countin' birdies and eagles, my man would've had this thing won already," Sidney complained to some of his fellow caddies on the eve of the last round.

"Yeah and if they was a prize for doubles and triples he'd get that too," Reefer Roy said.

They were seated at what had become the caddies' table in the pizza bar, waiting for a sport to buy them a round. Some of the players who'd shot themselves out of it and were resigned to a conditional card were shooting pool and getting drunk, but the losers weren't going to spring for a drink. Forbes bought the last round, and might've bought another if some girl hadn't come and gotten him and taken him into the dining room. Reefer Roy and Sidney were close, being two of the few black caddies on the PGA Tour. Reefer carried for Forbes Witherspoon, who was 12 under and leading the field by two strokes and likely to win the tournament tomorrow. This put Reefer in a good mood, as there was more than a thousand dollars in the caddies' pool, of which Reefer stood to make 70 percent. Sidney's bag on the other hand, whose scores had gone up and down like a ball on the cart path, was 2 over and would be lucky just to get his full Mini card.

"It's them fuckin' Hogan's ashes," Sidney grumbled, twisting his empty beer bottle.

"Hogan's ashes?" Reefer asked.

"Some pills he always be takin'. One minute he be playin' like a fuckin' turtle, then the next he be like a jackrabbit."

"Drugs?"

"Medicine. He got a fucked up hand like me."

"Hah! That white boy got a fucked up hand like you and playin' golf like that, that must be some fuckin' medicine," Reefer said.

"If he just throw that shit away he could be leadin' this fuckin' tournament and I could make me some money tomorrow."

"Coulda woulda shoulda didn't," another caddie put in. "Who's buyin'?"

"He could still make the cut. It ain't impossible," Sidney said.

"Yeah if he shoot fifty-nine," Reefer said.

"It's been done."

"Not at Grenelefe."

"Hey, Reef, you're gonna win seven hundred dollars tomorrow, why don't you buy us a round?" the thirsty caddie suggested.

"Ain't won it yet," Reefer said.

"Sid says his man's gonna make the cut, let him buy," another looper proposed.

"Ain't done it yet," Sidney said.

It occurred to Duff that he'd been expecting too much of his caddie. When he'd first grasped Sidney's withered hand he perhaps sensed a kindred spirit, a man who understood both the golf swing and their shared affliction. But of course no one but himself could know anything about his damaged nerves. His aggressive and reckless play had so far been less than successful—he had virtually no chance to make the low 35 tomorrow—but would he have made it if he'd played cautiously? Or was that just the excuse he'd need to come back next year? And if he failed again, what would his excuse be then? How many years before he came to know the real reason he failed?— that he just wasn't good enough.

He was sitting by himself in the corner of the resort dining room, listlessly eating his dinner while trying to decide if it was his strategy that had failed him or his confidence. He had played as well as his twitchy nerves would allow, and it just wasn't good enough. If he couldn't even place in the top 35 at Q-School, what chance did he have of ever winning on the PGA Tour? Probably none, he realized. Then did he want to be a

Minitour player for the rest of his career? No, never, he said to himself.

Still, a single attempt was hardly a fair chance. . . .

His self-examination was interrupted by the entrance of the attractive young woman he'd seen earlier around the clubhouse, apparently casing the players. When Forbes stepped in behind her and took her arm, Duff saw that she had settled on the leader of the pack. Forbes gave a benedictional wave to the crowd as they followed the maitre d' to their table. Duff nodded as they passed by, she in a little black cocktail dress that nicely set off her curved, tanned limbs, trailing a scent that left him lonely. That was another thing about the Tour. . . . He realized he was staring and looked away, affecting an interest in his cold pasta. He was, he realized when he looked up a minute later, just about the only one in the room not watching the couple. And why shouldn't they? Forbes was the tournament leader and a Tour veteran and he was having dinner with the best-looking woman in the house. There wasn't a golfer in the room who didn't want to be in Forbes Witherspoon's place.

Forbes had been in contention a few times during his several years on Tour but had always collapsed on the fourth and final day. It was to be expected at first—too much pressure too soon, not enough experience, something a good player would soon get over. But if he didn't, there would come the day when the young man with a lot of promise became just another choker. He would never hear the charge directly—it was tantamount to a slap across the face—but one morning he would arrive at a tournament to find it written across the foreheads of his competitors, and know that the promising first-class player had been suddenly reassigned to third class. It had happened to Forbes last year when he'd failed to earn enough to keep his card, but he was determined to get back out there and prove they'd been wrong about him. All he had to do was hang on for two more days, win the Q-School championship and reemerge a first-class player.

But it was so damned hard. In most sports the tension vanished after the first moments of play, but with golfers the pressure grew as the game progressed, until the final putt on the fourth day when a healthy athlete might feel as if he were experiencing a heart attack. And after the fourth day of Q-School, a player still had two more days of it! Although Forbes hadn't yet won the tournament, he had finished two strokes ahead of the pack after four days, and this was enough to convince him that he'd finally shaken the monkey from his back.

However, after an only-mediocre fifth round, Forbes felt the familiar specter of self-doubt lurking in the trees. He had played too safely, steering the ball, hanging desperately on the club a split second too long. But it wouldn't happen again. Tomorrow he would play as he had over the first four days—swing as loosely and freely as the teenage prodigy he once was. He had gotten this far by playing aggressively—he was certain to make the cut—he would go back on the attack, play for birdies and eagles!

When he bogeyed the first two holes the next day, his caddie cautioned him to take it down a key.

"I've lost two strokes to the field, how the fuck can I take it down?" he complained to Reefer.

Chastised, Reefer clammed up, which didn't help the situation. When Forbes was playing well, his caddie tended to chatter like an infielder, buoying his player with positive thoughts; but when he played badly, Reefer grew silent. Nor did his new girlfriend's occasional absence from his small gallery do anything to restore his confidence. He'd taken it as a good omen when she'd picked him out of the crowd, confirmation that he was a winner. They'd had a great night together and now she was drifting off. He didn't mind at first when she would wander across the fairway to find out how another player was doing and then report back to him, but after still another bogey it didn't help to be told that somebody else was making birdies. And when she told him that Duff Colhane was 3 under after nine holes, he was forced to remind her that he was trying to concentrate on his own game, not somebody else's. After that she disappeared more often.

Forbes didn't need his girlfriend to tell him that Duff was playing well. After he'd eagled the 10th and birdied the 11th, word flashed round the course like lightning that an unknown first timer was threatening the course record. The television announcers in the tower and out on the course, former players themselves who had seen a lot of flashes in the pan over the years, knew that a green kid who'd gone off with the dew sweepers at 2 over par was far more likely to collapse on the closing holes than make a serious run at the course record. But it gave them something to fill the airtime while the leaders were only on their early holes.

There was nothing in Duff Colhane's bio to account for his play today—no big amateur victories, no college association. . . .

"He's playing out of a muni for gosh sake!" the announcer gasped.

But when it was noted that he'd finished just three strokes behind the leader at Gulf Shores and had shot a couple of very low rounds here to offset the disastrous ones, the announcers quickly began to weave a dramatic tapestry from these few threads.

"He's obviously a volatile player, but he can go low," the anchor announced.

"Yes, but he'd have to shoot what—sixty-four to make the low thirty-five?"

"At least."

"And the storm's starting to blow . . ."

Later, when they were off camera, the anchor said, "God knows, the way Witherspoon's choking we need something to happen."

"Better find something else, because no rookie's going

to shoot sixty-four on this course," the veteran announcer
advised.

It was like pitching a no-hitter: you tried not to think
about it. But when Duff learned from the PGA official
who'd begun following him that he needed just two more
birdies to break the course record, it was hard to think
about anything else. A 9-under-par 63 would put him at
7 under for the tournament and virtually assure him his
PGA Tour card.

Or would it? What if the guys behind him were also
shooting lights out? What if the cut was moving down to
8 or 9 under? Then in that case he had no choice, he had
to play for eagles and birdies. But if the leaders were
faltering, if 6 under, or even 5 under would make it, then
all he had to do was par in. The math was driving him
crazy, he couldn't be sure of the simplest addition and
subtraction, and the extra pill he'd taken was only making
it worse. He had to compartmentalize, decide what he had
to do and then think about nothing but the shot. The trouble was, he had no way of knowing what the leaders were
doing now, let alone what they would finally do. Not only
were all the leaders playing far behind him, half of them
were playing on another course. Why couldn't golf be like
tennis!

"Just take it one shot at a time," his professional caddie
advised. His player was pacing about the tee box like a
caged leopard while waiting for the fairway to clear.

"Great—thank you, Sidney." This professional caddie
bullshit was greatly overrated. "I don't want to know
about *my* game, I want to know about their game," he
said, pointing back in the direction from which they'd
come.

"Can't do nothin' 'bout them," Sidney said. The boy
was getting that crazy look in his eye. "Jes stay cool,
baby."

Duff glanced helplessly at the large gallery that had

lately joined him. If they had somehow learned what he was doing, why didn't they know what anybody else was doing? It was then that he saw Forbes's girlfriend standing at the edge of the tee. When their eyes met, she smiled.

"How's Forbes doing?" he asked.

The smile gave way to a hopeless frown. "I think he's three over."

"And the guys he's playing with?"

"They're doin' much better."

"Damn."

"We can hit now," Sidney said.

Duff stepped up to his bag, where Sidney's hand rested suggestively on the 1-iron. Duff shook his head, like a no-hit pitcher shaking off the curve sign. He was going for the fast ball, blow it right by.

He knew the split second the driver struck the ball that it was perfect.

"We got all that one," Sidney said. It was just the club he would have recommended had his player asked.

The girl waited until Duff charged down the fairway after his ball, then started back to Forbes on the front nine. It wasn't unreasonable for a player to be charged up when he was going for a course record, she supposed. But that boy was positively in danger of OD'ing on testosterone. It was too bad she hadn't noticed him earlier. That underbite was kind of sexy.

When Duff walked up onto the tee and saw the crowd surrounding the 18th green 561 yards away, he was both amazed and unnerved by the unusual sight. Until today he had seen no more than a few hundred spectators spread out over two golf courses, but now there were hundreds of people focused on everything he did. He felt like an actor who'd been pushed out onto the stage in a strange play, and the audience was waiting, but he had no idea what he was to say or do. When Sidney came forward— the only actor on the stage who recognized his problem—

Duff placed a steadying hand on his shoulder. Then, as
suddenly as it had come, he felt the fear flow from his
body, replaced by a warm and comforting fire in the belly.
There was nothing strange or frightening about it after
all—this was the part he was born to play.

"Smooth swing," Sidney said, as he handed Duff his
driver.

They both knew he needed a birdie. That would get
him to 8 under, 6 under for the tournament, right on the
bubble. After that he'd just have to wait and see what the
others did. It was time for his big scene; he knew his lines.

He stood behind the ball and sighted down the cork-
screw fairway, a slight dogleg right followed by a turn to
the left, diabolically shaped by Trent Jones so as to require three shots to the green . . . unless he could hit a
power fade over the right corner, get it out far enough to
take the second dogleg out and go for the green in two.
It would require a drive of more than 300 yards followed
by a second shot of more than 250 yards, both of them
pure and perfect. Under ordinary circumstances it was an
insane play, but these weren't ordinary circumstances. He
had a lock on his full Minitour card even if he made
double-bogey, while a birdie might get him his PGA card,
but an eagle definitely would. To fade the ball, open the
club and take a normal swing, the great Nicklaus advised.
But Duff was a feel player, he had to open his stance,
hang onto the handle and slide the clubface across the
ball. It wasn't a shot he was comfortable with—he'd
much rather draw the ball—but it was the only shot for
this time and this place.

He looked up a split second after impact, perhaps a split
second too soon, and saw the ball fading over the right
corner. The gallery · applauded his might, but the hitter
knew he'd taken too much off the ball, that it probably
hadn't cleared the trees. He looked anxiously at Sidney
who was craning to see around the trees, but the caddie
could only shrug.

Duff stood poised like a runner at the starting line until

the last player hit, then raced forward, leaving the others far behind. When he rounded the corner and saw his ball resting on the edge of the tree line, scarcely an inch from the deep rough, he was filled with relief—followed by a familiar, sudden exhaustion. He hadn't counted on the effect of so much excitement, he should have taken still another red pill, he realized. Too late, suck it up, just one more shot.

He pulled his 3-wood from the bag, went through his preswing routine, then set up and swung almost as hard as he could at the ball. It went off low, then started rising and banking to the left. It landed short of the green, took two long bounces, then got down and ran through the opening onto the front of the green. The crowd at both ends of the fairway roared as the ball raced to the hole, on and on, stopping finally near the back of the green.

"Two putts for birdie!" Sidney exclaimed.

"One for eagle," Duff corrected, taking his putter from Sidney.

"Let's have us a look," the caddie grunted, as he hoisted the bag on his shoulder and followed his player down the fairway. "And jes stay cool." Please God, keep him cool.

The applause began well before he reached the green. Duff knew because he could see their hands moving, but he could hear nothing. He felt as if he were under water, unable to move his limbs freely, and he was running out of oxygen. What the hell was happening to him? This was unlike any drug effect he'd ever had. Then he remembered his doctor's words: It sounds to me like you can't take the pressure. Bullshit! I never choke! he told himself. I never choke!

When he stepped onto the green, he burst suddenly through the surface and the crowd noise became a roar and his limbs were suddenly free. It was as if he'd briefly blacked out, his body moving awkwardly on its own, disconnected from his brain. But now the two were back together and he was striding gracefully and surely across the green. He doffed his cap and tried to smile politely,

but it came out a Novocaine grin. He was still not totally
in control of his nerves, but it was all right, he'd get
through it. He was no choker. The applause continued
until he'd marked his ball and flipped it to his caddie to
be cleaned, just like the Tour players. He looked up at the
tower and saw the announcers talking animatedly and realized it was him they were talking about, that he was
being filmed for all the world to see, and his smile became
even goofier. He seemed to have lost control of the muscles in his face and his skin felt as if he were being
pricked by a million needles.

When it came his turn to putt, he chided himself to
settle down and just take care of the business that remained. Just make this putt for eagle—thirty feet straight
uphill for a 9-under-par 63—and I'm a Tour player! I've
got that putt, he told himself as he took a position over
the ball. But his muscles wouldn't receive the message.

He looked up as the putt was rolling up the hill to the
hole, then watched as it rolled past, propelled by the an-
guished groan of the gallery to a spot ten feet away. The
sensation of needle pricks changed to something like
snapping rubber bands and he saw that the fingers of his
right hand were twitching uncontrollably. Okay, easy putt
downhill, just get it started on line, he told himself, as he
stood shaking the twitch from his hand.

When the twitching stopped, just as inexplicably as it
had begun, he struck the putt. And watched as it rolled
another ten feet past the hole. Then he putted twice more
for a bogey-6. He was 4 under for the tournament. He
stood no chance.

Duff sat alone at the pizza bar, drinking beer while trying
not to think of what could have been. When the bartender
asked if he'd played in the tournament, Duff told him he
hadn't. Some time later however, after he'd drunk a few
beers, several wet, drunken fans burst noisily through the
door and his identity was revealed.

"Hey, the guy who four-putted!" the first fan pointed.

"Man that was sad," a second supplied.

They were all sorry he'd blown the tournament on the last green, and to prove it they offered him a chance to explain how he'd 4-putted from 30 feet.

"I don't know how it happened," Duff said, sliding off the barstool. "Excuse me."

"Wait!" the big one who'd fingered him ordered, blocking his escape. "I know why you missed that putt. Jimmy here does it all the time—especially when he's my partner."

"Fuck you," Jimmy said.

"You know what your problem is?"

"I don't have a problem," Duff said. When he tried to move, he found himself penned in by his fans.

"I'll tell you what your problem is."

"I don't want to hear it. Now would you please step aside?"

"Hey, we're just tryin' to help."

"If you don't mind, I've already got a teacher. But even if I didn't, I wouldn't look for advice from an amateur I'd just met in a saloon."

"I'd rather be an amateur than a fuckin' choker," the fan said, clutching his thick neck.

Duff saw an opening, but the big man stopped him with a stiff-arm to the chest that knocked him against the bar. He bounced back with a cocked fist, catching the pusher cleanly on the jaw. The large man fell heavily to the floor, and a second later his friends were all over his assailant, raining wild punches from all directions—until the bartender came around the bar and finally managed to put a stop to the mayhem. He pushed the golf fans away and turned to Duff.

"You okay?"

"Yeah," Duff said, wiping his bloody mouth. A few punches had found their mark.

"Then get out," the bartender ordered.

"Me? He started it!"

"You hit him first," the bartender charged, setting off a chorus of affirmation from his assailants.

"After he pushed me!"

"Makes no difference, you're eighty-sixed," the barman pointed. Duff started to protest, then thought better of it. He lurched painfully down the hallway, across the lobby and out the front door, where he was again slammed in the face, this time by a strong, wet wind. The sky had gone from gray to purple, splattering large raindrops on his bruised face, and the palm trees were shaking noisily in the wind. He looked at his watch, realized the leaders were still out there, and ran for the scoreboard.

"Where the hell you . . . ?" Sidney began, then stopped when he saw his bloodied face. "What the fuck happen?"

"Nothing," Duff replied, scanning the board for numbers. He saw his name with a 66 beside it, 4 under par for the tournament. There was no score beside Forbes's name. "What's happening here?"

"So far the cut's six under!"

"Not good enough."

"But they ain't all in yet!"

Duff was a bit drunk and still reeling from the punches he'd taken, but he knew his chances weren't good. Still, he thought, gazing up at the thrashing trees, this was a good 1- or 2-stroke wind.

Several minutes later, when the scorekeeper posted three more scores from the South Course, the cut had dropped to 5 under and Duff at last dared to hope. There were still six more players, including Forbes, out on the more difficult West Course. And the rain was coming down harder.

When the second to last group appeared on the 18th fairway, the umbrellas moved from the scoreboard to the green. Duff watched as all three players made par and the cut remained at 5 under. Meanwhile Forbes and his two playing partners, hitting against a stiff wind, were approximately 150 yards off the wet green. When all three of them hit serviceable but not spectacular shots, it ap-

peared they would all make par, although for the moment
no one knew how they stood to there. Then Duff saw
Forbes's girlfriend making her way up to the green under
a red umbrella and he called to her.

"How's he doing?"

"He's six over," she replied mordantly. "What happened to your face?"

"Cut it shaving. What about the other two?" Even if
Forbes 2-putted for par, he'd still finish at 6 under for the
tournament, not enough to lower the bar for Duff.

She didn't know. She was too concerned with Forbes's
dismal performance to monitor anyone else's. So Duff
waited in silent ignorance while all three players putted
to within a couple of feet.

"Damned double-bogey," the girl muttered, after Forbes
tapped in.

"Double?" Duff exclaimed.

"He had to chip out," she said, shaking her head as she
walked off to console her fiancé.

Forbes shot 80! he realized. They were both 4 under
for the tournament. And the others? What did it mean?"

"Congratulations, Mr. Colhane."

Duff turned a puzzled face to a man in a blue blazer
standing under a dripping PGA umbrella, a PGA badge
twinkling in his lapel.

"What?"

"You made it," he said, grasping Duff's scarred hand
and shaking it fraternally.

Up in the booth the announcer was explaining what
Duff had not yet grasped.

"This wind and rain took a terrible toll on the leaders
over the last nine holes," the anchor solemnly informed
the television audience. "And when Grady Tolson, playing in the last group on the South Course, shot seventy-
nine to put the cut at four under, that moved Duff Colhane
into a tie for thirty-fifth."

"Along with Forbes Witherspoon, who was leading the
tournament for the last five days," the coanchor added.

"Incredible."

"And because the cut is the low-thirty-five and ties, the rookie will be joining the veteran on the PGA Tour next season."

"Anything is possible," the anchor intoned.

When Duff phoned his father at Sal's to tell him the good news, Sam's initial exuberance was interrupted by a sharp gasp.

"Dad, what's wrong?" Duff cried.

"What have I done . . . ?" Sam mumbled.

"What? What happened?"

Sam's sigh was audible from Montauk. "Last Sunday I went to church—first time since your mother's funeral. I took a solemn vow—if you was to make it to the PGA Tour I swore to God I'd never take another drink."

Duff covered the mouthpiece long enough to suppress a laugh, then released it. "Dad, I'm sorry, but I'm sure your vow doesn't count, because you're an agnostic."

"Not anymore," his father replied woefully. "I'm very happy for ya, kid. And I'm proud of you, really proud," he added, voice choking.

Duff thanked him quickly and hung up, knowing he too was about to choke up.

Next he phoned Gena and left a message on her machine. "Your horse came in," it said.

3

The purses and the crowds were larger, the accommodations better and the competition a notch higher, but basically, Duff decided after his first few tournaments, the Big Tour wasn't much different from the Minis. Strip away the sponsors' tents, the media coverage and the pro-ams and it was just a bunch of guys teeing it up for a lot of money. But whether a player putting for a hundred thousand dollars at Pebble Beach faced more pressure than one putting for a thousand dollars at the Hardscrabble Country Club, depended entirely on how much money he already had in the bank. At the Q-School it was the silence; on the Big Tour it was the deafening noise of money. A PGA tournament didn't resemble a sporting event so much as a medieval market, with its great tents and corporate burgees flying, money and goods changing hands, deals being made and broken.

Money was everywhere on the PGA Tour. Duff had never felt its aura so much as he did from behind the ropes at a golf tournament. Marquee players commuted to work in private jets, bringing with them an entourage of family and friends, business managers, business partners, financial advisers, lawyers, accountants, coaches, caddies, trainers, sports psychologists and assorted hangers-on. Between shots on the practice tee, players made million-dollar deals to endorse everything from training aids to housing developments, designed golf courses, bought and sold large companies, built palatial hobby homes in paradises throughout the world, and plotted ways to avoid taxes on all of it.

It occurred to Duff, while flying back from Honolulu after the Hawaiian Open, that for the past couple of months he had been exposed to only servants or millionaires. The talk was no longer about good cheap restaurants or roach-free motels as it had been on the Minitour. It was now about IPOs and business opportunities and the new Mercedes and tax stratagems. He flew from golf resort to private country club in a hermetically sealed missile where he was met by police and marshalls who escorted him about the workplace, keeping the public outside the ropes, banishing them entirely if they spoke or attempted to capture him on film. Even the civilians—the bankers and CEOs and movie stars who paid thousands of dollars to play with them in the pro-ams—were fairly oozing and glistening with money. But the amateurs, unlike the pros, were not there in search of money; they were there in search of praise. The 20-handicap wanted only to be told by his pro partner that he had a good swing and, had he devoted himself to golf rather than commerce, could have been a damned good player.

Most players hated the pro-ams but managed to grin and bear them. Zeb Johnson, who'd grown up dirt poor in the Texas Panhandle, was one of the few players who claimed to enjoy them because, as he told Duff on the plane from Honolulu, "It gives us a chance to be with ordinary people for a change."

"An exercise in pure democracy," Duff remarked drolly from under his cap. Having missed the cut in Honolulu, he and Zeb and several other players, including Forbes Witherspoon, were taking an early flight to Tucson for the Chrysler Classic. "In fact they're so successful I understand they're thinking of introducing pro-ams to other professional sports," he went on. "Pro-am football, pro-am basketball, pro-am baseball . . ."

"Pro-am baseball!" Zeb spluttered.

"It's coming, mark my words."

"Bullshit. How's an amateur gonna play a team sport?"

"Nothing to it. Every player gets an amateur partner to help out in the field. So now you got two players at every position, the amateur backing up the pro."

"What about battin'—how they gonna do that?"

"They take turns—first the pro, then the amateur. Of course the amateur gets slow pitching—like playing off the members' tee," Duff added.

"Colhane, you so full a shit . . ."

"Just a little ahead of my time, Zeb, that's all," Duff droned.

Forbes, sitting on the aisle seat next to Duff, laughed softly. "You *better* be fond of those pro-ams, Zeb,'cause the way you're playin' that's all you're gonna see."

"I notice you didn't make the cut," Zeb growled.

"Me and Duff are savin' ourselves for the Tucson," Forbes said.

"You're a funny boy," Forbes remarked later, as they made their way through the Tucson airport. "But you bettah remembah, there's nothin' us Southern boys resent more than a wise-ass Yankee."

"It's too late to switch to hockey," Duff answered.

He knew Forbes was joking. Still under the impression that Duff was the son of a wealthy yachtsman, he had taken him under his wing soon after he got out onto the Tour. He thought his father was a little eccentric, Fed-Exing his son cash through the PGA office at each tournament, but he supposed what Duff told him was true: The rich are different from you and me. He supposed that also explained why a kid who didn't need the money would enter a golf tournament under a phony name, but it was not the sort of failing a gentleman brought up. *Droit du seigneur,* as his own father would say.

Duff was witty, attractive and wealthy, quite clubbable, and therefore fit company for a gentleman, Forbes decided. Things came easily for Duff—not even a broken hand could stop him—and that was the true mark of a gentleman.

"That 'If at first you don't succeed' stuff is just prole bullshit," Forbes had opined to Duff just a month before, over a *bubun* and branch water at the Palm Springs Tennis Club on the eve of the final round of the Hope Classic.

Forbes had played badly and was feeling depressed, but Duff was playing fairly well in only his second PGA tournament and knew he shouldn't be sitting here commiserating with his friend over cold beers. However he was both flattered and grateful for the attention paid him by the veteran (rookies were largely invisible to the more established players) and felt it was his duty to sit and listen. He would just sit and nurse a couple of beers and listen sympathetically, then get away as soon as possible, he had decided earlier. That had been more than two hours before.

"Things should come easily or not at all," Forbes went on. "If golf hadn't come naturally to me I wouldn't be here now. Unlike some of those fucking Texans. Fucking grinders." His hero was Bruce Leitzke, who scarcely ever practiced, and although he lived in Texas he was originally from Kansas City, so that didn't count. "Same with money—you either have it or you don't. I mean if you don't have it you've got no choice, you hafta work for it. But that doesn't make it any less grubby. God how I pity my father. Fucking insurance . . . Investments, that's cool. When am I gonna meet your father, Duff?"

"Soon, I hope."

"It's the same with women—they should come easily or not at all. That's why I like hangin' with you, you're a fuckin' chick magnet. That Gena is hot, man."

Forbes had met her when she'd surprised Duff by flying down to Florida to congratulate him on his induction into the PGA. Except in the movies, few of his fellow inductees had ever seen a woman like Gena Hall in her Barney's resortwear and five-hundred-dollar sunglasses. Duff didn't explain that she was just his backer come to pose in the winner's circle with her horse.

There had been a tense moment following his miraculous finish at the Q-School when it looked to Duff as if he might not get into the PGA after all. The guy he'd punched in the bar had gone directly from there to the PGA trailer to file a complaint against their newest player-elect, and was promising to sue him for assault and battery. Duff explained to a solemn panel of PGA officials just how the fracas had occurred (an account considerably at odds with that of the drunken fans) and waited while they decided what to do about this unseemly incident. A short while later he was introduced to Boris Stiffel.

Duff had noticed the gawky young man over the past several days—he was the only man at the tournament wearing a black Armani suit—and assumed he was employed by the resort in some unusually formal capacity. Either that or he was a hearse driver sneaking off between burials to watch some golf. But no, he was a players' agent.

"I also have a little legal experience," he added, as he led Duff away from the PGA trailer.

"You're a PGA lawyer?" Duff asked. He had sad, entreating eyes and a long, skinny neck poking out of a loose, starched collar, and a protruding Adam's apple that made him look like a vulture in a broad-shouldered suit.

"Forget the PGA. I'm only here on your personal behalf," he said, hands flourishing innocently in the air. "To see if I can help you out of this little mess."

"How?"

"The green poultice. Money," he added, rubbing his fingers together. "You got any?"

"A little. . . ."

"How little?"

"About five thousand dollars"—what was left of Gena's money.

Boris whistled appreciatively. "I think that should do it. Here's what I want you to do—write me a check to the claimant, leaving the amount blank and I'll . . ."

"It's not a check, it's cash," Duff interrupted.

"Cash?"

"I was afraid checks would be a problem."

"No," the agent said, shaking his head, "checks are cool, plastic is cool—money is a problem. But give it to me anyway."

When Duff took him to the parking lot and pulled a pile of twenties out of the trunk, Boris was incredulous. "Crazy bank, man."

Duff counted out two hundred and fifty twenties and waited in the car as instructed, while Boris went to the lodge to negotiate with the complainant. He knew that under ordinary circumstances only an idiot would give a stranger five thousand dollars and then sit in the car and wait while he ran off with it, but these weren't ordinary circumstances. If he was denied admission to the PGA simply because he'd defended himself, the money would be the least of it. Too, Boris wasn't a stranger. He'd been referred by the PGA—even if they wouldn't acknowledge it. Is it genetic destiny, Duff mused, that the son of Sam Colhane should be denied admittance to the PGA due to a barroom dustup?

A short while later Boris returned with a satisfied grin and a folded sheet of resort stationery, an informal though legally binding, signed release, he crowed. "For the sum of two thousand dollars the undersigned agrees to forego any and all claims et cetera, et cetera, balderdash and boilerplate," the lawyer said, handing over the release and his change.

Duff was nearly speechless. The man was a magician. He had gotten him off and saved him three thousand dollars besides. "Is that all—will the PGA forget about it?" he asked, uncertainly.

Boris brought a finger to his lips. "As far as the PGA is concerned, it never happened—the record is expunged."

When Duff tried to pay the lawyer for his services, he raised his hand like a traffic cop and shook his head, then reached into the breast pocket of his Armani jacket and slid an envelope out. It was an agency contract, Boris explained. He'd soon be making big money on the Tour, there'd be appearance fees and product endorsements to be negotiated, and the Boris Stiffel Agency was equipped to handle all his needs.

Duff took the contract in his hand and said he'd have to run it by his father—just to gain some time. He knew he'd need an agent, most of the Minitour players had them already, but he'd intended to wait until he was established so he'd be able to pick and choose carefully. But Boris was persuasive. His was a small agency and he didn't yet represent any marquee players, but Duff would get his full attention and not get lost in the crowd.

"You heard the one about the actor who was asked who his agent was and the actor said: 'I don't have one. I'm with the William Morris Agency'?" Well that'll never happen to you with the Boris Stiffel Agency," he promised. "And if you're ever unhappy with my representation, for any reason whatsoever, you can tear up the contract. I'll put it in writing."

What have I got to lose? Duff asked himself.

In the end he signed with Boris.

The big contracts with Titleist or Cadillac or other prestigious golf sponsors were scarcely available to an unknown rookie who had barely scraped through Q-School, but Boris did manage to patch together a batch of lesser-known sponsors that brought him a few hundred dollars a week in return for tricking himself out like a stock car. He agreed to use a little-known putter that resembled a hammer, in return for a promise of fifty thousand dollars should he win a tournament with it, but he abandoned it after missing several putts on the last day of the Phoenix Open. Boris understood why his client had to cancel the contract, (he'd been in the top thirty going into the final day) but he was still sad, it had been such a beautiful deal. Several days later, when Boris phoned him at Pebble Beach to tell him he was negotiating a deal with a major shoe manufacturer, Duff became excited.

"How much does it pay?" he asked.

"You get three pairs of shoes per season, free," Boris answered.

"No money?"

"Plus one replacement pair should they get scratched or damaged."

"What about the fee?"

"There's no money."

"Forget it," Duff said. "And I'm not going to wear that stock brokerage cap either; those guys are a bunch of crooks." By the terms of the contract, Duff got a hundred dollars each time the sponsor's logo appeared on television.

"They were only indicted, nothing's been proven," Boris argued. "And what are you doin' reading the papers anyway? You should be concentrating on your game."

"I don't need the money that badly."

"You still getting those care packages before every tournament?"

"Who told you that?"

"People talk."

It had to have been Forbes, Duff knew.

When he pulled Forbes aside on the practice tee the next morning and asked about it, he shrugged easily and replied, "Why should it matter if your old man's an eccentric millionaire?"

"It's something we like to keep within the family. So do me a favor, don't mention anything about the packages, okay?" Duff asked.

Forbes didn't understand what all the fuss was about, but he promised not to mention it again to anyone.

Duff was in the top twenty at Tucson following the Saturday round, and managed to get his face on television a few times (without the brokerage cap) which he learned from both his father and his doctor when they phoned him that evening. He wasn't surprised to hear from his father, who had taken a keen interest in the game when his son went out on Tour, but Frank Promer's call was unexpected.

"How's your friend Forbes doing?" he asked, after congratulating his patient and inquiring about his medication.

"Not very well. He missed another cut."

"What seems to be his problem?"

"Who knows? He's hitting the ball well but he can't get it in the cup."

"Tell him if he's interested I'll be happy to see him."

"Yeah, sure . . ." Duff replied.

What's he think I am, a drug pimp? he asked himself, as he replaced the receiver.

Playing somewhat uneasily with a superstar the next day, Duff started out birdie, birdie and quickly jumped several rungs on the ladder. After an eagle on the par-5, Tom Lehman seemed to notice him for the first time.

"Hey rookie, you trying to win this thing?" he asked, as they walked to the next tee.

"I haven't made any other plans today," Duff replied.

Lehman, who had spent more than his fair share of time on the Nike Tour before his break-out victory at the British Open in '96, smiled bemusedly as he watched the brash youngster launch another large tee shot, this one unfortunately into the barranca bordering the left side of the fairway. When he bogeyed that hole and 3-putted the next one, Lehman went back to ignoring him. He was just another rookie beginning to melt down after getting too close to the fire, and it was too painful to watch.

Duff thought he'd finally gotten the dosage worked out, but something was terribly wrong. He was feeling the same way he had when he'd stepped onto the last green at the Q-School, as if brain and body had become disconnected. Each bad shot fell like an added weight on his shoulders, retarding his swing, slowing his step. He saw the fearful look in Sidney's eyes and realized his caddie was helpless to lift the weight from his back. The only person who could help him was Frank Promer, and he was in New York, watching his experiment melt down.

When he finally got to the last green and stood over his putt, he was unable to take the putter back. Only when he watched the ball rolling far past the hole did he realize he'd hit it. He remembered hitting it two more times and he remembered Tom Lehman shaking his hand and saying something that must have been encouraging because he was smiling, but it all transpired at another time and place and he couldn't be sure of anything.

"At least we broke eighty," Sidney said, as he led his player, like a zombie, to the scorer's tent.

For the next tournament, the Nissan Open in California, Duff cut back on the dosage and played three of the best rounds he'd yet had on the PGA Tour. Unfortunately on Sunday afternoon he felt his game slipping away, but still managed to get into the clubhouse without hurting himself too badly and finished in 19th place, earning his first sizeable check. He was disappointed, he had been hoping for a top-10 finish, but he hadn't blown sky high on the last day—he was maturing.

The money itself meant little to Duff, so long as Gena's generous FedEx packages kept arriving at the PGA trailer, but it was necessary that he earn a minimum amount to gain entrance to the next tournament. He had originally thought that finishing among the top 35 players at the

Q-School guaranteed him a spot in each PGA event over the next year, but later learned that it only guaranteed him a place in the game of musical chairs. The way it worked was that the top 125 money winners of the previous year were guaranteed invitations to each 144-man PGA Tournament; eight otherwise ineligible players were granted sponsor's exemptions, and the rookies fought for the spoils, often leaving 35 or more hungry golfers scrambling for just 11 places. Six times a year the rookie ratings were changed, based upon how much each player had earned up until that time. The top player got first crack at a vacant spot, followed by the rest in the order of ranking until the field was filled. Because the first reshuffle would occur after the West Coast swing, Duff's high finish in the last Western event assured him a place in the top-10. At least until the next shuffle, which would take place after the first major tournament. It seemed the pressure would never end, but at least he was assured several more chances to earn enough to make the top-125 money list. Was there any other sport, Duff wondered, where an athlete's ability was measured by his wealth?

It was on the final day of the Nissan, as he limped up the 18th fairway, that Duff Colhane first came to the attention of the statisticians and announcers in the television booth who are always on the lookout for a little excitement. Mercurial, the tower announcer dubbed him, after noting that he had shot a 67 over a very difficult Pebble Beach course, followed by a 79 over a Tucson desert resort course just the week before.

"The young lad is able to smite the ball a mighty wallop, if not always accurately," the on-course commentator added in clipped British tones.

A mercurial long hitter, the producer thought while watching the action on several screens, visions of John Daly dancing in his head. "See if the kid can talk," the producer instructed his OC over the headphones. So few of them could.

When Duff emerged from the scorer's tent a short while

later, he was startled to have a microphone thrust in his face for the first time.

"Duff, congratulations!" the announcer greeted, as if they'd had dinner together the night before.

"Thanks . . ."

"I'm sure you'd like to play those last few holes over again, if you could . . ."

"Can you arrange it?" Duff interrupted.

The producer nodded happily while his announcer laughed shortly and went on, "I'm afraid not. But you've had a good tournament all the same for a lad just out of Q-School."

"I was hoping to do better."

"You like to just grip it and rip it, don't ye?" he asked, sounding a bit like Teddy McGill.

"Length is my strength," Duff responded.

The producer's eyes glinted greedily at such unusual chutzpa, while his announcer, quick to get it, went on about the rookie's overpowering style. The producer made a lot of money producing golf shows and he loved the game, but privately he hated most of the players and PGA officials who made his job so difficult. They didn't understand that golf wasn't just a sport, it was show business. Or they understood but weren't willing to perform. Once in a blue moon a star like Gary Cooper appeared, an Arnold Palmer; or a Fatty Arbuckle bad boy like Daly; or a Red Skelton clown like Jacobsen; or a rare black Tiger! But they were few and far between, and in the meantime the producer had to get to the refreshing personalities before they could be squelched by the suits.

At the conclusion of the short but promising interview, when the camera shifted back to the player-announcer in the tower, a notoriously short hitter, he remarked laughingly that, "The woods are full of long hitters."

When Duff later heard about the remark from a player in the locker room, he wasn't bothered by it. Hell, he could still hardly believe he was out here playing on the Big Tour, so even a less-than-flattering mention of his name on national television was grateful assurance that he wasn't just dreaming. Therefore when he passed the player-announcer in the parking lot later that day, he spontaneously quipped, "So is the leader board."

The rookie thought it an amusing rejoinder, but to the scarred veteran who hadn't putted for eagle in years, it was the insolent remark of a brash newcomer.

There were two kinds of golfers on the Tour, Nice Guys and Others. The Nice Guys tended to be family men who took their kids to Disneyland, went to church on Sunday, had cookouts, hunted and fished in the off season, and were always respectful to their elders—while the Others did little or none of that. Others needn't be playboys or deviants to earn their reputation, it was enough if they were perceived as somehow different from the PGA ideal. Unless a player did something outrageous, like get drunk and beat his wife, there was no defining moment when he became an Other. In Duff's case however, it began the moment he said, "So is the leader board."

Not that it might not have happened sooner or later anyway. Even though he grew up a hundred miles from the city, Duff was a New Yorker, and that was as Other as a golfer could get. Although they all played the Westchester Classic every year, just a short commute from Times Square, few of them ever ventured into the city. The image most players had of New Yorkers was provided by television news and cop shows, where white citizens lived in fear of being mugged or shot by dope-crazed punks while riding the subway and everybody talked like Joe Pesci. The more sophisticated elders of the PGA—bankers, lawyers, corporate officers and the like—who'd had some personal and professional experience with New Yorkers, tended to be tolerantly amused at the provincialism of their young players. They knew from worldly experience that New Yorkers were basically no different from anyone else—except that they could be pushy.

•   •   •

When Duff got back to his room there was a call from his father congratulating him on his high finish. The number he left was their home number, not a bar, Duff noted, as he picked up the phone.

"You did great!" Sam exclaimed. "I musta seen your face on TV at least a dozen times! Everybody's been phonin' me!" he said, and began ticking off the names of the well-wishers.

"That's nice, tell them I said thanks."

"Maybe there's somethin' to this God business after all, cuz the longer I go without a drink the better you play."

"Keep it up, Dad."

"You too, kid."

Next he called Gena's apartment and punched in his number on her new beeper. She called back while he was in the shower.

"I just wanted you to know, we made some money today," he said, dripping water on the carpet.

"I know, Frank Promer called. He was really pleased." With me or himself? Duff wondered, as his sponsor prattled on happily over her investment. Monte's horse had finished dead last at Hialeah last week. "Where do you play next?"

"Doral."

"The Doral Spa?"

"They also have a golf course."

"I'm coming!"

"What?"

"Where are you staying?"

"A Holiday Inn near the golf course. The PGA has a deal . . ."

"Forget it, I'll get us a suite at the Doral."

"Gena, it's a big week . . ."

"Monte's connected," she assured him. "Stay by the phone, I'll call you back."

•   •   •

A few nights later Duff stood outside on the patio at the Doral Resort while a Cuban band blared brassily from inside, and golfers and guests roamed about with plates heaped with shrimp and meatballs and large flutes of sparkling wine. He was waiting for Gena—who'd checked in and gone directly to the spa for a de-stress aromatherapy massage and a detoxifying herbal wrap—while staring at the moon and thinking of the last Minitour event he'd played. It had been over an unkempt golf course surrounded by unsold cinderblock houses in a small town somewhere in the center of this same state but now seemed no closer than the big Miami moon hanging over the palms. He had been told on the 18th tee that he needed only a bogey to win his first professional tournament, worth $750, then promptly knocked two drives out of bounds that ricocheted among the cinderblock houses, and finished with a snowman. That was the day, almost four years ago, when he had decided to pack it in. And now here he was at the Doral Golf Resort, about to play four rounds of golf for more money than he could make in a lifetime on the Minitour.

"Beautiful, isn't it?"

Duff turned to the young woman standing near him. She had thick, chestnut hair in a long roll hanging down over her right shoulder, covering one breast. The other pushed against a tan, cashmere sweater, and below that a pair of plaid culottes. Golf groupie, he said to himself.

Duff glanced at the fountain where a nearly naked woman poured water endlessly from a vase and replied, "Even if a bit gaudy?" Her short laugh, as if he'd said something hilarious when he hadn't, was nevertheless pleasing. He had thought Forbes was having him on when he told him about the groupies that awaited them on tour—until he arrived at his first tournament and found them hanging about, neatly coiffed young ladies in golf shorts, pearls and cashmere sweaters, scarcely the pierced, stoned, flamboyantly costumed sort to be found hanging around back at a rock concert, but groupies just the same. Most of them were looking for a rich golfer husband, but many would settle for a run-of-the-tournament affair. Being handsome, young and single, Duff and Forbes were quite popular with the girls; and being alone in one luxurious though strange golf resort after another, they very much appreciated having them around. The girls were understandably unpopular with the wives (as well as some of the blue-nosed players and PGA officials) so he and Forbes could count on some disapproving stares whenever they introduced them at dinner or brought them along to a sponsor's party. They were all cast from one mold—attractive, country club, party girls—but there was something about this one, an assured serenity the others lacked, that made Duff wish Gena hadn't decided to join him at this particular tournament.

"I thought you were admiring the moon," she said, her large green eyes pinched with amusement.

"Oh—no," he answered, a bit flustered. Groupies did not laugh at the golf gods. "Actually I was thinking of something that now seems much farther away than the moon."

"That sound terribly romantic for a golfer."

"Golfers are terrible romantics," Duff corrected. "We go off like knights with our faithful lance-carriers at our sides, to fight dragons and bring back the Holy Grail. . . . That's hardly the pursuit of a practical-minded person."

"Then how do you explain *them*?" she asked, pointing toward the buffet table where the sponsor's guests, businessmen in jackets and ties smoking twenty-dollar Macanudos, were piling their plates with lobster tails and lamb chops. "Surely they aren't romantics."

"They're amateurs," he sniffed. "Knights are like artists; they have to be supported by the merchant class."

"And are all golfers such snobs?"

"Only the best of us."

"I see. And what big tournaments have you won?"

"The Doral will be my first."

"To think that I'll be a witness to history," she said, pressing her hands mockingly to her cheeks. "But do you know what I think?"

"No, tell me."

"I don't think golfers are knights at all. I think they're hunters."

"Hunters?"

"Instinctually—metaphorically . . ." she added. "It's the celebration of an ancient genetic urge—the way they go off like hunting parties with a bag of clubs slung over their shoulders, like a quiver of spears and arrows, shooting birdies and eagles. That's why the game is popular with people like them," she said, pointing a thumb in the direction of the wealthy gentlemen at the buffet table. "They're the hunters of modern society."

This is no groupie, Duff said to himself. "Let me guess—you're a psych major at the University of Miami."

She shook her head. "Art, Risdee."

"Risdee—?"

"Rhode Island School of Design. I'm studying to be a painter."

"Aha! So you're just as dependent on the fat cats as we are."

"But far more deserving," she replied, in a mockingly haughty voice. "Unless you think Ben Hogan's contribution to the world is greater than Leonardo da Vinci's. Or Bach's, or Shakespeare's."

"You're not a golf groupie."

"A what!"

"No offense. I meant fan."

"I know what you meant," she said. "Somebody told me all about them."

"Who?"

"My lips are sealed."

"Just tell me where he's from."

"He's an old friend from the Vineyard."

"Martha's Vineyard?" She nodded. "This friend—does he go with groupies?"

"Of course not," she answered, with a whiff of reproof. "But he has a friend who tells him all about them."

"Duff Colhane?"

"You know him?"

Duff nodded sadly. "The man is a disgrace to the profession. Nobody can understand why a gentleman like Forbes Witherspoon would run around with him."

"Unless they both like to chase groupies . . . ?"

They both laughed. "How did you know who I was?"

"Forbes told me to find the one with the pugnacious jaw and stay with him until he got here. When did you know?"

"When you mentioned the Vineyard. When I first met Forbes at Southeastern about five years ago, he told me his family had a place on Martha's Vineyard. As a matter of fact he was going to have me up that summer and introduce me to all the best-looking girls on the Vineyard, but he didn't."

"Why not?" she asked.

Duff grimaced. "I don't know you well enough to tell you that story."

"But if he had we'd be old friends by now," she pointed out.

"Probably married with a couple of kids."

"So tell me."

"It might destroy our relationship," he said, extending the hand under discussion. "Forbes told you my name, but he didn't tell me yours."

"Priscilla Donne."

She gripped his hand firmly and they both held on for an awkwardly long time. It was surely unwilled and meaningless, yet an expression of embarrassment passed between them, as if each of them had unintentionally revealed an intimate secret. He was both unnerved and pleased by the unusual sensation creeping over him. He'd known her for only a few minutes and yet he felt as if they were indeed very old friends. He felt an inexplicable urge to tell her what she wanted to know, confident that she would understand why he did what he did in Vegas. And he wanted her to tell him everything about herself, things she would never tell anyone else because he was the only one in the world who could be trusted with her deepest secrets. It was only a flash of time, yet in that brief moment when their hands lingered together he felt an understanding pass between them that was as solid and as sure as the tiles beneath their feet. And he had to quickly regain control of his emotions before he blurted out something that would convince her he was crazy.

That was when Gena, fresh from her aromatherapy and herbal wrap, burst onto the patio like a blazing meteor in her hip-hugging pants, bare midriff and filmy camisole, accompanied by Forbes who hurried along beside her like a frisky blond retriever.

"Look who I found!" Forbes called.

"Incredible!" Gena howled. "You need a spa advisor just to explain the program! So far I've had a facial, a manicure and a pedicure; I've had shiatsu, Trager therapy, craniosacral therapy, body gommage and a total body fango, and half a dozen other things I can't even pronounce or remember, and I haven't even scratched the surface! I tell you, darling, this place is so great I could give up sex for it!" she said, clutching Duff's arm.

But not coke, Duff said to himself, as he introduced her to Priscilla.

"Wonderful to meet you. I'm going to take you all to dinner at Ian's place in South Beach, on me. The place is impossible, but I called Monte and he arranged it. And he told me about this club in Coconut Grove . . ."

"Gena . . ."

". . . a not-to-miss."

"We have to play tomorrow."

"Darling, you surely don't think I'd do anything to destroy your career, do you? But we do have to have a little fun. And I promise I'll have you in at a decent hour. What do you say, darling?" she asked, swinging from Duff's arm to Forbes's.

"Well—we have to eat."

"I thought we were having dinner here," Priscilla reminded gently.

"And we don't have a car," Duff added.

"I've spoken to the concierge, we have a limousine at our beck and call," she announced, as she snatched a flute of champagne from a passing tray.

"Cool," Forbes said.

Duff and Priscilla tried to dig their heels in, but in the end they were easily overwhelmed by Gena's manic need to party—and Forbes's need to follow her anywhere. They would stick around here for a while, have a drink with the stiffs, then go off for a little dinner and dancing.

"I'd like to meet Tiger Woods," Gena announced.

"*I've* never even met Tiger Woods," Duff replied.

"I have," Forbes said. "But I don't know if he's here."

"Well let's go see," she said, lacing her arm in his.

Beaming, Forbes went off with Gena to find Tiger Woods while the guests and golfers stared after her, and Duff and Priscilla waited behind.

"I'm sorry," Duff said.

Like a bomb survivor, Priscilla asked, "Who is she?"

"My sponsor."

She cocked her head and regarded him skeptically. "Sponsor?"

"Honest." Until now he'd let people think she was his girlfriend, but not Priscilla.

When they returned much later, Forbes was a little drunk. They hadn't found Tiger Woods, but he had happily introduced her to every other golfer he could find, as well as the many guests and sponsors who had shown interest. Gena was bored by it all and wanted to blow the place right away.

Later, as she was fairly pulling them through the lobby to the waiting limousine, she stopped suddenly and turned an elevator eye on Priscilla's sweater and culottes. "Darling, would you like to change?" she asked sweetly.

"No thank you, darling," Priscilla answered sweetly.

Gena and Forbes stood in the moonroof waving at the South Beach strollers as the driver drove slowly down Ocean Drive, past the art-deco hotels emblazoned with iridescent neon, while the sounds of salsa and reggae and metal and Stones and Sinatra and the Beatles ebbed and spiked as they passed each place. They drove up and down from 8th to 14th Street several times before Duff was able to get her to stop in front of the hotel where they were to have dinner.

As they walked up the stairs and into the 1920s lobby, strewn with bamboo furniture and palms twitching under the slowly revolving ceiling fans, Duff whispered into Gena's ear, "No drugs around Forbes."

"You're kidding!" she exclaimed. "What do you think we were doing while we were driving up and down the street?"

That's one player Tiger Woods doesn't have to worry about tomorrow, Duff said to himself. As for himself, he would have one glass of wine, dance one dance and be in bed by midnight, he vowed. Watch out, Tiger.

However it was well after midnight when they dropped Forbes and Pris off and returned to the Doral. And even then, Gena insisted on roaming the grounds from bar to bar, snorting dope and gargling champagne until she finally crashed and Duff was at last able to haul her back to their room. He only hoped he'd be able to break 80 the next morning.

Like a circus, Duff thought, as he watched the big tent come down at the Doral. A three-ring circus with the headliners in the middle, the lion trainers and trapeze artists and all the clowns in the outer circles. At the end of each run they folded their tents, packed the wagons and

headed north to Bay Hill, Sawgrass, Augusta, Harbour
Town, Greensboro, Fort Worth, Memphis, Rye, Milwau-
kee, Medinah, Akron, Brookline, Williamsburg and doz-
ens of other tank towns where the fans came out to marvel
at all the daring young men.

There were times during the first year when Duff appeared briefly in the center ring, poised to somersault
through the air and grab the trapeze, but each time he
grew dizzy at the last moment and missed the bar. It was
to be expected, everybody has to learn how to win, it
would come with time, the writers and commentators and
some of his fellow players said at first. But as the months
went by and the missed opportunities multiplied, their
words of encouragement changed to speculative diagnoses
and finally silence.

Through it all, Duff tried hard to keep his own counsel.
Nobody understood him like he understood himself. He
was aware of the many good players who had won during
their first year on the Tour, and at the start of each tournament he had expected to find himself among them. But
that hadn't happened, so now he had to remind himself
that a great many players didn't win until their second
year, and he had to keep his confidence if he wanted to
be among them. Confidence was what separated the winners from the also-rans, not just ability. After more than
a year among the greatest players in the world, he knew
that he could match any of them shot for shot. Everybody
on Tour could play the game, but there were only a couple
of dozen at a time who approached a tournament knowing
they could win it. Confidence was what he needed more
than anything else.

That and the pills. It was the pills that contributed to
his loss of confidence which, in turn, caused him to lose.
He knew he couldn't get along without them, yet the way
they sometimes worked against him, he wished he could.
The nightmares were growing worse and more frequent,
leaving him almost constantly fatigued, and he was becoming increasingly impotent.

"I just need a long rest," he told Forbes after their last tournament together in October.

They were having dinner in an ersatz eighteenth-century tavern in Williamsburg after the last round at Kingsmill. Duff had two more tournaments before returning home, but Forbes was finished for the season. He had played poorly all year, lost his card and would have to return to Q-School in a few weeks. Although Duff was disappointed with his own finish on the money list—he could've been in the top 50 had he not had so many disastrous closing rounds—he was enormously relieved that he would at least be spared that nightmare.

"I don't know that I'll be back next year," Forbes said, poking idly at his steak.

"Don't worry, you'll make it," Duff said. It sounded hollow even to the speaker.

"I'm thinking of not going back to Q-School."

After a moment of silence, Duff said, "You'll feel better after a rest." Nobody quits golf.

"I'm thinking of going into the family business."

"I thought you hated insurance."

"I do. But I'm thinking of getting married."

"Married? To Priscilla?" Duff said, leadenly.

He'd been afraid it was coming. As long as Forbes was playing well he hadn't thought about marriage, but when his game turned sour he began looking for something sweet, and Priscilla was close at hand. Through the winter and spring, while he was still hopeful that his game would soon come around, he scarcely mentioned her. But as the summer progressed and he continued to play badly, he invited her to join him, first at Westchester, then at the Hartford Open, and each time, she dutifully came. She was several years younger, so their summers together on the Vineyard had been innocent, he explained. Then there were a couple of years while he was on Tour when he didn't see her at all, and when he next saw her she was a beautiful young woman, and that, he told Duff, was when he had begun to fall in love with her. But Duff didn't believe it. Nor did he believe that Pris truly loved him. She was just another impressionable young girl who had been in awe of a good-looking older boy who had grown up to be a professional golfer who now couldn't hack it and was throwing in the towel. Given time, she would realize that he wasn't the blond god she had admired on the beach, but rather a quitter, and she'd drop him. And given time, she might fall in love with Duff, who had never stopped thinking of her since the night they had met on the patio at the Doral. But Forbes wouldn't allow her any time.

"You don't sound very excited," Forbes remarked after the long silence.

"I'm stunned."

"Yeah, me too. I always thought I'd marry a rich glamorous woman like Gena. Not that Pris isn't good-looking, but she's poor as a church mouse. Her father's the summer pastor on the Vineyard—they don't even own a house there."

"Tragic. Have you asked her?"

"Not yet."

"What makes you think she'll say yes?"

"You kidding?"

Only myself, Duff replied silently. "If you want my opinion, I don't think you should do anything rash. Go to the Q-School, see how it goes. Then make your decision."

Forbes shook his head. "The decision's been made for me. I've been out here too long and nothing's happened. I'm not gonna be one of those thirty-five-year-old guys bouncin' back and forth between Q-School and the Tour and not havin' a fucking thing to show for it. I've got a good business waiting for me, but it won't wait forever."

Duff regarded his friend across the table with a resigned, forlorn expression. "Whatever you decide, Forbes, I wish you luck."

"Thanks, buddy," Forbes replied.

• • •

Gena left her new Porsche in a dark corner of the lot near the party boats and walked quickly out to the docks. She walked away from the saloon lights and noise that oozed at intervals along the waterfront, past the empty fishing boats rising and falling on the midnight tide, out to the dark end of the pier where a sliver of moon hung like a scimitar in the sky. She'd taken a lot of risks in the dangerous business she'd somehow stumbled into over the last several years, but she was more frightened by what she was about to do than by anything she'd done before. It wasn't the narcs—they were always there. And it wasn't Leo Hover—he was cool. Amazingly cool. Leo had been in the business longer than anyone she knew—except for Monte—and the narcs didn't even know he existed. Leo was smart and he was careful. But that was true of a lot of dealers who were doing twenty to life in Attica. Leo, however, had one other thing the others, especially Monte, lacked, and that was humility. Leo was content to be a small dealer on the East End of Long Island where the surveillance was light and the competition wasn't cutthroat. And because New York was becoming increasingly dangerous, with the feds tightening down and the Colombians killing suspected informants on little more than a whim, it was time to move to the country.

Unfortunately, she hadn't saved as much as she'd intended. And that was why she needed Leo. She wasn't yet able to fully retire, but if what Leo said was true, she soon would be. And then, of all things, she'd become the wife of a professional golfer. She'd wear flowered skirts and golf shirts from all the clubs and spas they'd visit, and she'd have a couple of kids who would run out on the green and hug their daddy when he won a tournament. It all sounds so fucking corny but you know, you might just be ready for it, she said to herself as she approached the end of the pier.

There was an idling launch waiting at the end of the

pier, just as Leo had promised. And behind the wheel was Nick Spoto, little changed since high school when he was cruelly called Spotless. Now he was neat and trim in a glove-leather jacket and silk slacks.

"You look hot, Nick," Gena said as she stepped into the launch.

"You too," Nick said as he swung the launch about and headed for the yacht in the middle of the harbor.

It was a big boat, Gena saw as they edged closer to the loading platform at the stern. Much too big for a drug dealer. Maybe Leo wasn't so smart after all. Then a door opened and Leo stepped out onto the rear deck in a blue blazer with brass buttons the color of his long hair. He waved to her and flashed his teeth like a beacon in the night.

"Ahoy," Gena said as she reached for his hand. She had forgotten how good-looking Leo Hover was.

"Gotcha," he said as he pulled her up onto the deck. He put his arms around her and kissed her on both cheeks, as if he'd been spending time in Europe. "Glad you came." Then he stepped back and presented his yacht. "How do you like her?"

"To be honest, I was hoping for something a little more modest," she said, peering into the salon, a blaze of neon and mirrors and polished wood and red leather banquettes.

"Don't worry, it's not mine," he said, opening the door for her. She stepped inside and he closed the door after them, leaving Nick to tend the launch. "I'm part of a group that owns the boat and charters it out, only we don't really, we just move money around among ourselves if you know what I mean. It's cool," he assured her.

"You mean it's a laundry boat," she said, a little relieved.

Leo laughed. "Yeah, a laundry boat. I forgot you were also funny."

"Oh? And what else am I?"

"Gorgeous—and smart. That's why I called you."

"Because I'm gorgeous or because I'm smart?"

"Both. You and Duff still a pair?"

"We're good friends."

"And Monte?"

"Good friends."

"How's his business?"

"Since when did you become interested in the restaurant business?"

Leo grinned and shrugged. "I hear he's being squeezed—the Colombians are flipping out . . . ?"

"I wouldn't know."

"Right. You're just a low-level operative, like me. That's smart. How's your business?"

Gena pointed her chin at the bar and asked, "You gonna buy me a drink?"

"Sure, what'll you have?"

"Champagne."

"Why did I ask?" he said, going to the bar. He reached into the cooler and came out with a Fleur de France, which he held questioningly aloft.

"My brand," she said.

Leo popped the cork and filled a gold-stemmed flute, then filled the matching one with mineral water. "To business," he said, handing her the wine.

"Old times," she said, lifting the glass to her lips.

Leo sipped his water and returned the glass to the bar. "I don't drink," he announced. "Or do drugs."

Gena nodded. Leo was looking like a prospect. "I don't do drugs either." It wasn't true, but she intended to quit soon. A golf pro's wife could not do drugs. She wondered what the wives drank. Something with an umbrella sticking out of it, she supposed.

"Let's hope it doesn't catch on," Leo said, gesturing toward the leather banquette. "Sit?"

They both sat and Gena found herself staring at their combined reflection in the mirrored cabinet wall across the room. They made a damned good-looking couple, she decided.

"How's Duff doing on the Tour?" Leo asked.

"Good. I think he's about to break out."

"I hear you're sponsoring him."

"Where did you hear that?"

"Montauk's a small town."

"I help him out a little, that's all."

"Like my laundry boat?"

"No, not like that," she replied, shaking her head. "Do you want to tell me why you brought me out here?"

"Ecstasy," he said with a widening smile.

"Pills or pleasure?"

"Either one, or both."

"Business first."

"Okay. I can supply all the pills you want, lab certified, two dollars a pill."

"Two dollars?" That was very cheap for a pill that went for twenty or thirty dollars in any of the clubs out here. It was this price, which he'd quoted on the phone while calling them cough drops, that made her wonder if he was really talking about cough drops and not ecstasy.

"That's a special price to you only."

"Why?"

He shrugged. "Old times . . . Because I know things are getting hot in the city and I think you need a change of scene."

"How do you know that?"

"I deal with the Colombians too. Or I used to," he added. "Now I work out of Amsterdam where everything is legal. And safe."

A safe and prosperous business, she said to herself. She could do ten or twenty thousand dollars a week in the Hamptons all by herself, or even more if she hired agents. And Duff wouldn't even know she was in the business.

But Monte would. Not for a while perhaps, but eventually. Unless he first got nabbed by the feds or blown away by the Colombians, either of which could happen at any time. So if she could just split amicably from Monte and lay low for a while, just until he took his fall, then she'd be in the clear. She always knew she'd have to get out one day or else take a bad fall herself, but until now she had no way out. Then Leo came out of her past like a knight on a white charger and suddenly everything was cool. She could scarcely believe her luck.

"Can I see the stuff?" she asked.

"Did you bring the money?"

"Twenty thousand," she said, patting the bag beside her. Old friends or not, Leo had insisted that she bring the money with her.

"Be right back," he said, getting to his feet.

He opened an inner door and disappeared into the next room. A few minutes later he came back with a gym bag which he placed on the cocktail table in front of her. He pulled out a clear plastic bag of small white tablets and announced, "Ten bags, a thousand pills each. Care to count or sample them?"

She shook her head. "I trust you." She reached into her purse and withdrew two banded stacks of hundred dollar bills which she placed beside the pills.

"And any time you want any more, just give me a call."

"I have the feeling this could be the beginning of a beautiful friendship, Leo."

"I hope so."

Leo picked up the money and waited while she replaced the loose bag of pills in the gym bag and got to her feet. She smiled at Leo and presented her cheek for a European kiss as, a moment later, doors flew open and the room was filled with men in dark windbreakers with the letters DEA stenciled across the back. While an agent recited her constitutional rights, she caught Leo's eye across the room. He waved his hands helplessly and shrugged.

Duff's homecoming was the biggest event to take place in Montauk that winter. His father had saved hundreds of fan letters for him, including invitations from strangers with impressive letterheads to play a round at Shinnecock Hills, Noyac or the National. He was interviewed on television and written about in the local papers, and a photograph of him swinging a club on a palm-lined fairway was posted prominently in many of the shops and restaurants of this iced-over summer resort town. Everybody on the East End claimed to be an old friend, or at least they'd met him. Wherever he went people greeted him with, "Saw you on TV!" If he hadn't occasionally made the leader board and gotten his face on television, if he'd just been one of the anonymous grinders at the bottom of the pack, like Forbes, would he still be a celebrity, or just a local kid trying to make it on the Tour?

Of all the skeptics now turned fans, Sam Colhane's conversion was clearly the most remarkable. Only a few years ago a game for sissies and social climbers, golf was now one of the most demanding tests of athletic ability ever devised by man, and anybody who said otherwise was liable to get a punch in the mouth. Although Sam was faithful to his vow never to take another drink for as long as his son remained on the PGA Tour, sobriety had not entirely changed him. He had never told anyone except his son about the vow he'd made, not even Rita. He simply announced one day that he no longer had a taste for the stuff and had therefore quit drinking. His friends gathered at the bar and waited all winter for the night he would come crashing down off the wagon, but spring came and summer and winter, then another year, and Sam Colhane was still sober as a sheik.

Duff was amazed when he saw him. The man had lost twenty pounds and ten years and looked very much like one of the old pictures of himself that hung on the wall at Sal's, standing straight and slim on the deck of the Night Star, ready to battle wind and waves or anything else God put in his way. The image put Duff in mind of Captain Dobbs's offer to help his father finance a boat, providing Duff be along to keep him sober. Now he no longer needed anybody to keep him sober, nor did Duff need anybody else's money. Or at least he soon wouldn't.

When Duff told his father he'd made almost three hundred thousand dollars for the year (of which little was left after expenses and Gena's 25 percent and Sidney's 15) and offered to help finance a fishing boat, Sam flatly refused to take a penny from him. "That money's yours. You got it with no help from me, and I ain't takin' none of it."

"You helped me, Dad. You helped me in ways you don't know."

"Thanks for that," Sam said. He reached out suddenly and hugged his son, one of the few embraces Duff could remember. "But just the same, I don't want ya givin' me no gift," he added, blinking back the tears that welled in his eyes.

"I'm not talking about a gift, Dad, I'm talking about an investment, a tax write-off," Duff explained. "If I invest in you I expect to make a profit, just like Gena did with me. Only not right away. I'm thinking of next year."

"So we'll talk about it next year."

"Fine."

"If you find you need a tax write-off."

"Naturally."

Sam's tone was begrudging, but there was a light glimmering in his moist eyes that Duff had seldom seen.

When he phoned Gena in New York to tell her he was home, she didn't sound very excited. "I can't talk right now," she said abruptly. "Where are you?"

"At home," he answered. "But I'm coming to New York tomorrow to see Frank Promer and I thought we might get together."

"No," she said quickly. "I can't. I'll call you later."

"When?

"Soon. And Duff?"

"Yeah?"

"Don't call me at this number anymore, or on the beeper. I'm sorry—I'll explain when I see you."

"Gena, what's wrong?"

"Nothing. I'll call."

"When?" he called, as the phone went dead in his hand. He replaced the receiver and lowered himself slowly onto the kitchen chair.

"You get blown off?"

He looked up to see his father standing in the doorway, a football game flickering on the television screen in the room behind him. "I'm not sure. How's the game?"

"Giants are down a touchdown but it's still the first half."

"Plenty of time."

"Yeah. You know I saw her mother a couple weeks ago—Gena's."

"Yeah?"

"Apparently she don't know Gena's backin' you."

"You didn't tell her . . . !"

"Not exactly. I mean I pulled back when I could see she didn't know what I was talkin' about."

"But she knows."

Sam shrugged helplessly. "She might know somethin'."

"Shit," he said, rising from the kitchen table.

"Well, you didn't tell me not to say nothin'."

"I know. It's my fault. I shouldn't've told you—but you kept asking," he said, stalking across the linoleum floor.

"I was worried ya needed money, that's all," Sam protested. "I woulda send ya some for Christ's sake."

"I know—I'm not blaming you. But if Gena wanted her mother to know she was sponsoring me, she should've been the one to tell her. What did she say when you told her?"

"Nothin' much. Just that she couldn't understand where Gena was gettin' all that money."

"She's a model, models make a lot of money."

"Yeah but she said she never sees her pictures in the fashion magazines or on TV or anything."

"She does fashion shows. It pays well."

"How well? Well enough for a big apartment in the

city? Enough for a Porsche? Enough to sponsor you?"

"Don't worry, she makes plenty," Duff assured him, starting for the door.

Sam spread his feet in the doorway and wouldn't move. "But I am worried. Her mother thinks she's got something goin' with Leo Hover. You know anything about that?"

Duff shook his head. "Gena has nothing to do with Leo."

"I hope not," Sam said. "Cuz Leo's deep in drugs, everybody in Montauk knows it. And if *they* know, how long's it gonna be before the cops know? In fact I heard the cops are already on to him."

"Where did you hear that?"

"It's around, that's all. Somebody saw one of Leo's guys get busted in a club in Southampton with a bag of drugs, but there was never any mention of it in the papers. That Greek kid you went to school with . . ." Sam said, churning his hand.

"Nick Spoto."

"Yeah, Nick. Anyhow, him and Leo disappeared for a while right after that, then suddenly they're back in town like nothin' happened."

"Maybe nothing did," Duff dared hope.

"Or maybe they're cooperating with the cops. And if they are, I don't have to tell ya—stay away from Leo."

"I haven't seen Leo in years."

"But you are seein' Gena."

"Dad, I promise you, Gena has nothing to do with Leo."

"Good, I'm glad to hear that. But what about that restaurant guy?"

"Monte?"

"Yeah, Monte. Her mother ain't so happy with that guy either."

"I don't know anything about him," Duff said.

"That's what I told her—Gena's mom. But she ain't stupid. She knows Gena's got too much money and now she knows you're gettin' some of it and it's bound to make her think."

"I can't help that. Gena and I have a perfectly straight business deal," Duff replied.

"You got somethin' on paper to that effect?"

Duff shook his head. "She didn't want a contract."

"Didn't you think that was kinda funny?"

"No, Dad, I didn't. We're friends, we trust each other."

"And where'd you think all that money was comin' from?"

"From her modeling."

"Duff, Duffy . . ." he said, shaking his head sadly. "If your own father don't believe that, who the hell will?"

"I know you're trying to help, Dad, and I appreciate it. But I can't turn my back on Gena."

"No, I didn't think you would. But when you got a man-eater on the line, it's sometimes best to cut him loose," Sam advised before stepping aside to let his son pass.

Duff sat in the top deck of the train and watched the Long Island farms passing by as the train hurtled smoothly and silently toward the city. He was trying to make himself believe that there was no connection between Gena's strange behavior and Leo's arrest, but having little luck. On the one hand it seemed unlikely—Leo had been a small-time drug dealer when he was still in high school, before Gena even thought of getting into the business. And when she decided to get into it she went into it in a big way, assembling a network of dealer-models to sell to a lucrative market, while Leo was still selling nickel bags to the locals.

But then on the other hand, he suddenly thought, a lot of Gena's customers are in the Hamptons in the summer. Maybe there's a lot of business going begging because she's got no representative out here she can trust. Then she remembers her old friend Leo, just sitting around the gas station with nothing to do, and she has a great idea. The synergy is perfect—a whole new market just waiting

to be exploited, and Leo Hover is the man to do it! And
it would be just like Leo to walk away unscathed while
the roof caved in on everybody else, Duff remembered.

And, he asked himself, does that include me?

Duff sat on the edge of the examining table while Frank
Promer, in his white lab coat, stood proudly surveying his
creation. He had seen him on television several times over
the year, most recently at the JC Penney Classic where he
had played well until the final day.

"I thought that tournament was going to be your first
win," Frank said.

"So did I. That's the problem. I get close but no cigar."

"Patience, patience," the doctor chided. "Just the fact
that you're in the hunt is no small accomplishment."

"I'm sorry, Frank, but blowing it on the last day is no
accomplishment at all. I can play as well as anybody from
Thursday to Saturday, but not on Sunday. It's like the pills
don't work on Sunday."

Dr. Promer laughed softly. "I can assure you, the laws
of chemistry do not distinguish between the days of the
week."

"I understand—but I'm sure my reaction to the pills is
different after taking them for three days."

"Then I suggest we look to the patient, not the medicine. Find out what it is that might've changed in you."

"Nothing changes. I'm the same on Sunday as I am on
Thursday. I take the same combination and the same number of pills each day, but on Sunday I get an entirely
different reaction."

"Different in what way?"

"I don't know—different in different ways. Sometimes
I take just one red pill and my heart starts beating like a
drum. I swing so fast I can hardly keep the ball on the
golf course. Then I take a blue one and either nothing
happens, or my heart almost comes to a complete stop.
Other days I can sense what I need and regulate the dose,

but on Sundays I just seem to lose the feel. So why should Sunday be different from any other day?"

"It isn't," the doctor said. "But you are. You're tired after three days of play, both physically and mentally. You're more susceptible to the effects of drugs than at other times. But probably more than anything else, you're under greater pressure on the last day."

Duff shook his head. "No, Frank, this has nothing to do with pressure. This is about the pills, nothing else. The pressure is always there, right from the first hole on the first day."

"You're the player, Duff, not me. But I've followed your tournaments quite closely, and I've noticed something that you seem to be ignoring. If you don't mind me exchanging my medical hat for a coach's," he added.

"Go ahead," Duff said.

"I've noticed that when you're well back in the field after three rounds, you often shoot a very low final round. You're aware of this, I'm sure."

Duff shrugged. "That happens to everybody."

"That's what I thought. Until I went back and checked the scores and discovered that your drastic spikes are most unusual. The great majority of players in the bottom half of the field are there because they played four consistently unexciting rounds of golf; while those in the top half played four consistently good rounds. There are exceptions of course," he added over Duff's objection, "but your highs and lows are remarkable. You only play badly on the final day when there's something riding on it— when the pressure's on. And with that I'll change back to my medical hat," he concluded.

"Let me be sure I understand this . . ." Duff began slowly. "You're saying I only play badly because of the pressure?"

"I'm only saying there's a statistical correlation here that's hard to deny."

"Which lets you off the hook, doesn't it? It's not a medical problem, I'm just a choker."

"That's not the word I would use."

"That's what I heard. 'Let me change from my medical hat to my coach's hat?'"

"Each and every one of us is subject to anxiety syndrome under certain situations; there's no way to avoid it. But the way each of us handles it is entirely up to the individual. The difference between the winners and the losers is, the winners have learned how to cope with their anxiety, and the losers haven't. The drugs can only do so much, Duff. After that it's up to you."

"It's not the pressure," Duff said, shaking his head from side to side. "If anything I play better under pressure. I always have."

"You're talking about a time when you were a healthy young boy playing for a tin cup. You're no longer the same person, and now you're playing for a lot more than tchotchkes."

Duff wanted to respond, to shout, but there was nothing he could say. Of course he wasn't the same person. He knew life wasn't as romantic as Fitzgerald had led him to believe, but the doctor was supposed to fix that! He had taken him this far, shown him what might be, and now he was turning back, leaving him to go on alone.

"I think I recognize my responsibility," Duff began in a deliberately calm voice. "My emotions are my concern, but my nerves," he added, waving his scarred hand, "are yours."

"I'm sorry, they're the same," the doctor assured him.

"No! I can feel it, I know the difference. What if it's not me, what if I'm just taking too much? What if the drugs keep building up in my system over three days and by the fourth day I'm overdosing? Wouldn't that explain it?"

"It's highly unlikely."

"But how can you be sure? You said this was only an experiment."

"And a successful one, I'd say." He walked around behind his desk and settled into his leather chair. "When you came to me you had one goal—to get through Q-School. Well, I got you through and you've had some pretty good tournaments. But there comes a point when you have to do the rest by yourself."

"Frank, I'm not asking you to hit the shots for me. I just want you to seriously consider the problem I'm having with the pills."

"As I've told you—"

"You told me I'm choking!"

"If that's the way you want to characterize it," he said, tossing his hands helplessly in the air. "My area is pharmacology, not psychiatry."

Frank Promer wasn't urging self-reliance, Duff realized, as he watched him burrow deeper in his chair. He was just laying up. He had gotten a crippled golfer through Q-School and onto the PGA Tour. If he couldn't win—well, there's only so much a medical genius can do.

"So I'm on my own," Duff said.

"I'll always be here to help you with your medical problem," Frank assured him.

"Always . . ." Duff repeated, as he thought of the endless nightmares and sickness that awaited him. What was the point if it only led each week to a Sunday crackup? "Tell me, Frank, what do you think would happen if I tried playing without them?"

"You'd crash and burn."

"You're sure?"

"Positive. If you want to win, you'll have to continue treatment for as long as you play. Which reminds me, you'll need a new prescription," he said, sliding his pad across the desk.

Duff waited while he wrote the prescription, then inquired casually, "Have you seen Gena lately?"

"I saw her last night at Monte's."

"How is she?"

"Fine," he said, handing the prescription to Duff. "You haven't seen her?"

"Not yet. Did she seem—upset or anything?"

The doctor shook his head. "Should she be?"

"It's just that I haven't made a lot of money for her, you know . . ."

"I'm sure that doesn't bother her," he said, getting to his feet. "And you're doing a lot better than your friend Witherspoon."

"Yeah, Forbes is going through a rough patch," Duff said. "He's even thinking of quitting golf."

"No!"

"Going into the family insurance business."

"Umm—that's too bad," Frank said, throwing an arm over Duff's shoulder as he walked him to the door. "If there's anything I can do, be sure to tell him I'd be glad to see him."

"Sure."

"Or anybody else!" he called as Duff closed the door.

Shortly before Christmas, Gena called in the middle of the night from Monte's house in East Hampton and said she had to see him right away.

"Why didn't you answer my calls?" he asked, fumbling for the bedside lamp.

"I told you, Monte's watching me."

"Where is he now?" She was high on something and possibly reckless.

"In St. Bart's with his mother. Get dressed and come on over. You know where it is?"

"Yeah, I know where it is. I'll be there in half an hour."

"Make it sooner," she said, and hung up.

What kind of guy takes his mother to St. Bart's? Duff wondered, as he drove his rented car to Monte's house on the beach. Although he'd never been there before, Duff and most of the locals knew the house quite well—a flat glass box perched on a dune between two classic, shingled cottages, like a lottery winner flanked by his bankers. All the oceanfront houses were dark—their owners off to one of their other houses in Aspen or Palm Beach or someplace—except for Monte's glass box that glowed like a Japanese lantern.

Gena opened the door as he stepped out of the car, then kissed him hungrily as he stepped inside. She wore jeans and a sweatshirt and smelled of alcohol and perfume and her hair was combed carelessly.

"Merry Christmas, let me look at you," she said, releasing him and backing away. "You look terrific."

"Thanks, you—"

"I know, I'm a mess. Come in, come in," she said, pulling him along.

"Why all the lights?" he asked, looking about the vast living room. It resembled a museum, with several abstract paintings on the smooth white walls and a minimum of furniture.

"To guide you by. I can turn them off if you like," she said. She skipped across the floor to the panel and plunged the house into darkness.

The only light remaining was the moonlight on the ocean poking through the tinted glass overlooking the beach, giving everything, the breakers and the sand and the very air in the house, a smoky gray color. He walked across the enormous room and stared at the roiling sea, then watched Gena's reflection in the glass as she slipped up behind him and wrapped her arms around his waist.

"Is that better?"

"Very romantic."

"I've missed you."

"Then why didn't you call me?"

"I called tonight didn't I?"

"Gena, are you in trouble?"

She tightened her arms around him and he felt her warm breath on his neck. "No, I'm not in trouble, and that's not why I called you here. Look at that ocean."

"Beautiful."

"That's a five-million-dollar view," she said. "In Montauk you can see the same thing from a trailer park, but it's not the same." She bit him lightly on the ear, then released him and danced across the room and switched a lamp on. "Come on, I'll show you what a five-million-dollar house looks like."

She took his arm and led him into the dining area, dominated by a long table and 22 chairs. She struck a spokeswoman pose and recited, "The popular restaurateur is fond of intimate dinner parties." Next came the African safari bedroom with its canopied bed and a marble bath, separated only by walls of living bamboo. Next to that was a large gym, sauna and tanning room.

"I'm surprised at how little five million dollars gets you anymore," he said.

"Looks like shit, doesn't it? Monte chooses architects like racehorses. How about a Christmas drink?"

"Sure."

She steered him to the long low couch where several empty wine bottles lay scattered on the floor in front of the cold fireplace. An ice bucket with an open bottle lay on the cocktail table beside a bowl of white powder. "Want to do a line first?"

Duff shook his head. "Frank says I can't mix drugs with my pills." He hadn't taken any pills since his last tournament, but he didn't want to get started again with cocaine.

"You're still taking those things?" she asked, dipping a small silver spoon into the bowl.

"I'd like to try playing without them, but Frank says I'll have to stay on them as long as I want to play golf."

She brought the coke to one nostril and snorted it, followed by a satisfied sigh. "I thought he told me you'd be able to stop taking them pretty soon."

"He said that?!"

"Didn't he?" She dipped the spoon again and repeated the procedure, this time in the other nostril. "Aahh . . ." she sighed pleasurably. "I don't know, maybe I just imagined it." She filled two glasses with champagne, handed one to Duff and raised hers. "Merry Christmas!"

"Merry Christmas."

"And may you have a great year on Tour," she added.

"Thanks," he said, as they lifted their glasses and drank. "That reminds me, I have a check for you."

"I didn't invite you here for that."

"Business is business. I would've mailed it but I expected to see you before this." He pulled the check from his pocket and pushed it into her hand.

"Thank you." She leaned forward to put the check on the coffee table without looking at it, then kissed him lightly on the lips. "I sure as hell did better with you than Monte did with his fucking race horses." She laughed.

Duff picked an empty bottle from off the floor and placed it on the cocktail table. "Did you drink all these by yourself?"

"Hell, I've been here all day."

"So why'd you wait until the middle of the night to call me? Who are you afraid of?"

"I'm not afraid of anybody."

"Then why can't I call at your apartment anymore?"

"I told you, Monte listens to my messages."

"So what? He knows about our business, he knows I have to call you."

"Monte's changed. He's paranoid, he's doing a lot of coke," she said, dipping her spoon again into the bowl. "He's unpredictable."

Duff watched as she sniffed it up one nostril, then another. "You're doing rather a lot yourself, aren't you?"

She shuddered with pleasure and replied, "This is a special occasion—first time in weeks."

"Just a way to celebrate the birth of Christ . . ."

"Hey, when did you get religion?"

"Maybe it's time you did," he said.

"What's that supposed to mean?"

"You heard about Leo?"

"Leo Hover?"

"Yeah, Leo Hover."

"What about him?"

"He and Nick Spoto got busted."

"No!"

"Yes."

"Poor Leo," she said.

"It might be bad for a lot of other people, too," Duff said. "You know how it is with Leo—he screws up but somebody else ends up taking the rap. Leo's going to have to give up a lot of his friends to get out of this one."

"They'd still have to prove something," she said, reaching for the champagne bottle. "It's not enough just to name somebody."

"But if he were to name somebody, would it be you?"

"Yeah, right. Why would I be involved with Leo?"

"You were involved with him once," Duff reminded her.

"That was high school shit; this is now. It's too bad about Leo, I liked him. But believe me, darling, he's got nothing to do with me."

"Your mother thinks you were involved with him."

"You talked to my mother?"

"My father did—he ran into her someplace."

Gena took a drink and replaced her glass on the cocktail table. "She's a worrier, that's all. My mother knows nothing about my business."

"She knows you have a lot of money and she knows Monte has something to do with it. She also knows you're sponsoring me."

"There's nothing wrong with that."

"The feds might not think so. They might call it money laundering."

"Bullshit."

"It's not bullshit, Gena. Not anymore. It's time you got out."

"I know, I'm working on it."

"Working on what? What are you doing?"

"I can't tell you," she said, pressing a finger to his lips. "You'll only worry and it'll fuck up your golf swing." When he tried to speak she pressed down on his lips. "I promise you, everything is going to be fine." She removed

her finger and kissed him full on the mouth, then got to
her feet and pulled him up after her.

He followed uncertainly as she led him through the
living and dining rooms, into the white hunter's jungle
bedroom. She removed his shirt and tossed it over a chair,
then sat on the edge of the bed and unbuckled his belt.
Through the side window he saw a car standing in the
driveway across the road, its grill reflecting in the moonlight like silver teeth. He didn't remember seeing another
car in the neighborhood when he arrived only a short
while before, but perhaps a short while ago he wasn't so
vigilant.

"All this talk has frightened you," she observed. "But
don't worry, I can fix that," she said, pulling him down
beside her.

She was able to fix it, but it took longer than usual.

4

When Duff arrived in Hawaii shortly after the start of the new year, he was amazed to run into Forbes in the lobby of the Kapalua Resort.

"I thought you were getting married and going into the insurance business!" Duff said, happily shaking one hand while scanning the other for a wedding ring.

"I was going to—until this happened," Forbes said, holding up a book.

Duff peered at the dog-eared book that Forbes held aloft like the Ten Commandments and read: *"The Spiritual Side of Golf* by the Mahatma Maharishi. You're kidding me," he said, sad and incredulous.

"No, my friend, I am not kidding," Forbes replied gravely. "I have been there, I have met him and I am the living proof. It works. The Mahatma Maharishi got me through Q-School!"

"Congratulations!" Duff exclaimed. "I didn't know."

"Of course you didn't. You're a PGA regular now, and regulars aren't concerned with the Q-School."

That was true, he was now a regular, Duff realized as he apologized for the oversight. He hadn't thought about the Q-School since the last time he'd seen Forbes, when he'd advised him to go back and give it one more try rather than marry Priscilla Donne. Well, he'd done it! And if Duff had the Mahatma Marsharini or whatever he was called to thank for it, then so be it. Praised be the Marsharini!

Suddenly he had a sobering thought: What if Forbes still planned to marry Pris? He had to know, yet he couldn't be too obvious. Just let Forbes run down, then sooner or later he'd tell him. But he wasn't about to run down. He was describing his miraculous finish at the Q-School, shot by shot, and he was still on the front nine.

"Listen, Forbes—I want to hear all about it, but first I have to go up to my room and take a shower and—"

"I'll come with you. I gotta tell you about the Maharishi. He's fucking incredible. You should go see him, Duff. I guarantee it, you go and see the Maharishi and you'll be able to throw away those drugs."

"Medicine," Duff said, as Forbes steered him across the lobby.

Duff listened while Forbes followed him up to his room. He listened while taking a shower and he listened while getting dressed. He listened to him at the reception in the Tiki Room, and while having dinner in the Lanai Room. He listened while Forbes read some of the more inspirational passages aloud, most of which sounded to him like Hallmark cards. In fact the Maharishi's teachings seemed to be nothing more than a collection of mystical metaphors that applied as much to fly fishing or plumbing as to golf, although Duff was careful not to say so. There were many superstitions on the Tour, all of them sacred for as long as they worked.

The next morning, however, when he saw Forbes coming at him on the practice tee, clutching his sacred book in both hands, like a crazed missionary come to convert the heathen, he cried, "Enough! All I want to know is, are you going to marry Pris?"

"Pris?" he repeated, as if hearing the name for the first time. "What's Pris got to do with the Maharishi?"

"What do I have to do with him?" Duff replied. "If he works for you, that's fine. But I prefer Western medicine to Eastern religion, so please, lay off."

Forbes regarded his friend with a stunned and wounded expression. "The Maharishi is more than Eastern religion, Duff," he said sadly. "He understands the golf swing. He's even got a driving range on his ashram."

"Only a range? Not a whole course? And a dozen Rolls Royces? What kind of a swami is that?"

"Okay, Duff, if that's the way you feel. If you want to make fun of the Maharishi, I won't stop you. But you just watch how I play this week and see what a change the Maharishi has had on my game. Then," he said, tapping his book, "then you'll know what the Maharishi can do for you."

"I'll watch," he promised.

Satisfied, Forbes moved off, looking perhaps for a more likely convert.

Duff watched Forbes through the first two rounds which, true to his prediction, he played very well over a windy par-73 golf course, but he wasn't around to watch the finish. Duff missed the cut by one stroke—due to the effects of jet lag on his medication, he was sure—and left early for the next stop at Waialae, where he again missed the cut, this time the result of plain bad luck, the kind of thing that happens to every player once in a while. There was nothing to do but forget about it and move on to the next tournament.

He played a little better at the Bob Hope in Palm Springs, making the cut but finishing near the bottom of the field.

"I'm just a little slow getting started," he told Gena

when she phoned him at his hotel. Their new plan called
for him to leave his number with his father when he
checked into his hotel, and Gena would phone his father
for the number. She was still FedExing his money to the
PGA trailers as before, but the amount had lessened considerably. Making small purses, he didn't need as much
as he had, which was just as well as he sensed she no
longer had as much as she once had. When he offered to
end the arrangement—for as much as he still needed the
money, he had become increasingly nervous about taking
it—she had adamantly refused.

"This is my stash. You're not forcing me out on the
streets," she had joked. At the moment he wasn't terribly
sorry that she had insisted on sticking to the deal, as he'd
spent a lot and made nothing on the Hawaii swing. California would be better to him, he predicted.

"I'm sure it will," she said.

"How are you doing?"

"I'm doing fine."

"No problems?"

"No problems."

"Heard anything about Leo?"

"There's no reason I should," she answered. "I gotta
go. I'll be looking for you on TV."

"I'll try to be there."

Duff's performance at the Hope didn't merit even a brief
glimpse of television time. Nor did he play much better
at Pebble Beach. He was in a slump unlike anything before. Certainly the medication was a part of it, but for the
first time it wasn't everything. He was simply inconsis-
tent, hitting one or two good shots, followed invariably
by a bad one—like an amateur! Sidney and several players watched him closely on the range, but they saw nothing different in his swing from the year before. Some had
a suggestion, a minor adjustment here or there, like dec-
orators dabbling with a finished room, and Duff tried them

all. But nothing worked. The ability remained intact, his swing was sound, yet the strokes mounted like debts, driving him closer and closer to bankruptcy.

Forbes Witherspoon, in the meantime, whether the result of the Maharishi's magic or simply because of one of those inexplicable hot streaks that happens to all golfers at some time in their life, continued to play better than he had for some time. Even though he hadn't finished in the top 10 in any of the Western tournaments—or even in the top 20—he had made every cut except for the last one at Pebble Beach. But that had been his fault, not the Maharishi's.

"I lost my errant," he seemed to say to Duff, after they'd both shot themselves out of the tournament. "I'll have to talk to the Maharishi about that," he said, fishing his cell phone from out of his locker.

"Can't you just slip into an altered state of consciousness?" Duff goaded. Forbes had only had one bad round, his had all been bad.

But Forbes would not be goaded. "Why don't you let me make an appointment for you?" he asked in a kindly voice.

"I need a golf lesson, not a religious teacher," Duff grumbled, as he pulled his damp shirt over his head.

"He's a golf instructor too," Forbes said. "He started out as a caddie at the Bombay Country Club when he was just a kid. As he said to me, 'I was a veddy good stick,' " Forbes imitated in an Indian tenor voice. "And I can believe it; he's got a good swing."

"So how does a Bombay caddie end up a swami on an ashram in California?"

"That's a good question," Forbes replied thoughtfully. "He told me that years later, while he was studying religion and philosophy at some university, he experienced an epiphany."

"Epiphany?"

"Yeah. Like when St. Paul fell off the horse? He said he suddenly saw the connection between the noble eight-

fold path to Nirvana and a round of golf. And that's when
he wrote this book," Forbes said, taking it from the locker
and handing it reverently to Duff.

Something in the ceremonial presentation caused Duff
to take the book in his hands for the first time. Forbes
watched, smiling warmly as perhaps his first disciple
turned back the brown-edged pages. "To win is to lose;
to lose is to win . . ." he began.

"But to strive is to strive," Forbes finished.

"Heavy," Duff said, closing the book and handing it
back.

"It all becomes clear once you've finished the course,"
Forbes said, returning the book to his locker, like a priest
replacing the monstrance. "See the Maharishi and see Nirvana!"

Duff stepped out of his shorts, wrapped a towel around
his waist and started to the showers.

"What've you got to lose?" Forbes called after him.

That was yesterday. Now, approaching the ramp to the
Golden Gate Bridge, Duff began wondering what he could
have been thinking. He who believed in nothing he
couldn't see, was on his way to see an Indian fakir who
believed golf to be a religious experience, and had built
his church on a driving range!

And it wasn't St. Patrick's Cathedral, Duff saw, when
he finally arrived at the Maharishi's headquarters at the
end of a gravel road near Tomales Bay. The driving range
was a hardpan field surrounded by a motley collection of
Quonset huts, one of which served as pro shop, veggie
snack bar and ashram. There were several dilapidated cars
and trucks in the dusty parking lot, along with several
expensive sedans. Duff parked next to a Mercedes and
stared incredulously at the strange sight. A group of ten
or twelve men and women in flowing robes were slashing
away at golf balls under the watchful eye of a bearded,
cinnamon-skinned man in saffron robes and jeweled tur-

ban. Seeing Duff, he smiled, touched his fingers together and bowed to his new disciple.

I must be out of my fucking mind, Duff said to himself, as he nevertheless climbed out of the car.

"Ah, Mr. Colhane, the golf professional!" the Maharishi greeted in a paper voice that closely resembled Forbes's imitation. "We are most pleased and honored by your visit."

Duff returned each greeting awkwardly as the Maharishi introduced each of his acolytes by their adopted names, Prairie Grass, Primrose, Sea Glass and other names that sounded like paint samples.

"Perhaps, Mr. Colhane, you might demonstrate to we untouchables how a master does it?" the Maharishi invited, offering the pro his Hogan driver.

"Actually I'm here because I'm not hitting the ball all that well," Duff said, accepting the club.

A barefoot young woman in a long white robe placed a ball on the rubber tee, stepped back and smiled invitingly. Duff stepped up onto the frayed mat and took a few practice swings, then lofted a soft fade down the range that evoked an undeserved chorus of adulatory utterances from the Maharishi's students.

"That was veddy good, Mr. Colhane, veddy veddy good!" exclaimed the pleased instructor.

At the urging of the Maharishi and his awed followers, Duff hit several more, each a little longer than the last as his travel-stiffened muscles warmed and loosened up, but none of them very accurate. The balls were old and the club much too whippy.

"I think you are as long as Mr. Witherspoon, yes?" the Maharishi observed.

"Yes," Duff said, then grunt-hit a very long one for proof.

Each successive grunt elicited an onomatopoeic chorus from the onlookers, suggesting a primordial liturgical chant—uh-ooh! uh-ooh! When the Maharishi decided that his students had seen enough, he sent them off, leaving the two of them alone on the practice range.

"You have read my book?" he asked abruptly.

"I didn't have to, Forbes read it to me."

"You do not have your own copy?" he asked, crest-fallen.

When Duff said he didn't, the Maharishi called to an assistant in the pro shop to bring him one.

"I will be most pleased to inscribe your book when we have finished the lesson," he said, bowing and handing it to Duff. "Now please, tell me about yourself, why you have come."

Why indeed. Because I was desperate and willing to buy into anything, so I let Forbes talk me into this nutty trip. "I guess I'm here because of my medical problem. Although Forbes thinks it's psychological or something, and because you were able to help him . . ." he trailed off, finishing with a shrug.

"Ah yes, Mr. Witherspoon is a singular success story. He is playing veddy good now, yes?"

"He's playing with a lot of confidence," Duff acknowledged.

The Maharishi smiled and bowed humbly. "I merely gave him permission to esteem himself. Only then can one be *arahant*."

"Arahant?" It sounded familiar.

"It means worthy. But tell me of your medical problem, Mr. Colhane."

"Duff. It's my hand," he began, exhibiting the scars.

The Maharishi listened sympathetically as Duff described the broken bones and surgical scars that impeded the nerves and sometimes caused him to jerk the ball uncontrollably. He told him about the pills he took, one to calm the nerves, another to pump the heart.

"Body and spirit are one," the Maharishi cautioned. "The nerve paths can be opened or closed by the force of the will alone. Master the will," he said, tapping his head, "and you will master your fate."

"I'm afraid my surgeons overlooked that," Duff replied.

The Maharishi smiled tolerantly at this sarcasm and replied, "Science is but another level of apprenhension of truth." He then removed the clear stone from his turban and, holding it in both hands, extended it to his doubting student. "Take this crystal. Hold it in your injured hand."

Feeling foolish, Duff obediently closed his right hand over the pear-shaped crystal. It was the size and weight of a good throwing stone.

"You will feel the stone growing warmer as the heat passes from your hand into the stone. Can you feel it, Mr. Colhane?"

"It's getting hot."

"You must not say so if it is not so."

"It's warm."

"Veddy well. Now picture a vast network of dark tunnels filled with thousands of tiny blind mice, all of them struggling to find their way out and into the light. Can you see this, Mr. Colhane?"

"Quite clearly, Mr. Maharishi."

"Just Maharishi. They are no bigger than germs. Do you see them, Mr. Colhane?"

"Clearly."

"Excellent, excellent. These little blind mice are your nerves, Mr. Colhane, trying to find their way through the dark nerve passages of your hand. But they cannot see and hence they run up many blind alleys. Much too many blind alleys. Hence they require light to guide them on their path. And where will they find such light?"

"Just a minute, Maharishi. . . . I thought these mice were blind."

"Blind, yes."

"Then what good is the light?"

The Maharishi shook his head impatiently. "This is a trifle, Mr. Colhane. You must not let a small trifle stand in the way of a larger truth. From where is the light coming?"

"From the crystal in my hand?"

"Veddy good. Now imagine the warm light penetrating

your hand, illuminating the path for your lost nerves. Do you see it? Do you see the nerves moving freely through the lighted tunnel and out into the light of day? Concentrate, Mr. Colhane. Concentration and meditation are indispensable to enlightenment."

"Tell me, Maharishi, is this the same advice you gave Forbes?"

"There are many paths to nirvana, Mr. Colhane."

"I'm sure. But I'm only interested in getting to the last hole in fewer strokes than everybody else."

"And is that not nirvana?" the holy man asked, with the conspiratorial grin of a fellow golfer. "Can you describe your feelings when you played the greatest round of golf in your life?"

"I was ecstatic, I could do no wrong."

"As if someone else were in control?"

"Exactly."

"But you are a skeptic, I think, Mr. Colhane. You do not believe in a force outside yourself, yes?"

"It's just semantics—golfers call it playing over their head."

"Buddhists call it a beatific state, a state of supreme enlightenment and blissful detachment. But unlike you, Mr. Colhane, they believe it to be a state that can be achieved and maintained through the powers of the mind, by concentration and meditation. If a Buddhist plays a round of golf like the great Ben Hogan, he knows that he has played to his potential and that he is capable of doing it again and again. Your friend Mr. Witherspoon knows this, and that is why he is playing—over his head. When you know this, you too will play over your head."

"Is this like the power of positive thinking?" Duff asked. He could have gotten that from one of the sports psychologists hanging around the fitness trailer.

The Maharishi shook his head wearily. "You speak of selfish desire, I speak of detachment."

"Detachment being unselfish desire?"

"It is neither selfish nor unselfish, but it is surely more

unselfish than selfish. It is a state of its own, it is the state of *arahant*."

"Worthy."

"Exactly."

"And how do I become worthy?"

The Maharishi smiled and opened his hands in voluptuous revelation. "By freeing yourself of the desire to win."

"Because it's selfish. . . ."

"And therefore unworthy."

Duff stared blankly. Until now he'd thought the Maharishi just another sports psychologist in a nightgown, but he was wrong. The Maharishi was a loose cannon on the deck of Western ideas.

"So to win, I have to want to lose. . . ." Duff tested.

The Maharishi smiled as if he'd finally gotten it, but shook his head. "Nirvana is a state to be wished for, but it can only be achieved if the motive is pure."

"So if I achieve nirvana I'll play better golf. But if that's my purpose I won't achieve nirvana?"

This time the Maharishi didn't shake his head when he smiled. "I think you might be ready, Mr. Colhane."

"Ready for what?"

"Come."

The Maharishi took his acolyte by the elbow and steered him to the Quonset hut. Inside, the floor was nearly covered with stacks of his book, and the walls and racks were filled with sets of golf clubs, all of them marked SALE.

"Where are we going?" Duff asked, treading carefully between the books and golf racks.

"I have a film I would like you to see."

He led Duff through the pro shop and into a dark room filled with folding chairs. He sat him in a chair in front of a movie screen and left the room, promising to return at the conclusion of the film. A few minutes later, a movie flashed on the screen. It was *Follow the Sun: The Ben Hogan Story,* starring Glenn Ford.

• • •

Duff grew steadily angrier as he drove back to San Francisco, not with the Maharishi but with himself. It was insane to have stayed through the end of that movie, but he had never seen it before and had gotten caught up in it rather quickly. He had enjoyed it but he had no idea what the hell it had to do with nirvana. Nor did it matter. The Maharishi was just another con man. And not only had it cost him a thousand dollars to find out, the sonofabitch had charged him $24.95 for the autographed book.

After his session with the Maharishi, Duff was determined to devote himself even more wholly to the promise of Western medicine. He bought a notebook the size and shape of a yardage book, where he noted the time and dosage of each pill taken, then periodically monitored his pulse during the course of a round and entered it in the book, all in search of the ideal balance of neuromuscular function. It might've looked a bit odd when he occasionally stepped off to the side of the green and stood for a couple of minutes of silent meditation while gripping his wrist, followed each time by a mysterious notation in his yardage book. However, in a profession whose members believe that bracelets hold a magical power to harmonize the body's bio-energy frequency and balance the yin-yang ions, superstitious tics aren't all that unusual. And after he made the cut at La Jolla and finished in the top 30, a few of his fellow professionals became more than a little interested in his strange bahavior.

"I don't understand it," Forbes complained, after failing to make the cut for the second time in two weeks. "I still have faith in the Maharishi, and suddenly I'm playing like a dog. You come back thinking he's a fraud, and you shoot a pair of sixty-eights."

"Believe me, the Maharishi had nothing to do with it," Duff said, examining his shoes. According to the contract

Boris had negotiated for him, he was presently entitled to another pair, but until today he'd been loath to ask. When he calls I'll tell him to get me another pair, Duff decided. He hadn't heard from his agent in weeks—he never called when his client was playing badly—but Duff was sure he'd hear from him after today's round.

"You wouldn't kid a kidder, would you?" Forbes asked.

"What do you mean?"

"I mean your partners told me about the wrist-squeezing and head-bowing thing you were doing out there today. What's that, some kind of mantra?"

"Oh, that. Actually, it's a spiritual exercise for summoning energy," Duff came up with after a moment.

"Really?"

"Really."

"How does it work?"

"Hey, you saw what I shot."

"No, I mean how do you do it?"

"Well, you bow your head and close your eyes tightly and grip your wrist as hard as you can for a couple of minutes every few holes."

Forbes clenched his eyes, bowed low and clamped a viselike hand around his wrist. "Like this?"

"You feel the energy beginning to surge through your body?"

"I don't know. I feel something."

"A little tighter," Duff said, turning and walking away.

"Yeah, I feel it!" Forbes called, as Duff started upstairs. "Duff? Duff, where are you?"

A lot of players scoffed when Forbes divulged Duff's secret to them. After suffering through his praise of the Maharishi over the past several weeks, only to witness his angry denunciation of the man when his game suddenly soured, Forbes's reputation as a golf seer had become badly sullied. However after Duff finished tenth at the Nissan, closing with a torrid 65 on the final day, more than a few players could be observed at the next tournament, stopping occasionally to pinch their eyes closed and squeeze one wrist until the hand turned blue. Although Forbes clenched and squeezed as hard as any of them, his game continued to spiral downward at a frightening pace.

"I can't figure it out. I must be doing something, but I don't know what. I can't see it," went the familiar lament, as he hit ball after ball into the gathering dusk at Tucson.

Duff, who'd shot 64 that day and was on the leader board, watched critically as Forbes swung with the rhythm of a metronome, knocking shot after shot onto a small green 200 yards away.

"I've never seen you hit it any better," Duff said.

"But why can't I take it to the course!" he exclaimed, slamming his 5-iron into the turf.

"It's all in your mind," Duff said.

That was what everybody said. But what did that really mean? Forbes began to wonder while standing under a hot shower a short while later. That he made mental errors, bad choices? Was it a lack of concentration, psychological weakness, failure under pressure? Or was it possible that these vague psychological and neurological explanations were only a secular evasion of a greater spiritual question? Could it be that God didn't want him to win?

For Forbes, never more than a Christmas Episcopalian among serious Southern Baptists, it was the first time in his life he'd ever thought seriously that God might require something of him, rather than the other way around. Being rich, talented and good-looking, Forbes had never had much need for God's help and, having drawn very little on his account, he'd always assumed he owed God nothing. The thought that he might have been wrong all these years struck him like the proverbial bolt of lightning.

All of my life I've wanted only one thing—to be a great golfer. I've never once given any thought to the effect my selfish desire has had on my parents, my sister, poor Priscilla. I've always assumed that everybody was there for me, but it never occurred to me that I might owe *them* something. I'm not a truly bad person, I wouldn't kill to get what I want—except maybe for the Masters. But what about all the nonfatal wounds I've delivered along the way—the long absences from home, my refusal to take my place at the head of the family business, the way I use women and then discard them . . .

"Is it any wonder that God has forsaken me!" he cried aloud in the shower.

January and February is golf's silly season. For the fan watching on television while the snow swirls outside his window, it's a wrenching anachronism that engenders nostalgia and self-pity; while for most of the players strolling the balmy fairways, they'd rather be at home watching the playoffs and the Superbowl. For them it's funny hats and cigars with the movie crowd at the Hope and Pebble Beach, while for the wives (with whom the Western swing is quite popular) it's the spa at La Costa and the beach at Hawaii. It's spring training. Many of the stars show up late or not at all, while for those who do it's an opportunity to sneak off with a win or a large chunk of cash while the stars are home watching football. But when the Tour returns to Florida in March for the Doral, the Honda and Bay Hill—warm-up events for the Players and the Masters—then the long knives come out.

Duff still hadn't won a tournament after the Western swing, but he'd had a top 10 and made a couple of good checks, and was beginning to smell victory amidst the orange blossoms. Frank Promer had been right after all; it wasn't the medicine, it was up to the patient. And the patient had finally mastered his medicine. He was more in control of himself and his game than he had been at any time since the accident, and it showed in his scores. That 64 at Tucson had finally proved to him that he could go low. He wasn't just another competent golfer, always around par, sometimes a little under but never much. He was able to mount a charge at any time, to thrill the crowd and unnerve his opponents with unnatural feats and majestic shots. Not just able to withstand the pressure, he thrived on it. He was a steamroller requiring nothing more than a full head of steam to send him rolling down the fairway, crushing everything and everyone in sight.

"God bless Dr. Promer!" he said aloud, while showering at the Doral.

When Duff arrived at the course early the next morning, he saw Forbes waiting on the practice tee. It was the first time he'd seen him in a couple of weeks, as he'd missed the last two tournaments, and he knew he'd need some cheering up. As he pushed through the crowd and stepped over the yellow rope, he saw that Forbes was standing with his head bowed and his hands joined.

"Hey, Forbes, don't you know I was only kidding?" he said, as he walked toward him.

Forbes took his time before lifting his head. "Pardon me?"

"That spiritual exercise shit," he explained, clutching his wrist. "It was only a joke."

"Oh, I know," Forbes said. "To you most things are a joke, aren't they?"

"Some things anyway," Duff replied with a shrug. "Not all things."

Forbes's stare was unsettling. "I'd like to know what isn't."

Duff laughed shortly, like a boiler releasing steam. "Isn't it a little early for this?"

"The Maharishi is a joke."

"I'd agree with you there."

"There's only one true way."

"What way is that?" Duff asked.

"The way of Christ."

Duff laughed nervously and replied, "I didn't know He played."

"I don't find sacrilege funny," Forbes said.

"Holy shit," Duff breathed. "The pod people got you."

"Pardon me?"

"You've joined the Bible-thumpers."

"I've joined the Bible study group, if that's what you mean."

"Oh, man," Duff lamented, shaking his head. "First the Maharishi, now the Born-Agains? Are you nuts? I know you're depressed, nobody likes to lose. But Forbes, this is not the answer."

Forbes smiled indulgently and replied, "Christ is not the answer?"

"Not to this question, no. I've got nothing against religion, but if that's all it took, the Pope would be out here whipping everybody's ass, and he isn't. Because golf is a secular game, a manual game, not a fucking spiritual exercise. Didn't you at least learn that from the Maharishi?"

"The Maharishi is not Jesus," Forbes said.

"Right, Jesus is Lord. And being the Lord, don't you think he just might have more important things to do than fix a fucking golf tournament? Because that's all these self-righteous Bible-thumpers are praying for. They're just a bunch of guys getting together to ask God to let them beat the shit out of everybody else in their prayer group so they can get all the money. They call themselves Christians but they're really nothing but a bunch of selfish, sonsabitches!"

"That's not fair!" Forbes charged. "I have dedicated my work to Christ and pray that my offering be worthy of Him. The money means nothing to me."

"I don't believe that."

"Are you calling me a liar?" Forbes challenged.

"You're lying to yourself, Forbes. I thought you were smarter than those guys."

"So I'm not just a liar, I'm a stupid liar," he said, taking a step forward.

Duff raised his hands in a gesture of peace and stepped back a step. It was only now, when he looked into his friend's empty eyes, that he saw the depths of his despair. He was so eager to dedicate his game to the Prince of Peace that he'd kill anyone who tried to stop him.

"Take it easy," he cautioned, as the words from his religious youth sprang inexplicably to mind. " 'And now abideth faith, hope and charity, but the greatest of these is charity,' " he recited. "The next time the brethren meets, ask them how much of their winnings they give to charity."

"The Tour raises millions for charity."

"Right. Turf research, junior golf . . ."

"Hospitals."

"Private hospitals that don't need the money."

"What are you, a socialist *and* an atheist?"

"Forbes, this is me, remember? The guy you used to go drinking and whoring with?"

"That was then," he shot back.

"You're still the same guy."

"No," he said, shaking his head surely. "No man is beyond redemption, not even you."

"Thank you, Forbes, but I've already been redeemed. I think you're making another mistake, but I wish you luck all the same," he said, turning and starting back to the ropes. Several players in the area had stopped hitting balls and were watching curiously.

"Redeemed with drugs?" Forbes called after him.

Duff stopped. His first thought was the source of his money, then he realized what Forbes was referring to.

"The drugs you refer to have been prescribed by my doctor," he replied pointedly but calmly, aware of the probing stares of his fellow professionals.

"To calm your nerves? Nerves that were damaged when you got caught playing in a golf tournament under a false name? I'd say you have more need for redemption than you think."

"Now who's being unfair?" Duff asked, walking slowly

back. "I tried to explain, but you didn't want to hear it."

"And I don't want to hear it now," Forbes replied, before turning his back to him.

Duff stood rooted for a moment, faced with an urge to spin the self-righteous sonofabitch around and make him listen. But there was no talking to a zealot, he realized, and he turned around and walked away.

When he was awakened by the phone in the middle of the night, he knew it could only be Gena, for whom day was night. He fumbled in the dark for the phone and, without asking, said, "Hi, Gena."

"Duff . . ." she said, her voice a drunken muffle.

"Yeah, it's me," he replied after waiting a moment. "You okay?"

"I'm shitfaced."

"I'm sorry."

"Not as sorry as me. I'm so sorry," she whispered, her voice trailing off.

"Why don't you go to bed and call me tomorrow?" he said. "I'm playing well, we should have a lot to talk about."

"No. Can't . . . Can't send you any more money."

Duff switched the bedside lamp on and threw his feet to the floor. "What's happened?" he asked.

"I'm sorry." She was crying softly while trying to speak, choking on her words.

"Never mind the money, just tell me what's going on," he urged.

"Forgive me," she cried, then the phone went dead.

"Shit!" He bounded across the room for his address book, dialed her New York apartment and got her answering machine. "Gena, pick up," he pleaded. "I know you're there, please pick up the phone!" Reluctantly he hung up and started walking around the motel room in tight circles, his injured hand hooked around his neck. He tried telling himself that nothing was wrong, she was just shitfaced, as she'd said, and didn't know what she was saying. But he knew better. Something had happened, and if she wouldn't pick up the phone, he wouldn't know what it was. Then he remembered their only mutual friend who might know. He picked up the phone and punched in the number for the 631 information operator. "Montauk. Leo Hover, H-O-V-E-R."

The phone rang for a long time before Leo picked up. "Hey, man, you know what time it is?" he asked sleepily.

"It's Duff Colhane."

"Duff?"

"I want you to tell me—is Gena in trouble?"

After a pause, Leo asked, "Where are you?"

"In Florida."

"Give me the number, I'll call you back."

"Don't bullshit me, Leo."

"I promise, I'll call you back."

Duff gave him the number, then paced about the room until Leo returned the call on a cell phone just a few minutes later.

"What makes you think I'd know if Gena was in trouble?" Leo asked.

"Gena told me all about it," he bluffed.

"Then you know as much as I do."

"I want to hear it from you."

Leo sighed audibly. "Look, I'm sorry it had to be this way. All I can say is—nothing bad is gonna happen to Gena as long as she tells them what they wanna know."

"You shit, you gave her up!"

"Hey man, that's the way it works. She knew that goin' in. First they grab the little guy, then the little guy trades for a bigger guy and so on and so forth."

"So all she has to do is give up Monte?"

"That'd certainly help. But it's the Colombians they're after."

"But Gena's not involved with the Colombians. All she has to do is give up Monte and she'll be out of it, right?"

"Not exactly," Leo said.

"What do you mean?"

"I don't like to say it, but your girlfriend and Monte were pretty close. She was right there at the table with him and the Colombians when a lot of bad shit went down."

"Bad shit? What are you talking about?"

"I mean she knows some shit it'd be better if she didn't know."

"Like what?"

"Like a murder."

"A drug murder?"

"A federal agent."

"Aw fuck," he groaned. "How do you know this?"

"She let it slip."

"To you?"

"Yeah."

"And you told the feds . . ."

"Hey, I was trading. Gena would've done the same."

She already has, Duff knew. Yet she might still go to jail for withholding murder evidence, and he might go along just for doing her laundry.

"You're amazing, Leo," Duff said wearily. "You walk on hot coals and everybody else gets their feet burned."

"Yeah, I seem to have a gift," Leo agreed. "But Duff, I didn't give them anything about you."

"What could you give them about me?"

"About the money laundering."

"Fuck you, Leo!"

Duff hung up and tried to go back to sleep but he couldn't. In just four hours he had to be on the tee. He was six strokes off the lead after the first day, he'd been thinking Doral might be his first win, and now he had to play three rounds with the DEA on his back.

When he stepped up onto the first tee a little more than four hours later, he glanced nervously among the spectators for likely cops. There were plenty of uniformed state

police around, and a few guys in suits who looked more
like resort employees than federal agents, but none of
those guys with DEA baseball caps you saw on television.
Being within reach of the lead, and known to some of the
crowd as a long hitter, Duff got a warm hand from the
fans as he teed it up. The cheers would soon change to
silent boos, Duff knew, as he reared back and let it fly.
But he heard only cheers as the ball flew more than 300
yards down the middle of the fairway.

"You musta gassed up on them red pills," Sidney commented, as they walked off the tee.

Only then did he realize that with all that had happened,
he'd forgotten to take his medicine.

"Fuck the pills," Duff said.

Sidney smiled. "I got a feelin' we gonna do real good
today."

His caddie proved to be right. Between shots he was
thinking of DEA agents, but when he got over the ball,
he forced himself to think only pleasant thoughts. He en-
visioned his approach shots bouncing on the green and
rolling to within a few feet of the hole, and many times
the ball did just that. He was stunned to find, when he
walked off the 18th green, that he had had the lowest
round so far that day and had climbed onto the first page
of the leader board.

What would I shoot if I was in real trouble? he mused,
as he signed his scorecard.

On Saturday night, after still another inexplicably hot
round of golf that brought him to within three strokes of
the lead, Duff found himself seated with his agent and an
automotive sales manager in the main dining room of the
Doral Resort. Boris was excited, his player was about to
break out, and the car salesman was eager to sign his
client to an endorsement deal before that happened. This
was what Duff had been working for since coming out on
Tour the year before; he should be bursting with dreams

of a rosy future, but he felt as if he were locked in a nightmare. Boris and the car man were excited enough with their own plans that they were able to fairly ignore the golfer after failing to draw him out.

"He's very intense," Boris confided to the car man over the soup course.

"Intensity wins games," said the salesman, who'd played football at Carleton College.

At the end of the meal Boris and the sales manager fought politely over the check until Boris graciously conceded.

"Thank God, that was more than I have in the bank," Boris joked when the salesman went to the men's room. "Hey, cheer up, this guy's gonna make you a rich man."

"I'll need it," Duff replied gloomily.

"Listen, I'm gonna have an after-dinner drink with him and try to do a little business, so if you don't mind . . ."

"That's fine," Duff said, relieved to get away from them.

Duff waited until he got back, and then made his excuses. The salesman gripped his hand tightly, wished him luck the next day and said, "We'll talk."

"Those shoes are coming!" Boris called, as he walked off.

As he wound his way through the tables, a few players who'd scarcely noticed him before nodded or lifted a fork in acknowledgment of his play over the last three days. Strangers smiled at him and called him by name. He was among the tournament leaders, but it did little to lift the gloom. Then a familiar voice called his name, and he looked across the room to see Priscilla seated at a table with Forbes, and a smile crossed his face. She waved him over before Forbes said something to her that caused her smile to fade and her hand to fall slowly.

Fuck him, Duff thought, as he made his way to their table.

"Is it spring break again?" he said, bending over to kiss her cheek.

"Nope, just trolling for golfers," she replied. "Congratulations on your fine round today."

"Thanks," he said, then turned to her silent companion. "Hello, Forbes."

Forbes, who had barely made the cut, replied with a grunt and a cursory nod.

Duff turned to Priscilla and asked, "What are you doing now that you've graduated?"

"I'm working at an ad agency in Boston," she answered.

"Like it?"

"Hate it."

"What do you want to do?"

"Paint."

"Then do it."

"I can't afford it," she said. "But I admire your optimism."

"It's blind faith," he said.

"I don't think that's funny," Forbes growled like a waking bear.

"I didn't mean it that way. . . ."

"The hell you didn't."

"Forbes's new religion discourages humor," Duff explained for Priscilla. "Are you here for the golf match or the prayer meeting, Pris?"

"Prayer meeting?"

"Bible study group," Forbes corrected.

"What are you two talking about?" she asked.

"He joined the Bible-thumpers," Duff answered.

"No!"

"Last month the Buddhists, this month the Christians," Duff said.

"Forbes, is he joking?"

"It's no joke," Forbes replied. "I'd invite him, but he's got more faith in chemistry than God."

"The way you played today, maybe you should think of joining my church."

"Let's see how you do on Sunday, Slingshot."

"Slingshot?" Priscilla repeated.

"He calls me that when he plays badly. Which is quite often, which is why he joined the Bible-thumpers."

"He used to have a big slingshot, until somebody snapped it for him. Ask him to tell you about it some time."

"I offered to tell you about it, but you wouldn't listen."

"I heard all I want to know from Earl Cawthon."

"He doesn't know the whole story."

"You played under false pretenses, what else do I have to know?"

"Gentlemen, please," Priscilla said, raising her hands for silence. "I thought golf was a game of friendly competition."

"Assuming it's played fairly," Forbes answered.

"You think I got on the leader board by cheating?" Duff asked, amused.

"What else would you call playing with performance-enhancing drugs?"

Duff's jaw tightened, exposing a pair of lower incisors that seemed ready to tear out Forbes's throat. "I don't use performance-enhancing drugs, Forbes. Do you understand that?"

"I understand you got some New York doctor to write you a prescription."

"Then you understand everything you need to know. And if you ever so much as imply anything else, you'd better be prepared to prove it."

"Guys, please . . ."

"Are you threatening me?" Forbes said, throwing his wadded napkin on the table.

"If I hit you it'll be with a lawsuit, not this," Duff said, showing a clenched fist. "After all, you'd only turn the other cheek."

"I'll make an exception in your case," Forbes replied, getting to his feet.

"Forbes, sit down!" she said, grabbing his wrist.

Forbes glanced around the room at the horrified onlookers, then allowed Priscilla to pull him back down into his chair. "Get him out of here," he muttered.

"Duff, you'd better go," she said. "Please . . . ?"

Duff turned and walked out of the restaurant under the watchful eyes of most of the players and wives in the room.

It took several moments for him to realize where he was and why his head was throbbing. Then he remembered— the cocktail lounge he'd gone to after the blowup with Forbes, the English girls, then it all became vague . . . He looked at his watch. It was after eight.

"Shit!" he wailed, bolting to a sitting position.

Then he remembered that for the first time in his career he was among the leaders and would be one of the last groups off. There was still time to get straightened out, he reminded himself, as he sank to the pillow and closed his eyes. The thunder continued to roll through his head, punctuated now by flashes of light pecking at his closed eyelids. When he groaned and opened one eye, he discovered that the light was from the morning sun glinting off the Maharishi's crystal which was lying on the night-stand beside him, along with his keys and wallet. He had originally meant to throw the piece of cheap glass away, but had been carrying it in his pocket for some reason ever since. Was it possible that he was no more rational than Forbes, that he secretly believed the stone might contain some magical properties? Absurd. Nevertheless he reached for the stone, felt its cool smoothness in his palm and placed it against his fevered brow. It was no icepack, but it felt good while the coolness lasted. After a minute or so it began to warm—the mice were coursing through his lighted veins, bringing water to his burning brain. It was a soothing image—concentration and meditation are indispensable to enlightenment—one he held for as long as he could.

Until, amazingly, the throbbing in his head disappeared! He got out of bed and stood waiting for the pounding to resume, but nothing happened. He shook his head and waited some more, but still the pain didn't return. The Maharishi's crystal had cured his hangover!

An hour later, dressed to win in freshly pressed linen slacks and a tropical-print golf shirt, Duff emerged from the locker room and walked confidently toward the practice tee where Sidney waited. As he passed the 18th green he saw Priscilla standing among the wives and children, awaiting their high-scoring husbands and fathers who had gone off while the dew was still on the grass. He turned away and speeded up, but he heard her call his name and had to stop. He pretended to look for her—she was hard to miss, standing out as she did against the pale wives in pastels and prints, she in black shorts and T-shirt with a long roll of chestnut hair falling over one shoulder. Finding her, he smiled hesitantly and waved. The wives watched alertly as the woman who had nearly set two men to blows the night before made her way down the slope to the other man. Her greeting was surprisingly cordial.

"I'm sorry if I ruined your evening . . ." he began.

"Ruined? Two men fighting over me in public is scarcely a ruined evening."

"We weren't fighting over you," he gently reminded her.

"I know, but I'm not telling *them* that," she said, with a backward toss of her head. "Besides, who'd believe it if I told them you were fighting over religion?"

"It was more than that."

"I know it was. I had a long talk with Forbes last night," she said, reaching for his hand. She studied the scars with a pained frown. "It must have been horrible."

Duff shrugged. "Unexpected anyway. Someday you must let me tell you my side of the story."

"I intend to." She crooked her head to the leader board and remarked, "You're still holding your position nicely."

Duff pretended to search the leaderboard, saw his name in glowing black letters halfway down the board and replied, "In this wind the scores will be high."

"Is that good or bad for you?"

He traced his jaw with his fingertips as he looked up at the thrashing palms. It was blowing hard and was expected to continue until late in the afternoon, at about the time he'd be making the turn. He'd have a chance to make up some ground on the closing holes, but the leaders playing behind him would stand an even better chance. If he could go low on the windy holes, he was sure he'd move up the ladder. That's where the tournament could be won. Then if he could just get a little hotter than everybody else on the back. . . .

"The wind brings out the best ball strikers," he said.

"And are you one of the best ball strikers?" she asked with a teasing smile.

Duff shrugged and replied, "One of them."

"I rather thought so." Then she peered down the fairway and announced, "Here comes Forbes."

Duff turned and looked. It was obvious from his body language that he was playing badly. "How's he doing?" he nevertheless asked.

"Not well at all, I'm afraid."

"There are always the Muslims."

"Try not to be too hard on him, okay? He's very upset about his father."

"What's wrong with his father?"

"He didn't tell you?" Duff shook his head. "He has prostate cancer."

"Ah, shit! So that's why he suddenly got religion."

She shrugged. "I suppose."

He glanced at his watch and said, "I'd better get to the tee."

"Kiss me before you go," she ordered. "It'll give the girls something to talk about."

He expected a peck on the mouth, but was startled when her lips parted slightly and she pressed tightly against him. Was that for the girls or him? he wondered, as he walked to the practice tee.

When weighed on the scale of natural disasters, the strong gusty wind blowing over the Doral golf course on that Sunday in early March would scarcely tip the scales. It wouldn't cause a tidal wave or blow any houses down or require federal emergency relief, but it was surely going to dash the dreams of a lot of golfers before the day was out.

Duff and his two playing partners were standing on the first tee, trying to gauge the effect of the wind on the most important shot of the round. There were no ominous clouds or pelting rain to see and feel, just a fearsome evanescence from which there was no escape. Like its Creator, it was capable of great kindness or capricious cruelty. Sometimes it blew fair, sometimes ill; it could carry a ball a heavenly distance, or leap up and smack it back in a player's face. The sound and buffeting was incessant, doggedly tearing away at a player's concentration, constantly testing his resolve. It could deprive him of his senses; sight and hearing and feel are altered, leaving him with only a tenuous connection to his surroundings; judgments become blind guesses, distances illusions, the swing unfamiliar.... It becomes a game of shifting allegiances: With the wind at his back, the player can tee it high and let it fly; when it's against, blocking his way like an invisible sentry, he must sneak under its flapping coattails.

To win in the wind today will require uncommon courage, Duff told himself, as he drew his driver from the bag. And unusual luck. He teed the ball high and let it fly more than 300 yards down the fairway.

Over the front nine he managed to play with scarcely a thought beyond the shot at hand. He hadn't completely forgotten about Gena and the trouble that probably awaited them both, but for a time at least, this was the only thing that mattered. The wind that snapped his linen slacks like a loose sail in a squall was no more than a cooling breeze, and the constant roar was but the soothing echo from a seashell pressed to his ear. He calculated wind velocity and direction as carefully as his natural instruments would allow, decided on the shot most suitable, then realistically calculated his chance of bringing it off. Sometimes he went with the risky shot, more often the safe one, and at the turn he was the only player in the group in red numbers. He was playing with uncommon courage and unusual luck.

On the 14th hole, with the wind gusting erratically, he miscalculated and his ball dived into the side of a greenside bunker like a blind pelican. When he got to it and found it all but buried, he worried that his luck had finally run out. When he placed his hands on his thighs and stooped over for a closer look, he felt the vial in his pocket and realized he'd forgotten to take his red pill at the 9th hole. He should be weak by now, especially in this punishing wind, yet he felt stronger and more composed than ever. Then he realized it wasn't the vial of pills he felt—they were in his bag—but the hangover-curing crystal he'd taken along on a whim. He had to be imagining it, but the crystal felt unusually warm between his hand and leg.

He decided on the shot, his only shot—hit down hard and hope—and managed to get the ball on the green. And, after rolling for several more feet, into the hole.

Despite the wind, the roar of the crowd carried back to the last group of the day. David Duval, waiting with his playing partners to hit his tee shot, turned his space-age shades in the direction of the cheers and remarked, "Somebody did something."

"Glad somebody's doing something," Tiger Woods, who had just made a rare double-bogey, grumbled.

As Duff and his group approached the final green, the

crowd erupted once again. He assumed it was for Phil
Mickelson, the marquee player in his group who was
walking a couple of steps ahead of him—until Phil slowed
and pushed him ahead and the cheering grew even louder.

It was incredible! He felt so light he was afraid he
might blow away. Objectively it wasn't difficult to understand—he was going to shoot 68 in near gale conditions and possibly take second place—but just now it was
hardly possible to be rational, let alone objective. He was
coming off the best and most intense round of golf he had
ever played, without taking so much as one pill over the
last nine holes, and the crystal in his right hand felt warm
as a baked potato. There was so much going on for which
he had no explanation—it was if he were watching all
this from someplace else.

"Smile," Phil suggested.

"Easy for you . . ." Duff said, removing his cap and
revealing his underbite as the crowd in the stands rose to
pay their respects to golf's newest hero.

He marked his ball and stood at the edge of the green
while Mickelson studied his lie in the greenside rough.
Duff knew the camera was probably on him and the announcer would be talking about him, and everybody in
Montauk would be watching, and he was afraid to look
up. So instead he put his hand in his pocket and closed it
around the crystal and tried to look like he was used to
all this.

Oh, Mama, you should see me now, he said to himself.

Phil Mickelson had decided on his shot, his trademark
flip wedge against a solid wall of wind. He lashed it high
and hard and it hung on the air like a hawk and he was
already grinning when it started to fall, knowing he had a
tap-in par. He waited until his playing partner had
2-putted, then tapped in for a 71, leaving the green to Duff.

He had a long sidehill putt from left to right, not a sure
2-putt even under ordinary conditions. But knowing he
could 3-putt and probably still hold second place made it
a lot easier. He heard a groan from the crowd and looked

up to see that Woods had lost another stroke, but it didn't matter, he had fallen far down the leader board. Except for David Duval who was 2 under for the day, most of the other players in the field had gone up like kites in today's wind.

"I wouldn't look for him to hit this hard," the player-announcer remarked from the booth while watching Duff line up his putt. "Notice how he keeps rubbing his pocket? What do you suppose that's all about?"

"Don't know," Jim Nance said.

Duff stood, took two practice strokes and addressed the ball. He hit it soft and wide, letting it take the slope and trickle down to within a couple of feet of the hole. But a moment after hitting it, he was nearly knocked off his feet by a sudden gust of wind that got behind the ball and pushed it downhill at an alarming speed. Hit the cup, he prayed, even while knowing it was going too fast to stop.

A collective gasp of disbelief went up from the crowd as the ball slammed against the back of the cup and leaped high in the air, then somehow dived into the hole for a 67. Duff stared in amazement—only a second gust of wind from the opposite direction could have saved that shot—as the gallery, like a trained choir, segued from an incredulous note to an explosive chorus of hosannas!

In the tower the player-announcer was exclaiming excitedly, "I wanna tell ya, I never would've tried to make that putt in a million years, but I guess that's why I'm up here and he's down there! You know, Jim, he could win this thing!"

"I know. We'll be back after a word from our host," Jim Nance said.

"Get that kid up here!" the producer ordered when the mike went cold.

But Duff begged to be excused after signing his card. He told David Feherty that he needed to prepare for a playoff should there be one, even though he doubted that there would be. Although David Duval led by only one stroke with two holes to play, that was a comfortable lead for a player like him. In truth, Duff was sure he would get in front of the camera and freeze. So instead he remained in the scorer's tent to watch on television as Duval finished his last two holes.

The camera caught Duval staring at the leader board on the 17th tee as Duff's name went up just under his, one stroke shy of a tie for first. Duff wondered what he was feeling, knowing he had to par the last two holes to avoid a playoff. Probably not a damned thing. He'd never played with Duval, who usually ran at the head of the pack, or hardly even knew him. He was always friendly when they passed in the locker room, but quiet, not a guy to stop and shoot the shit. In fact now that he thought about it, he couldn't remember David ever calling him by name. And as he watched him, still staring at the board and scratching his whiskered chin, he realized that Duval wasn't contemplating his position—he was trying to remember who the hell D. COLHANE was.

A short while later, after he'd bogeyed the 17th hole to share the lead with D. COLHANE, he was perhaps thinking he'd find out sooner than he would've liked.

Everybody in the tent watched Duff while he watched David Duval plotting his next move on the 18th tee, and the player-announcer did the voice-over.

"I'll tell you, if I was in Duval's shoes right now I'd hit fairway wood, take the water out of play. Maybe you still make birdie, at the worst you make par and go on to the playoff hole."

"Makes sense," Jim Nance said.

But having no television set along, Duval pulled a driver from his bag.

"I'll tell you, I don't like to second guess a player, but I don't understand that play at all," the player-announcer said.

Although he knew the camera would be waiting for him, Duff had to go outside to watch the finish. He wished now that he'd gone to the range to loosen up. The evening wind was chilly and his hand felt stiff. He put his hand in his pocket and wrapped it around the crystal, then looked over at the roped-off area where the players and their wives were all watching him. He saw Priscilla among them and she saw him and waved. Forbes wasn't anywhere to be seen. Duff smiled nervously and waved back as the camera zoomed in for his closeup.

Duff didn't see Duval's drive, but the deafening groan from the crowd left no doubt—his ball had found the water. At that moment he both understood and didn't understand what had happened. He remembered a silver-haired man grasping his hand, followed by a wall of bodies, all wanting something, like a horde of beggars. He remembered Boris pumping his hand, and the salesman from the night before.

"We gotta talk!" Boris cried.

Then he remembered being shepherded across the grass to a table where a gleaming trophy rested on a white linen cloth. He saw the big check with his name already printed on it and he wondered how they could have known. Or had more time passed than he realized? The announcer asked how it felt to win his first PGA tournament and he replied sincerely that he hadn't been expecting it.

"Neither was I," David Duval said, eliciting a laugh from the crowd.

Now he was holding the trophy over his head and the cameras were clicking like snapping teeth. Then a little while later, as Boris was leading him to the locker room, there were suddenly two men in suits standing on either side of him, and he knew the nightmare had begun.

"Don't worry, everything'll be okay!" Boris called as they led him away. "I'll get this cleared up!"

And Duff remembered thinking that he wouldn't. This was no barroom tiff, this was nothing Boris or anybody else could fix.

5

Duff had always assumed that on the morning after winning his first PGA tournament he'd find himself seated at a long table in a fancy office, fielding offers from Cadillac and Titleist and Rolex, but instead he found himself seated at a small wooden table in an outdoor cafe in Little Havana with a drug lawyer. He'd imagined his picture in newspapers and magazines and everywhere he went strangers would come up and congratulate him, but of all the people who'd stopped by Raymond's table to speak to him in Spanish, not one of them recognized the golfer who had won the Doral-Ryder Open the day before.

"Do you ever get the feeling you're not the person everybody thinks you are?"

Duff asked, studying the grounds in the bottom of his demitasse.

"Relax, nobody thinks you're a money launderer," Raymond assured him. "To any federal prosecutor in the country, a couple of thousand dollars a month is simply not worth his time. Those guys were just using it to squeeze whatever other information out of you they could."

"That's not what I mean," Duff said. "I mean I'm finally living my dream, I'm a professional golfer and a gentleman, and yet I have the feeling I'm going to be revealed as a fraud."

The young lawyer laughed, flashing very white teeth against his olive skin. "Yeah, I know that feeling very well. Growing up in Ybor City I never expected to be a lawyer, but here I am, an officer of the court. Only I'm still afraid somebody's gonna find out I conned 'em and they're gonna send me back to the cigar factory."

"With me it's a fishing boat."

"No kidding. I don't know much about that," the lawyer said, gesturing at the men sitting around the scarred wooden tables. "If I see a Cuban coming in on a boat, I know he hasn't been fishing."

"You represent a lot of drug dealers?"

"A few."

"Colombians?"

"Some."

"Let me ask you this. If one of their dealers knew something about a murder, and they got a little worried about that person, what would you advise that person to do?"

"I assume we're talking about your girlfriend." Duff didn't reply. "I'd tell her to disappear."

"What about protective custody?"

"That's an option, but for me it'd be my last resort. They promise you everything—full immunity, round-the-clock surveillance—but they fuck up. Believe me, if she rats out the Colombians they'll probably get her. You tell her that."

"It's too late," Duff answered.

"Why do you say that?"

"Because they asked me about the Colombians and a murder. I told them I didn't know anything about it and I don't. But Gena does, because her good friend Leo told them about it. And she certainly wouldn't have given them my name but withheld something like that, would she?"

"No," Raymond said, shaking his head. "If she expects to stay out of jail, she can't hold anything back."

"So you think the Colombians will kill her?"

"No—I didn't say that!"

"You said the feds will fuck up and the Colombians will probably get her," Duff reminded him.

"I was talking in general terms. These are New York feds. They've had a lot of experience in witness protection."

"So you think she'll be okay?"

"I'm sure of it," the lawyer said.

"Yeah, me too," Duff said.

A short while later Raymond eased his Mercedes to a stop in front of Duff's motel room.

"I think you're clear on this," the lawyer said for the second or third time, as if trying to convince himself. "But if they come after you again, you tell 'em you want your attorney, and you tell 'em nothing else. You got that?"

"Yeah, I got it," Duff said, shaking his hand.

"One more thing . . ." he added, as Duff climbed out of the car.

"Yeah?"

"I'll need your billing address."

"Right." He gave him his agent's address and watched the big silver car disappear around the corner of the building. Is that all? he wondered.

Despite the rumors circulating about his police encounter, Duff amazed himself by finishing near the top again at the Honda Classic in Coral Springs on the following Sunday. Whether it was due to the pills or the crystal, or if he just required added pressure to play his best, he didn't know. He just knew that something within him was work-

ing better than it ever had before, and he felt that he actually stood a good chance to win the Players
Championship at Sawgrass. And that would be a very big
win.

Although the Players lacked the cachet of the British
and U.S Opens and the Masters, the PGA was doing
everything it could to establish it with the players and the
public as a world-class event. And to get the best foreign
players to compete, the winner was granted an exemption
to compete in all PGA tournaments for the next 10 years.
For Duff, the thought that no matter how badly he played
he wouldn't have to go back to Q-School for 10 years if
he could win the Players was all the incentive he needed.

When he arrived at the PGA headquarters in Ponte Vedra,
he was amused to find a message from the Maharishi congratulating him on his first victory and asking for a complimentary quote to be added to his book. In my opinion,
you're a fraud and a . . . Duff began to write on PGA stationery, then crumpled it up and threw it away. He was,
after all, still hanging on to the Maharishi's crystal for
dear life, just like all of his other mantra-mumbling duf-
fers.

The second message, however, was not so amusing. He
was directed to report to the Commissioner's office immediately upon checking in.

"He probably just wants to congratulate you," Boris
assured him over the phone. "I talked to Raymond; everything is cool. If the Commish asks, you weren't arrested,
you were just called in and asked to give some information. Beyond that you can't say anything because the matter is under investigation. You got that?"

"Yeah, I got it," Duff said.

"Good luck."

Duff thanked his agent and hung up. He'd said nothing
about the car deal.

• • •

I have nothing to worry about, Duff assured himself as he sat, surrounded by portraits of the greatest players in the game, waiting for the Commissioner to call him in. He tried to imagine his own picture hanging there with Bobby and Walter and Ben and Jack and Arnold, just to take his mind off the interview. It was a long shot, but who knew he would've gotten this far?

"The Commissioner will see you now," the receptionist informed him, as a pair of PGA officials in blue blazers emerged from the office and walked past him with a wordless nod.

"Thanks," Duff said, as he got up and followed her.

The Commissioner came from around his desk with a practiced smile and an extended hand. He was a trim middle-aged man who favored well-tailored suits to the ubiquitous blazers of his subordinates, and always looked as if he had just come from an expensive barber. Duff, who'd never been alone with him before, found him to be taller than he'd expected, their eyes at the same height.

"Thanks for coming, Duff," he said, indicating a pair of plaid couches flanking a large coffee table, inviting him to choose.

Duff sat on one and the Commissioner took the one opposite. He congratulated Duff on his first victory, using his name a lot, and made some pleasant small talk about its significance. Duff was relieved. Boris had been right, this was no more than the welcome-aboard meeting.

"Unfortunately, I understand your victory was marred by an arrest," he said, getting abruptly to his feet and walking to his desk.

"Arrest? No, sir, I wasn't arrested," Duff replied.

The Commissioner picked up a blue folder from his desk and put on his reading glasses. He glanced at the first page, then looked over the rim at Duff. "You weren't arrested?"

"No, sir. I was asked to come in and give some information, which I did. They told me I was free to go at any time, but I wanted to give them as much help as I could."

"And you stayed all night?"

"Not all night. And I slept most of the time. I was exhausted after the tournament so they found a cot for me and I napped for a few hours."

"Until your lawyer showed up put an end to the questioning."

"I think they were pretty much finished with their questions by then anyway," Duff answered.

"And what was the tenor of these questions—what were they about?"

Duff shrugged helplessly. "I'm sorry, they told me not to say anything to anybody. Part of an ongoing investigation, you know . . ."

"We're well aware of that," he said, turning a page. "We were also paid a visit by the same agent who questioned you. And I have to tell you—they think you know more than you're letting on."

"Really?"

"Really."

"Then they're wrong," Duff replied firmly. "I told them everything I knew."

"Do you know a woman named Gena Hall?" he asked abruptly.

"Yes. She's my sponsor."

"Who sends you large amounts of cash by Federal Express, using the PGA van as your pick-up?"

"It's not a large amount."

"And you in turn have been sending her your personal checks?"

"I give her a percentage of my winnings, just like any other sponsor."

"Did you have a lawyer draw up a contract?"

"We have an oral agreement."

"A bit irregular, isn't it?"

"We're good friends."

"Your girlfriend?"

"No—I mean we're not engaged or anything."

"But you're sleeping with her . . ."

"I don't think that's anybody's business but ours."

"I think you've already involved the PGA far too intimately in your affairs to take that position now, Mr. Colhane. You were taking drug money and we were the dupes."

"I don't know that it's drug money and neither do you," Duff shot back.

"Come on, Mr. Colhane. Where did you think she was getting all that money?"

"From modeling," he answered hollowly. It was the story he had given the feds and he was stuck with it.

"Do you really expect anyone to believe that?"

"They didn't arrest me," he replied.

"There's still time."

"No," Duff said. "My lawyer has assured me that they're finished with me. I told them I don't know anything about drugs, and they believe me."

"You know nothing about drugs?"

"Nothing."

"Never taken them?"

Duff shrugged. "I experimented when I was a kid."

"But not recently. . . ."

"No."

The Commissioner pulled a sheet of paper from his blue folder and placed it on the desk in front of him. "Let me ask you, Mr. Colhane. Did you threaten Forbes Witherspoon with physical violence in the dining room at the Doral Resort?"

"I did not," Duff replied firmly. "I threatened Forbes with legal action, not physical."

"Witnesses say you raised your fist."

"They misunderstood. You can ask—"

"And when you assaulted a fan at the Q-School, was that a misunderstanding too?"

"No, that was self-defense. As the PGA knows."

"This was the first I heard of it," the Commissioner said, rapping the file with his knuckles.

"The PGA sent Boris Stiffel to take care of it. He got a release from the guy and that was the end of it," Duff informed him.

"If Mr. Stiffel took care of anything, it was on your behalf, not ours. And whatever the disposition, I'd say it indicates a certain tendency toward violence which—considered along with Mr. Witherspoon's charges—creates a rather strong presumption that you might very well have threatened to strike him."

"I did not threaten to hit Forbes," Duff said firmly.

"All these witnesses?" the Commissioner cautioned, waving the file.

"The Bible-thumpers."

"The what?"

"Nothing. They were sitting across the room, they don't know what happened. Did Priscilla Donne sign that statement?"

"Who is Priscilla Donne?"

"Forbes's girlfriend. She was sitting at the table. She saw it all. Ask her, she'll tell you what happened."

"Very well," he said, making a note in the file.

He has no intention of calling her, Duff thought, as he watched him leaf through the report. He thinks I'm a drug dealer and Forbes is an upstanding Christian.

"I understand there was also an incident in Las Vegas—some confusion with names . . . ?"

"Las Vegas!" Duff exploded. There was no longer any confusion—Forbes intended to annihilate him any and every way he could. "That happened a long time ago—when I was a teenager."

"You entered a tournament using a false name?"

"My partner did. I didn't know about it until it was too late to pull out."

"When is it too late to pull out of a golf tournament which you've entered under false pretenses?"

"In hindsight, never. But for me at the time it was very

complicated. I was away from home for the first time, my partner was holding my return ticket . . ."

"You seem to have plenty of excuses, Mr. Colhane. But no contrition. You don't regret what you did?"

"Of course I regret it," Duff said, regarding his damaged hand. "That was the dumbest thing I ever did in my life and there isn't a day goes by that I don't regret it."

"Because you cheated, or because you got caught?"

Duff closed his eyes like a child taking medicine and replied, "Because I cheated."

"That's rather glib, isn't it?"

Duff took a deep breath and answered, "I'm sorry if it sounded that way."

"How it sounded is not the point, Mr. Colhane. This isn't about the appearance of wrongdoing, it's about wrongdoing itself. Golf is a game of conscience. The integrity of the PGA is dependent upon the morality of each and every member. What you did in Las Vegas you did a long time ago, before you joined the PGA. If we'd known it then it would've made a difference. But it's too late now, you've gotten away with it. And if we'd known you were taking money from a drug dealer, that would've made a difference. But you say they're not going to prosecute, so you've apparently gotten away with that too. And when you strike a fan and threaten to strike a fellow player—maybe we can even overlook that. But if what I'm told is true," he said, picking up the blue folder and waving it at Duff like a stick, "that you're competing while taking performance-enhancing drugs, that is something the PGA can not and will not overlook."

"Did Forbes tell you that?" Duff demanded, springing off the couch.

"Sit down, Mr. Colhane."

"It's not true!"

"Please sit down!"

Duff sat. He had to put Forbes out of his mind and concentrate on the man who held his future in his hands.

Be calm and rational, he cautioned. Forget Forbes, go to the doctor. Doctors have authority.

"The only drug I'm taking is the medicine prescribed by my doctor in New York—Dr. Frank Promer. You can call him."

"The medicine you call Hogan's ashes?"

"That's a joke."

"A rather tasteless joke, I'd say. This is nerve medication?"

"Not just the nerves, it's for everything," Duff said, displaying his hand. "Bones, muscles, tendons, nerves . . ."

"What exactly is this medicine you're taking?"

"I don't know, a couple of pills. You can ask my doctor."

"You're taking pills and you don't know what they are?"

"He had to try a lot of different things . . . I'm no longer sure. . . ."

"Amazing," the Commissioner said, shaking his head. He closed the blue file and looked across the room at Duff. "We're going to have to have a urine sample."

"Urine!"

"You may refuse, of course. But I can tell you, it won't help your case if I have to report it to the disciplinary committee. And if you're only taking medicine that's been lawfully prescribed by a licensed physician, you have nothing to fear."

"Then I have nothing to fear," Duff said. "When do you want it?"

"Now."

"Now?"

"Until we have the results of the drug test, you won't be allowed to play in any PGA event."

"How long will that be?"

The Commissioner shrugged. "We've never had to do this before. You'll find a jar in the bathroom."

The Commissioner walked across the office and opened

the door to a stark white room where a jar rested on the sink. Duff got up slowly and walked across the room and pulled the door closed after him. It took him a long time to piss.

There was a long silence at the end of the line after Duff finished telling his agent everything that had happened at his meeting with the commissioner.

"Boris . . . ?"

"I'm thinking. You actually played under a false name?"

"That's not the point!" Duff exclaimed. He was being suspended and tested for drugs, and all Boris could focus on was a teenage peccadillo. "He suspended me before he even had the results of the drug test. He can't do that, can he?"

"Maybe not according to the by-laws," Boris answered slowly. "But we have to ask ourselves, would we rather take a voluntary suspension, just until the drug results are in, or demand a full hearing and air all that other dirty linen in front of all the players and everybody else? And my advice is, take the suspension."

"But it might be for weeks," he complained.

"If we fight 'em it could be permanent. What kind of drugs are you taking?"

"Something my doctor prescribed for my hand."

"Beta-blockers?" Duff hesitated. "I can't help you if you don't tell me," Boris prodded.

"Yeah."

"The golfer's drug of choice. But not to worry, the PGA has no rule against drugs. Their attitude is, no PGA player would use 'em so we don't need a rule. Even if some players have used them," he added.

"For medical reasons," Duff supplied. This was the heart of his defense.

"Supposedly. But there was this unknown player who won the Senior Open while he was taking them for a heart problem, and suddenly a lot of players got interested. Mac

O'Grady admitted he used 'em when he beat Tom Watson and got to the semifinals in the Seiko Match Play. He told the Commissioner a lot of players were using them to calm their putting nerves in the ninety-four Masters and the PGA should investigate, but nothing came of it. If they investigate it, they're admitting there might be a problem and they don't want that. And that's why I think your problem will go away if you don't rock the boat."

It both made sense and didn't make sense. Sooner or later it was going to come up again, and the PGA was going to have to deal with it. But as long it didn't involve him, Boris was right, Duff supposed. He would not rock the boat.

"But just to be on the safe side, there are still a couple of things you gotta do," Boris added.

"What's that?"

"Get hold of your doctor. If the PGA should ask, make sure he tells 'em you came to him for medical therapy, not to cure the yips."

"Don't worry, Frank's cool," Duff assured him. "What else?"

"Forbes's girlfriend. What makes you think she'll back you up?"

"Because Forbes didn't have her on his list of witnesses. That must mean she's not willing to back him up."

"I'd make sure of that if I were you. And Duff . . . ?"

"Yeah?"

"Don't worry, I'm in your corner."

Duff thanked him and said good-bye. He threw his bag up on the bed and repacked the few things he had taken out. He wasn't sure where he was going, he just knew he didn't want to be here when they were playing without him.

He wound his way slowly north along the water until he happened on a small town with large gingerbread houses scattered along the beach. He parked in front of one advertising a vacancy and was shown to a room at the top of a pointed turret. There was no television, and the bath was off the hallway on the floor below, and there wasn't much to do in Fernandina Beach, but that was okay, Duff told the middle-aged woman who showed him the room. When he went downstairs to check in, she asked him how long he was going to stay. Until then he hadn't thought of it.

"A couple of days . . ." he said uncertainly. "Just until I get the results of some tests."

"Our policy . . ." she began, then halted. "I hope everything will be all right."

Duff thanked her and remembered. "I have to call my doctor."

Judging from the sad look on her face, he worried that the phone was out. But no, there was a phone in his room, she informed him.

She looked up from the desk a few minutes later to see him struggling into the lobby under a bag of golf clubs and a large suitcase. "Let me help you!" she cried.

"I can manage," he said.

But the small woman wouldn't take no for an answer. She pulled the heavy suitcase out of his hand and hauled it all the way up to his room, stopping on each landing to rest. Feeling guilty, Duff tried to give her $10 but she wouldn't hear of it. After she left, he picked up the phone and called Frank Promer. He was with a patient but he took the call, anxious to congratulate his patient on his first victory.

"Thanks, Frank, but I'm calling about something a little more urgent," he interrupted.

"What is it?"

"I just want to know—if anybody asks about the drugs I'm taking—you'd be able to say they're therapeutic, wouldn't you?"

"Yes. . . . Why do you ask?"

"Because somebody from the PGA might call."

"The PGA? They know you're taking beta-blockers?"

"They soon will."

"You're going to tell them? I'm not sure that's a good idea, Duff."

"I had to take a urine test."

"Oh, shit."

"But there's no need to worry as long as it's for a medical condition," Duff assured him. "My agent checked. The PGA doesn't even have a rule against drug use."

"But the AMA does. Why in God's name did you submit to a urine test?"

"I had no choice. But don't worry, they might not even call."

"Let's hope so. Listen I have a patient. . . . Good luck, Duff."

"Yeah, thanks," Duff said, as the line went dead.

It was only natural that Frank should be a little upset at becoming involved in his patient's personal problem, Duff realized. But in the end he was sure he'd be able to rely on his doctor. I'll be with you all the way . . . that's what he had said.

He phoned Gena's apartment at odd times over the next twenty-four hours, but got nothing. Finally he phoned her mother's house and left a message on her machine asking that Gena call, but by the next day he hadn't heard from either of them. In the meantime he stayed close to his room, trying to concentrate on one of the paperback novels he'd been carrying around unread for so long, while nervously awaiting a summons from the PGA. When the manager passed by his table at dinner and asked the name of the book he was reading, she seemed almost shocked by his answer.

"Couldn't you find something a bit more cheerful?" she said.

"It suits my mood," Duff replied.

She shook her head sadly and hurried away as he slid

the book across the table. It was *Heart Of Darkness*.

He finished the book that evening and was about to take up *Billy Budd*, when he decided instead to try to get in touch with Priscilla Donne. He phoned information in Boston where she was working, but they had no listing. Then he remembered her father's church in Marblehead and found a number for the Reverend Thomas Donne.

"Oh yes, Forbes Witherspoon's friend!" the cleric exclaimed, before Duff was able to complete his introduction. "You won your first tournament, you must be very excited."

"A little," Duff said. "I wanted to speak to Priscilla about something that happened there, but she has no listing."

"She's sharing an apartment with a girlfriend and hasn't gotten around to adding her name. She's very much up in the air, I'm afraid. Do you have a pencil?"

Duff copied down the number and thanked him.

"Good luck in your next match. I hope we'll have a chance to meet."

Duff said he hoped so too, thanked him and said goodbye. He dialed the number he had given him and found Priscilla at home.

"How did you find me?" she asked after a surprised hello.

"I just had a very cordial conversation with your father. He wants us to get together."

"You and me?" she laughed.

"You wouldn't want to hurt his feelings, would you?"

"I'd never do anything to hurt my father's feelings. Have you come down from the clouds yet?"

"With a great crash. I'm suspended from play pending an investigation."

"Investigation!" she exclaimed. "Of what?"

"Forbes didn't mention it?"

"No."

"So at least he's ashamed. I guess that's a good sign."

"Ashamed of what? What's he done?"

"Well, among other things, he claims I threatened to hit him that night at the restaurant."

"But you didn't! Why would he say something like that?"

"I don't know. Because he's playing badly and wants to blame somebody besides himself?"

"It's true, he's miserable," she agreed. "But I can't believe he'd do something like this to a friend."

"I'm afraid that's all over, Pris."

"Don't say that," she said. "He's depressed right now, but I'm sure I can get him to withdraw his complaint."

"I don't think so," Duff said. "Forbes threw everything at me he could, and the worst of it is, he accused me of using illegal drugs."

"What! After you explained?"

"He doesn't want to hear it. He won't be satisfied until I'm off the Tour. I don't like to put you on the spot, Pris—but if I need a witness, will you tell them what happened at the restaurant?"

"Of course."

"And if it embarrasses Forbes . . . ?"

"I won't lie, if that's what you mean."

"No, I didn't think you would," he said. "And who knows, maybe it'll never come up."

"Let's hope not. I'm going to talk to Forbes. I'll make him see the light," she vowed.

Duff knew better, but he thanked her just the same.

"Where will you be?" she asked.

"I'm not sure."

"Will you call me?"

"If you'd like me to."

"I'd like that very much," she said.

"Then I'll call," he promised.

Then they said good-bye and he slowly replaced the phone. He was very grateful and very angry at the same time: grateful for her decency, and angry that a sonofabitch like Forbes should have her.

•   •   •

At the end of the week, after learning that the PGA hadn't yet received the results of their tests and he was therefore still under voluntary suspension, Duff packed up his rental car and checked out of his small hotel.

"I've enjoyed my stay," he told the sad-eyed woman who had hovered about throughout his stay, as he paid his bill. "I just wish I had more time."

She seemed to choke as she suddenly clasped his hand in both of hers and fairly gasped, "I just pray to God everything turns out well."

Duff thanked her and hurried to his car. These small hotels were charming, but from now on he would settle for something a little less personal, he decided.

He drove idly through the tidal wetlands of southern Georgia over the next few days, staying in chain motels and eating at Shoney's and Burger Kings. He finished *Billy Budd* at the Ramada Inn on Jekyll Island and began *The Sun Also Rises* at a Holiday Inn outside Savannah. Each day he phoned the PGA office at Sawgrass, and each time he was told the office had no information for him. Finally he'd had enough.

"I'd like to speak to the Commissioner."

"I'm sorry, he's in conference," his secretary informed him. "Would you like to leave a message?"

"I've left a message every day. Tell him I'm coming in tomorrow and I want to talk to him," Duff said.

"I'm afraid he's unavailable tomorrow."

"Tell him if I don't meet with him tomorrow I'm going to meet with a sportswriter from the *New York Times*," Duff said.

"Just a minute Mr. Colhane," she said, and left him listening to some sappy music.

Now what have I done? he asked himself. Bullshit! He works for me, I don't work for him, he reminded himself.

After what seemed a very long time, the secretary came back on the line.

"The Commissioner will see you tomorrow," she said.

Duff thanked her and hung up, then pumped his fist in the air like Tiger Woods and shouted, "Yeah!"

The Commissioner made him wait in the reception room for a punitively long time before sending his assistant to escort him to the conference room. He was seated at the end of a long table, flanked by a silver-haired man whom Duff had never seen before. The commissioner introduced him—his name was Hagis—and motioned to a chair opposite him.

"In view of the change in tone these proceedings have taken, I thought it would be best to have Mr. Hagis along," the commissioner prefaced cooly.

Lawyer, Duff decided. Should he break off the meeting and get his own? Probably. But he was anxious to hear what they had to say. And somehow he had the feeling that he might do better with a new guy than with the Commissioner, who was obviously pissed off at him.

"We have the results of your lab test," the Commissioner said, brandishing it for him. "It shows you've been taking large doses of beta-blockers and amphetamines."

"I only took what my doctor prescribed," Duff answered.

"Yes, we've spoken to your doctor," Hagis said. "When we told him how much you were taking, he claimed he had never prescribed that dosage and that you were abusing your prescription."

"That's not true!" Duff exclaimed. "He and I worked together on the dosage! If he thought it was too much, why did he keep renewing the prescription?"

"Why indeed," Hagis said. "Obviously your doctor was prescribing drugs without any guidance and now he's afraid his license is in jeopardy. Did he tell you your damaged nerves could never be repaired?"

"Yes."

"And did you ask him for something to calm them?"

"No. All I did was ask him to fix my hand."

"After he'd told you it couldn't be fixed."

"That's not what he said!"

"Let's not confuse things," the Commissioner interrupted. "Even assuming you went to your doctor with the best of intentions, the fact is he prescribed a performance-enhancing drug and you took it, knowing it was illegal. Can we agree on that much?"

"No, we can't," Duff replied. He just hoped Boris knew what the hell he was talking about.

"Pardon me?"

"Show me the PGA rule that says beta-blockers or any other drugs are illegal in tournament play," Duff challenged.

He could tell from the exchange of looks that Boris was right.

"We're not talking about a written rule here, we're talking about an understood rule," Hagis said.

"The spirit of the rules," the Commissioner added.

"And what happened to those players who violated the spirit of the rules?" Duff said, then began reciting names. "Were any of them suspended for using beta-blockers?"

"Those players were taking them for a legitimate medical purpose," the Commissioner replied.

"How do you know? Did you call their doctor? Or did you just sweep the problem under the rug—pretend it doesn't exist. Well it does exist, and if you want to make an issue of it with me, it's going to be a very public issue."

"I don't think threats are the answer, Duff," the silver-haired lawyer put in.

The hell they aren't, Duff now knew. "That's not a threat, that's information," he said. They might not be afraid of *him*, but they were scared to death of being embarrassed. And he was a hot potato, a druggie, capable of violence! He was a public-relations bomb ready to explode at any minute, and he mustn't let them forget it. "I just think we should all know what we're in for."

"I assure you, no one wants to make you the scapegoat," the Commissioner said. "And it might be that the PGA's position on drugs is a bit . . . fuzzy. Unfortunately for all of us, however, your case has put it in sharp focus. A player has made a charge against you, and other players corroborate his charge."

"I did not threaten Forbes Witherspoon."

"We know, we talked to his girlfriend," the Commissioner said, nodding dismissively.

"But we're still left with the drug issue," Hagis said. "Which we'd like to resolve as discreetly as possible. In other words we'd like to avoid a formal disciplinary hearing if we can. That'll be up to you."

"I'll do what I can," Duff said.

"I'm sure you will."

"If you hadn't just won your first tournament when this came up, the players might have been a little more forgiving," the Commissioner said. "As it is, they know about the shipments of money from your friend, and about the incident in Vegas."

"Thanks to Forbes. . . ."

"He is persistent," the Commissioner allowed. "Nevertheless, some of the players think we'll have to deal with the drug issue sooner or later anyway, so why not now."

"They think you're an easy target," Hagis said. "But as I said, we'd rather avoid a formal disciplinary hearing if at all possible."

"So we went to the players with an alternate proposal," the Commissioner continued. "First of all, you have to give up the drugs entirely. Do you agree to that?"

Duff's hand went instinctively to the crystal which he now carried in his pocket at all times. After playing the last nine holes at Doral without his red pills and winning, he was beginning to think he no longer needed drugs, despite what his doctor said. Until now he was undecided—should he cut way back on the dosage for his next tournament or quit cold?—but now it seemed the decision had been made for him. And surprisingly he was more relieved than angry that someone else was deciding for him.

"I can agree to that," Duff replied carefully. "But I'd like to hear the rest."

"You'll have to submit to testing before your next tournament. . . ."

"Okay . . ."

"And you'll have to agree to a voluntary suspension."

"For how long?"

"Until the U.S. Open."

"What! That's not till June!" Duff wailed.

"It was the best we could do," the Commissioner assured him.

"Some of them wanted much worse," the lawyer put in.

"I'll miss the Players Tournament!"

"You won't be able to play in any tournament this spring."

"What about the Masters? That's not a PGA event," Duff reminded them.

"I'm sorry, it's all or nothing," the Commissioner said, shaking his head.

"Not that it's any satisfaction, but the Masters won't be sending you an invitation," Hagis added.

"You went to them?"

"Some of the Masters champions took that upon themselves."

"With a little help from Forbes?"

"That's not the issue. You've heard our offer," the Commissioner said.

"That isn't a fair offer," Duff replied, pushing away from the table.

"It's non-negotiable, they're insistent about that," the lawyer said. "It's either this or a formal hearing, which could result in a lifetime ban."

"You don't have to decide right now," the Commissioner said. "Talk it over with your advisers, get back to us in a week."

When Duff stalked angrily out of the conference room a moment later, he was resolved to make a public fight of it. However after phoning Boris a short while later and listening to his bleak assessment of his chances, he realized he had no choice. He phoned the Commissioner the next morning and told him he would accept his offer. The Commissioner assured him it was for the best and told him he looked forward to seeing him at the Open at Shinnecock Hills. With nothing to do for a couple of months, Duff phoned the airlines and booked a flight to JFK.

He could tell from the look on his father's face when he struggled through the door with his clubs and bag that something grave had occurred between his announced homecoming and his arrival. His first thought was that the Commissioner had phoned to tell him the players had rejected the deal, that he was being banned altogether. But it was a fate more final than banishment weighing on his father.

"Dad, what's wrong?" he asked, letting his clubs slide to the floor.

"You didn't see the news?"

"What news? What happened?" he asked, knowing already.

"Gena's dead."

"No!"

Sam stepped away and gestured at the flickering television set in the living room, as if all the answers were in that box. "It come over the news a little while ago. She was missin' for a coupla days. Until they found her in the trunk of a car at JFK."

"JFK . . . ?" How could that be? He'd just come from there.

He moved unsteadily across the room and sank to the

couch. He felt as if he'd been struck by something unseen
and knocked nearly unconscious. But not entirely. He remained cruelly conscious of the undeniable fact that Gena
was truly dead, murdered by Monte or the Colombians or
somebody. His lawyer was wrong, the feds had fucked up
real bad. His thoughts and feelings were an incomprehen-
sible mass of contradictions. He was both sorry and angry.
Not just anger at the people who had done it, or at Leo
who had set her up, or the clumsy cops who'd allowed it
to happen—but anger at Gena as well. If she'd gotten out
when she should have—or if she'd been home when he'd
called—or if she'd just been more careful . . . ! She was
like a child who knew the stove was hot but had to touch
it anyway. He was angry at himself for his helplessness,
and sorry for himself, and concerned that his emotions
weren't as pure and selfless as they should be. Or was
there no script for death?

"You got anything to drink?" Duff asked.

Sam shook his head. "It don't help anyway."

"What does?"

"Time. Just time."

"I got a lot of that," Duff said, pushing himself up from
the couch and walking into his bedroom.

He spent a mostly sleepless night in bed, finally falling
into a deep sleep shortly before the sun rose over the
ocean. He was awakened soon after by his father.

"There's a New York homicide detective on the
phone."

"New York?"

"You wanna talk or should I tell him you're asleep?"

"No, I'll talk to him." Might as well get it over with,
he thought, climbing sleepily out of bed. The money-
laundering charge might still be hanging over his head,
but he had nothing to fear from a homicide cop.

Nor did he sound at all threatening. He told him he was
a golfer but not a very good one, who played at La Tour-

ette on Staten Island, and he'd watched him win the Doral
on TV. When he offered his sympathy because he wasn't
playing right now, Duff knew he'd been briefed by the
DEA. After the preliminary questions, he asked about the
money, and once again Duff explained that Gena had been
sponsoring him on the Tour. The New York detective apparently found this explanation more acceptable than the
DEA had, which gave him some relief. It indicated that
Raymond was right, the DEA didn't seriously think he
was a money launderer. And if the cops believed Gena
was supporting him on the Tour, they surely didn't think
he'd killed her.

After establishing that Duff had been at the PGA headquarters when Gena was killed, the detective quickly
wound up the interview. He was plainly satisfied that Duff
had nothing to do with Gena's murder, yet he asked him
to stay at home or inform him if he was leaving town in
the next few days.

Duff said he had no plans to leave but would inform
him if anything came up.

Then, before the cop could hang up, he asked, "Do you
have any suspects?"

"A few," he answered.

But Leo Hover's not one of them, Duff knew. He
wanted to go after Leo, to at least confront him over what
he'd done, but he knew better. It wouldn't accomplish
anything, and there was probably a law against beating
the shit out of a federal witness. But one way or another
Leo had to pay for what he'd done, and when things
cooled down, Duff would see that he did. That's a promise, he vowed silently to Gena.

Later in the morning he received a phone call from a
sportswriter from *Newsday*. The writer lulled him with
some questions about his first victory on Tour, then asked
why he hadn't competed since then.

"I'm resting up," Duff answered.

"For how long?"

"Until my hand feels better."

"What's wrong with your hand?" the writer probed.

"I injured it when I was a kid."

"How?"

"Doing something stupid. Do you have any more questions?" Duff asked, anxious to get away from this reporter.

"Let's talk about something other than golf," the reporter suggested. "You were a close friend of the woman who was murdered, Gena Hall . . . ?"

"Yeah, we were good friends," he said carefully.

"She was sponsoring you on the Tour?"

"Yes."

"Is it true that she mailed large sums of cash to you through the PGA offices?"

"What?"

"And that she was involved in drugs?"

"No! Who told you that?" Duff demanded.

"Have you been suspended from the PGA for using drugs?"

"Medicine, not drugs! And it was voluntary!"

"Did you voluntarily withdraw from the Masters?"

"Look—I'm not answering any more of your questions until you answer mine. I want to know who told you this."

"I'm sorry, I can't reveal my source," the journalist recited. "But from what you've told me, it would seem that he's reliable."

"Forbes Witherspoon is not reliable!" Duff shouted and slammed the phone down.

The phone continued to ring for the rest of the morning, with Sam acting as secretary, informing not just the several newspaper and magazine writers who phoned but radio and television journalists as well that his son was unavailable. Finally they disconnected the phone and Duff paced about the house like a caged animal. He was sorry he had come home, but he didn't know where else to go.

A short while later, when a Channel 12 television van

pulled up in front of the house, he realized there was no way to escape anyway. As long as that camera remained in the front yard, Duff was a prisoner in his own house.

There was a common theme running through most of the stories that appeared in the papers and on television over the next few days. It was a sad but typical tale of a beautiful girl who had gone to New York to find fame and fortune as an actress, but had instead found drugs and death. There was no mention of Monte or Leo Hover— Forbes knew nothing about them and the cops were being closemouthed about their investigation—although the golfer she'd been supporting with her drug proceeds got plenty of ink. There were rumors that he had taken a temporary leave from competition due to a drug problem of his own, possibly brought on by an injury sustained after playing in a Calcutta under an assumed name. No one claimed his win at Doral was the result of performance-enhancing drugs, but the implication was clear.

"They didn't only kill Gena, they killed me too," Duff said to Priscilla when he phoned her after most of the publicity had died down. He had called to thank her for setting the Commissioner straight, and because he'd promised to call, but mostly because he wanted very much to hear her voice again.

"No, Duff, you beat them. Forbes told the Commissioner he's withdrawing his charge against you."

"No!" he gasped. He'd lied to the Commissioner in the first place, then launched an all-out media blitz to destroy him, and now, just when he'd gotten what he wanted, he'd just as irrationally withdrawn his charge? "What made him do that?"

"Me," she answered. "I told you I could be very persuasive."

"I had no idea."

"Try not to be too hard on him, Duff. He thought he was going through a spiritual redemption, when in fact it was more like a mental breakdown. He's also quitting golf."

Somehow Duff wasn't surprised. Yet he had to ask, "Why?"

"He's going into the family business."

"So I guess this means you're going to be the wife of an insurance agent."

"Broker," she corrected. "And no, I'm not marrying Forbes."

"You're not?" he asked, as if afraid he hadn't heard correctly. Or afraid there was more coming. I'm marrying my boss at the agency. "You've broken up with Forbes?"

"I'm officially an old maid."

"I hope it's not because of me," he said.

"No you don't," she said.

"You're right, I don't. A minute ago I was totally despondent. My friend was murdered, everybody thinks I'm a drug-addicted golf cheat, and right now I'm happier than I've ever been in my life! When can I see you?"

"This weekend?"

"What about tomorrow?"

She laughed. "I have to work."

"I don't. I'll come to Boston!"

"When?"

"Right now!"

"Yes!" she cried. "Yes! Come right now!"

One day a caravan of tractor trailers arrived, and only a short while later the hills of Shinnecock were dotted with striped tents. From a distance the scene resembled an ancient military encampment, with thousands of soldier ants going about their mysterious maneuvers; or more likely, perhaps, a vast medieval market, with goods and stores arriving by giant carts hauled by invisible devils. The biggest tent of all—larger than an archery range, pitched close beside the narrow road that led up to the stately Stanford White clubhouse with its broad, columned

porches—was the merchandise tent. Nearby was a restaurant tent that offered full dinners and adequate wines to
the more sedentary sportsman; while spotted elsewhere
around the course were smaller tents offering hot dogs
and beer to the more venturesome golf fan. There were
press tents and communications tents and medical tents,
official USGA trailers and unofficial trailers; there were
powerful television cameras mounted on towering cranes
and floating blimps, and hundreds of miles of electrical
cable thick as garden hose strung everywhere, so that all
the world might see and hear what would happen here
over the four greatest days in all of sport.

No, it wasn't the World Series or the Superbowl, where
teams of hired hands played for a title whose outcome
was fairly predictable. This was the U.S Open, where
Everyman, amateur golfer or professional, had the opportunity to emerge the champion. A few weeks ago there
had been more than seven thousand of them, well known
professionals and unknown amateurs, vying in two 36-
hole local and regional matches for fewer than 100 non-
exempt places. Now they were down to 146 of the best
golfers in the world, and Duff Colhane, fisherman's son,
winner of the Doral Open, was one of them. How ironic
it was that the most aristocratic of games, where the cost
of membership at some clubs was more than a string of
polo ponies, was so democratic when choosing its champion.

Perhaps for this reason, Duff felt for the first time in
his career that this was a tournament in which he truly
belonged. Here there were no men in blue coats watching
him, telling him how to dress, how to talk, how to think.
If he won the U.S. Open there'd be no one at his sleeve
reminding him to thank an insurance or truck-rental company for their contribution to golf. Here there were no
cars floating on ponds, or corporate logos behind every
tee and green—even the brand name of the official clock
was taped over. This was golf as he knew it; pure, stripped
to its essentials, golf as it was meant to be. Of course they

were still playing for a lot of money, but even if they were playing for just a tin cup they'd still all be here, because this was the U.S. Open.

Most of the players, whom he hadn't seen in several weeks, came by his locker on the first day at Shinnecock to welcome him back, but some didn't. Duff was grateful to those willing to give him the benefit of the doubt, but dignified in his response. This was almost his home after all, they were merely visitors. He had caddied it and played it until he knew every bounce and break the course could offer. Those who'd never played the course wanted to know how Shinnecock should be approached, but it was just an ice-breaker, an excuse to talk about something other than Duff's recent troubles. They all knew that Shinnecock, like any Open course, could be seduced but not raped. A few players said they'd disapproved of his suspension, but most pretended he'd just been away. There were still a few who believed he'd forever stained the profession and should be banned for life, but they said nothing to him nor he to them. It wasn't an unusual arrangement on the Tour, where few friendships ran deep. Like gladiators before the games, they were as friendly as they could afford to be while knowing they would soon be going into the arena to try to kill each other.

Duff didn't know whether to be pleased or wary, but for some reason he was more confident going into this tournament than he'd ever been before. Not having taken any drugs of any kind for several weeks, not even a beer, he felt better than at any time in the past several years. True, he hadn't played competitively over the last couple of months, but he had been practicing diligently at Montauk and Shinnecock, and his game was the best it had ever been. Whatever competitive edge he had lost he more than made up for with his home-court advantage, he was sure. He would be playing in front of family and friends, sleeping in his own bed and eating his father's fish stew.

He would be playing without his manager—Boris had sent him a registered letter soon after Gena's murder, revoking their agreement for violation of the morals clause—but Duff understood. His corporate clients were interested only in squeaky-clean golfers, and a struggling agent who represented a player associated with a drug victim would be as popular among golf's CEOs as an IRS agent. But after he won the Open he'd be beating off agents with a wedge. He had also lost his caddie, but that had turned out all right too. Sidney had jumped to another bag after his boss's voluntary suspension, but Teddy McGill, who knew him and his game better than anyone, had leaped at the chance to help his student win the Open.

"There's nobody here playin' better golf right now than Duff Colhane," Teddy boasted to his fellow caddies on the eve of the Open. His player had broken 70 in practice rounds almost every day since arriving at Shinnecock. True he was only playing hundred-dollar Nassaus against some of his fellow pros, not competing under the stress of a U.S. Open, but he had won all the money, hadn't he? And for the first time since his injury, the lad was once again playing with the cool nerves of a teenager. If there was ever a tournament made to be won by Duff Colhane, this Shinnecock Open was it, Teddy knew.

Because Duff was a rational man, he didn't attribute his new-found confidence to the crystal he carried in his pocket and rubbed to a high heat whenever he felt in need of help from an outside agent. He knew it was just a piece of glass and that he could play just as well without it as with it. He understood this perfectly well, yet he would not flush it down the toilet as he had the drugs. He was confident but not that confident.

Opening day dawned in a misty rain and ocean fog through which the fairways and greens of Shinnecock Hills glowed luminously, and the players shimmered spectrally behind a pewter scrim. It was a quiet and inert scene, sound disappeared quickly in the grainy wet air and the players moved leadenly, as if afraid of dislodging more water from the sky. But this was no real rain, the fisherman's son was sure, just ocean fog the onshore winds would scud away before it was his turn to tee off.

However, by late morning the rain had taken hold and was coming down harder, and it was obvious that those who had gone off earliest had drawn the best time. The other two players in Duff's group—one a member of Forbes's Bible class who hadn't yet spoken to him— grumbled about the weather as they waited on the first tee.

"The farmers need it," Duff remarked. Both players looked curiously at him. "The tension makes me say dumb things," he explained. They laughed slightly and the tension lifted a bit.

When his name was finally announced, the rain-soaked locals responded enthusiastically. Duff smiled and waved, then teed it up and knocked it over the corner onto the dogleg right fairway for an easy approach. Both of his playing partners laid up short and the game was on.

"Don't know why there's no sun up in the sky. . . ." Duff sang in a passable baritone as he strode down the first fairway, his healed hand clamped tightly around his pocketed crystal.

Four and a half hours later, Duff climbed the steep slope behind the 18th green and made for the locker room for a hot shower and a change of clothes before reporting to the press tent. He had shot even par, not a great score, but he was so far tied with Ernie Els and Tiger Woods for first place, and it was likely that no one would go any lower in this wind and rain.

On a sunny summer weekend in the Hamptons, the beaches, golf courses and tennis courts, the backyard pools, the restaurants and shops and all the roads are filled with the rich, the beautiful and the famous, all of them desperately intent on having fun. But on the last day of the U.S. Open, when a young man from Montauk was tied for the lead with Tiger Woods, something dubbed Duffmania by David Feherty took hold of the jaded denizens of the East End, and they were all either at the tournament or watching him in front of a television set. Fans who'd had the foresight to buy tickets early were able to sell them outside the gate to desperate bond salesmen and stock brokers for thousands of dollars, while hundreds of others were willing to scale the fences and dodge the security guards to witness this possibly momentuous event. Not since the glory days of Carl Yastrzemski had the sports fans of the Hamptons such cause to cheer, and they weren't holding back.

It had begun slowly. After falling three strokes back of Colin Montgomerie on the second day, the initial enthusiasm of the sophisticated golf fans gave way to reality. How could a one-tournament-winner with a drug problem be expected to hold up under the pressure of a U.S Open? But after coming back with a blistering 67 on Saturday to go into a tie for first with Tiger Woods going into the final day, there wasn't a pundit in the East End who didn't think Duff Colhane could win the U.S. Open.

"Heck, I played Tiger in the Open hundreds of times before at the Montauk Muni and I always beat him," Duff told Jim Nance after posting his Saturday score.

"I don't know if he can beat Tiger or not, but I've never seen more confidence in a player in my life," Nance commented after Duff left the booth.

On the first hole on Sunday afternoon however, after Duff tried to cut off too much and left his ball in the intractable gorse to the right of the fairway, a collective groan went up from the local fans. Miraculously, however, Duff managed to slash the ball out of the thick grass and down the fairway to within a hundred yards of the green, then get up and down for par.

"Nice par," Tiger said, as they walked to the second tee.

"You too."

Both players played reckless and sometimes erratic golf over the next seven holes, risking driver where more cautious players hit fairway woods or 2-irons, and the fans loved it.

"It's almost like there's two matches goin' on between these two players," the player-announcer observed excitedly as they approached the ninth green. "One for the Open title and one for the macho title. And I'll tell you, Jim, it doesn't get any better that this."

Both players had seen more bunkers and rough on the front nine than a serious contender should, yet they were both 1 under going to the 10th hole, despite two birdies each. When the crowd stirred, Duff and Tiger looked automatically to the leader board. David Duval had just made his third birdie in a row and joined them in a tie for first. He'd been so intent on taming the Tiger that he'd forgotten there were still half a dozen other players out there who could win this thing. A second reaction from the crowd and he saw that Colin Montgomerie had climbed back to within one.

"You're up," Tiger said.

Duff reached into his pocket for his crystal, then stuck out his jaw and walked up to the markers. The 10th was a treacherous hole, a blind drive over the top of the hill, then down to a narrow landing area at the bottom of a deep valley. It was here that Nicklaus lost his ball in the left gorse in the '86 Open, and possibly the tournament as well. Difficult as the first shot is, the second, up a steep hill to a narrow hogback of a green that slopes away, is one of the most infernal approaches in golf. A wedge might land a foot short and roll back down the hill to where it started, or land a foot too long and roll down the hill behind the green. Then a strong chip might roll across the green and back down the hill, leaving the shaken player to start the damnable process all over again.

Duff gave the crystal one last rub, then stepped up and calmly laced his drive over the hill. But it began to hook as it disappeared over the crest, and he waited anxiously until Teddy signaled from the top of the hill that his ball had landed safely. Relieved, he stepped aside and let Tiger have the tee. His drive was perfect.

When Duff reached the top of the hill he saw his ball, not on the fairway as Teddy had signaled, but in the first cut of rough.

"You trying to spare my feelings?" he asked Teddy as he approached.

"It's better than fairway," Teddy assured him.

It was a good lie, but not entirely to Duff's liking. He had developed an unusual shot into this unusual green. Rather than mortar the ball onto a small green at the top of a steep hill that was little more receptive than a car roof, he had taken to chipping a mid-iron crisply into the side of the hill near the top, letting it bounce and drop before running a short distance. It wasn't a pretty shot, but it was one he had practiced thoroughly and was comfortable with. However he hadn't practiced the shot off a fluffy lie.

He waited and watched as Tiger hit a high soft lob that was obviously too long. He would have a tough chip to a hole that was cut very close to the front edge on the last day, dangerously near the precipitous slide that could take him out of contention. Duff put his hand on the 6-iron and looked at Teddy.

Teddy nodded. He hadn't liked this exotic shot at first, but after watching Duff make it every time in the practice rounds, he was sold.

Duff slid the 6-iron from the bag and brushed the top of the rough with it several times while Tiger waited in the center of the fairway, head bowed. He was angry, he had hit the short iron too long and quite possibly lost a stroke to this kid who was now rubbing his damned leg again. He acted nervous, but he wasn't missing many shots. And when he hit this one into the side of the hill, Tiger thought he'd made another one. But this time the ball didn't bounce as it should have; it hit softly and failed to rise above the edge, then trickled back down the the hill.

"It got up on me!" Duff said, slamming the turf with his club.

"Take it easy," Teddy cautioned. "We can still make par."

He felt rooted to the ground. He was walking to the ball, but he couldn't feel his legs moving. And when he stood over the ball, he couldn't feel the club in his hand. He knew what he had to do, take it back and hit the ball, but he couldn't move. Finally he forced it back and released it and watched the ball skitter up the hill and onto the green.

"That's close!" Teddy cried. "Very close!"

Relieved, Duff followed him up the hill. When he crested the hill and saw two balls, one lying within ten feet of the pin, the other in the swale behind the green, it took him a moment to realize that his was the close ball. He looked at Teddy, who was grinning like a leprechaun, and he tried to smile back, to let him know that he was all right. But the smile came out twisted. The muscles in his face seemed to be dancing to a different tune from the one he heard in his head, yet Teddy was still grinning as if nothing was wrong. Couldn't he see? Couldn't anybody see what was happening to him? He saw Tiger's ball bounce and roll to within a few feet of the hole.

Duff replaced his ball and lined it up from one side of the hole. He wanted to line it up from the other side but he didn't trust himself to walk. He felt like his legs and arms were in danger of becoming detached from his body. When he felt ready, he struck the putt and watched it roll directly at the hole, then stop half way there. He had no memory of making the next putt.

Nor would he ever remember much about the next eight holes. After making his last putt for a 43 on the back nine, he lurched away like a shell-shocked warrior. Teddy waited while he signed his card, then led the way to the locker room, pushing through the crowd, silent as mourners. They watched with incredulous grief as the hollow-eyed golfer who might have won the U.S. Open if only he'd had the nerve, passed by like a zombie.

TEN YEARS LATER

Sam Colhane had seen too many yachts in his time and place to pay much attention to any of them. But there was something about the one that eased in next to his fishing boat that sparked more interest than usual. For one thing, she was named Fore, which could mean get the hell out of my way, or might simply mean that her master would rather be golfing. She was big but not too big, just dripping with continental snootiness, ports big as store windows and almost too dark to see through. There was a big white piano and lots of chrome and leather furniture in the main salon, and a gleaming mahogany launch hanging from her starboard davits, along with a bunch of those jet skis for the towheaded kids hanging over the rail. The father, who was doing a nice job of docking his own boat while the captain stood by, was a tall guy in a well-cut nautical jacket that shouted money—the kind of guy Sam used to hate on sight. But now he'd mellowed. Although he was sure he could dislike that wife easily enough. She was a pretty enough woman, but with that embalmed homecoming-queen look popular with rich husbands. When Sam waved back at the kids, she looked at him and smiled twitchingly, as if smelling fish.

She was annoyed with her husband at staying over, Sam gathered after listening to them for a while. She'd wanted to continue on to the Vineyard where the staff was waiting, but he'd insisted on laying over in Montauk for the night and arriving the next day. Exasperated, she finally disappeared into the main salon with the children, angrily slamming the hatch after her.

"A minor mutiny," the yachtsman said, when he caught Sam's eye. Sam nodded understandingly. "How's the fishing?"

"Great. Like to go out?"

"Any other time—Captain . . ."

"Colhane."

The yachtsman's mouth fell open. "Duff Colhane's father?"

Sam nodded smartly. "You heard of him?"

"Yes, I've heard of him," he answered, as an image of the young golfer popped into his head—on the driving range at Southeastern, swinging with a graceful viciousness unlike anything he'd ever seen. He could see the resemblance now, the same defiant jaw beneath the gray seaman's beard. "He almost won the Open ten years ago."

"That's right! You must be a real fan," he said, pointing to the name on the bow.

"I played with your son."

"In the Open?"

The golfer shook his head. "I was retired by then."

"No kiddin'. What's your name?" Sam asked.

The golfer hesitated before replying. "Forbes Witherspoon."

"Sounds familiar . . ." Sam glanced appraisingly at the yacht and asked, "What'd ya do after ya quit golf?"

"Insurance," he replied with a fateful shrug. "Is he married?"

"Yeah, he's married. Got three beautiful kids. His wife's a very talented painter."

"Priscilla . . ."

"You know her?"

"I did," he answered.

"Well, if you're gonna be around tomorrow I'm sure they'd love to see you. I'd tell you to call tonight but they're busy gettin' ready for the president's dinner. He's head pro over at the Noyac Golf Club—very fancy."

"I'm sure. Well, it was nice meeting you, Captain Colhane. Please tell Duff and Pris that I wish them the very best."

"I will," Sam said, as the golfer walked to the stern and disappeared around the corner. *If I can remember that name.*

The Noyac clubhouse glowed like a lighted pyramid atop a high hill overlooking Peconic Bay, shimmering silvery in the full moonlight. A column of expensive cars snaking up the hillside stopped briefly in front of the canopied entrance to unload their privileged passengers, slim women in summery gowns and flashing stones, along with their counterparts, sun- and martini-reddened sportsmen, bulging comfortably against their formal jackets and cummerbunds.

The tall blond man in nautical garb attracted some attention when he stepped out of the Montauk cab, until, instead of entering through the broad front portals, he walked around to the side of the clubhouse. Extra help or a tardy musician, they assumed. But the man in the naval officer's jacket didn't go in through the service entrance, nor, when he continued on around to the outdoor dance floor, did he join the musicians on the bandstand who were beating out an up-tempo number. Instead he stood behind the hedges, beyond the light from the Japanese lanterns that encircled the patio, and searched the tables for the golf pro and his wife. Some of the younger members were dancing energetically, but most were content to sit at the tables and watch while being served drinks by the pretty waitresses in club uniforms, or mingle at the bar while replaying today's round.

The music ended and a few of the dancers clapped. Moments later, when the band played a slower number, the romantic and the less adventurous joined the dancers already on the floor. Then, from amongst the dizzying swirl of beautiful dancers, he suddenly discovered Duff and Pris. He was leading her by the hand through the dancers, her bare arms poised like wings, chin high, her dark hair swept up off her long thin neck, trailing black voile after her. Ten years and three children, and she still glowed bright as the day she'd left him. They halted directly in front of him, like performers on a stage. She made a laughing pirouette and collapsed against her partner, and they danced so blithely together it brought tears to a sailor's eyes. Then the music ended and they walked back to the president's table and everybody clapped. Why? He'd won one tournament and his career had fizzled and these people acted like he was Tiger Woods. It wasn't fair. He'd come expecting to find a dowdy couple sharing a table near the kitchen with the club manager and his wife, but instead he got Scott and Zelda!

Yet he was happy for them. And sad. He remembered the three of them as they once were, filled with hope; and saw them as they were now, filled with hope of another kind. All ambition ends as accommodation, he supposed. But that was okay. It might not be Tommy Dorsey they were dancing to, but they were still his arrangements.

"Sir?"

Forbes turned to find a uniformed security guard standing next to him. "Yeah?"

"Can I help you?" the guard asked.

"I was just looking for an old friend," Forbes answered.

"What's his name?"

"Name . . . ? Donne."

"I don't know who that would be. . . ."

"I must have the wrong party," Forbes replied, lifting his chin and tugging at his lapels. Then he squared his shoulders and walked away, dignified as a captain surrendering his ship.

When Duff suddenly stopped dancing, Priscilla asked what was wrong. He was staring across the dance floor at a spot behind the hedges where a guard stood.

"Nothing's wrong. I'll be right back," he said.

"Duff . . . ?"

The guard was staring undecidedly after the departing stranger, until he turned and saw the golf pro walking across the dance floor.

"Who was that?" Duff asked from behind the hedge.

"Just some crasher in off a boat," the guard answered.

"From a distance he looked familiar. . . ."

"Said he was looking for somebody named Don or Dun . . ."

"Donne . . . ?"

"Didn't give me no last name. You want me to go after him?"

The pro stared into the darkness for a moment, then shook his head. "He was probably just curious," he said, then turned and walked back.

Half way across the dance floor, Priscilla glided into his arms and they resumed dancing.

"What happened?" she asked.

"Some clam digger wanted to crash the party, but I told him we already have one here."

"I hope they don't find out," she said, as he suddenly spun her around and dipped her low.

Priscilla threw her head back and laughed, and he was suddenly overwhelmed by something beyond love, and overcome by a feeling that this had all happened before. They had entered the kingdom where music played and people laughed and glasses tinkled and Japanese lanterns cradled the dancers in a warm light of golden promise for all the nights to come.

"I'm a lucky boy. . . ." he sang.
"And I'm a lucky girl. . . ."
"What comes next?" he asked.
"I don't know," she answered.